- A t[...] [...]ngs back the [...]
- A we[...] [...] programmed sex. .
- A man[...] [...] of human dreams—and reality. . . .
- A chess game played for the fate of the universe. . . .
- A boy genius who controls people's minds and behavior. . . .
- Dracula's diary as the Count himself might have written it. . . .

This is Barry Malzberg's unbeatable best— a giant treasury from the award-winning author of *Phase IV*.

"Malzberg, a big frog in the biggest pond, continues to grow and grow in richness of ideas, excellence of prose, daringness of themes and ability to set down the harsh truths of the world. . . . Malzberg is a true hero!"

—*The Magazine of Fantasy and Science Fiction*

THE BEST OF BARRY N. MALZBERG
is an original POCKET BOOK edition.

Books by Barry N. Malzberg

The Best of Barry N. Malzberg
Beyond Apollo
The Destruction of the Temple
The Gamesman
Herovit's World
On a Planet Alien
Phase IV
The Sodom and Gomorrah Business

Published by POCKET BOOKS

The Best of
Barry N. Malzberg

Barry N. Malzberg

PUBLISHED BY POCKET BOOKS NEW YORK

THE BEST OF BARRY N. MALZBERG

POCKET BOOK edition published January, 1976

Ł

This original POCKET BOOK edition is printed from brand-new plates made from newly set, clear, easy-to-read type. POCKET BOOK editions are published by POCKET BOOKS, a division of Simon & Schuster, Inc., 630 Fifth Avenue, New York, N.Y. 10020. Trademarks registered in the United States and other countries.

ACKNOWLEDGMENTS AND COPYRIGHT NOTICES

A RECKONING, copyright, ©, 1973, by Robert Silverberg. All rights reserved. First published in *New Dimensions 3*.

LETTING IT ALL HANG OUT, copyright, ©, 1974, by Ultimate Publications, Inc. All rights reserved. First published in *Fantastic*.

THE MAN IN THE POCKET, copyright, ©, 1972, by Robert Silverberg. All rights reserved. An abbreviated version of this novella appeared in *New Dimensions 2*.

PATER FAMILIAS, copyright, ©, 1972, by The Mercury Press, Inc. All rights reserved. First published in *The Magazine of Fantasy and Science Fiction*.

GOING DOWN, copyright, ©, 1975, by Barry N. Malzberg. All rights reserved. First published in *Other Times*.

THOSE WONDERFUL YEARS, copyright, ©, 1973, by The Macmillan Company. All rights reserved. First published in *Tomorrow's Alternatives*.

ON ICE, copyright, ©, 1972, by Ultimate Publications, Inc. All rights reserved. Published in *Amazing Stories*.

iv

FOR THE EDITORS:

Roger Elwood   Harry Harrison
Robert Silverberg   Joseph Elder
Virginia Kidd   Ben Bova
Edward L. Ferman   Robert Gleason

CONTENTS

INTRODUCTION

The idea was to be a short-story writer. *Playboy* was paying two thousand dollars on acceptance; *Esquire* was always looking for up-and-comers at a thousand a throw, and *The Atlantic Monthly,* although chintzy in its third-generation New England way, was still collaring a new writer a month for five hundred dollars for the Atlantic Firsts . . . well, wasn't it? And just below the major slicks were all those fine literary quarterlies paying two or three cents a word on publication, and just beyond them the Foley and O'Henry collections picking off the best of the best, and once you had O'Henry in hand, well, then, you would put together your volume of short stories for Scribner's or the Atlantic Monthly Press, publish it to the kind of reviews received by *Good-Bye Columbus,* and then . . . well, then you could write a novel. Wasn't that the way to approach the problem? In the meantime, of course, you continued your career as an assistant professor of English at the University of Maryland or Ball State University. It all looked pretty good in 1964. How could the situation not fall to honest effort? Everybody knew I was good.

Unfortunately, the *Writer's Digest,* Anatole Broyard (then merely a humble instructor of creative writing at The New School, not the distinguished A. B. we know and revere today for his thrice-weekly insights in the *Times Book Review*), and George P. Elliott had neglected to tell me that the short-story market for the literary short story had collapsed (except for Ivan Gold and Leonard Michaels) ten years ago and had sunk without trace, carrying the few survivors in the undertow to the *Nautilus* under the sea, but had left the rest of us on the shore eyeing the carnage through opera glasses, blinking rapidly through watery eyes, and trying to describe to one another (always inaccurately) what had happened. In other words, I failed dismally in all of my attempts to sell literary short stories and decided at about that time that I did not want to be an *unpublished* assistant professor of English at Ball State U.—or whoever might hire the ex-Cornelia Ward Writing Fellow. Accordingly, I left the writing program along with most of my hopes and savings at the upstate university where some of these lessons had been acquired and returned to New York City where I became, through means initially coincidental, the fastest, the most fluid, the deftest, and the most brilliantly skilled employee that the fee department of a certain major literary agency had ever seen. They called me the Golden Eagle, the Flying Feeman. I set records that old-timers still talk about. Five novels, eighteen short stories read and commented upon (three thousand words of commentary on a novel, a thousand on a short story) in a single working day. A thousand pages an hour! Twenty-two short stories rejected in a morning! They say that one is young only once, but the Golden Eagle was not truly young (he had not been young since his twenty-fourth birthday); he was merely desperate—for money—on behalf of his adoring wife and helpless infant daughter who, during one of the G.E.'s spates of life affirmation, had been conceived and later born.

Meanwhile, the G.E., who was only intermittently myself, was in the process of making himself a writer for the commercial markets—science fiction, mysteries, sex stuff, you name it—because he still wished to be a writer (he needed more money) and the conversion of his refined *Prairie Schooner* talent toward Softcover Library and *Wildcat* was excruciating. It had become clear to the G.E., surrounded as he was by the appurtenances and hack writers represented by this certain literary agency, that if he wished to be a writer he had no choice but to go to the commercial markets. This he was willing to do; in fact, he begged to be permitted to do so.

The G.E. made two discoveries that were to frame the next ten years of his life:

a). The commercial markets were oriented toward the novel, and if one wanted to be a working writer one would have to write novels as a steady source of income and short stories only for incidentals. With some astonishment, the G.E., who had thought himself incapable of being a novelist, wrote seventy within the next nine years.

b). If one wished to write serious short stories, if only as a release and escape from the pressures of novelistics, the science fiction magazines and original anthologies represented the only consistent paying market for a body of literary work. Science fiction had a deservedly bad reputation—ninety percent of its practitioners being hacks with concommitant results—but the reputation was not deliberately arrived at. There was a place for serious literary work in S-F, and the editors—most of them—could recognize it and publish it welcomingly or grudgingly. Also, because the market was so relatively open and a reputation so relatively easily acquired within the field—since so few of its practitioners could write at all, a modest literary talent that could write a little looked very good—you could, after just a little while, write and publish what you wanted to write and publish almost at will . . . you only had to make minimum obeisance to the hardware or props of the field to cover yourself, and that was easy enough; it was, in fact, a pleasure. What else is really worth writing about today except the effect that technology has upon people, that people have upon technology? This is, after all, the machine age.

The G.E. (after slight stutter-stops editing a men's magazine and a couple of bottom-line-pulp S-F magazines) became a full-time writer. His distinguished body of work grew and grew under his sure and shaping hands: sales to Midwood Books, Belmont Books, Berkley Books, Pocket Books, Avon, Random House, Bobbs-Merrill. Within the framework of the commercial markets the G.E. had the game beaten almost cold in a period of seven years. The distance from Brooklyn to Manhattan's west side, Norman Podhoretz to the contrary, may after all be measured in a matter of miles, but who other than one who has made the journey can truly know the distance between Midwood Books and Random House? Not I, the G.E. said . . . I merely kept my head down and did the best I could, no less for Midwood than for the House.

Meanwhile, however, the Eagle, no longer Golden (his tail feathers were rumpled and he was becoming distantly conscious of his age the way that one may become aware of a crippling disease only after the process is well advanced), kept on writing short stories. He never stopped. Nor, despite the fact that his reputation rested and will continue to rest upon his novels, did he ever think of himself as anything other than a short-story writer who had been forced into novelistics in order to survive. He was able, over this seven-year period, to produce over two hundred short stories, almost all of them for the science-fiction markets and almost all of them published. The stories were written through and up to the level of his literary range and the markets did not resist. If they did not fall on his work with ravening cries, they did not, either, reject it. He had tolerant editors who gave him his head. He had readers, most of whom did not think that what he was doing incited to lynch law. . . .

This short-story collection, my fifth, is the one I consider definitive. Two earlier collections, published as Ace half-doubles, are long since out of print (although most of the stories therein are still being anthologized here and there) and involve, in any case, earlier work. A third collection in the inventory of a publisher not to be named may or may not have been released as of publication of this (most likely not), but it involves stories written only through a period of a year to a year and a half and is itself only 60,000 words long.* This one, at 180,000 words —what I understand to be the longest collection by a modern S-F writer ever to be published—takes work

---

* It has been published as has a minor collection elsewhere.

from many years (grouping, of course, toward the near end, but do not let the copyright dates dissuade you: some of these stories took several years to sell) and through a consequent range. It may even establish what I have wanted to establish for many years and at no denigration of the novels—that I am a better short-story writer than novelist, that there are a few contemporaries in my field who are better novelists than I (although not many, he hastily added, his beak trembling), but none to whom I will defer as a short-story writer. There are some as good —Disch, Silverberg, Lafferty, James Tiptree, Jr.—but none who I would say are better.

The prefatory comments to the stories can be read or skipped; as a writer I have a morbid and thorough interest in the facts of composition and marketing behind a published work, but I never thought it a healthy interest or one which a non-writer would share. Take them for the record, then, or let them be.

This is written under the assumption, of course, that there are non-writers and non- would-be writers among readers; that the writer has an audience greater than those who would like to emulate him or want to see what he's up to or how he managed to get away with this.

I hope that this is the case. In commercial writing it probably is. In literary writing it isn't. That's why this book is labeled S-F.

February 1974: New Jersey

The Best
of Barry N. Malzberg

Introduction to
A RECKONING

A Reckoning is a pastiche of the work of the late Cyril M. Kornbluth, a writer to whom I have been often compared in reviews and for whom I have great affection. I never knew him—he died tragically in 1958 at the age of thirty-four when I was but eighteen—but I wish very much that I had. His novels, at least those written noncollaboratively, were weak, but his collaborations with Frederik Pohl, notably *The Space Merchants* and *Gladiator-at-Law,* were strong, and his later short stories show the outlines of what would have been a black and definitive body of work. Two of them—*The Last Man Left in the Bar* and *Notes Leading Down to the Disaster,* both available in his last collection, and *A Mile Beyond the Moon,* published by Doubleday—have been stitched together and transmuted in his story. The style and vision are as close to that of C. M. Kornbluth as I could make them while not appropriating the sense of his work. The theme—which is an overly characteristic one—is clearly mine.

Kornbluth in his last years was a black and bitter man wronged by personal circumstance and by the field of science-fiction, to which he felt condemned and which he felt did not give full range to his enormous talents. He was a genuine child prodigy: a consistently publishing writer at the age of sixteen, and before he went into the service during the war, he must have authored or coauthored a hundred short stories of all kinds for a whole range of pulp magazines. The Kornbluth who emerged from the war might have, like so many others, been wounded in a subtle and terrible way, but he was also a mature artist. His *The Little Black Bag,* published in *Astounding* in 1950, is an enduring classic, and his work, alone and collaboratively, improved from then on. Able to sell John W. Campbell—another novelette, *That Share of Glory,* appeared in *ASF* in 1952 and a novel written with

1

Judith Merrill, *Gunner Cade*—he became one of a number of writers who became too good and ambitious to sell him anymore.

He suffered from hypertension, which worsened as the decade went on. Donald Wollheim said that Kornbluth had been a bitter man as far back as Wollheim had known him, into the 1930s, and as he got older he "just got more and more bitter until you knew he was going to have to die because he couldn't go on anymore that way." Laurence Janifer remembers him at a party in the mid-1950s slightly drunk and muttering, "Don't do something if it comes too easy. If it comes too easy you're finished." And Fred Pohl says that when severe hypertension had been diagnosed, his doctor put him on a salt-free, no-alcohol, no-tobacco diet and told him that if he did not obey it faithfully he would be dead in a year. Cyril tried it for two weeks and decided he'd rather be dead than live that way, so he went off the regimen and, as predicted, he was dead in less than a year. There appears to have been some choice here operative.

Reviewers have compared me to Kornbluth: spiteful, angry, bitter, dark, brooding. They ignore Kornbluth's astonishing range which in stories like *The Altar At Midnight* trembled into great compassion, or *The Marching Morons* with its piercing (terribly prophetic) social observation . . . to say nothing of my own. Nevertheless, I am honored. I miss him very much. I miss a man I will never know very much. He was a brother.

———◆———

A RECKONING

Researcher's efforts disclose definite evidence that the subject, Antonio Smith, was insane. "I can't stand it anymore," Smith wrote in one of the cache of secret, unmailed letters found by the researcher and remaining exclusively in his possession. "First we fail on the Moon, then on Mars, Venus is a total disaster about which the less said, perhaps, the better, and now they want to solve our problems by going to Jupiter. What good is Jupiter going to do us, I want to know. We must stop this insane foraging, this conveying of our lunacies from one segment of the solar system to the next; we must, I say, stay on our home planet and work out our problems in the arena of our birth." The letter, apparently intended for the President, terminates here. There is no dating, although objective data would place it somewhere in the month of July, 2151. I am sure of this. There is clear internal evidence, which I am keeping to myself.

Antonio Smith was mad. The study unearths huge blocks of data which only direct us, further and further, into this central insight. The researcher has, so to speak, "lived" with Antonio Smith for five working years; he has pored over documents public and private; he has come into exclusive possession of the aforementioned correspondences (no, I will not reveal the source, nor will I, despite all threats, turn them over to the agency: you put yourselves in this fix, gentlemen, and you will have to work out the consequences without aid from me); he has, through the use of his celestial mind and the three principles of fixation, been actually able to "dwell" with the late and obscure Antonio Smith, thus sharing not only his thoughts, but his actual visceral reactions. The study is now almost complete, lacking only the footnotes and proofreading, and in due course will be presented, under binding copyright, to the archives of the Second Committee. In the meantime, this more general prospectus, outlining the "highlights" of the study as well as addressing certain "tentative conclusions," will suffice. The files are under time lock. Any attempt to tamper with them or to release the sources of the information will result in the triggering of a massive explosion that will destroy Block K to the thirty-second level. I will give no further warning. Any more visitations by obscure "agents" or "correspondents" simply desiring to "talk" with me will result in the setting off of the detonators, whether or not the files are actually touched. I will say no more.

"You must tell my story," the madman Smith has said to me during our most significant conversations while sharing the Cosmic Connection. "You must make it clear to them that none of it was my fault and that I was forced by the actions and reactions, the stresses and the strains of the time, to do exactly what I did. I could have done no other. A reasonable man may chart no other course." This is not true. Antonio Smith was not reasonable, but, in fact, psychotic. Evidence permits no other conclusion. Nevertheless, Smith, no less than the others in the Jupiter Project, has motives for his condition. It could have been worked out in no other way. The researcher is aware of this, being tolerant, experienced and flexible. Smith found himself the man on the key, alone in the evacuator, assigned to be the first man to land upon the surface of that large and tortured planet, Jupiter. I will make no attempt to tell this chronologically. The completed study will have everything in order. The purpose of this prospectus is as a preliminary, so to speak, setting out the basic points and protecting the copyright. I know that there are other, false, researchers in the process of preparing spurious reports and it is necessary to file early to establish my primacy. Smith found himself the man on the key.

Alone in the evacuator, he considered his condition. Thoughts of his past flooded his mind: dim obsessions, fragments of scatology, somewhat larger, more metaphysical speculations of his future and the purpose of the voyage. Thirty-seven years old at this time, born in the old Gardens and given, by perverse parentage, not only the name of an ancient conqueror but some of his spirit, Smith checked the tubes in the evacuator, the controls, the dials, the visual plates and so on, all indicating that the capsule was in proper order and would not fail him in his speedy flight to and return from the remarkably large planet of Jupiter. "I don't think that this is sensible or possible," Smith said, clasping his hands in the evacuator and lending this chant some of the lilt if not the tonality of the popular song of his day. But of course he said this quietly, being aware that his actions, not to say speeches,

in the capsule were available on viewplate to the other
eighteen men charged with the responsibility of the conquest of Jupiter, and that anything he said to discomfit
them or to suggest the possibility of failure could only re-
bound against him to stunning effect. He had been assigned to the key, since, in the judgment of superiors in
the controlling mission, he was the most competent, not
to say phlegmatic member of the crew, and if he could
not succeed in landing upon Jupiter, who could? How
wrong they were! Not judging Antonio Smith's bizarre
mental condition and the twisted heritage that would fail
him in the very synapses at the most crucial moment . . .
but I am getting ahead of myself, at least somewhat. It is
difficult to keep these notes in order. I am terribly excited,
even at this distance, by all the details of Smith's disaster
and then, too, I am turning this out under enormous pressure, trying to make completion-and-delivery before the
offices close for the cycle. Early. They will close the offices early, knowing with their constant and weird cunning that today, of all days, I am working frantically on a
deadline. They are alert to my purposes; they will try to
thwart me at every juncture. Nevertheless, I have a cunning in excess of their own. I will not be defeated. The
recording clerk, however reluctantly, will accept my prospectus as binding.

"After all," Smith said very quietly, rubbing his hands
for warmth (it was kept chill in the evacuator, twenty
degrees below the temperature maintained in the mother
ship in order that the environment would be self-
maintained against atmospheric pressures, and there
would be safety margin in the event of failure of the con-
densers), "the record is not good. We abandoned the
Moon, failed to achieve Mars and lost the Venus project
when the only ship ever sent out returned with one man
missing and the other insane. In light of our . . . so to
speak . . . past performances, we cannot be too optimistic
about the conquest of Jupiter. How did I ever get into
this? All that I wanted to do at the start when I joined
the agency was find tenure and a good retirement plan,"
he said as the evacuator, with a slight whisk, detached

itself from the holding clamps and began its voyage, however unceremoniously, to the extremely grandiose, if hostile, planet of Jupiter. Gravitational forces would bring it at drift fifty miles to within a five-mile radius at which point retroactive devices would fire, enabling a soft landing. After fifteen minutes in the capsule on the surface of Jupiter, reporting all the time his impressions and opinions of the planet from this close range, automatic timers would trigger the capsule again, lifting it in a carefully charted arc toward the ship, whose orbit was then calculated to intersect that of the capsule in another soft landing. Smith had not chosen to be the first man on Jupiter, but it had been the decision of the Committee, in constant consultation with the crew, that Smith was the most qualified.

Falling toward Jupiter at a graceful and easy rate of speed (internal evidence charts this as five hundred fifty-nine international kilometers per unit, but I take this to be a canard; it was actually much faster than that, and the distance covered far more than the fifty miles maintained), other and interesting thoughts paraded through Smith's rather solemn and befuddled consciousness, most of them sexually retrospective in certain ways that I have chosen to delete for the satisfaction of the censors who might otherwise quibble with this altered portrait of a "major historical figure." Statements concerning Antonio Smith's heterosexuality from bureaucratic sources may be dismissed as self-serving: I will leave the matter at that. It was during this time that the transceiver was put into operation and Smith engaged in dialogue with the Captain, who, tense in the mother ship, was monitoring the voyage through various devices and gauges in whose use he had been carefully instructed. "We seem to be losing contact, Smith," the Captain said. He was not actually a qualified member of the Jovian expedition, but instead a government agent given minimal training and a fast clearance in order that the government, by proxy at least, would be close to the situation at all times. This decision, a bad one, had been dictated by previous disasters in the Moon, Venus and Mars programs. I will not discuss this further. "I said, we seem to be losing contact, Smith," the Captain repeated, looking nervously at indicators that yielded only the dimmest portrait of the interior of the evacuator, Smith a glum, huddled shape toward the amorphous center. "Do you hear me?"

"I hear you," Smith said. His mind was less on the transceiver than on a certain obvious insight into his condition that had never previously occurred to him but which now seemed perfectly clear as he looked through the one clear pane at the approaching specter of Jupiter, gaseous and purple in the light of the tensors.

"Then why are we losing contact?" the Captain said somewhat irritably, trying not to convey his discomfiture to the sixteen other members of the crew who huddled around him in various postures, gaping at the disappearing image of Smith. "We have almost completely lost visual contact. Talk to me. Adjust one of the tensors."

"I can't be bothered with that now," Smith said, abandoning sexual retrospection (believing that he had finally settled something about himself that had always been obscure and that he would be a better man for it: now, if he returned to the ship and hence to Earth, he would begin a new life by requesting a transfer to a new type of living unit). "Can't you see that I'm concentrating on the landing?" And, indeed, despite his proven insanity, Smith was not dissembling at this juncture, for he could see Jupiter coming rapidly upon him like a vast set of indigo dishware being alternately hurled and handed to him by enormous, disappearing hands, and at that moment he could feel the bucking of the retrofire, sending surges of power and fear through his slender, fit frame as the evacuator capsule slowed in its descent and eased toward Jupiter at a corrected (rumored) rate of ten kilometers per standard time. "I can't do everything," Smith said with increasing irritation, leaning to look through the pane at a network of green and interesting tendrils, very possibly alive, which appeared before him as the ship sunk ever closer to its destiny. "I can either land on Jupiter, I mean, or give you a travelogue. This is a decision you're going to have to make, but I really can't be concerned with any of this now." And, saying this, Smith lifted a hand to the wall of the craft, and pulling a switch that he had been given to understand controlled all monitored contact, turned off communication.

That is to say, he was under the *impression* that he had turned off all communication; in fact and by nature, the mother ship had been provided with a free override switch that the Captain merely hit to restore contact . . . but the difficulties in connection of which the Captain had already complained became even more serious. All that the intent crew and the Captain were able to see through the viewplate was a thin glaze in which a deformed parody of a human shape could be seen struggling against a nebulous background. Aural communications, similarly afflicted, yielded only a static from which random curses, like stray flies from decayed sugar, emerged only occasionally and without energy. "Are you there, Smith?" the Captain said, and the appalled crew, moving even more closely toward the viewplate (in the crowded quarters of the mother ship's communications center, it became increasingly fetid and some of the crew made hostile gestures toward one another while trying to fixate their gaze on what they erroneously took to be important), saw at that moment a vague impression of several large forms seemingly coming into the evacuator and surrounding Smith, whose own form was so indistinct that it was difficult to establish identity, although there was a clear impression of struggle before transmission for the last time winked out and all contact with the capsule was lost during the remainder of the conquest of the Jovian landscape.

Looking at that landscape, his senses filled with wondrous impressions and visions of that largest of the located planets of the Solar System, Smith felt an alteration of his consciousness so profound that he knew he would never be the same again (in our last and most pointed conversation he added that "It was before me all the time, though; just extraordinary to have to go to Jupiter to see what was staring you in the face . . . so to speak . . . all of your life, but then there's no reckoning for human perversity, now, is there?" I solemnly agreed, although by that point in our dialogues I had begun to lose all patience with Smith, whose increasing lunacy and wavering stream of consciousness were taking him further and further from those simple and obvious conclusions that we should have been making evident by then . . . but so much for my problems as researcher; I do not expect you to have any more sympathy for me than you did for the pitiful Smith, who, as we know, lives on, although no one except the researcher has taken the trouble to establish his point of view and then make the simple and earnest conclusion that the man was mad), but then, as the Jovians overcame his increasingly feeble struggles and slapped their rescusitator-and-chains upon him and prepared for the triumphal return to the mother ship for the purposes of capture and the ensuing and long-delayed capture of Earth, Smith was not so sure. It was not so clear what you could accomplish by going to Jupiter that you could not by staying in your own bed. It was not so evident what men had to gain by leaving their still essentially alien planet to voyage out except for a great deal of trouble. It was not clear exactly what he was going to accomplish by all of this, despite his elegant name and tangled heritage.

But this is something of a different nature entirely and not germane to the purposes of this study, which, when completed, will remain at the explicatory point of reference that Antonio Smith was insane, and thus could only give the Jovians entirely the wrong impression of our race. A different representative might have led to a gentler conquest, but remaining as I will in my field of specialization, I do not wish to speculate unduly upon the tragic area of the new government operations.

Introduction to
LETTING IT ALL HANG OUT

Letting It All Hang Out is a story that could have been written by Stanley Elkin, and who is to say that if he had not written it he would not have found a proper ending? The idea is the kind of conceit with which he works so well and the character is pure Elkin . . . but I couldn't find an ending.

It came into my head all in one piece one Monday night, everything but a conclusion, and, instead of writing it straight out (which I almost always do with the ideas that are furnished; to not do so would be to spurn gifts), I sat on it a few days hoping that an ending would materialize. By Friday, when it had not, I wrote the story because I was afraid that I would lose it if I didn't, but I *still* had no finish. It was marketed by the capable Virginia Kidd to the incapable *Fiction* and *Esquire* and rejected, but in neither case because it lacked a conclusion. (Literary markets need no excuses, having manufactured all of their responses in advance.) It was sold to the occasionally capable Ted White, who said that he would have liked it more with an ending, but he did not welsh on payment—the largest I have ever received from *Amazing*—on this account. It appears in this collection in the same form, slightly cleaned up, tightened, literatified . . . but it *still* does not——

If anyone out there can speak to the story's condition or my own, I would be delighted to hear from them.

Stanley Elkin . . . do you read science fiction?

LETTING IT ALL HANG OUT

To come straight to the point, I am the man who invents the clichés, catch-phrases and aphorisms of the times. Yes, although it may sound highly unlikely, all of these emanate from these deft hands, this twinkling brain, this small furnished room, ditto those figures of speech that you hear from disc jockeys and television hosts, perhaps as recently as last night. *Freak out, tough shit, hanging loose, uptight, give me five, ask the man, cool it, baby, jammed up.* All of them had their origin in this bullet-shaped head likewise these fingers that poured the words out to clean paper and then, via my various distributorships, to the world. You didn't think that these things were spontaneously generated, did you? Even the universe had an origin. *Big bang. Tough bananas. Sixty-nine.* How did I get into the business? Looking back upon it, this is hard to say. Unable to settle on my life's work in the late teens like most people of my generation, I guess that I simply fell into it. The pay is not bad and the job is necessary; there are worse careers.

It is difficult, difficult to be responsible for all the clichés of the world. Also, this has had a ponderous and rather sopoforic effect upon my own rhetoric, which swings casually between my instincts and trade, my narration thus mediating uneasily between passages of the most shocking insight and moments that fail to come alive due to inevitable hackneying. Nevertheless, I must get this all out as best I can; my confessions are no less interesting than any actor's, and I will keep a cool and cunning hand upon the second serial rights.

Here I am, the day's completed work before me. Twenty-five phrases and figures of speech that will slowly descend into the public consciousness until they emerge on July 7, 1977. I must work several years ahead like a good comic strip to guard against illness or sudden death.

11

Winking out the Border, Lilydark, Skintight, Mars Maze.
I am paid four cents a word for my efforts on acceptance
for all rights. Several years ago I secured an agent who
attempted to retain some of the performing rights and to
grant me some kind of royalty arrangement based on use,
but my employers became very ugly and threatened
to terminate my services. I was forced to release the agent
who had only been trying to do his job, but as a result of
this failure, I am given to understand, he became severely
depressed and, his confidence shattered, was out of the
markets within a year. He is now in manufacturing,
although I cannot obtain more specific information.

Four cents a word is not ample payment, but on a good
day I can generate eight to ten typewritten pages, each
averaging two hundred words, which means that my gross
pay before deductions is somewhere between sixty and
eighty dollars a day, or, perhaps, seventeen thousand a
year. This is not inadequate to my purposes—I live simply, I have no hobbies, I have a horror of relationships of
any sort—and, although I have been at this job for five
years now without any significant raises or promise of ad-
vancement, I am not discontented. It was understood at
the outset that this job was a dead end; there is, after all,
very little place in the outside world for my highly specialized skills, and in any event, I could hardly declare them
on a résumé. Interviewers would not believe me. You do
not believe me . . . do you? *Giving me jive.*

It is five P.M. My day's work has been done for half an
hour and I have been filling in time awaiting the arrival of
the messenger for half an hour or so, idly typing these
notes. Now the messenger comes, a few minutes late as
usual, slipping through my open door and standing rather
humbly before me on the other side of this desk, waiting
for me to pass over the copy. The messenger is my only
contact with my employers, who I have never met. All of
my dealings with them have been through intermediaries.
In the course of my agent's negotiations, to which I have
previously referred, I received a rather hysterical phone
call from a woman who said that she was a secretary and
that one of the employers would be down to fire me personally if I did not desist from my demands, but this is as

close as I have gotten to personal contact. I got this job through answering a small classified ad, box number included, in the local newspaper.

"All done?" the messenger says. He always asks this; it is our ritual. Sometimes I think that he is as compulsive as I. My work is always ready for him; there has never been a time when the pages, neatly polished (I still do second drafts, although my facility has reached the point where they are necessary only for the sake of conscientiousness), were not on the far side of the desk, awaiting his pickup. "I see you are."

"I'm always done," I say. "I love my work." This, too, is part of the ritual.

"That's important," the messenger says. He is a small man, no older than his early thirties, perhaps as young as twenty-five or so, although intensely nervous. He has his own responsibilities; they must be overwhelming, and the pay, merely to vet and fetch copy, cannot be too good. He looks through the pages quickly. *"Mars Maze,"* he says. "Explain that one."

"By July 7, 1977, there will be renewed interest in a Mars expedition with the change of administrations and the bottoming-out of the aerospace industry. Extended probes of Mars will have indicated a soft terrain and an accommodating atmospheric situation making a landing feasible by no later than 1982. On the other hand, reformist and libertarian elements will persist in their loathing of the space program and will need a catch-phrase to symbolize their feelings. Also, by inference, the phrase will refer to all situations that seem indeterminate or manipulative. It will even have a sexual connotation."

"I think that that's perhaps a bit specious," the messenger says. This is routine; he will quibble over one or two phrases daily, whether from honest doubt or from the rigors of his position, I cannot say. I know that he does not have the right of final approval, although his recommendations, of course, are important. "We have no assurance that the matter of a Mars expedition will be in the popular consciousness at that time."

"The phrase will plant that consciousness," I say, which

is absolutely true and unanswerable. I know my work. The messenger nods, folds over my copy and places the sheets in the small knapsack that he has strung over his left shoulder. "All right," he says, "I'll take it up with them and give them your point of view. Is everything all right otherwise?" This, too, is routine.

"Yes," I say. "There's a small possibility that I may have to find new quarters sometime next year; the landlady tells me that we're being investigated by urban renewal. But I see no urgency, and she says she's going to fight it, anyway."

"Good," he says, "good." He nods. Now is the time for him to move away, but, strangely, he does not move away; instead, he removes a package of cigarettes from his knapsack and lights one uncomfortably, flicking the match into a disheveled corner of my room and then inhaling and exhaling in large scattered puffs. "There's one other thing, though," he says, looking over my shoulder. "I don't know how to put this. Something came up."

"Well," I say, "what is it?" It is disconcerting to have the ritual broken in this way. I am a man of small habits, great order and defined activities through which I block out my life and which make my work possible. If I were not so ordered I am sure that I would have long ago found my life and work untenable. "Tell me."

"Yeah," the messenger says, "yeah." He grinds out the cigarette, looks from corner to corner of the room, and then, putting his hands on his hips, confronts me straight on. "I have to tell you that you're going to be laid off for a while. They think that you're so far ahead now that the stuff might kind of . . . uh . . . lose touch if we don't wait it out. They're thinking in terms of a year or two, until some of the inventory gets used up. They say they're having trouble coordinating the stuff already."

"You mean that I'm being fired?"

"Well, no," the messenger says. He seems very uncomfortable, backs away from me, leans against the open door. "Not at all, because you aren't going to be replaced. There's no need to replace you because the work's caught up ahead for so many years. It would be a layoff by mutual agreement, and in a year or two you could . . . uh . . . reapply and probably get preference." He nudges the door even further ajar with a toe, then steps into the hall. "I mean, it isn't my decision, you understand," he says. "I just kind of run the messages back and forth, that's all. I don't have anything to do with it. But they think that this would be best because the stuff is . . . ah . . . as I say, getting a little out of touch and not coordinated too well, and you got to consider my position. I may get laid off, too. I do other stuff for them but this is the primary job, and if they cut this off they may be able to shift jobs around and let me go. It's a question of cutting down the payroll. They say like everybody else that they're a little overextended and have to make adjustments." The messenger now seems voluble. "I don't mind saying," he says, "that I think you're getting a real screwing on this deal after the way you took it on your own hook to build them up an inventory, but that's the way it is. It isn't my decision. I had no business getting in with them in the first place; I just needed some kind of job until I could get back to school and then I got hooked in. Maybe it's all for the best; with your talent you should be a writer, anyway —a real writer doing real stuff."

"When does this layoff start?"

The messenger looks at the floor, puts his right hand on the knapsack and adjusts it. "Sort of today," he says quietly. "I mean, tomorrow. Today is the last day. They'll mail you your check right up to today and probably pay you through the end of the week, although I can't be sure. They don't tell me anything. You know," he says confidentially, "sometimes I get the feeling that we got absolutely no control over what's going on here, that even *they* don't know what's going on, but I figure that that's not my problem." And then he leaves, closing the door quickly. I sit at my desk over the typewriter facing the door, waiting for the messenger to return and add to what he was saying, but he does not, and after a while I understand that our relationship is terminated.

It is only a little while after that when I come to accept the fact that my job has been terminated as well, and that is the most dismaying thing of all, but years of working in terms of aphorism enable me to control my feelings. *Stick it in. Tough it out. Hard-nosed. Making the rounds.*

They cannot do this to me, I say to the empty spaces of my room. *They cannot abuse my skill and experience in this way.* Mad thoughts of going into the business for myself afflict me, but I realize immediately that I lack the distribution sources and would not know where to begin.

Then it occurs to me. I realize both how I can solve the problem and pay back the employers. This is only a brief of my situation; I have much more to divulge, plus thousands of my writings, which for some reason did not make it into the common language. The tools for analysis are there; it will be fascinating for the ethnologists to decide why some phrases made it and others did not. This is only the beginning of what I could tell, a brief, if you will. For a contract and advance, I am ready to write the full story.

I want to hang in there.

Introduction to
THE MAN IN THE POCKET

The issue of this story is one of my five or six obsessive themes (others: paranoid astronauts; wives who know their husbands are crazy; husbands who know their wives are crazy; horse-racing and another Not to Be Mentioned), and I am heartily sick of it, finally. It first appeared in a short story, *In the Pocket,* written in 1967; it was expanded to considerable length from another point of view in the version that follows and then cut (this version) for a Robert Silverberg *New Dimensions* anthology in which it was still fourteen thousand words. Not satisfied, I spliced together those two pieces, found another voice and published it as *The Men Inside* (Lancer Books, 1973), which, according to my records, appears to have been read by five or ten people. (Every prolific writer has a Book Praised Beyond Its Merits and a Book Unjustly Ignored, and *The Men Inside* fits any definition of the latter, although the reasons are clear . . . it is not precisely upbeat.) The following is the original version submitted to *New Dimensions* and my favorite of all the treatments for the purity of its style, and because I think it could have been published in my favorite S-F magazine, the *Galaxy* of the early 1950s, as edited by Horace Gold. It has the feel.

Reasons for the obsessive nature of this theme are private. Purists may find a partial clue in the dedication to *Beyond Apollo* . . . but I have had nothing to say on this issue in public or private for some years, and this will continue.

THE MAN IN THE POCKET

PROLOGUE

To COMPREHEND HULM: THE SIMPLE,
MAD CONSTANCY OF THE MAN

In the night after his first Experiment, Hulm has a dream, and in that dream the process has been perfected. Institutes have been opened all over the world, staffed by trained workers to speed relief to the millions, and, now, as he hovers cloudlike over this agglomeration, all the workers turn to him. Reduced by the process to five-eighteenths of an inch, they confront Hulm, an army of elves, singing in a massed chorus, their little lances poised deftly in their hands, and what they are saying is, "You are a vain man, Robert Hulm, a vain and stricken man, because none of it turned out the way you thought it would. None of it, none of it; corruption, corruption." And they turn from him then to assault a phalanx of patients, lumps of flesh lying in the distance. Hulm rises, contorts, raises his fists and says, "But you don't understand; it had to be that way, it had to be a corporate entity to survive. I didn't want it but it had to be!" Somehow, it seems, he has gotten the whole gist of the argument from his tiny Messengers, none of whom pay any attention to him as they march off toward pockets of metastases. "Oh, yes, you did," one of them calls back, "yes, you did, Hulm, you loved it, you saw it all, the potential and the reward; it was *profit-making,* and it was that more than any other thing that drove you through your mad researches. Not to cure, but to prosper, but the joke is on you, Hulm, because it's all been taken away, every single part of it; only your name remains. Because, although you had the greed of the entrepreneur, you had none of the

18

skill. None of it, none of it." The Messengers march away giggling and Hulm screams, screams and screams in his cloud, bellows himself to frenzy, but none of them are listening; no one, it seems, wants any part of him and he says, "I wanted to do good; that's all I wanted to do— good: how did I know it would have this effect upon you?" And he comes to realize then that he should have given thought—a lot more thought—to the Messengers, because, after all, these were people who were going to make the whole scheme work, but no time for that now, none of it at all; stretched in ice, freezing in dreams, he wakes dying to the dawn, and before anything can be done for him it is late, far too late. Only the Experiments and their notations can be saved.

Poor old bastard.

I. Telling It All to the Priest:
How I Wish My Hands Were Stone

The night after I graduated from the Institute I went down to the Arena. Perhaps it was rage of disillusionment, perhaps sheer perversity, but I got drunk, very drunk then, and destroyed a Priest while only trying to make my position clear. Later on, when all the factors coalesced, I discovered that things weren't quite as simple as I had taken them and that I had, possibly, been a little melodramatic. By that time, however, the Priest was fragments. So, for all I know, was my sensibility. Resignation comes only after the fact.

I am not trying to say that the job is good. The job, in fact, is a disaster in every conceivable way. But it is terrible in a fashion that I did not understand, good in a way that I could not have suspected. One learns. One cultivates perspective. One turns twenty-one and begins to see implications. By that time, however, the damage has been done. The night that I ripped the Priest, I thought that I was dying, conventionally.

"Let us face it," I said to Smith, who had come with

me that night, not because he was a friend of mine (no Messenger ever has any friends), but because he was one of those off of whom I could bounce the rhetoric without back talk. Part of this submissiveness of Smith came from stupidity (idiocy runs rampant in the downside these days), and part of it came from something that I only discovered later might have been love. "Let us understand. We're menial laborers. Hod carriers. The lowest of the low in the post-technological age. The machinery has given us a wider range of skills, has provided a title, but that's all of it. In truth we have spent four years in the most dreadful kind of training imaginable simply so that we can move in mud. Disgusting, it's disgusting. Of course, there's no way that you can understand that, so I won't even try. Instead, take this one. The whole thing is for a fast buck. It was contrived that way. It's profit-making, and they've got fear working for them. It's out of control. Totally."

"Oh," he said, "oh, Mordecai," and finished his drink one-handed, his dull eyes turning wide and large in the aftertaste, looking around hopelessly for a waitress, "oh, Mordecai, I can't argue with you, you're so much smarter than the rest of us, but do you really think that's so? The work is so important. And it's dedicated. Scientific. It's like religion; even doctors can't do it."

I should point out that I am changing Smith's name for the purposes of the integrity of these notes. It is not my intention to slander people or to hold up the limited for ridicule. Like most of the people from his downside, he had a long, unpronounceable ethnic name that sounded like a curse. My name, however, *is* Mordecai, and you will find me useful and credible throughout. A pity that there is no audience for these reminiscences, then.

"Pick and shovel," I said, "moving the caboose. That's all. They've trained us for four years their way to make the optimum profit, and now we're to breathe their religion. I can't stand it. I can't stand it anymore. Of course, there's no percentage in that. We're in on a five-year up."

The Arena, of course, is dedicated to the most practical pleasures, but there is a small anteroom of a bar of which you may have never heard where serious drinking may be done, and it was there that Smith and I had gone. I knew that it was only a matter of time until I left him for the more realistic activities—hadn't I come to the Arena to pleasure myself?—but we were stupefied with drink and I had still not managed to say what I had on my mind. Whatever there was on my mind. No Messenger can really handle liquor; we are not trained that way. The kind of mind that can be manipulated into being a Messenger would adapt poorly to liquor.

"You're an orderly," I said. "At best, you're one with dignity. That's the furthest that they dare push it. Be realistic."

"Cancer," he said, shaking his head, "cancer, Mordecai, just think of that. We're going to be able to cure it. Fifty years ago no one knew the answer and now people like you and me can make it. We are the answer. Besides, where else would we have gotten all this free education?"

"They'll get it back from us tenfold. The whole thing is calculated. Don't you understand the factor of turnover?"

"Education, Mordecai. It's all education and it's free. We've made something of ourselves. I was afraid. I didn't want the cold gut," Smith said, and stood up to go for a drink . . . but fell instead heavily over his feet. Alas, drinking Messengers! He fell with a clatter tableward to land in a sighing heap.

"Stupid," I said. "You're stupid and naïve and scared. They didn't even have to hook you in; you were sold when you were born."

The fine, sensitive Smithian hands that would soon cleave out colons twitched and he muttered *Kyrie* in a high guttural; I decided to leave the bastard where he lay. In due time—there is always due time—he would come back to himself and deal with the situation in his way, and that would be time enough. There were five years ahead of him. In the meantime, he was entitled—or in any event, this was the way that I thought at that time—to all the oblivion that he could get. (I could only envy his low threshhold.)

On the other hand, there was always the chance that Smith might get himself beaten and roughed up, even in this most aseptic of the Arenas, in which case he would not be coming back to himself for a while. They might have to reroute him. In either case, what the hell did it matter?

He had no future to look forward to; that was how much it mattered. He was no different from me, the percentages were the same; the only difference, in fact, was that he *thought* that it mattered. He did not have my perceptual advantages. I did not wish them upon him. We were, therefore—or would have been, to use a fair word —even.

I left him there. I left the drinks, too, went out into the corridor and toward the fluorescence of the Arena. The attendant caught me at the rope and decided that I was undrunk enough to be safe and asked me what I wanted. She did not say it graciously, but then Smith and I were not in Clubhouse. Grandstand was the speed for Messengers and enlisted men.

"I want a confession machine," I said, "right away."

"A confession machine?"

"Isn't that what you call them? All right, I've been out of the world a while. A Priest. I want a Priest."

She looked at me with some puzzlement on her middle-aged face (I detected a fine brown wart that would flower into metastases in five or six years; one could see the intimation of the filaments it would cast: burn it out fast and horrid with a knife.) and said, "We don't get many requests for that these days."

"People don't want to confess?"

"Not that way."

"I do."

"Well, the thing is, it isn't working too well. The demand fell off so greatly that we have only one Priest and the machinery isn't right. I don't know if it's dependable."

"I'll take my chances," I said. "I said, I'll take my chances. I want to confess. Do I have the right to confess?"

Something in my voice must have caught her, or only

perhaps the frenzied caper of my hands; she looked and
shrugged and pressed a bell. "I'll have an attendant right
here," she said. "You aren't out of the Institute, are you?"

"That's right," I said. "They just graduated a flock today."

"Oh, I know that. I just wasn't sure for a minute. Most
of them you can tell right off. Congratulations. You must
be very proud."

"I'd get that wart looked at," I said. "I see desiccation
and death."

"What? What's that?"

"Desiccation and death; intimations of waste. It could
go rampant at any time. Get it looked at," I said, then
went off with the attendant, a girl of twenty-four or -five
who looked at me strangely and held me at arm's length
as we went down a corridor. Behind me I heard moaning,
which was fine with me. The girl dragged me into an alcove halfway toward a door and, putting her arms around
me, said, "Want some flesh?"

"No," I said. "I'm neutered."

"Neutered? I don't understand that." She squeezed. I
could feel the horrid pressure of her rising breasts under
one layer of silk, with wicker of lips against the ear.
"Come on," she said, "I can tell. We can do it off the
tables. Private rates."

"Don't touch me," I said, pushing her away, feeling her
resilience cave into waste under pressure, all yielding, all
devastation, all loss. "Don't touch me, you fool. I'm contaminated."

"Contaminated? Are you crazy? What the hell's wrong
with you?"

"You don't understand," I said. "I'm a Messenger—
a man of cancer."

"Oh," she said with a shrug and took my hand wearily,
and we started down the corridor again. "That explains
everything. Why didn't you tell me kicks no?"

"No."

"Oh, it isn't all that bad," she said, her features
congealing around an asexual slant, perfect for celibates
and lunatics. That wonderful adaptability. "It can be a

great thing. Besides, think of the honor of it. How many ———"

"I just graduated. I graduated from the Institute today. I don't know about honor. All I've learned so far is reduction."

"I don't understand any of you," she said. "Not one."

"We're not crazy, just realistic."

"I know you just graduated from the place," she said, tenderly guiding me through a door. "I just knew it. I should have been positive when you ordered the Priest. Tens will get you dimes, the ones who graduate always take the Priest. Well, that's up to you what you do; I don't care. I only try to hustle a little in private."

"I admire your spirit," I said.

"No you don't. If you admired my spirit, you wouldn't talk bad," she said, then wandered away somewhere with my credit balance in her fist to do whatever attendantly things are done in the Arena when they are not more directly in use. It is not a pleasant job, but then, again, the Arena is not really a pleasant place, merely a necessity. "Don't worry about nothing, nothing to worry you," she said on the way out. "It's a defective, so that's a discount right there, and I have a friend's mother who just lost cancer the other week, thanks to one of you. I'll arrange a discount. I have special influence; I'll work it out nice."

"I don't care."

"Yes you do," she said. "Even Messengers will take the money."

There seemed little enough to say to that, so I shook my head, looked at the Priest for a while and then went inside. It was an older model, no reclining chair, just stiff wood and without color, but all of that is merely polish. I put the machine on, waited until the green cleared and said, "I have come to you, Father, for I have sinned."

"You have come to me, for you have sinned," the machine said in a pleasant tenor, the voice only slightly creaky. Defect or not, it had been a good model in its time.

"I wish for you to hear me because my sins are dark and grievious."

"Confess and be blessed," it said and rasped, coming to an effeminate yowl on the *blessed*. Gears ground dismayingly somewhere in the background. The attendant had been right; the machine was almost shot. A small plate on the seat said that it was 1993, which was about right, for I discovered it didn't even have a visual. Without visuals it is almost impossible.

"Be blessed," it said again and clicked. "Confess and be known."

"I have just graduated from the Institute, where I took my training to become a Messenger."

"That is a fine undertaking of which you can be very proud. Messengers ————"

"The Institute is a profit-making institute run under medical sanction as a monopoly. It exploits its one stroke of genius and the terror of its dependents for crude gain. It is utterly cynical and destructive. I have discovered this."

"Messengers often react to circumstances in this way." The damned thing, apparently, did not even have an automatic override so that it could cue into the direction of speech. "Go on," it said, "go on, relieve yourself."

"It is in the hands of a very few greedy men who, having controlled the rights to the Hulm Projector, use fear as a means of maintaining power."

"How long have you felt this way?"

"Listen," I said, "listen to me. I have not come to this lightly. I have learned. I know the three causeways of metastases; I know its lesser and greater pathways, its colors and symbiosis. I learned the seventeen manual and forty-five automatic methods of incision; I learned of filamentation, mitosis and the scattering of cells. I saw demonstrations; I performed my own tasks. I learned of the history and implications. I ————"

"That all sounds very interesting; however, you have not yet detailed your problem. Please detail your problem."

"You're not giving me a chance to finish. You won't let me explain."

"Confess and be blessed ————"

"I could have come here for anything, you know. Who uses Confessors anymore? You could show some consideration."

"What is this personification?" the machine asked rather sullenly. "Why do you have this compulsive need for special iteration? The important thing is to come to terms———"

The new Confessors have special circuitry. Even though demand for the machines has fallen off to nothing, special circuitry is available that blocks the Confessor at certain points so that you can ride straight through. (I know of this from those who have used the newer models; I have had no experience with them.) The vintage of this one, however, seemed to preclude the possibility of dialogue. Also, the machine was hooked into a familiar Freudianism, which by now was completely archaic.

"Impossible," I said, "it's impossible."

"I am begging your pardon?"

Disgraceful. It is wholly disgraceful that the Arena would have equipment of this sort still in use while the sex machines were all of the newest and most powerful model. Perhaps this will only illustrate the eternal difference between purgation and escape, but I do not think so; something more ominous seemed to be at work. Even if the demand for Confessors fell off with my generation, there is still no point for functioning of this sort. No point at all. I was perfectly justified in doing what I did. Perfectly. Justified. I had a right to express myself. I had a right to let my demands be known. No less human than all of them, despite the pain of reduction, I felt fury boiling.

(I should point out that all of this happened sometime ago. I no longer wish to confess. I have no interest in confession. Confession can be accomplished in acts, not words. All of this has been outgrown; it took place a long time ago. Let me keep this in front of you at all times. I have changed. I am not the same individual. I am in all senses now Blount Transmogrified.)

"Let me finish," I said, trying it one last time. There was no point in getting exercised about a machine, this being the first and most basic level of the successful Confessor. "Let me finish this up. I learned all the means of reduction and expansion, to say nothing of the very interesting history of the Hulm Projector, a splendid but simple piece of equipment whose commercial application began only after the sudden death of its inventor, and the full details of whose functioning remain suppressed, even to Messengers. I learned about Hulm himself, the father, the psychoneurotic old bastard; I learned about the vision that drove him in darkness toward a sense so enormous ————"

"You are sweating. Your pulse is extremely rapid. Why do you react to this cold data with such excitation? It is only fact. It is known to all. Try to be reasonable and calm."

"I don't want to be reasonable. Reasonable men got us into this."

"You cannot confess unless you are calm. You must learn to suppress ———— "

"I'm perfectly calm. How do you know my mental state? I simply want to confess."

"Why?"

"Why not?" I said and tried to ride it out, deciding that on this most fundamental of all days the machine could be said only to pose another challenge, slightly more hideous than most, but hardly consequential. Also, as I have explained, or should have explained, I was quick drunk. Very little drinking is done in the Institute in the first place, and in the second place, Messengers are small men."

"I took the oath today," I said. "I came from the Institute. I have been educated to all the greater and lesser evils into which the corrupted Messenger may stray, and I have learned the ways of their avoidance. I received a drill and a beam; I received a lance. I received an engraved diploma and memory book, the cost of which will be deducted from my first salary check. In short, I am now a professional awaiting his first assignment."

"You must be very proud."

"Listen, now: I will make thirty-nine thousand dollars

a year before taxes, and this is only the beginning grade, mind you. Soon I will go to fifty if I keep my hands straight. I have all the advantages of which I would have otherwise been deprived by coming, like all Messengers, from a rather deprived background. From the downside."

"What do you think of this?"

"I think nothing of the downside. I had no future; the Institute nourished me. I had no possibilities; the Institute made them manifest. I had no hope; the Institute gave me a profession."

"That must make you very grateful."

"That is not my question," I said. "You must listen to me now. All of this has been done for me, just as I have established it for you. If this is so, and surely it is . . . if this is indeed so, why do I hate them?"

The machine blinked its light. "Pardon me," it said, "I am now on automatic. There is an overload in the circuitry. It is only a slight problem that can be swiftly prepared. All will be corrected. An attendant will come."

"I hate them. Why do I hate them so? If only I knew the answer. Everything else I think I can understand, but not that."

"My circuitry is overloaded. Please be patient. There is some small problem in the mechanics. An attendant will come and all will be corrected. In the meantime, you must show patience. Very little time will elapse when I will again be functional and you may continue."

"Listen to me," I said, pounding metal, "listen to me, you son-of-a-bitch. . . ."

"Do not personify. My circuitry is overloaded. If you will . . ."

"I paid my money and I want to make my confession. I'm going to make it. *I want to kill.* Do you understand that? Not to cure, but to strike. All my life I have been maimed, burned, blasted, sullied and then coin-turned off my deprivation. Now they have taken me from those terrible streets and told me of a future, but I do not want a future. I do not want the Hulm Projector. I want no part of it. I do not want to clamber inside people like an itch to burn out cancer. I realized that during the ceremony; it all came to me terrible in its white completeness. I hate it. I hate it. I do not want to . . ."

"I am not functional. My circuitry overloaded is. Patience and mendacity, lying quietly. Signals for an attendant and soon the attendant will pass and then all well again you must speak but now it be . . . "

"Shut up, you bastard, and listen to me! *Listen to me!* I have no desire to cure the disease. I have no interest in diminution; indeed, I fear it. I hate the forty-five ways. I want to kill. I want to kill . . . "

"Coming attendant is."

"And kill," I said.

I rose to my full height, full of liquor and intent, five-feet three-inches of power and rage (Messengers, among other things, are recruited on the basis of their small height; one should not only be a slum denizen, but a *tiny* s.d.) and hurled myself against the metal, battering my tiny hands into the walls; smashing my little feet against the damned iron couch. Then I began to work on it in earnest application, spinning controls, wrenching dials, moaning and screaming and gasping as well. "You, too," deponent shouted, "you, too, you're just like the rest of them, profit-making, profit-making, profit-making! It's all rigged, all of the machinery!"

Oh, I · was very drunk, indeed, drunk so that I only wished that my hands were stone so that I could smash the Priest instead of feeling the blood run down the craven flesh while the woman returned and saw what I was doing and perhaps sensed what had happened (but how much do the attendants know?) and came to clutch me in an embrace as fierce and warm as death. "Don't worry," she said, "don't worry, it's not so bad; you only think it is, but you will learn to live with it." And she nuzzled me with lips like steel.

But I did not want any of that stuff, either. There was nothing the Arena could offer me that I would take: like the luckless or lucky Smith, I was beyond all of it by then, beyond all of it, and without aplomb I fainted.

But I fainted not soon enough to miss hearing what she

said over me as she cradled me, oh, ever so lushly, in her enormous arms.

"Messengers," she said, "Messengers, have you noticed? All of them like that and not a word to explain. What are they doing to them there? Is it worth it if they become people like this? It must be the equipment."

Deponent paid for it. A battered Priest, vintage 1993, is still a Priest. Eight hundred sixteen dollars and forty-five cents, payable in ten-percent deductions from my salary for the first eleven weeks. I was given the machine as a souvenir—the Arena, as a corporate enterprise, tries to meet its obligations—and there it sits, *there,* right this very moment before deponent, right in his foul little rooms where he continues to transcribe these notes. He has, at the present moment, so little else to do, your faithful deponent, although he could always stroll out a window or phone for Protection. All of this is useless speculation; deponent has no plans, has come around to the belief that all energy is merely a cover for the Void, has bigger and better things on his mind as soon as he can, so to speak, turn the corner. Things will get better, or worse, depending upon one's point of view; the important thing is to maintain a caution and open-minded reserve.

All harmless. All harmless. The Priest says nothing (certain blockages in the wire), but its contemplation keeps time purring along for dwarflike but vigorous Blount as he sits in the highest room in the clinic and decides exactly what he will Make of His Life.

Ideas. Ideas? Any ideas?

II. MEETING THE DIRECTOR;
THE STRANGE CONSTANCY OF THE MAN;
THE MASKING OF OBSESSION

The thing was that at the beginning it seemed like it was set up in almost a pastoral fashion. If they had edged off into the hard lines, if there had been some sense of the madness, I would have locked up my intimations toward outcome and everything would have fallen into place; there would have been a sense of control. But it didn't happen that way. I got thrown off the scent, came back late to it and assward. No easy answers for Blount; he comes from a deprived background.

The entrance interview:

"Good to have you in here, Blount," the Director said, winking at me across the desk. "It's always good to have new personnel, and in your case we've gotten excellent reports. People seem to think the best of you; they figure you to be one of the best."

"No I'm not."

"Don't even think of that. It will be good to have a competent new man breaking in here. Of course, we won't build you up to quota for a while. We'll give you time for that. Quota is one a day, but that won't be for four months; you'll have a full three days for a while, then cut back to two."

"One every three days? I thought that it was one a week."

"Well," the Director said with a merry laugh, "training isn't reality, you know, and the policy of the Institute is pretty much of an ideal. I'd hate to tell you that some of the clinics are turning over quotas of two a day. But we can do very nicely on one as we work you up to that. Lots of illness, Blount, lots of tragedy and loss. We have an enormous job to do here; we have to meet our obligations. The treatment is a responsibility, you know."

"But you don't understand," I said, looking from my valise to the wall, then to his face, a fine panel of blankness that looked at me with rising light. With a feeling of vulnerability coming from that face, surely anything could be impressed upon it, even a simple Blountish opinion. "You don't understand any of it. Qualifications for nothing. I don't want the job. I had this problem ————"

"Don't worry about it, Blount," he said with an elfin chuckle and removed a bottle from his desk, taking a hearty swallow. "Happens all the time—coming from four years of insulated training can be quite shattering."

"It wasn't the insulation."

"Pardon my informality with this wine. I should apologize, but I come from a generation more abused than yours, my friend. Liquor is still quicker."

"I don't care. I don't use anything."

"Well, how could you, my boy?" He leaned forward, a horrid confidentiality spreading over his features. It occurred to me that, with the door locked behind us, almost anything could happen, although there is really very little of that problem in the Institute. "Let me tell you something: you would have no way of knowing this, of course, but almost every new Messenger with whom I've had this interview comes into the office feeling exactly as you do."

"Is that so?"

"Of course it's so; in fact, you almost use the same words, the very words that you are now using, Blount—the feelings of ambivalence, and so on. It's the shock of transition. In a week you won't even think of it anymore."

"I'm not ambivalent," I said.

"Of course you are. Everybody's ambivalent. Examine your feelings, Blount, your real desires. Be realistic."

"I said I'm not ambivalent; I'm repulsed. I want no part of the whole thing. It's a disgusting exploitation; it's profoundly evil. There, I've said it to you."

This statement was made, of course, with my luggage beside me, my biography in hand and little lance nestled under my clothing to one side. There is truly nothing like a fine gesture of disavowal when there is no place to be gone. Images of the Priest roiled thickly in the brain. I belched excelsior, a whiff of wood shavings, with a hint of nausea uncoiling slowly in the anterior reaches. On the wall were pictures of the Director and other personages, inscribed in affectionate ways. I recognized none of the people, but that was to be expected; downsiders know little, and where had I been since downside but into the pit? It occurred to me that the office smelled faintly of money, not an unpleasant smell at all, really, but mixing poorly with nausea.

I leaned back on the chair, closed my eyes against the pictures and tried to imagine that I was in control of the situation and he the petitioner. He was a very fat little man, rosy, about forty-three or so, archangelic in appearance, but thin at the edges. Still, one could see the kind of confidence he might have inspired in the inscribers of the pictures. It was all there if he wanted to use it.

"You're disillusioned," he said. "You feel the Treatment should be a free process, Government-supported, available to the least as to the greatest, all as public charges. You feel that the Treatment has been exploited, that it has become an institutionalized process for profit. That's it, right?"

"So, you're clever," I said. "So you've heard it before. Does that make it any less valid? I don't think the Treatment has been exploited; I think it's doing the exploitation. For fear. The manipulation of people at a level . . . "

"You talk well, Blount. You're highly articulate."

"I studied rhetoric and composition in the second year as an elective. I thought that I might write my memoirs or an exposé. Of course, I found out about that soon enough."

"Well, of course," he said, nodding, "of course, nobody wants to hear about it, Blount; they just want the treatment to *work,* which, fortunately, it does."

"For the Institute."

"For *all* of us, Blount. All of us. I'm not unsympathetic to your reaction; all of us have had it at one time or the other. Once I did. Let me assure you that things all do work out and that there is no other way. Our facilities are still entirely too limited . . . "

"That's why you take a Government subsidy."

His eyes narrowed and he said, "I don't really think that any of this is necessary, Blount. There are matters far beyond your control or understanding, and I can only assure you that they will become comprehensible and will work out as time goes on. That's one of the virtues of maturity. We have a long way to go, and I'm the first to admit it, but we're catching up."

"How much does the Institute really own? Can it take over the world at this rate? What are the economics of it?"

"Overhead," the Director said, "terrific overhead.

Really, Blount, you're not being reasonable, and I'm beginning—just beginning, mind you—to lose my patience. Receiving initiates is not my only duty, you know."

"I thought that was all you did—that, and take pictures."

"Now, come on," he said and took another drink from the bottle, put it carefully into his desk and slammed a drawer. "There are limits to this kind of thing, and you're approaching them. You're uncivil and disturbed, Blount, because you've decided that the Institute really has no reason to hoard the Treatment by patent and limit its application by payment; you think that this should be a Government utility. I might point out that this sentiment is neither original to you, nor very useful, and I might point out finally that I'm mighty poorly paid and dressed to be one of your exploiters. What *is* important is that we've beaten the disease."

"Only in the Institute's terms."

"Terms, terms, what are terms? Cancer is an expensive toothache now; that's all it has to be. You ought to count your blessings. You've got a wonderful opportunity to make something of yourself here and receive the Treatment free yourself, should anything ever happen to you."

"Isn't that wonderful!"

"You listen to me, Blount," the Director said and leaned his elbows on the desk, looked at me with bright and piercing expression, seemed to emit a luminous wink from one stricken eye, "you listen to me, I've heard you out and I'm not entirely unsympathetic. There's a lot about the Institute itself that can be very brutal, and the way that you fellows are recruited has always seemed to me to be a little cynical. Maybe Messengers should be taken in another way."

"You wouldn't get anyone with any alternatives to *be* a Messenger."

"Yes, that has been the problem. I know that from where you're sitting it all looks a little calculated and cruel and somehow limiting. But it's all training, it's all maturation. You'll find that it runs into a large context and you've got to understand that it's a question of total-ity."

"The hell with that."

"You should only know how many generations of Blounts have sat across from me at this very table with the same grief, the same rage, the same feeling of particularity."

"He worked on corpses in the Institute," I said. "Corpses. For the first two years it was only working on people who couldn't afford the Treatment. You learned a lot that way."

"There was no alternative."

"And they made it religious. How did the religion get tied in? It's purely a business."

"You're a bright man, Blount, but the Institute was not created to frustrate and torture you. Maybe the disease was. But don't confuse the one and the other; we are, after all, on the side of light. I don't like metaphysics."

"I got all that," I said. "I got it in the orientation course they give you just before you get graduated. They have an entire half term just on the philosophy of it: the history, the sense of mission, Hulm, his passion, the oath."

"Well, that was something."

"It's all bullshit. Bullshit. The whole thing is nothing but lies. But I'm stuck."

"Of course you're stuck, Blount, and now you're talking sense."

"I'm stuck on a five-year term and nothing will get me out, so I'll make the best of it. So you have no worries. You've got a bed for me; give me the bed. You have a quota assigned it. But nothing more. No lectures. No metaphysics."

"You've become considerably more reasonable now. That's more even."

"How can I not be reasonable?" I said. "Where can I go?"

"I don't blame you for feeling bitter," he said, standing and giving me a warm smile, the kind of smile that probably would go over well with a notification of irreversibility. "We need that kind of idealism and energy."

"I'm not bitter. You have it all wrong; you misunderstand entirely. I'm not in the least bitter; I'm *grateful* for the opportunity you gave me."

"That's not necessary."

"Certainly it is. Without the training I'd be breaking people up downside for a few hours or less in the Arena, or they'd be busting me. The training freed me from all that, that and my old man the foresighted bastard. You gave me identity, mission, a sense of purpose. I even have a goal now. But I won't hear ... "

"You're in for hundreds," he said softly and touched my hand, a stinging clasp that would indeed be calculated to make me turn solemn, to make me think. "You're in for hundreds, Blount, because now you're saying it . . . what did you have?"

"Nothing."

"That's right. You had absolutely nothing. You would have been another downside alley death, off at twenty-three in a shuffle. They wouldn't have even packed up the corpse."

"Is this better?" I said and thought of downside, thought of the alleys, thought of the Clout. I had not been there for four years. Nevertheless, deponent could recall all of it, every bit, not a string missing. Perhaps a shudder ravaged my delicate features; perhaps a premonitory twitch of the shoulders brought the blade home. "Yes," I said, "yes, this is better. Okay. Okay."

"You're a paraprofessional, Blount."

"Why not say professional? It sounds just as good."

"The distinction has to be made. You aren't medical staff. But you are what you are. You can't misunderstand everything all the time. You know that."

"Oh, forget it," I said, some downside ooze still baking through my veins, and I stood up then, feeling the oppressive slant of the walls, the clamor in the distance, the dim scent of clinic oozing in through unoccupied spaces. I had then a sudden understanding of the Director that came unbidden, but with force for all of that; his job could not conceivably be pleasant. There was too much mediation. He was not a Messenger, and that was good, but then he was not one of the entrepreneurs, either, which meant that he was paying the price without a ticket. Call him a front man. I had had the whole thing figured out, and he was strictly public relations. The ones in Operations would be invisible, would be seen only in dim glimpses of policy, faint trickling memos passing somewhere in the distance.

Horrible. It was horrible. It was not worth two semesters of rhetoric and composition to be able to see things in this way. But there was no other way of seeing it; even the Priest had known that. I could feel the pity like nausea rising within me then, and there was really nothing that would make any final sense of it. His clasp was firm on my arm as he guided me toward the door; his fingers clasping me like lances. "You don't know," I said. "You just couldn't know. The process. The Institute. The things that are done to you there. And all for what? It isn't metaphysics. It's just profit."

"I know," he said. "I think that I do know. Would it do you any good to tell you that once I was a Messenger? Would it? I started off that way myself, you know."

"No, it wouldn't. I don't believe you. And if you were, then you're a traitor, the worst of all of them. How could you stand it?"

"What was I supposed to do? It makes some people well, Blount. Not everyone can be cured, but that's the price you pay for the society. Money makes a differential."

"That's why they recruit from downside."

"They can't do it from easterly," he said absently. "Anyway, we'll have someone take you to your room, get yourself settled in. You'll find that our accommodations are surprisingly adequate once you get used to them. It really isn't a bad position at all, and you'll feel much better about all of it shortly, as soon as you get acclimated."

"That isn't the reason," I said. "That isn't the reason at all."

"What's that? Pardon me? I don't think that I quite . . ."

"That isn't the reason that it wouldn't make any difference. Not because I don't believe you, because I can see where anyone could have been a Messenger; that's the horror of it, anyone could be. But I can only hate you the more."

"I'm sorry."

"It's nothing personal. I hate Messengers. Every single one of them I hate. I can't bear to see or touch them or to hear their horrors when they get drunk. To listen to their muddled shallow fantasies when they think they are sleeping; to know their self-pity and fear. I can't stand them."

"This revulsion is common."

"I don't care if you were or weren't, because it would only make it worse. Do you understand? Am I clear?"

"You're clear," the Director said. "You're a very tough case, but you're clear. I don't think that I can misunderstand you. They don't usually come in as bitter. Or as articulate."

"I'm not your ordinary Messenger," I said. "Maybe you can understand that. I have feelings. I *suffer.*"

"Certainly you suffer," he said, "but the suffering is all self-directed, and that's what concerns me."

"Out in one piece," I said *mysterioso* and left him there then with a quavering laugh while attendants showed me to my room.

And in there I took out the Projector, reduced myself to the size of a roach and, for comfort, huddled in a socket all night dreaming—all night, that is, until reconstitution, damn it, took over again as always and I tumbled out on the floor, fuming, twitching my kneecaps and examining the ceiling.

So much for my introduction to that center of enlightenment, sacrifice and dedication, the Clinic for Metastatic Diseases: Clinic Number Five, the Easterly, located at Bushwick and Flash, as any of you researchers may know.

The air is becoming increasingly foul in here. Nevertheless, I must continue. I have so much more to say and have not yet even gotten to Yancey . . . the pig.

III. A BRIEF ESSAY ON REDUCTION:
WHAT THEY DO NOT UNDERSTAND

It hurts. It hurts, it burns, it is a feeling of compassion and helplessness coming over in waves of sickness and impotence from scalp to toes, the body curling in on itself, the flesh becoming desiccated and sickly and then folding in upon itself in a series of snaps, like a ruler. Disproportionate it is, terribly disproportionate, so that the limbs are already gnomish when the shoulders and head have not begun to gather, and the feeling is one of terrible foreshortening: gloom and extended concentration, the kind of emotions that, I understand, might be known in sexuality or gymnastics when the body, sighing, departs from its humors and takes a more ominous direction. And throughout . . . throughout the pain, the pain that sears and rends, and the helplessness, because, once begun, reduction is irreversible.

Even with the wish to supersede clamoring within . . . it is irreversible.

My God, my God (but Messengers do not pray), can they not understand? This is being done to *people!* At the tormented center, the small fuse of a soul struggling (a downside soul, but nonetheless sacred for all of that, or, so I am taught to believe).

Are the souls of patients larger merely because they can contain us?

And at the core of the fuse, a light as wicked as death. As constant as night.

IV. A MOOT HISTORY OF INVOLVEMENT:
HOW THEY LIGHT THE DOWNSIDE

The way that they work it is this: flyers are pasted all through downside, vandalized all the time, of course, but simply repasted the next day so that you grow up with them. Grow up with pictures of the Institute and songs of the Messengers and six times a year there is an enormous recruiting campaign complete with festival band. Politicians will come in during the campaigns, enclosed in glass, to talk through megaphones of the virtues of dedication, the power of paraprofessionalism, and, although there have been one or two really spectacular assassinations through the years, by and large the technique is effective. I love, to this day, to meet celebrities, particularly politicians: it is the sense of *connection* they provide that is so exciting. Everyone from the downside understands this right away.

It seems that the bare facts of the case are enough. In any event, there is a certain paucity of returned Messengers who have come to tell the tale, and all of this, all of it, must be too abstract for the good and simple folk of the downside to handle. Be a Messenger and make something of yourself. Come to the lance, be a man. Enlist in the war against disease. Fight a fighter; takes one to know one. My old man didn't even know about the bonus. That is some indication of the kind of stock from which I come.

Even without the question of a bonus, it appealed to him. It appealed to him very much. For my eighteenth, as a coming-of-age present, he pulled me out of a pocket Arena and took me to the enlistment office. There they told him of the bonus and their gratitude as well; he wept with humility. He took the bonus and attempted to hit the multimutuels for everything that they had taken from him in the forty-odd years intervening between transfiguration and death. He did not succeed.

Were this his story rather than mine, I would go into the particulars of his failure, but the hell with him, the hell with all of them! The center stage is Mordecai Blount. He did not succeed; he failed utterly, in fact, because I learned through channels recently that he had applied for admission, as a subsistence patient, at the Clinic Number Five in Houston. A subsistence patient! Charity! Of special value! He claimed relative-privileges, of course. Somewhere he had gotten the idea that the families of Messengers received special priority.

He found out differently, I am sure.

But at this moment, even now, I am convinced that that collection of angles and systems he had accumulated in four decades stood him in good stead when confronted by the Ninth Race, and that even at the odds, he probably beat the game. Do not bet fillies against colts. Never bet maidens in a mixed field. How painfully acquired, how preciously he submitted these dicta to me!

It hardly matters. The tentative maturity I have elected post-Yancey assures me that ninety-nine percent of what involves one is sheerest abstraction, and almost all of the remainder—*all* of it—can be handled as if it were. Nothing matters. None of it. All lies and small entrapment, manipulated cunningly in the dark.

(A speculation for old time's sake: I see him lying on his bed somewhere in the final of the sequence of miserable furnished apartments that he has occupied all his life. His eyes glint, his face sags, he looks through drugs at the ceiling. He is finally aware that he is dying and can even bring himself to say it—*the game is up, laddie, the machines have now closed*—but, inescapably, at some corner of the consciousness, he is not sure of this. He wishes to think differently. Perhaps it is all a final elaborate hoax rigged by the Telegraphics to tax his patience.

(Three or four insects scuttle across the sheets, chatting to one another, and wander on his palm. His eyes flutter, screams of children outside, the noise of downside flooding the room in an expiring moan. Watch for sudden drops of weights. He gathers to absorb the sound, rises, gasps; air comes into his wizened old lungs. Look out for lightly raced three-year-olds in allowances for threes and up. Now he feels pain: pain in filaments and fragments, pain working through him at all levels and he tries to hold it off. He shakes his head, mumbles, the noise rises, his breath sags, he falls back. Watch the condition factor carefully. He expires dreaming of four figures on the tote, rolling gracelessly from bed to floor, exhibiting an acrobatic he has never shown previously. All reverence. All reverence to this discovered grace of my father, whose limbs insects now occupy. Insects and metastases. Metastases and apprentice jockeys.)

(Messengers can envision well. They should not . . . but how can one not have a good imagination in this job? If I only knew that . . .)

"Be a professional," he said to me in chronotime. "Make something of yourself. You're nothing now—you and me both—but you'll really be something if we can get you into the Institute."

Lucky enough to get into the Institute! "You don't understand, father," I said (I was only eighteen), "the Institute takes everyone. *Everyone*. Why do you think they push it all the time? Why the campaign?"

"Because that gives them the widest selection of young men to choose among; that way they can sift and get only the cream of the crop."

"You've fallen for slogans. It isn't so. They'll take anyone."

"No sir, no sir!" he said and fairly leaped for emphasis. "No sir! You are wrong. They want you to feel that it is easy when it really isn't. The requirements are high, the processes are testing. Some of the best cannot make it. You'll be in by the hundreds if we can get you in there."

I was not naïve then, not at all—an upbringing in downside, while perhaps no preparation for Messengership, is an education against vulnerability—but his intensity was alarming. "I don't know," I said, "I don't know. I hear stories. I don't want to be a Messenger."

"What's that?"

"I said it's disgusting. I don't want the job. It sounds horrible to me."

"Coward," he said. "Now you take me, the old man who has raised and nurtured you. I'm too old, too cold, got no slack in the limbs, got no potential or possibility. They wouldn't take anyone like me now. If they had had this thing around when I was your age, it would have been the making of me. If you think that I wouldn't take it right now you got a flasher coming. They just didn't have it when I was younger."

So I went down, down the corridors of downside, holsters at the ready, two steps behind my old man, into the main sector and right into the booth that was hot and cramped and smelled of ozone. On the wall were posters showing Messengers twelve feet high advancing upon some enemy in the distance, spears at the ready. The Messengers were very clean and solemn, bright faces washed into vacancy by commitment, and in one of the posters a minister of some sort was delivering a blessing under the line: YOU'LL HAVE NO NEED OF BLESSING WHEN YOU BECOME A MESSENGER. The booth was occupied by a fat man who breathed poorly, and every time he exhaled the papers on the walls and desk jumped. There was something about the aspect of the office that indicated he had not had company for a long time. Small marks of vandalism around the door hinted, however, that in its own way the district was keeping him in mind.

"Take him, take him," my father said with a series of antique flourishes resembling those with which he encouraged horses by the teletape. "Take this boy. He's just a young lad with a streak of cruelty and bad manners, but he's mine own son and he has potential. I told him that you'll make a something out of him, bring him to his purposes. It's all in the training; training is a wonderful thing when it works with the young animal. He wants to serve humanity; he only needs a direction."

"Of course," the recruiter said, shuffling for some papers in the desk. "He looks like a very promising lad, and his height is good, too; he has the right height."

"I told him, I told him that small was tall," the old man said and winked. "It's grace, that's what it is, and entrance into small alleys, moving in and out in the good way."

"I have to ask a few questions, of course," the recruiter said. "It isn't automatic, you understand; we have a selection process here. It's a prestigious position. Firstly, to whom should the bonus be made payable?"

"Bonus! Bonus? You say there is a bonus?"

The recruiter eyed my old man, an intense, arch, rising look and said, "Surely there's a bonus. It varies to the conditions, the length of enlistment, the qualifications and so on. . . . You were not aware that there was a bonus?"

The old man put his hand on my shoulder and I felt the grip move toward pain. Of simpler stock than the rest of us, he showed emotional reactions in blunt physical ways. "Of course I knew there was a bonus!" he said. "I knew all about that. You're not meddling with an old fool and his tiny son, you understand. I just wanted to make sure that we would get all that straightened out first."

"Of course there's a bonus," I said. "You mean you didn't know that?" At that instant, my appraisal of my father shifted subtly but for all time; it occurred to me that he was probably insane. He had driven me toward the Institute for commitment's sake; this was inexplicable.

"I said I knew it, didn't I?" he asked sullenly and looked at his nails, uneven and greenish in the pastel light. "I knew all that stuff."

"You don't think that they'd get people into this for nothing, do you? Just stuff them inside for the cuff?"

The recruiter gave me a look, an expression strangely paralleling that of my old man, and I took the papers and began to sign them indiscriminately. My insight into him had changed my life; I had not realized until that instant how badly I needed to get away from him. There is no future in influence from a man who believes that the Institute can induce people on the emotions.

"It should be several thousand dollars," I said. Large money in downside. Large money for a Messenger, now come to think of it.

"Several thousand dollars. Well, that's interesting. Just what I expected, and one of the very reasons I brought down my boy this morning. He's a fine boy; brought up to be of the highest quality, and in these filthy circumstances that is not easy, of course, but you will find him more than up to par. You do not get candidates like this walking in here just any day. When do I get these thousands of dollars? Surely it should be on the day of enlistment."

"Why should you get it?" I said. "Then, again, on the other hand, why shouldn't you?"

"Why shouldn't I, indeed? Who raised and nurtured

you into this condition. In a way, it's only a small return for all I've done for you."

"It's several thousand," I said. "Maybe ten. Quite a bit of money."

"We still have to get the questionnaire completed," the recruiter said, moving his palms against one another. "We can talk out those arrangements a little later. Firstly, this, however: it's a simple process, but not entirely automatic. If you'll just take a few inquiries now . . . "

Most of the recruiters (I learned soon enough) are ex-Messengers whose nerves have gone irreversible, but whose enlistments are a long way from totality, and who thus must be utilized in other useful ways. This is not to excuse or even to defend them, but to point out that the job is several unpleasantnesses, and in its own way worse than the process, because the process can be turned around. I do not seek to release the recruiter entirely from my rage, but there are larger reasons, larger angles to be explored, and in any event, I am hardly naïve enough to think that it was he alone who got me into this. What can diminution, over and again, do to a faltering psyche? What would the job do to a claustrophobe? What is it like when one begins to think of the implications of the job while in the pocket oneself? As you can see, it is necessary to cultivate tolerance, perspective, etcetera.

"Just give me that dough," the old man said, having settled on the essential thread of the interview and wishing to think of nothing else. "Just pass it over to me; I'm entitled. It's all mine for raising him. Just give me that generous bonus. The boy isn't really of age yet, but there'll be some good investments for him, too. I'll think of everything. I have plans."

The recruiter and I looked at one another in some horrid comity of understanding, and then, perhaps, put it to one side. "Your history," he said quietly, "your biography, the details if you will, if you want it. It's not necessary, but it's a good option, to tell you the truth. Don't hold back on anything. The Institute wants to know the best way to train you . . . any problems which might come up, better sooner or later."

So I filled out the forms. Filled them out in three minutes in their full complexity and meaning and was then rewarded with a moist recruiter's handshake, a winsome recruiter's wink, and a deft recruiter's check, payable only after two weeks, and to a bank of the Institute's choice. The check I turned over to my old man, on the reasonable principle that he deserved it. What I am trying to make clear, possibly with only a residue of success, is that money did not interest me then or now. Life in downside, surprisingly, exists on the same level with or without money, and the Institute is one of the very few ways out. If he wanted money to color the question of his existence, my old man was entitled to it. This is the kind of thinking that one can entertain at eighteen; later on, as one's horizons expand, one is supposed to assimilate the value of money. I am not sure of this yet, however.

I took my travel orders and went.

There's no waiting for the Institute. A new cycle begins almost every month, and in the meantime they give you a very fine dormitory to lie around within and interesting puzzles to perform. The point is that one is not allowed time to think the thing over. This is a good thing, at least from the point of view of the Institute, it would seem, because one is provided a long waiver to sign with lots of sub-clauses and qualifications; thinking of this waiver, among other things, might turn a speculative soul around. The waiver contains phrases like IRREVERSIBLE REDUCTION and ACCIDENTAL MORTALITY or DISCLAIM INFECTIVE CONTAMINATION, and even though a good deponent could not read or write very well at this time (ah, but I had potential!), I took note of some of them with interest. "Don't worry," the recruiter said, "just don't worry about a thing. It's purely routine, just a routine waiver. No one ever gets injured on the job; not really. Nothing ever happens."

"This check," the old man said, folding and pocketing it, "this check, I see I got to wait some weeks to cash it. I don't know if this is really fair to the boy."

"He has to report," the recruiter said.

"Of course he'll report. Don't you think my boy knows proper respect?"

"That's the policy and procedure."

"Well, I don't know," the old man said, "I respect policy and procedure as much as anyone in downside, learned to live by it good, but I wonder if this isn't stretching it a bit. Not that I'm complaining. Not that I can't really wait if I have to. I have resources; the resources can wait. Just inquiring is all. Don't worry; I don't mean to give the check back."

This is the nature of the way in which I became a Messenger. There is little more to say. The background is fairly typical of that time. One must revert to archetype to understand how the Institute even now is able to maintain its flow.

The year after, of course—the following year, I mean —there were those riots in downside that brought a few politicians to quivering attention, to say nothing of the Institute. Seventeen of the booths were bombed or burned out; one unfortunate recruiter happened to be working late when all this occurred. Since then recruiting is allowed only at certain times of the year and in very special circumstances; this means only that instead of being empty most of the time, the booths, when they are opened, have huge lines. It seems that most of the residents of downside are not interested in the protection and benefits that their leaders want to offer them.

Still, a few things have changed: a different quality of man was coming into the Institute in the last years, a kind of Messenger who was, perhaps, more inclined to jive in the intestines or find a mission hummable. Consequences do not seem as immutable. Nevertheless, superficial change only covers the fact that there is really no change at all, and they will still not recruit women, Hulm's inheritors being a very proper sort. Not that women have shown undue eagerness.

Three years later I met the recruiter in a bar while on leave. (They give you a pass every few weeks in the later years, after they are confident that the spirit is broken and that there is nowhere you can go . . . they are interested merely in the complete exhaustion of motives.) He was drinking solemnly and heavily, draped over the bar. I had no rancor. Blount had become generous. Blount was compassionate. By the middle of the third year Blount had had his rhetoric and composition and was a more patient, not to say a metaphysical, man. I went over and introduced myself (he remembered; there is this thing about Messengers—one never forgets a single one of them) and said, "Not to look for riots, but why do you do things like this to people? Can't you reconcile?" My mood was elevated, sanguine. I had no hatred. It could have been any recruiter.

"Have a drink," he said. "Have two, I'm buying. I'm buying for threes; you're one of us now."

"Not quite."

"The day you signed the application. No later. Conscience has nothing to do with it, son; it's just something that has to be done. Recruiting is a tough job; so is reduction. I still shake when I think of that."

"Is it necessary?"

"Of course it's necessary, son. Where would you have the recruiting be done? In the farmlands? Or Easterly? Downside is downside, and you'd better remember that the Institute didn't create it; it was just there."

"I didn't create it, either."

"Well, whoever said you did, son! Drink up, time is nigh. It's all sociology, sociology and metaphysics; downside created itself. You have to take it on in that way. There wasn't anything personal about it; we didn't put you people there."

"There's money in it," I said, with the first edges of my new and subsequent insight. "There's a lot of money in it."

"Of course there is; I would hope so. But it's nothing personal. Money comes to need—that's it—time and again. What was your future, anyway?"

"Who knows?"

"Indeed, who knows? Speaking for the personal, I had none of it."

"None," I said. "Well, then, tell me this: is this any better?" I motioned, an implicatory gesture meant to take in him, his condition, the bar, the slow dribble of liquor and saliva that spewed from a forgotten corner of his mouth. "Tell me, is it?"

"You're still in the third year. You're cynical; you're just learning reduction. That would explain it."

"We get reduced in the first month," I said. "The curriculum changed. Don't dodge it. Is it any better?"

"I don't know," he said. "'I can't answer that. I was out of downside, too. I'm not an unsympathetic man. I would have had an ax in the head when I was eighteen."

"I might have carried it."

"Anyone could have carried it; that's downside. There isn't even a burial overhead."

"You're dodging it," I said and poked him in the shoulder, feeling the faint, curling rigidity of flesh grown brassy through reduction, a common effect. He, too, had been inside limbs. "Just answer the question."

"I was a Messenger only six months; then something went wrong. They gave me this, instead. I really didn't have the fullest dose. How can I say?"

"You served, you know. Was it worth it?"

"Why do you want to know? Why is it so important? Does it make any difference?"

"To me, yes. I'm still in training, you understand. I'm entitled to be naïve. Was it better?"

He sighed and shrugged. He finished his drink and said, "I don't know. I don't know. It's a close thing, I can tell you that. Very close."

"How close?"

"An ax in the skull or Messenger, maybe the one or the other. Don't ask me anymore, kid. I'm all torn up inside. I'm not the same anymore. It all gets to you," he said and then fainted dead away for me, thoughtful of him and spectacular as well, falling in a whoop across the bar in a shower of glasses, liquor dancing in the air like fire.

Or, perhaps, he did not faint dead away. Maybe that was only the time that the evening began to go out of focus for deponent, who was much drunk (or did it go out of focus for him?), and things turned bright then— bright with that terrible clarity known only to the very drunk or grief-stricken, and it all began to wander out of apprehension. Perhaps I fell into an alley somewhere, my neutered soul shrunk before the prospect of a woman.

As to whether it was better in his case, I do not know. But in the case of faithful deponent, now listening with some apprehension to noises in the corridor, in the case of faithful deponent, that is to say, I think that I can answer that.

I truly think that I can answer that.

Consider: consider. Clatter of wood in the distance.

V. Seeing the Clinic, Burning Like a Flame in the Heart of Night: A Small Lecture for Constancy

But things, once established, settled in at Clinic Number Four. Much of my revulsion was of the longer-term variety, not to be confused with apprehension; nevertheless, *le directoire* had his messages. Clinic Number Four, this was, of the Hulm Institute for Metastases, Easterly division, deposit upon admission. Landscaped grounds: an aura of green for brief, recuperative walks. Private toilets for Messengers. Erected only in 2019, it was a modern facility. Diamonds glittering in the fixtures.

Deponent was given a private full at the end of a corridor a mile long and half a mile high, a full plug into the music system. Deponent was given full access to the employees courtesy shop, the employees lounge, the employees cafeteria and the employees recreational facilities. No possessives. No mingling with the patients. Enough corruption is enough. Deponent was given a uniform with his pseudonomic stenciled on it in red. He was given— with all due ceremony, although a certain winsomeness permits me to be succinct at this point—his very own Hulm Projector. My Hulm Projector, to switch pronouns. Mine to keep and treasure forever, liable to pay for the damages for the duration of my term as Messenger. My pseudonomic was *Jones,* which was in fashion at that time. I had requested but been denied a Hebraic name. There is no sense of humor in the Institute at any of its myriad levels.

I was given a tour of the facilities and an orientation lecture. Miss Greenwood, the head of employee services was (is) forty-five years old and of a somewhat restricted passion, as was suggested to me in an alcove, not that this would be construed to do either of us any good whatsoever. It is impossible even for the employees of the Institute to fully understand that Messengers are functionally neutered. If it is not congenital, it is none the less pervasive for all of that. It is not strictly speaking a requirement of the job—and some Messengers have been known to copulate—but it simply seems to work out that way. Sex is a mystery, and how much of a sense of mystery can we sustain? It is all too obvious. Besides, the job may well attract that kind of individual in the first place. All circular. Hard to understand, difficult to embrace. I will think about this more.

(Perhaps it is all a metaphor for Entrance, and that most basic of all Entrances precludes the other. Or it may only be my repressed homosexual tendencies, of which I am very aware, and while declining to investigate them, I can sense their power, their rage, their need. Messengers are complex people: do not rush to understand me.

(Also, I have a low threshhold for exercise. Also, I have never been able, during moments of sexual attempt, to avoid scatological images, clownish fantasies: dwarfs scampering in mire or fantasies of deflation. Perhaps I attempt to rationalize all of this too much. Perhaps I should simply rejoice in the fact that I have no sex drive and worry no worry no more no more. Tra-la.)

Miss Greenwood's tour did not surprise me. I was not disconcerted. I was prepared for all of it. The only thing that disconcerted me, and this just a little, was that all of them—patients and doctors, nurses and attendants— treated us like orderlies. Perhaps *thought* we were orderlies. This they had not readied us for in the Institute. They spoke only of the unusual status of the Messenger and the special and privileged position he occupied in the war against death.

The Institute prepared us for very little, outside of the technological question. Everything outside of machinery was rhetoric, and poor rhetoric at that. (By then I had learned to discriminate.) "Dedication is the first obligation of the Messenger, respect his reward, paraprofessionalism his outcome. Full professionals then work together in unified and sacred accord under this benevolence of technology in an atmosphere of probity," etcetera, etcetera. This was one of the lines. Another had to do with the religious instance, some refraction of what might have been Hulm's own obsession. It seemed that he had been a reverent man. "Purgation of the body and the blood, the holy lamb," and so on and so forth, mixed in with a strange blend of Easterly and the divine; snatches of Judaism as well. Like the prophets of old, we cast our words against doom and the other evils.

Bravery, too. Bravery in the intestines as tiny swords poised like those famous warriors who are our heritage, we move into battle. "Remember this, gentlemen, remember: we are soldiers, we give no quarter!" An old lecturer told us that we had taken upon ourselves the front line of the battle for the world to follow.

I do not mean to down it entirely. Not at all: some of it was very effective, and all of it was partly effective. They taught machinery well; whatever else they did was just filler, but it was *good* filler for its purposes. Kept them in line. Whatever we expected of the job when we moved in, we knew this, for they had told us: we would be treated with a dignity upon which our skills were incumbent. They had their reasons. I can even see them now and they are explicable. Defensible I cannot argue . . . but they have merit.

Nevertheless. Orderlies. We were treated like orderlies. In fact, at odd moments, it was possible for one to think that one *was* an orderly; a certain kind of grinning shamble seemed to overtake the walk, a certain vacancy around the eyes. The downside stupor: seeing everything, registering all of it, understanding nothing, rising only through small humiliations and grief to rage. One could well *have* been an orderly, of course, save the Institute. This they kept reminding you of, anyway.

Part of the problem from the patients came from the fact that we were introduced in exactly that way. Messengers and their function are not, after all, particularly appealing, and it suits the public relations and policies of the Institute to make things as aseptic as possible. One does not go in to have cancer burned out; one goes in for a "little job," something coming out of a "little weariness," and shortly rejoins the world joyfully, having acceded to cosmetics. This is the thrust of the Institute's public relations: a stay in there is a happy stay; cancer is a *happy* disease. So one met the patients very much out of role: this is your "helper, Mordecai," your "little watchman, Mordecai" or whatever the effusive Miss Greenwood had in mind at that time. The fact that this grinning, genial, nicely shaped and dedicated helper would shortly go crawling inchwise into their gut was something to come by only peripherally and after the relationship had been established. Even then there was little interest; the impelling thing about the patients was how willing they were to function as if the little job took care of itself and attending the Institute were essentially a social obligation . . . a rather weary one, but necessitous, like attending one coming-out party too many.

(A certain rage about the patients seems to be filtering. Let me make it clear that I bear them no grudge; the position of money or status has never struck me as ipso facto grounds for my hatred. The patients are manipulated; they come from the only population to which the Institute will minister; they react as the Institute will have them. One must look somewhat nearer or deeper, therefore, to get into the matter of culpability.)

Reinforcement on the employee end, to be sure. Rule seven: the one thing that a Messenger may never divulge to a patient is the exact nature of his responsibilities. A

certain modesty and secretiveness of demeanor are recommended, should there be inquiries (there are rarely
inquiries). It is put down somewhat more elegantly:
*a Messenger is technology's servant; it is not his position
to call upon himself particular reverence. Humility is the
soul of all strength.*

Policy and procedure; procedure and policy. All of it
carefully conditioned. The manuals even now fall quickly
into line in mind's eye: regulation and ordinance, containment and meaning ruled neatly on the lined paper, the
printing large for the functional illiterates among us.

Little did we know, however, that we would become orderlies.

It was something else; there was one thing, perhaps,
that we (or, at least, this faithful deponent) allowed ourselves to be fantasized into, and that was that we would
be benign priests of reduction, striding through the wards
to the awed gasps of doctors and nurses, nurses and attendants, performing our green and terrible tasks in an
oozing isolation of ease and strength, under rich beams of
fluorescence, to occasional gasps and whimpers of ap-
plause, much like a tennis match. It was the Hulm Projector that, in its magnificence and patented simplicity,
would make us go; nevertheless, even the Projector's Pos-
sessions were entitled to a little bit of common respect, or
perhaps somewhat more than that. We had struggled for
four years to learn to play our motions against the body's
cave; we had practiced on a hundred corpses so that we
could take on the precious husks of the World's Finest;
weren't we entitled? Weren't we? Was this not only a reasonable way of considering things?

The question is rhetorical, gentlemen; do not answer.
Neither peer through the cracks in these doors in an attempt to see me; Blount has shrouded himself in smoke
and haze, towels stuffed in every crack to block vision.
There is no way that you can get at me unless I let you in,
and I am not ready; not quite yet ready, thank you very
much. How my little fingers tremble on these threads!
How my eyes bulge, how my brow emits its antique and
finely chiseled beadlets of sweat! Time, gentlemen, time!

Everything will come to its conclusion. I will even tell you about Yancey. Presently.

For now, stay away from the doors.

Deponent's visions were incorrect. Things did not work out in that way. Disillusion is the condiment of the reflective life; nevertheless, I suffered. Bedpans were the lot of the Messenger; bedpans and strange prosthetic devices. This enamel was poor enough reward for four years of study, but there were also changes of clothing to be made, rollings over and regurgitation; pattings in the night (post-operatives become very nauseous from the remembered effort to expel us, and who can blame them?), heaving and retching, clawing and moaning, patting and wondering—the small activities of the post-metastatic patient being conducted in the smells and tightness of their rooms, which, for all the highly vaunted decor of the Institute, still had quite a twentieth-century cast. Amorphousness and sleek panels of doom, overlaid on emptiness. In the dark they would grasp at us to whisper terrible confidences. "I'm afraid," old or oldish men would say, bending their arms to crook's edge, staring from luminous eyes, the metastatic pall bringing strange knowledge to their faces, "terribly afraid. You see, I don't think that it would work out; I just don't see it."

"The process is infallible," I would say, "just relax. It's like a toothache, just a toothache. It's as antiquated as diabetes. Be reasonable. Be calm."

"But the pain," they would murmur, "still, the *pain* . . ." And I would not have the heart to advise them that the pain was mostly illusory, encouraged by the pre-operative drugs that the Institute itself passed on to them so that their gratitude at elimination would be that much more profound, their resistance to charges impossibly reduced. Instead, I would assure them, or at least at the beginning I would take the trouble to assure them, that it would work out, everything would work out, no problems at all; it was only a question of machinery—machinery and technique. Calmness and patience. The days had already, I would say, shaped themselves into a pattern that would see them walk out of the ward, easy and even strutting, freed of their terrible complaints . . . but still, the Institute counseled a certain amount of fear in lieu of credit agencies, and while I could deal with the men, the most of them, the women defied me. I could not deal with feminine emotions; no male neuter can. And then there were the younger ones, too; even a couple of children of the very rich who I found particularly trying. (Why should I? Had I been a child of the very rich? What would have happened to me if *I* had contracted me-tastases in downside?) And then there were the semi-informed who had picked up knowledge on the side, and these were the ones who knew the true function of the Messengers, and these were apt to be the worst of all, because when you came in the night to do the process one might find them sitting at terrible ease, drugs discarded in a washbowl, looking at one through ominous eyes as the Projector was repaired. Those were the ones the nurses had to condition with needles, and it was difficult, difficult.

Too much indirect narration. A specialty of your de-ponent, who, when he is not letting his eidetic memory run away with his mouth, literally tumbling in his tiny skull, is busy encompassing huge chunks of data without spirit, without care. (Still, some sections of this strike me as rather well written; I think that the scene with the Priest was quite well done, setting the stage as it did, and then the portrait of my old man was chillingly accu-rate and precisely fair to him. It is not that I lack talent, as my rhetoric teacher suggested, but only that I try to make up in verve what I miss in patience. Or so I ration-alize, so I rationalize. The hell with it: I am not writing for publication, anyhow.)

One must illuminate instead, get into the core of the problem as best as one can. A scene. A patient. A proc-ess. "Boy," he said to me, "boy, I'm sweating. I'm really sweating. You'd better do something for me. You'd better clean this stuff up. I feel like I'm sitting somewhere in a pool." A middle-aged man, verging toward senility since he is pre-operative, who is, I understand, the founder of the largest commercial mask company in the nation, providing masks for all of the major Arenas. He still, apparently, connects vaguely to a sense of command (give him a little time).

"I've already done that," I said, reading. (*Journals of a Nihilist: A Reminiscence.*) "I've already cleaned you three times today. You've got to rest now."

One must attempt to transmit the full picture. The book is poised, flapping in my hand, an unopened magazine for good measure on my knee, sweating quietly myself in the cool heat of the room, very neatly drenched my attendant's whites. Not five hours from now I will go inside and take it out of him: a glowing filament placed in the deepest pocket of his stomach. A nauseating task; many capillaries to be bypassed. No subject of anticipation. Pre-operative, however, and knowing it, he is restless. "I'm not comfortable," he says. "You've got to show some consideration and care. You've got to clean me up."

"That's been done. Time and again. Why don't you just try to rest for a moment?" The request is moving the other way, of course. A slight edginess snakes into my tone; it is not by the book, but it is there. I am entitled to apprehension. The process is safe, very safe (the Projector has, after all, never lost a Messenger or injured one, and it has had millions of opportunities by now), but it is taxing, terribly so. Hours after the reduction, one still feels a sense of compression in the joints, liquid unease, a feeling of disassembly. Also, there is the question of archetypes to be posed; this is not respectful work we are doing. Perhaps the body is entitled to go metastatic and we have it the other way around; by preserving it against devastation, we are making things more difficult in the Other World.

Still, one must stay with the patient through the end of the conventional shift, apprehensions or not. One is obligated to maintain the full responsibilities of the Messenger, which embrace an orderly's duties. This is procedure. This is long-standing policy. The patient must be soothed, relaxed, must have utter confidence in us. Only the Messenger may be the patient's attendant; only he can train him along to the insights and mood that the situation de-

mands. (It also cuts the overhead, and this fact cannot
be ignored. Do not ignore it.) "You don't understand,"
I say. "I can't be in the service of your every whim. I'm
tired. I have a schedule to meet, too. Besides, it
isn't proper, procedurally speaking."

"I don't care if you're tired, son," the patient says, as
if he were ordering up a consignment of ghouls and
greens, "you've got to make me comfortable. What am
I paying for, if not my care?" One would like to pity him
his ravaged frame and fear; one would sense that in
health he will again be wistful, gentle, attracted to shining
monsters and friendly elves, but the illness and its syndrome have made him cantankerous, have thrown upon
him fully the aspect of the senile fool he will now, due
to the blessings of the treatment, become. It is hard to
maintain much tolerance in the face of this insight.
"You're my orderly," he says, "that's what you are. Let's
face it. And it's my right to treatment and concern."

I stand. It is not easy, and the book flaps uncomfortably floorward, but nevertheless, it is done. A pity in line
of all this impressive effort that my height can hardly be
calculated to close the issue. "Listen," I say (what I am
about to do is bad policy, but I cannot really contain myself), "listen, you can't order me around like that. Don't
you know who I am? Don't you know what I'm going to
do for you? I'm not an orderly; I'm not even *your* orderly. I am a Messenger."

He shrugs. "I know all about that. I understand that
whole part."

"In not five hours, well, make it six, I am going to
crawl inside you, slither in your gut like a fish, use fork
and forceps to take the matter out. Can't you show a little
respect? Nothing uncommon, but just a little common respect? What do you think is really going on here anyway?"

(Although there is precedent for this kind of thing, and
it is winked at in complaint, there is really no excuse for
business like this. Messengers are, by the book, to be def-
erential, kind, modest, civilized, all hints of their slum up-

bringing having been purged by the Courtesy Class. They are not to deal in the specifics of evisceration, the quality of the machine, the nature of their tasks, and so on . . . because this simply unsettles the patients. The question at the heart of it is one that deals in blood.

"Come on, now," I add, picking the magazine up off the floor and tossing it toward a corner of the room (it is one of our Trade Journals, full of glistening equipment and Helpful Hints to the specialized voyager, written by advertising copywriters and largely involved with two-tone projectors), "I really don't have to take any more of this." A pity my rage is largely contrived. "There are limits, you understand, limits to anything. Why do you think that most Messengers go insane? I can't clean you up; I can barely clean you out. I'm not an orderly, you fool, I'm a paraprofessional."

"You're frightening me," he says, rearing in the bed, and I think of his little gut quivering inside, the metastatic loss already reducing it by three-fifths, the accretion of acids, the lava of amino; I am really making my job only that much more difficult. "Stop it. Stop it now."

"Lie down, you ass!" I scream in a different mood. "Don't you understand that you're going to make it impossible by infiltrating your gut that way?" I move toward him, pummel pillows, slap sheets and begin to talk to him in a high-pitched but comforting tone, taking another line entirely. I have, after all, been a fool. I snatch alcohol from the bedstand, begin to rub, pummel, converse; his flesh feels like slate under my hands. In the distance I can feel the puff and tick of his heart, quivering with terror. He is harmless, I understand that now, and shame comes to replace the hatred. Nevertheless, I say, "I can't stand this anymore. I can't stand any of it. I'll never last out five years. I know that now. How could anyone? How can you take it?"

"You frightened me," he says, apparently having set on a path of conciliation. I can understand his position. "I didn't mean to say those things, but you did frighten me."

"Forget it," I say, rubbing, "there's too much at stake

here. Just be calm. Forget it. It's all over now." An orderly's whine creeps into my tone: is it possible that one
can become what they say one is? "Just rest. Rest."

"I was sweating. I really don't feel very well. I don't at
all."

"All right," I say, seized by something that is not exactly remorse, but which, like certain minor symptoms of
metastases, can mask the real thing. "All right, all right,"
I say, and then push, pummel, knead, slap, release, relieve, work on the slate-gray flesh until the end of shift-
time comes at last and the moment for reduction approaches. I skulk to the relief room, light glittering before
me, light shuddering and receding, the filaments of his inhabited gut seeming to weave their way past my stricken
consciousness and toward some deeper center. Push, pull,
pummel, knead, and who knows how long the night is
until it is done? Until the Institute itself sinks past re-
demption into some gutted eave of its own?

There is no future in this. That is the point of the previous essay, if point must be made. Nevertheless, one is
led to understand that it is a job, and a job is a job, and
if one can see poignance in reduction, sentiment in fear,
release in metaphysics, then it is definitely the job for you
. . . although, I should hastily add, not the job for me.
Not by elevens.

He got out of the hospital three days later, after being
switched to automatic care. Some months later, I received
a card. (This is really quite rare; patients are not encouraged to think of a Messenger as anything other than another functionary in staff. An orderly, right? Beyond that,
patients do not like to recall their illnesses; ipso facto,
they do not recall Messengers.)

Hello there You, just wanted to drop a line of
memories. Why don't you try to get a decent job and
make something of yourself? *the card said*. I am
available if you are interested in any opportunities;
something might be done. No one should be in a
situation like yours and hate so much, so much.

They passed it through without comment. They do not care. They have the five-year enlistment, for one thing, and for another, they know the secret about Messengers, which even the Messengers do not learn for a long, long time. A secret that, incidentally, I shall never tell. Not here. Not now.

So I filed it away; filed it with the one letter my father had ever sent me, this letter coming shortly after I had commenced training:

The sistem wuks, it's all a question angles is all I should have known it a longa time ago.

A longa time ago I received that card. A longa time ago I received both cards. And both cards placed in one damp sock underneath a journal of my dreams in the Institute.

My correspondence file. My history, my memory. My death my dreams.

Something new. Now they are pounding at the door. Their voices rasp insistently in the hallway; it would be interesting to know what they are saying. I have toward this the kind of clinical interest that toward the end I was able to sustain toward Yancey.

But only toward the end.

Eventually they will begin to get forcible, try metal and hooks, but long before that this all will have been finished, all of it placed inside the drawer with the sock, and I will await them only with the dull glazed smile of the executioner, eyes narrowed, arms folded, a hint of arch in one brow, all quizzicality and compunction as they come toward me to take their due.

I have even formulated what I will say to them; the first words, that is, before they begin to ask their foolish, hammering questions. "Gentlemen," I will say, "gentlemen, listen to me and you will understand.

"Gentlemen . . . ripeness is all."

VI. A REFLECTION ON THE PROCESS ITSELF;
SOME HINT OF IMMEDIACY FOR RELEVANCE

"But," a voice says, somewhere in the distance (I believe I have succeeded in externalizing my father, a remarkable feat by all accounts; I have never been able to do it until now), "but you still haven't made yourself clear. For one thing, you haven't made it known what it's like, and for another, you keep on raving without specificity. You're taking any hint of point from the whole thing. Who cares? Who cares?"

One hastens to answer. The point is meaningful, well taken, clear. It is not quite as elegantly phrased as my father would have made it, but, then again, toward his last moments, I give him enough credit to suspect that he might have become metaphysical. Let me, my father, my conscience, my *doppelgänger*—let me, if you will—get to the point of it.

A word then about the process. (One has a desire to please, even at this point. One has learned the messages of the Institute all too well.) A word about how it works.

You stand before the Projector. It is cold in the dark, cold and damp, one stands shuddering, wet in the crevices, wet to the bone of nakedness, only the huddle of the patient, deep into anesthetic omnipotence, hints at the possibility of connection. Catalepsy moving from the even, trembling pores. In this night (for operations are always performed at night: for privacy and quiet, the dictum reads, but I believe, like the act of generation, that it is for stealth's end) the noises of the hospital seem to overwhelm, then. Tick of generator, wailing scream down the hall, patter of night nurses tossing scatology at one another, the singing of electricity. Power in the coils. It is possible in this moment to imagine that one is no longer in a hospital at all, nor is this a patient. One is standing instead in one's own room, perhaps, eight or nine years old, alert toward the dark and attuned to that very sense of possibility that seems to stream in through the windows.

The gasping of the patient is now only the sound of one's own dear parents fornicating in the hall, forcing fluid from one to the other in that slick transfer that we are told is Love . . . and then one touches the Projector. The Projector at least is there and brings one back to some sense of origins, destiny, the fishlike movements between.

One touches the Projector: the slick, deadly surfaces of Hulm's obsession and comes to know then (over and over again, it is always the same: learn everything, forget everything, they will never learn) that it is a different quality of experience here. It is not at all the same as being eight or nine in the darkness. Here, one is not re-fracting possibility, but history.

Hit the starting switch. (It must begin somewhere, although it began to terribly long ago.) The batteries hum, pulse with energy, Hulm's madness seems to call upon the familiar of its inventor and issues then its whine: a strange, characteristic, whimpering clang. Lights flicker, indicating that the Projector is, hopefully, working. (It has a history of working. It is, in fact, as we are told at the Institute, foolproof.) One hopes that it is working. One knows that there has never been an authenticated case of a machine breaking down in process . . . but there are rumors, the kind of things that circulate around any population, and in addition there is always a first time. The thought of reduction continued, or the thought of a partial restoration within a capillary, is enough to keep even the limited imagination of a Messenger hopping. Hopping and hopping. Bounce and connect. On schedule, the reduction begins. It is all quite automatic from the moment the switch is thrown.

It begins: it begins slowly, then accelerates. The Geometrical Progression of Diminution, as it is called in the Institute, and they concede that they do not know themselves why it seems to work in this fashion . . . but it has long been graphed that while it takes five minutes to lose the first foot, it takes merely another five to lose all but the necessary percentage of the rest. It is during this time, then, as during none other, that the mind blanks, the corpuscles run free and there comes the slow, wild onslaught of epiphany known at no other time. One sees things, one senses things in the dark. One can, if one is very perceptive and insular, even understand at that moment precisely what has been going on at the Institute. (The insight is always forgotten in the skin, but there will be a next time.) Reduction is a narcotic, this being a theory I have, but I believe that it is based less on physiology than on the sheer involved sense of anticipation.

Anticipation! One never knows, after all, what one might find inside there, what differences might be uncovered. I am led to understand that less committed men obtain the same kind of reactions from sex. (I know nothing about this.) One thinks of the Ultimate Body, the Ultimate Metastases, the discoveries of the blood and becomes prone to talk to them.

One talks to them. Something must be done, after all, to make the moments and exhilaration go by, to push back the fear and the wonder and, besides that, they are so deeply narcoticized that for once almost anything can be said to them without it sounding strange, even to the Messenger himself. We have so few pleasures. Most of us are nondrinkers as well. One must take one's satisfaction where one may. I have many thoughts and insights of this sort; so many that once I thought I would prepare a book of essays called *Momento Capitula* (I admire all foreign languages that sound more mysterious and powerful than our humble own), but this, alas, will never be. One has to settle, at the root, for simple autobiography; untransmuted ravings, the delimitations at least woven into ferocity. *Momento Capitula* would, however, have said it all.

So, one talks to them. One perches on the edge of the chair and finally the center, exposing the body to the rays of the Projector and raving onward in a tiny voice in the still night. "You don't understand," one might say, "you simply do not understand what you are putting me through, you stupid, rich, self-indulgent bastard; you ought to show some appreciation; that's what you ought. . . ." Or one will lapse into neologism and rhyme such as, "Hitch, twitch, itch, rich, into the body's bitch and ride the rising blood," or, "Faster sees the metastases," or, more simply, "You ungrateful bastard, don't you understand that I—I, Mordecai Blount—could put a needle right in your liver and you'd never know the difference? I could kill as you lie, bobbing merrily in the circulation, and what would it all come to then? Tell me, what would the sum of it be: your remonstrances, moans, itches, pleas, apologies, compulsions, memories, resentments, confession and hope—what would it be? All for nought and within my power. You don't really think I have to take this, do you? I'm just passing through; I'm doing it for the experience. Actually, I'm quite independently wealthy; I only went to the Institute so that I would have an interesting trade to keep me occupied."

And so on. And so forth. All of it quite stimulating (in its way), serving to pass the time interestingly, in any event; one way or the other, there are those moments under the Projector to kill, and, meanwhile . . .

Well, in the meantime, reduction is working away— working away all the time so that the voice, even in the process of accusation, becomes gradually higher pitched, moving from a fine adult rumble to an adolescent whine and then into a childish squeak, squeak for mama Messenger, squeak for remorse, too, the voice finally taking up residence somewhere around the palate or just below the jaws and then, at last . . .

Well, at last . . .

At last one is something less than an inch tall (it is humiliating, but I might as well get it over with), dancing angelically, but upon the head of no pin, and then preparing, preparing for entrance. One slinks into the body.

(How entrance is made will be one of my few confidences. I will not say. Nor will any Messenger; you will find this to be a fact, no matter how great his disillusion. You will not find it, either, in any of the popularized essays, articles or books on our splendid trade; you will find it in no procedural manual. It is expurgated. It is carefully expunged by wise people. It is, in short, our single professional secret, blocked by part of the oath and the one confidence of any import that the Institute yielded in its four years. (The rest can be looked up biochemically and theologically.) It was not worth four years to know, nor all these years to exercise, but it is something, some kind of fringe benefit, in any event, and I will not reveal it cheaply. Not cheaply.

(Of course, if these memoirs find a *publisher,* a high-grade publisher who is willing to pay me what I am worth, or, in any event, what I have been conditioned to desire, and to assume the legal overlay, I might do a carefully prepared second draft in which I will at least *hint* strongly at the process. Then, again, I might not. Let it be the decision of a publisher: how curious are you? Is it worth it? Get the hell away from my door.)

(Let us say, then, that the mechanics of entrance unite simplicity and scatology, penance and immersion in equal proportion, and that in their calm, their force, their sheer practicality, these methods are the only fashion in which it could ever be done. But I will add this to counteract the inevitable easy grimace of those in the gallery, the mumblings of ex-patients, the grins of doctors: it is not made in the fashion that you think. Not in that way at all. If we were so simple-minded as to think of doing it that way, it would leave us, due to intestinal blockage, trapped in areas through which we could not successfully pass, and the incidence of blight in that area itself is, for all the folklore, surprisingly minimal. Few get ill there. I do not want to become coy or to dissemble, but that is the absolute truth of the matter, ladies and gents, that is the truth. Of course, a couple of maddened Messengers, later dismissed, *have* tried it in that fashion, Institute folklore indicates, but, nevertheless . . .

But, nevertheless. Into the bloodstream we stalk, little divers carrying our lance, the lance also cleverly reducible for crises (like us, it is conditioned to be beam sensitive). Now in the body's fever at last, the noises have changed: sharpened, heightened, strange whines and sirens in the distance, a clanging and receding, flicker and thud as we stroll our way, with surprising casualness, up those alleys and toward the appointed spot.

The spot, ah, yes, the spot: it has been localized for us,

painted red by radiation in the morning, turning orange by nightfall; nevertheless, it does not show up clearly in that darkness, a thick atmospheric haze descending like the soot of downside obscuring its buildings, and some illumination, cleverly provided by the tip of our lance (make of that what you will!), is necessary. In this cove, then, one can feel not only the humors, but the instances themselves: the very seat of the personality here. Twitches of culpability, seizures of continence, revelations and platitudes, even a fanatic shriek here and there, and the corridors seem to curl in spots, as if impaled. The siren rings faster, a bell knocks, we move upon the designated spots like assassins.

Oh, it is cold, cold! Temperatures are not adjustable through reduction, and so one must shudder within one's little outer garb until reaching that designated spot. Stalk, then, skitter, run, jump, sway, stagger, perch to a corpuscle, and finally, finally, tumble into the heart of that orange, now gleaming in the proximity. Doff the garments swiftly; plant them in a cell.

Gloves, indicator, goggles, all gone. They flap on a filament in the chill, the strange intestinal wind moving them slightly, and then the lance is carefully brought to fire through the old method—one droplet of heat applied and bringing it to burn. And burn, then, burn, burn! Eviscerate, quiver, until, at last, the burning, bright bulb of metastases emerges at the end of the lance. Who said that this was not a socially useful occupation, after all?

One looks at it then in the light, and one can see the whole of the lovely tumor, reduced to centimeters. It seems to have features now, some of them mimicking the faces of animals or men. A slash of mouth, wink of eye deep in the pocket, holding it then at tiny arm's length to avoid contamination (although it is not at all infective; we have been assured of that), removing the tag from the lance and slapping it in there. Don the goggles again (I have a feeling of accelerated lyric like the accentuated tempo of an idiotic smash ballad, but one must try to keep up), whisk the bag into the coat and then off into the boulevards again. A boulevardier. A stroller out for his evening's pastime, the wind a bit damp, but what can one do?

One shuffles much faster this time. Reduction exists only for a certain stated interval, and after that one is known to enlarge, whether the patient will contain one or not. Physics and Hulm cannot be embraced by simple willfulness. It would not necessarily kill the Messenger—enlargement within the patient, that is to say—but it would from the cosmetic and career standpoint do him little eventual good, and as far as the patient would be concerned, of course, it would be quite a pulpous mess, not saying a final one. Also, the fee would undoubtedly be collected then only through suit, which would inconvenience the Institute quite a bit. (Fees, it is stated by signed agreement, are due regardless of success, but it would be embarrassing to collect from the estate of one so spectacularly diseased.) Quicker and quicker on those roads, then, the heat now, the pulse pounding, the metastases deep in the pocket of the coat in the pocket, the metastases being carried like an awful little secret that the patient himself may never learn; a high, penetrating hum over all of this that might only be one's nervous reaction . . . although I believe differently. I believe it to be the song of the metastases, overtaking itself and making a carol of release (I took my metaphysics courses all too seriously, it would seem). And, finally, then to the exit point (I will not tell you about exiting, either; do you think I am a fool?) and into the light.

Perch on a tabletop.

Sing with the metastases.

One waits then, waits and waits. Sometimes one has exited too fast and there are terrible, terrible moments for the peculiar elf as he sits with legs dangling, wondering if this is the time that the roof finally falls in, and then at last . . .

Ah, at last! There is a feeling of unfolding, flowering, heightening and elevation as the reconstitution—the blessed reconstitution—at last begins. To come right to the point (I confessed this to a Messenger once, and he said that for him it was exactly the same, so I know that in this one detail at least I am not crazy), it feels like nothing so much as an *erection,* an erection not of that quivering useless organi that has not sustained one such for ten years—no, the hell with that; it is far more profound . . . an erection of the axillae, the papillae, the deltoids, the jugular and so on, blood filling all of the cavities as they rise to terrible authority, this contraption we call the corpus unbending and snapping out like a slide rule, and, finally, full height restored (it takes only seven or eight seconds this way, but how long can an orgasm last?), one stands, glinting out of angry, mature eyes, toward the form lying on the bed of life. For all that this form knows or cares, it might as well be on the Moon; it is beyond analysis, as insensate of what has been done to it as if it were roaming the blasted surfaces with power pack and nightmare, and one sighs, sighs; one packs up his equipment. It is all too much. Buttoning the little metastases securely into a flap, the figure trundles wearily through the hall to turn it in for superfluous analysis and inspection.

In the hall, they look at you. They know, it seems. They always know; they know that it has happened and what you have done, and there is a rim of terror underneath the inquiry and the smile. For the way they look at you, you might as well have been fornicating with a sheep or committing self-abuse in a sterile washbasin, and yet, I want to say to them, yet, how can you look at me in this way? It is only your Messenger, your faithful Messenger, dedicated servant of man and enemy of metastases, moving wearily through these outer corridors; can you not understand that? Can you not understand that for us it is simply a process, a process more difficult than most, but devoid of irony? Devoid of mysticism? (I am lying here.) In any event, why do they look at us in this way?

I think I know the answer.

Oh, yes, indeed, yes, indeed. There is no way that I can get away from it; I do think I know the answer. And understand why they must do this. And understand the quality of their responses.

Say it, say it and be damned: let it come, then, and no way around it. Say it once and for all time, gentlemen, this intimation buried like the ant at the heart of the blooded rose a century ago, deep in the gnarled gardens of darkness.

Say it:

I loved my work.

VII. Very Brief Interlude, Prelude to Yancey, Epilogue to Yancey: Upside, Downside, All Around the Town

Still, one gets into a schedule. One can routinize everything. The capacity we possess for subsumption is enormous.

Had Yancey not come, I might have squeaked through for all five years of it. I might have even re-enlisted, become like certain Messengers I have seen, old men lurking in the corners of the Arena, watching the lights with blasted eyes, dreaming of tumors and want in the center. I might have gone all the way, because in the center of my understanding was a desire to acclimate. And coming from downside, I knew the downside of the soul.

However: came Yancey on a three-day pass from the activities of his life, come to pay cancer routine penance.

And from then straight on to this.

There is really little more to say: Yancey being, as you may have already discovered, the sheerest afterthought of the hurricane. The extension of the problem. Or, if you will have it, the tiny breast of mitosis, after the long, stumbling search.

I hear steel in the corridor, which means they are coming with wedges, which means not too much longer now, but plenty time enough.

VIII. YANCEY, YANCEY: THE HISTORY COMPLETED, TRANSFERENCE BUILT, METAPHYSICS AND ALL THE OTHER IMPORTANT THINGS

Yancey. He is sixty-three, sixty-four years old, but already wrecked by what I take to be corruption, as shriveled without as he is porous within, talking, talking, inexhaustibly talking. Not a full day ago I burned the metastases from him, incurring the usual risks deplored, the standard humiliations visited. All of it by the book and so on. I am entitled to tell you about him as I see him; there is no explication without character, no understanding without guilt. I am, in fact, far more entitled to talk of him than he of me. I wish that I could establish this. I have suffered. I am sure that it is clear by now—listen, gentlemen!—that I am not your usual Messenger; I have suffered, I am articulate, not unacquainted with grief.

But he talks. Only he. He talks interminably, irresistibly, the drenching flow making almost impossible that clean incision of silence that I need so desperately for recovery. I am still in an apprentice position. I cannot do the operations one after the other. I need time to come back to myself.

Nevertheless, he talks. (I remit to present tense; it is too difficult the other way. I do not want to think that all of this has already happened, that it is beyond recovery, that in certain essential ways everything is in the past. No. No. I cannot believe that.)

The bastard. Oh, he is full, full of statements, platitudes, small explosions of pique, and all of them now he must share with me. Mostly, they have to do with the newfound purity of his body. (He, unlike most of them, has done some serious reading on the subject and knows what is going on.) Monstrously, he equates this purity with a cleansing of soul. When he came in the other day, I know that he had neither soul nor body, but, instead, lay staring at the ceiling with eyes the shape of doors, working out the slow beat of his mortality, ignorant of what I was going to do for him. Subsumed beneath feeling. Those were the good times, of course, although I was not permitted to know that.

I would ask him, now and then, how he was (occasionally, I will initiate conversations; it is not the rule, but I bend a little), and all he would say then was, "Terrible, just terrible, son; leave me sleep, leave that flesh crumble." But I awoke that morning in September, stumbling from dreams of downside, and tenderly acclimated his body and then went before the Projector, dwindled and went inside his inert form to clean him out right proper. Did so with unusual dispatch because *then* I wanted to cure him.

It was in his liver, yellow and green, busy as death, so powerful that it clung to and resisted my hand with a bird's beat when I dug it out. But I fought it; I took it— took out this lovely metasasis, lovelier than anything of Yancey's all his life, and clutching it to my tiny chest, impaled it on the lance and went home. Perched with a grin on tabletop because I had rendered him this service. Saw the restoration in his eyes, the growth of accomplishment, the sense of fragmentation restored to wealth.

Now, he is full of rhetoric. What can this be said to prove?

It must prove something. I know that it proves something, for through all of this I have held one thing to my chest tighter than eviscerated metastases, and maybe it is that alone that has sustained me: there is some purpose in this beyond what I see. It amounts to something: we are serving higher ends; the metaphysics must also be considered. Also the consequences. But what, Yancey now makes me ask myself, what can it possibly come to? How can his presence sustain meaning?

He has come in, like all of them, riddled cheek-through-jowl, terrorized into silence, and he touched me, touched me as few of them had, and so I took care of him with particular facility, particular involvement. He mattered. I became involved. Now I have become merely an object of his reformation. He finds me impure. As if an impure man could possibly perform my tasks!

I know what I have to do.

I know what has to be done; that is all there is to it. Complications, petitions, policies, procedures assault me. I know the consequences of this; I know what will happen. Nevertheless, I cannot escape the knowledge. "You are a corrupt man," he has said to me, "an irretrievably impure and corrupt man. Don't you reflect? Don't you think on what you are?"

One must excise, one must give back to the good gold earth. Why did I not see all of this a long time ago? What could I have been thinking instead? All of it coalesced toward this moment. "I know what kind of people you are," he has mumbled. "They get slum rats and train them to be technicians. But it's the same, the same; it never changes. How can it be different?"

I am his orderly. I am his orderly and his Messenger and his familiar, and after hours tonight, after hours I will creep into his dark with the drill reversed. There I will restore where I had laid waste, restore a thousand-fold. Then I will emerge, sit before the Projector and wait for the morning by Yancey. When they come they will see what I have done and they will understand. I know they will understand. "The whole technology is crazy," Yancey says. "It isn't worth the price. All it is, the whole thing, it's a racket. I didn't even want any part of it. Yancey has no relatives. Occasionally, dim men who I take to be associates come and consult with him while I sit by his bed glowering. They motion that I should leave the room and Yancey says, "Don't worry about him. They understand nothing. Absolutely nothing. If he heard it, it would be meaningless. Just don't take him seriously."

Don't take me seriously. But it is coming. If Yancey does not know it, I sense with a fanatic's skill that others must: doctors and nurses, even the Director, have eyed me cunningly today with a look shrouded by meaning. They know. They know that Blount can be pushed just so far before meaningful action must be taken. I'll teach them some respect. I'll teach them.

Only Yancey does not know. Whatever he says or senses, like all post-operatives, he has no intimation. Locked into his condition or released of it, he mumbles of the "twitchings of recovery."

"Clean in God's hands, son?" he asks me. (He varies between high religious plaint and low administrative rant; he must have had these streaks running co-equal within him and the mitosis, splitting everything, meaning that they can no longer fuse.) "Clean in the hands of Jesus, that is? Or does the filth and decay of your function possess your soul? Is your mind raddled and ruined? Is your heart truly pure? Can you face it? What do you know of your background, your motives, your condition? Sadness, sadness, you will never understand me.

"Corruption! Corruption!" he mutters. "But remember, remember this, son, the mind breaks first, and only then the tormented shell of the body. Boy, you may already be dying inside yourself with your filthy performances, your terrible guilt. Untenant your soul, throw away your drill, resign and let the breezes go free before you, too, are incurable. Listen to me, son, I know about these things!"

This is what he says to me. To *me*. Toward this coalescence, all of it has mindlessly drifted. Even the Priest, who now sits in these rooms, even the Priest was merely a step on the way. For Yancey has enabled me to see so many things.

(I know. I know that. I know he is a senile gentleman; I understand. This has nothing to do with the question. I have put up with too much. It has all been too great a price to pay for this, and I am most sensitive, far different from your average Messenger.)

(Also, his cancer was not senile. It was youthful, bright, quivering, reaching for the heart's moon, full of joy and first seeking. One is not concerned with the condition of the container, not at all, all or not.)

(I never answer him. I try not to speak with him. I avoid all dialogues; nevertheless, he will not stop. I cannot take it up with the board; they are not sympathetic to the complaints of Messengers. The patients *pay;* the Messengers *are paid*. That is the difference.)

Stay with me. Oh, God, I haven't called on you in thirteen years, but I'm calling now, oh, God; stay with me just a little bit longer and then it's all over. Hold the doors, bar the doors, lock the windows, hide in the Priest lurking head-high behind me, and just this little bit more. Stay, stay; listen, listen. It is night.

It is night, darkest night; in that familiar cunning I once again steal upon Yancey. Slide in quickly, tenant the now familiar flesh. It is late in his corridors as well, illuminated in the metastatic loss only by phosphorescent dust and faint refractions from the quarters below. In his room, in that night littered with prefiguration and doom, murky to the sounds of his stirring, Yancey's gut is where I laid it last, shimmering in the light of the lance. I hear murmurs. The blood's whisky travels home. It bathes my knife.

I change my plans; I do not re-implant. It is too complicated, too agonizing, too *patient* for my mood; instead, I do it with the knife rather than drill-reversal. It is, in addition, the soundest and most painful way.

One thrust then, one thrust into the stomach, another past the arteries, finally into the pancreas itself, hearing the panicked recession of the blood. It takes a very long time, but it takes no time at all. I think of my father. I see him once again dying on his bed. And in that seeing, I grasp everything. But far too late.

When it is over I emerge, perch on his pillow this time, blow in his ear, regard him. He has fallen heavily on his back, eyes diminishing. Eyes open, undrugged, awake to all of it. He gasps and turns.

"Why, son?" he says, with what I suppose is his last breath. "Why do that? Could you not escape your own corruption?"

And I try to point out then that it is the other way; that as always he has it wrong—that, in fact, it is my unassailability that broke *his* corruption, but my tiny lungs resist as inflation takes over. Frantic, I clamber to the foot of the bed. And by the time I could talk again, he is dead on his side. I am pleased, pleased. It is all over. I know what I will do now. I will return to my room quietly and await them against the bolt with reason and expectancy. Faint quizzicality will inform my eyebrows, faint resignation my breath. I will prepare my notes. I will bring my journals up to date. I will drink a little, sigh a little and know a song or two. It is all over now, and I can wait for them without suffering or fear. I am beyond their touch at last. It has been long and difficult, but I am beyond, beyond, beyond, beyond them.

And then . . .

(They have broken through with a lance. I see it turning in the door like a tiny phallus, poking and probing. Seconds then until they come. But I do not care. I want them now. I did not believe such suffering was possible. I did not believe it. Nothing has worked out the way it should. Instead of resignation there has been only terror. I want them now; I, too, want the knife.)

And then . . .

And then, from deeply within, hovering over Yancey, I feel my own fresh tumor, full-come and dancing for joy.

For joy in the forever dark.

Introduction to
PATER FAMILIAS

I've written very little collaboratively, mostly because collaborations don't seem like work. They are fun and (because they don't seem like work) gratifying, but in a way different than results self-administered. Just as the quality of art seems to be determined by particularity—the *narrowing* of metaphor so that the less it's about, the more it says—so the value of fiction seems to diminish in relation to the number of consciousnesses applied to it. With one notable exception freely granted—the distinguished collaborations of Frederik Pohl and Cyril M. Kornbluth, and even *they* turned out mediocre work along with the very good—can anyone think of an important work of science fiction or of literature, period, that was done collaboratively? Answers c/o the publisher, please.

This is not to say, to repeat, that collaborations are not fun: they aren't work; anything that isn't work in America *has* to be fun. ("Why am I paying seventy dollars a day and I'm still miserable here, honey?") I've enjoyed every one of them . . . three stories with Kris Neville, three with Bill Pronzini, and two novels, one with Harry Harrison, one with Valerie King. Of them, this and the King collaboration (which also appears in this book) strike me as being the best, and all of them have extended my range: the key to a good collaboration, of course, is the emergence of a style, a compound/chemical fashion that is neither yours nor your collaborator's, but some intricate melding of the two that is new.

Kris Neville, born in Missouri in 1925, is one of the best people in the world, and could have been, if he had gone in that direction (he's been a technical writer most of his lifetime and a brilliant one, knows more about polymers and epoxy resins than all but ten people in the country), one of the absolute best in the history of our field. For a quarter of a century his short stories have been appearing in all of the S-F markets, and he has published several novels. His most famous is *Bettyann* (*New Tales of Space and Time,* Healey & McComas, 1951), later novelized under the same title. But his best, I think, are *Cold War* (*Astounding,* 1949, widely anthologized), *Ballenger's People* (*Galaxy,* 1969, *not* anthologized; look it up) and *The Price of Simeryl* (*Astounding,* 1966, anthologized in *The Far-out People,* Robert Hoskins, Signet, 1971): He is a magnificent correspondent and knows everything about everything.

For the record, this collaboration represents Neville's deep revision of an unsuccessful short story that I had been unable to sell. That's the way we worked together. Pronzini and I, Harrison and I worked in alternate sections, and the King represents my reconstruction of *her* earlier draft. Like marriage, it all depends . . . as long as it works.

————◆————

PATER FAMILIAS

People keep saying the past is dead. Your hear it on practically every street corner. I think my father had something to do with it. But then I may be wrong. I may still tend to overvalue him on some level of my being to compensate for my real feelings.

The last time I saw him alive, there was something profoundly moving to me about his condition, considering all the times he had humiliated me, and considering that for all intents and purposes he had been dead for five years and five months.

When my father straightened, finally, from the Fox Temporal Couch, I passed him the remains of my drink.

"Ah, you bastard," he said, sipping. "You caught me in the middle of a TV program that time. I was lying straight out on the chair and hassock, watching the draft riots. I told you last time, I never wanted you to do this to me again."

"It isn't easy on me, you being dead these five years and five months," I said. "I was sitting here drinking and looking at the Transporter, just sitting around, and I said, 'Hell, I feel like having a chat with my old man again.'"

"Stop telling me when I'm going to die," he said. "There's absolutely no need for that." Still half-locked in the Couch, he managed to make it to his knees, clutching the glass, bringing it to his mouth two-handed as if it were a baby's bottle, which, of course, in at least one sense, it was. All of this was bringing back memories. I half-hoped, but did not expect, that he would begin one of his circuitous analyses of the world, as in times past, as though trying to teach me something that I again, as in times past, and in the last analysis, would not be able to completely figure out. Such was his way and mine, I guess. I think it may be the way of all parents, but I suppose some are more direct and maybe better organized and really teach you something, but I doubt it. Then, of course, it is a mistake to generalize like this.

Not the least of the Transporter's appeal, the brochure said, was its poignancy, the nostalgia of it all. It infused the present with the past, brought you back to your origins from which you were now so distant as not to be touched. And, also, as the brochure said, "You don't have always to be a child with your parents, now," although that may be wrong.

"Let's talk about the old days," I said. "Remember that time in 1982 when we were playing softball and I broke your finger with a pitch? And you gave me a shot and broke my nose? That's what I really want to talk about—the basics that we both understand. The cut-off is only five minutes from now, and we really ought to do some talking before I have to send you on your way."

"Five minutes, eh?" he said. "Well, what if I just don't go back? What if I sit right here in your basement and refuse to let you put me back in that circle?"

As if, any longer, he had the strength to resist my determination. And, besides, they wouldn't let him, anyway.

They turned everything upside down when people tried to do that, finding them. Some people said it was so you'd have to keep renting the equipment.

"It won't make a shade of difference," I said. "The past is immutable. That's the point of the construct . . . "

But, of course, what *was* the point? How could one really know the past was immutable: perhaps it was fluid or semirigid like gold gelatin, or something else entirely.

To pursue our ignorance on this point: how might one account for why the Transmitter could bring back only parents and no one else—except once in a great while, grandparents? Was there some psyche force between generations grown up from an early dependency? And yet, there were occasions when the father who came back was a stranger to the child, and so . . . Was there some transcendent genetic continuity, some scientological myth, that the Transporter responded to? Or was the circle that was necessary like the pentagram of old, and was this black magic entirely, as the world fragmented itself on the New One Thousand, having broken an obscure equivalent of the sound barrier? It's academic now, I guess, but no one admitted to understanding it, even Fox, any more than anyone admits to understanding time itself, or, for that matter, reality, either. Now, of course, Fox is working on a machine to let us visit the future. He seems to be having unexpected problems that perhaps my father also contributed to. I like to think something will go wrong with his research, but maybe this is merely because I have come in other areas to distrust the uses technicians make of science.

But then, I could not admit any ignorance to my father, could I? Was he ever less than certain with me about things of which he knew nothing?

"Come on, Dad," I continued, mindful of the time, "loosen up, relax. Let's tell a few old yarns. Yours is the first generation in recorded history that has been given the advantage of time travel to your descendants—the privilege of seeing your works in their fullest flower—when you're dead and gone."

"Know what I'm going to do?" my father said, managing to make it fully to the top of his warmed legs and stand at last. "I'm going to kill myself, that's what. Right here in your basement. That way, the way I figure it, none of this ever happened, then."

I wondered what he thought he was trying to teach me this time.

He reached into his inner coat pocket. "Get this!" And he waved the knife at me. "Been holding it for the time those draft rioters get too close to the old man and start to mess with him! Been my protection, this little sweetheart: clean and sharp, really does the job! Good luck, son. I can't take it anymore; I can't spend the rest of my life wondering when you're going to get the urge to pull the old man all to pieces. . . ."

He held the knife two-handed against his heart and then brought it all the way through his shirt.

He stiffened in the midst of a good deal of blood and kicked right out on the floor. Despite the fact that he didn't look good at all, there was a smile on the small fragment of face that hadn't gone completely white. I was sure then, and now, that nothing like this had occurred in temporal transport before, and I waited for something awful to happen.

I was scared. I admit it. If my father had really died here in my basement in 1988 rather than 1933, then my whole life would be unalterably changed, to say nothing of the consequences of his being found suddenly missing sixteen years ago. I would never have had the fight with him that sent me away from home, but that eventually got me into the job where I had made enough money to buy the Transporter in the first place. But, if so . . .

The only thing I could think to do was to get him back. This may have been a bad decision, and, if so, then I'll just have to take the blame for it.

I picked him up—it was the most disgusting event of my life—and staggered into the circle with him and tossed the corpse in, and, putting the Transporter on manual so as not to take any chances, set it for a quick return. Then I pressed the lever and closed my eyes.

I said "Thank God" when he vanished, although who

can possibly believe in God anymore, although, of course, I guess there are some who still say He's not really dead; He's just senile.

Well, it meant at the worst the old man would be found dead in 1988 instead of 1993, which would be very bad, but not as bad as the other way, or so I supposed. Perhaps the shock of his death like that would have sent me away from home. Best of all, it could be that the effect was self-negating.

I sat in the basement in front of the Fox Temporal Couch with all the doors locked, waiting for myself to vanish or something, but some time later, when nothing had happened and my memories hadn't changed, as far as I could tell, and it was fairly obvious, I thought, that nothing *was* going to happen, I let out a long breath and decided that I had beaten it. The Transporter had beaten it. Time, indeed, was immutable, as the brochure claimed, and my father's action had, for all intents and purposes, never happened.

I brought my father back twice after that. The second time, decomposition had progressively advanced. On January 4, 1999, I decided that I wanted no more part of it, so I gave up using the Transporter. When the Government call-in was announced. I was more than happy to turn it in. It was a pleasant novelty there for a while, but who in hell wanted to see corpses, lots of corpses, coming back, and have to think about all those moms like that, too?

And I still hope Fox keeps having problems, for there could come a day when some parent may wish to continue his instructions into the far future, thereby succeeding in killing it, too.

Introduction to
GOING DOWN

This comes close to being a characteristic story of its period (1969–1973); it is completely black, but the narrative style, by refusing to admit its thematic implications except in an occasional scream or two, works against the vision to try and be horridly funny. The tension between unspeakable subject matter and comic style gives the work what energy it has.

It is one of the few pieces that partake directly from my background as an investigator in the New York City Department of Futility, Resignation and Containment back in the early 1960s (Fort Greene and Williamsburg divisions), and it is a representation of what I believe the facts of the department to be. Like most departmental briefs, there is the aforementioned tension between style and comment, suggesting that this is not as original an approach as some might think, but, indeed, highly derivative. Has anyone out there ever NA'd a pending case?

————◆————

GOING DOWN

I

The subject will, through the devices of the Institute and the services offered, be enabled to explore all avenues of sexual release that tantalize him, but which, for one reason or another, he cannot enact in the "real world." Included, for instance, might be such practices as homosexuality, bestiality, pedophilia, generalized sodomy, specialized sodomy, necrophilia or rape. These processes will also enable the subject to "unblock" buried or unconscious fetishes which, once discovered, will be similarly gratified. Since all of the experiences are inducted, (needless to say!) through hypno-therapy and do not impinge upon "reality," the subject will be shielded at all times from the very serious consequences that he might incur if he were to perform such acts in the public domain. The hypno-therapeutically induced experiences will be no less vivid or satisfying, however, than their actual counterparts, and the guidance of experienced and specially trained Institute personnel will be available at all times to lead the subject through these diverse avenues in order to bring him to a fuller understanding of his drives and their fulfillment.

It is understood that such processes are guaranteed by the Institute under the mandates of the congress. It is further understood that those who psychologically desire entrance for prurient reasons alone will be summarily rejected. It is also a condition of entrance that a full release shall be signed by the patient—that is, the Institute assumes no specific liability for behavioral syndromes evidencing themselves subsequent to treatment—although all reasonable efforts will be made to avoid post-hypnotic shock. The possibility of adverse reaction is certainly low. Every subject who completes the course successfully will be granted a certificate available for display.

Unsuccessful candidates rejected by psychological profile may reapply after a waiting period of six months, during which time psychotherapy or meditation may be desirable.

II

"I want to be President," I said to the girl. "I want to design cities. I want to change the face of our time. I want to effect a change of consciousness so vast that no one will ever again look at the world in the same way. I want to survive death. Isn't that a perfectly normal set of ambitions? What do you think?"

"No," the girl said, a gentle, submissive girl whose name I do not recall; she must have been one of that succession of gentle, submissive girls I knew in those summers. "No, there shouldn't be anything wrong with it. What's the matter with ambition?" She leaned down to touch me again, and I felt the brush of her breasts at my knees, her hands on my back, the heat coming from her body in slow waves, "Let's just fuck now," she said, but there was nothing left of me even for this persuasion; we had fucked away the enormous afternoon of August, and now, slow changes inside and out, I looked at the fading light of her bedroom and tried to make order of what was building. "Come here," she said, but I rolled from her then, knees to chin, rolling and rolling to the far side of the bed where I reared to an elbow and spoke against the wall. "But I cannot do it," I said, "because I am trapped within myself, small obsessions, small desires, wracked by fantasies of the impossible. Everything the brochure says is true; I can never be free of them, nor with them can I design cities."

"I don't understand you. I know you're not crazy, but what are you talking about?"

"No one understands," I said. "Everybody's crazy, but you must believe that I have tested limitations of which you yourself would never be aware."

I talked that way that summer. It was a very long time ago and I thought that elevation of language was elevation of thought, pity me, but then, again, I had excuses. "I want to capture the world. I want my name to be world-famous. I want women who do not know me to feel desire, but this will never happen."

"Why should it?"

"I am going to enter the Institute," I advised the wall with some real decision, "and see if they can do the job for me. I have read the brochures and they make a good deal of sense, although, of course," I added gently, showing that I had a subtle grasp of reality, "you can never be entirely sure of everything from public relations copy."

"No," she said, "don't do that. Don't go into the Institute. What do you want to go into the Institute for? They're a bunch of crazy people there; it's very danger-ous. Let me help you," she said, touching me again, shadow's touch on the buttocks, easing within, praying for some lever of excitement to unlock me. "Can't I help you?" A nice girl; of course, I may be sentimentalizing her a bit, and this conversation did not exactly take place, at least not in this way, but it would be nice to think that it did, and from the standpoint of a finished (or even unfinished) work of art, it *should* have happened.

"I don't think so," I said. "I just wanted to tell you this, really. I've already applied and been accepted. I'll be starting next week and retreat begins tomorrow, so this is really the last time for us. But you were entitled to know why," I added, then pivoted from her, stood up, began to search for my clothing. "I wouldn't want you to think that I had just rejected you," I pointed out.

"No!" she said. "No!" And she sprang from the bed, the eaves and ledges of her body wobbling away, reached toward me with insistence and cunning. To the end I did not retreat further but leaped upon her, took her by instinct if without lust for the last time, moving my body in the old way, making the familiar gestures of penetration, my mind tight, hard, bound at some great distance, and finally, like a tree breaking from age, she came around me in little strings and lay quietly as I pierced here, poked there, stroked her cheek. Her chest heaved. Her eyes closed. She slept.

I came away from her and went quickly from the bed, dressed quickly, buttocks hoisted to the wall for balance, and then I left her quickly. Her breath was even and regular, with a slight gasping intake when I closed the door. I knew then that she had not been sleeping, but out of some understanding I could not touch . . . she had released me.

Well, it makes a pretty scene. Whether it happened or not, I have no idea.

III

"It's 2020 now," the assistance case said, sweat breaking from the ledge of her forehead and coming into her eyes, not entirely unlike this girl of many years ago (I leak associations like a foundering ship spews water).

"It's 2020 and a new era; I don't have to take this from you. I know my demands and rights; you give me what I need," she said, then leaned forward against the desk, shook her head in an effortful pause and then spat in my face.

I felt the spittle curve like blood off the chin, dripping then to the papers scattered on the desk. "Policies and procedures," I pointed out, using my training. "We must have policies and procedures. If you want larger quarters you'll have to explain . . ."

"Explain nothing, you old son-of-a-bitch!" the assistance case pointed out. "I demand!" Old I was to her, indeed—old at forty-five, hunched over my clerk's forms in clerk's posture (I tend to objectify myself nowadays; depersonalization is one of the signs of oncoming schizoid reaction, I calmly note), the sounds of the loft going on to the right and left of us, but locked into this booth one bare fan above putting out gusts of exhausted air. "Put it through for me," she said, "or I'll have you beaten out of the Government. Old fucker, we have rights!"

Rights. All of them have rights. Looking at her through the one necessary moment of flat confrontation, the drugs making her assume a somewhat sentimentalized posture (after all, she could have been a madonna, I reminded myself—a madonna in trouble), those sweeping, soaring hands which, if they were knives, would have cut me open, the garments parted drably here and there to give out whiffs of her body—looking at her in this way it occurred to me that I should stand, close down the investigation and leave this area. Just *leave,* prowl the streets, have some more drugs, consider the convolutions and difficulties of a public assistance program that in eighty-seven years had not changed from its original assumptions that themselves were wrong. This really occurred to me despite the fact that I would risk less of pension rights and the Ever Horizons Program offered by the agency. But, of course, I would not do this, attractive as it seemed, because I had accepted my fate, much as it had accommodated me, and what would be worked out would only occur within these spaces. Sound of fans, low murmurs in the center, isolation. Cases like this might have attracted attention (in an era of low confrontation, confrontation should in itself be interesting), but since the four murders committed in the center last month, staff tends to keep to itself. Any shriek here might be semaphore to more blood; certainly, I would not go near an agitated recipient. "I don't think that this is getting us anywhere," I said. "Maybe you should simply leave now and come back another time when you're somewhat calmer." Disassociative reaction; not interested now in my own identity, I can hardly be expected to pay much attention to theirs.

"I'm terminating this interview," I said. "I am terminating this interview," he said as well. He and I both said it.

Halfway through the corridor, however, she caught up with me. Clinging, grabbing, gnawing. Her earlier aggression had been tenuous; the drug had misled me into seeing menace where there was only despair. The usual error. "Please," she said, hanging on, "please, now, you've got to help me, sir. I'm really sorry that I cursed you before, but I'm so worried, worried about everything, don't you understand, understand, understand that? Got to help me, got to help me get a place." No, I do not. "Yes, you must. You've got to." No, I am afraid that I do not. Get away from me, cunt.

Away from her, leaving her sprawled on the floor, I strode the corridor like a demon, strong and calm, brave and free, in control for that instant of my destiny and the world's. Only, however, for a moment. These flashes will not carry anymore; increasing amounts of drugs must be taken just for little shy twitches of the way it used to be almost always.

Alone, alone at last, I found myself a booth on the next level and was able to sit before the spasms began. The spasms brought out tears that made him very sick; let me tell you that.

IV

The subject is a white, Anglo-Saxon male. Birthdate: 11/22/63. He states that the fact of his birthday has "always had a profound effect," since the incidence of that birthday with the assassination of Kennedy Number One has given him a feeling of "unique destiny and obligation." Subject is five-feet eight-inches tall; one hundred and forty-three pounds; blood pressure one-forty over seventy-five; reflexes and motor responses within the gross normal range. Health may be considered acceptable at the present time; the shocks of therapy involve no mortal risk.

Subject states that he "wants to be President, wants to design cities, be loved by women who do not know me," etcetera, but he does not feel capable of realizing his drives at the present time. "I am trapped within myself, small obsessions, small desires, wracked by fantasies of the impossible. That is why I am seeking treatment. I need and deserve treatment." The preceding has some air of rehearsal. It is indicated that the subject has planned out his approach. Spontaneity is lacking. Subject says that he "teems with sexual repression" and hopes that the Institute will provide the opportunity to "explore" said repression so that at last he will be "free."

In summary, although the subject appears to be reasonably intelligent and aware of the nature of the treatments, he is *not* aware of the intentions of the Institute.

Subject's questionnaire indicates interest in the following acts: pederasty, homosexuality, anal intercourse and bestiality. Under preliminary hypnosis it was discovered that the subject's obsessions verge upon an extreme sado-masochistic syndrome with possible fantasies of murder. Such drives are sublimated. Subject lacks insight into these drives. He has had a number of relationships of a hetero-sexual nature, all of them superficial. Most have been of short duration. He states, however, that he has never had much trouble in "meeting girls or getting laid," and judging from internal and external evidence, interviewer can agree with this!

Under hypnosis, subject disclosed a strong identification with John F. Kennedy, thirty-fifth President of the United States: 5/30/17–11/22/63. John F. Kennedy, the subject stated, "had none of the repressions that I have. Why, here was a man able to accomplish every conceivable act he dreamed of doing, desire equaling achievement. I want to be strong and successful just like him, and because I was born on the day of his death I'm entitled to that, the transmigration of souls and so on . . . but how can I get things done if I am constantly overwhelmed by terrible, unspeakable desires? Oh, my, I teem with urges, urges I can barely express, and if I cannot pass beyond them I know that I will always fail."

Subject also revealed a number of extraneous details that are excluded from the report since they are not relevant.

Subject disclosed accounts of $19,321 in conventional savings and stock-transfer holdings, assets that were the result of a recent inheritance from his father, who had died on 4/11/87, willing his entire estate to his son. It was the receipt of this inheritance, the subject stated, that made it possible for him to think for the first time of the Institute as the solution to his difficulties. "What is $19,000 now?" subject stated. "I couldn't live on it; I could barely die on it, but it would finance my way into the Institute, and then I might be found an interesting case, worthy of further treatment." Assignment of said assets has, of course, already been effected.

It is recommended, accordingly, that the subject be admitted. Only as much of the purpose and processes of the Institute have been explained to him as the interviewer felt minimally necessary at the present time. Subject should be an excellent candidate. He expresses resistance to treatment at no conscious or preconscious level. He can be expected to cooperate throughout. He is, therefore, an ideal candidate.

V

Later at night, merged with Antonio, sliding and blending with him, rising above him, I felt on the verge of a breakthrough, some reciprocity of feeling not known before, and then, with orgasm, the same grief and futility. Nothing, nothing: at the last moment I have been betrayed, as has happened time and again (note the self-pity, but I am entitled to it, friends), and I do not know if the fault is within Antonio (homosexuality is, after all, still a perversion, I feel) or in myself. I cannot tell; he cannot tell. Leaving Antonio then spent on the bed, not a word between us, because he understands my failure as I understood his (coming into him I knew that he, too, had felt nothing), and so I left the apartment, then, throwing on an overcoat, nothing else, naked under the wool, a perverse excitement reaching at me again, and I took the elevator to the bottom level, then went out on the path to an open space and looked out upon the city.

The wind tore at my body through the coat, tore at the man's body, stirring the ruined blood. At length I realized that there was someone on the overhang beside me, and I thought for a moment that it was Antonio, come to speak with me again . . . for at the end of all failures comes, in Antonio, anyway, the inexhaustible need to converse, whereas I desire only silence . . . but, turning, I could see that it was not. It was a little man from the second level, a clerk in the assistance center in which I work whose name I had never known and did not want to know . . . but in a terrified way this clerk has been pursuing me for weeks, scuttling through and around the trap of our mutual lives, happening on elevators as I did, joining me on the overhang, thrusting a frozen hip cruelly into mine when I had been wandering, alone I would have thought, on the grounds surrounding the complex.

"Beautiful night," he said, "isn't it? Even for the city it's a beautiful night."

I said nothing; gathered my coat more tightly around me. Surely if he sensed that I was naked underneath he would take it as an invitation. The man was naked underneath, I said; the feel of wool against him gave him a perverse sense of excitement. I control no situations anymore.

"It's just like the two of us are here alone in this wonderful city," the man said. "Haven't you ever felt that— that you're with someone you hardly know in an isolated spot and all of a sudden it could be only the two of you in the world, for all that that world cares? Feel the wind," he said, granted lunatic inspiration by my silence, or, then again, maybe he simply liked to talk that way. "Aren't you cold?" He reached forward to touch me.

"No," I said, stepping brutally from him. "I am not cold. Please leave me alone. I don't want to talk."

"Come to my room," he said, his voice thin and fragrant in the night. How I must have incited his desire! Well, this is only natural, I being a most attractive man. "Only for an hour. Why not? I've wanted you for weeks; don't you know that? I can make you happy." Something had opened up within the madman; he was no longer shy. I could feel the pressure of him more insistently now, digging in waves below the surfaces, lightening and deadening in alteration. It might have reminded the naked man in the overcoat of the girl he had once known, although I do not want to seek such easy cohesion. Quickly the man in the overcoat moved from him, leaned tightly against the balcony, then turned at last for a fuller confrontation.

Oh, my! He was old, old, disorder had eaten away, desire had shriveled, his mouth opened and he showed me his tongue. "Please," he said, "surely you know I won't hurt you. I know that you want to come with me. You don't care for the other at all; I know that. I've researched your life," he said. "You can't hide anything from me, not ever. The other will not work out. Come with me."

"No," the naked man in the overcoat said finally. After a pause, he then said, "You feel; do you think that

it would make any difference if I did? How can I give
you identity? I have none of my own."

"I don't want identity; I want to fuck you," the stranger
said hopelessly, "and, besides, I'll make you happy. . . ."

"There are no promises," the disassociative naked man
in the overcoat said. "There are no possibilities; there is
simply the infinite trap of self, the one refracting instant
when that frozen self is known again and forever." He
gestured floridly, perhaps repelled by his rhetoric. Then
he moved quickly away from the stranger, miming a violent gesture. "Find someone else," he said. "There are a
million others in the city who spend hours in the rooms
of others, and any one of them would give you more than
I. I have nothing; do you understand that?" And then
he added, after an instant, "I'm sorry," and he did not
know if he was extending mercy or a taunt as he went
inside, the wool sticky with perverse sweat, beating at him
with insect wings as he closed the door and headed toward the elevator.

He thought that he might have seen the stranger bend
on the balcony in a posture of tears; he thought that he
might have seen no such things—his perceptions are muddled, he is fifty-seven years old and rarely sees what he
used to, although in the best of health, of course, the
overcoat swaddling him as he trotted back to his rooms
carrying, as always, that eternal burden: the body.

VI

Under hypno-therapeutic block, the subject was given
the usual tapes and promptings. He was permitted to enact the fetishes and practices disclosed at the conscious
level. Subject was led through homosexuality, pederasty,
bestiality and other practices. This stage of treatment
lasted one week, at the end of which the subject appeared
for standard, checking interview. He was not articulate
about his reactions; had to be coached into response.

Under strong questioning the subject finally disclosed
that: "It was all right, everything I could have expected.

I mean, I'm not quibbling with the reality of it; it certainly seemed real enough. But I have the feeling that I'm missing something, haven't put it together yet." This response well within the normal range.

Subject hesitated and continued under prodding: "It's hard to tell what I'm missing exactly, because I did do everything I wanted to do, but there was a feeling of incompletion. Knowing through all of it in the back of my head that it was just a dream. That can hold you back and make you feel silly, and then, too, I wonder if I was telling the truth; I mean, I thought it was the truth, but evidently I was holding something back. There must be another level of desire, if you follow what I'm saying— things that I've wanted to do that I can't even admit to myself."

Subject, it can thus be said, showed an initial level of insight. The prediction of this interviewer that he would be an excellent candidate was therefore completely verified. I call the attention of the board to this.

"I'm ready," the subject stated. "I feel that I'm ready now, that the rest of it was just a preparation. Show me now. Show me what I *really* want to do. I'm ready for it; I'll never be what I can until I see where I've been, and I know this. Show me the dark heart of my desire, at least until the $19,000 is used up."

Subject's rhetoric has persistent flashes of this nature. He tends to become melodramatic at key moments and shows some lability of effect, manifested primarily in abstruse speech and florid, rhetorical devices. These may be discounted as potent defense mechanisms.

It is recommended that we proceed.

VII

Disassociative reaction much better, much better—I know exactly who I am, gentlefolk, thank you very much —and so onward, into the dark. Kennedy ceremonies at the center, a day off although attendance at the center is itself compulsory. Government employees must pay min-

imal homage, etcetera. My clerkly forms folded for the
holiday, my clerkish frame bent to an appropriate shuffle,
I proceed past the gate and to the great adjoining lane
where the ceremonies take place. It is necessary and just
that employees show affinity with their history by attendance at the ceremony . . . but if it were all the same to me
I would rather be elsewhere, even in a small room with
Antonio . . . and this morning, incidentally, I told the man
that all was finished. In my head. Extrinsically, not quite
yet. But soon, soon. Will he cry? There are still, I believe,
reservoirs of feeling here or there.

Kennedy Day? John F. would have been one hundred
and three if he had survived, the other merely ninety-six,
the third ninety, but I never saw powers of survival in the
two younger. It was that elder who interested me,
not only because of the coincidence of birthdate—and
sometimes I must smile, remembering what that meant to
me long years ago—but because it is possible to tell by
those old photographs, bedazzling in the light outside, that
he was a man who had passed all barriers of expression.
He had literally every experience that the simple accesses
of the body might accommodate, and it was this knowledge—every orifice satisfied, that is to say—that had
given him the power of command.

In youth, tantalized by this collision of his death, my
birth, I had scurried through the libraries and museums
seeking information on Kennedy Number One so that I
would be able somehow, somehow to emulate, and even
thirty years later (thirty years!) something within that
lordly memory must call to me yet . . . for I stand upon
the street during the ceremonies, transfixed once again by
their simple elegance. Their meaning.

Opening their masks, the dancers come for the ritual,
then the speeches and finally re-enactment of the assassination itself, a re-enactment that is simply a renewal of
that martyrdom that sent us on our simple way. In this
dense crowd, jammed comically among the bodies of
other clerks, I feel surges—for just a moment—of the old
desire. I feel that I could rise above and by the power of
my rage alone seek control . . . but this emotion,

too, passes, and as the assassins crawl from their high places to kill the dancers I feel the energy dwindle. It collapses within me. In place, drained, I remain.

"What's wrong?" Antonio says. We work close together in the center; it is impossible to avoid him, ever. There are no partitions in our relationship, then, which is one of the reasons why I have decided that it must end. "You look terrible." He laughs at this, touches me on the back. Winks. "Tonight," he says, reconstituting an old joke, "I will make a man of you." His humor.

I retreat from his touch, stumbling into other bodies. I wave my arms to establish between us a small, neutral area as the dancers crumple. And then, not entirely to my surprise, I find that I am screaming.

"Leave me alone!" I scream. "You have got to leave me alone now!"

"What's wrong with you?" Antonio says, looking keenly in the old way, then turning to some of the others as if to seek the approval he deserves. "You look crazy. What's happened to you?"

"Nothing happened. Nothing will ever happen." The gun, amplified, booms over the dancers and the great mask, sixteen feet high and five feet wide, is hoisted slowly into the air, dominating us, flapping by rotors in the still, dead little currents. Disassociation begins once more. "Nothing's happened," he says. "It's just that you must leave me alone."

The man of whom we are speaking—the clerkly protagonist of this narration—wants to run, is seized throughout his fifty-seven-year-old frame by an idiot wish for flight . . . but attendance at Kennedy Day is compulsory, and what would happen to him if he dived into the center, whimpering? What would they make of this man and what has happened to his control: he feels that he has become translucent.

Translucent, he is attacked by color: little red and gray fibers of fright coming alive under the skin, giving him the feeling, or should we say *impression* of phosphorescence. He reaches to the crowd. "Oh, my God!" the

fifty-seven-year-old clerk cries. "Oh, my God!" A definite
sense of inadequacy seizes him. "This isn't right."

The mask is hoisted, the solemn and dead eyes of that
long-ago murdered chief of state peering at and through
the clerk with distance as he huddles before that mask.
"What is going on?" the clerk avers. "What is happening
here?" He turns to pelt from the area, then, despite the
rules and regulations of the service, he staggers through
bodies and up against the implacable doors of the center,
beating, beating like a heart for entrance. "I identified
with him," he mentions, expostulating in a cold, mad, fu-
rious little voice, expostulatory and tearful by turns as he
tries to make this vital point. "I thought that I could be
like him if the Institute had done its dreadful work." And
now Antonio comes behind him.

Antonio's hands rush up and down his back as a matter
of fact, excess of connection, but it is not lust, not this; it
is inspection that drives him through his gestures and,
mumbling, the clerk submits to his grasp. What else could
he have done? The doors of the center, gentlefolk, are
locked.

"You thought you could be like him?" Antonio says.
He cackles in an unseemly way, but his laughter is no less
offensive than the clerk's; it streams and bubbles, rivulets
of laughter running like blood. "You like him?" And he is
all around the hapless clerk, pity him, and bodies are all
over. He must be having an attack of some sort, first heart
attack at fifty-seven, and events become magnified, events
become removed, dwindled and enormous, beating like a
heart around him . . . like ancient film—Zapruder, I may
say—near and far, far and near, the very best of it picking up in rhythm with the clerkly pulse, the pulse ragged
and frantic, and it must only be then, mercifully, that the
clerk faints, or at least this episode of his memoirs concludes: the ceremonies of memory, the mask dancing
above him, he thinks in his faint, and locked into position
he dies on the stones, a bullet in his neck, in his head, that
second bullet penetrating the shoulder. An Anglo-Saxon
white male. Think of that.

VIII

In the Institute, under the block, I fucked an old man. As I fucked I murdered him. Oh, my God, the ecstasy of it! To say nothing of the cunning of the Institute to give me such sweeping rejoinder to possibilities. Leaning over him on the bed, penetrating fully, opening like a flower inside him, and so I fucked him and struck, using the knife to make a swift cross-stroke from back to ribs that opened him like a vegetable. Nevertheless, those strokes would not kill him for a long, long time. He would suffer. Indubitably, in or out of dreams, he would suffer.

Who would have thought that I had it in me?

Who would have thought that this be my mean desire? But I believed them. I believed the Institute, for I had come there to be fulfilled . . . and, also, under the drugs, anything—*anything*—I believe would have been an ecstasy and a release, or so the technicians whispered as they shot me full. "Remember, remember that this isn't real," they counseled as I went under, every single time, "this isn't actually happening, no matter how concrete the interior reality, or, at least if it's happening, it isn't happening very often." How comforting! Did they think, then, that I would take all of this and disappear underneath in a conviction of actuality? Well, there must have been policies and procedures established.

"It isn't real, it isn't real," they pointed out as the drugs seized me, and then I was astride the old man, beating and flailing, screaming at him as I cut and pumped, and I could see life running out of him in small, bright pulses as I worked the incisions with the tenderness of a lover, biting away at his body.

I never saw his face.

His face lay buried in the pillows, and, try as I did to taunt and strike him into confrontation, he never would, the old fucker. All of his expression was in the line and heave of his body, that and in the small grunts he made as he took me in. The pumping and the knife. He never pleaded; he never protested. And he never resisted me at all.

"Take that, you old son-of-a-bitch!" I mentioned, driving at him. "That and that and that!" I cut and jabbed and the full darkness of my deed overtook then with a singing vault and I felt myself beginning to emerge within him. "And that!" I commented, putting the knife between his shoulder blades with all force.

And came within him then, colors of the blood intermingling. That queer orgasm was intense. I closed my eyes and in that enclosure had a view of his face: it was burned within the tormented eyelids, that face woeful and turned toward me at last in shades of red and green, and I looked at that face in the fluorescence for a long time, all the rivers running away, away: the face was that of my father.

I recall wondering at just that moment whether this treatment was quite necessary, after all. Or whether I had been misled.

Meanwhile, quite excited, I fucked my father.

IX

The next day, lying in that apartment, quite alone, stunned by the heat coming through the grillwork and the aftermath of the Kennedy ceremonies, the clerk was visited by the man who he met on the overhang, that man who had been pursuing him, that man who he had begun to think of (he has a very ordinary mind) as the Traveler.

The Traveler came in quietly through the open door, swept through the archway and into the bed nook where the clerk had been sitting propped up, reading memorabilia while dozing intermittently on the pillows Antonio had heaped for him. Too weak to battle, the clerk has agreed that it would be best for him to stay away from the center until strength was fully restored. He had feared the uselessness and boredom of idleness, but the apprehensions had been all wrong; that day had been pleasant and easy, restful and pleasant and filled with images of Anto-

nio, who had proved once again how well he understood
and knew how to take care . . . of the clerk. If for no other
reason, the clerk thought, the relationship with Antonio
must continue.

"Hi, there," the Traveler said, coming to the bedside,
leaning over, with great compassion. "I missed you there
today and heard that you were home. I wanted to come
and see you." He lays a hand on the bed clothes.
The clerk can feel the warmth trembling through the various layers, but he lies there quietly, giving no indications
of his true response, which is still in the process of preparation. He lies quietly underneath him then, that touch.

"Are you feeling better?" the Traveler asks. "That's the
important thing, of course."

"There is nothing to be done for you," the clerk says.
The weakness has led to a fusion of purpose, an impatience of gesture that guides him through dialogue. "You
must understand this now. I have nothing inside. All of
that disappeared a long time ago."

"There is much I can do for you," the Traveler says
blandly, sensuality darting in and out of that masking face
on bird's wing. The pressure of his hand increases.
"I want to do much for you."

"I can no longer feel," the clerks contributes. "I live by
convenience and endure life because it is too much trouble to resist." He is rather a self-pitying clerk, as has been
noted previously. "I have nothing for you. I have nothing
for anyone."

"You have not lost feeling," the Traveler says. "You
abandoned it."

"Not so."

"Yes, you did. It was the price." The Traveler's face is
deep and filled with knowledge; it hovers over the clerk.
"The other means nothing," he says, "so come with me.
Live with me and be my love," he says huskily. The clerk
smiles at the archaicism. He has little enough at which to
exercise his keen and highly developed sense of humor;
he can at least enjoy a sentimental archaicism when
it makes itself present. Grant him this. Have pity. Be reasonable.

"I am fifty-seven years old," the clerk notes. "I am an obscure man; I am deadened. There is nothing left." Memorabilia slide to the floor from his diminished grasp, portraits of the dull, elder Kennedy mingling with photostats of ancient newspaper pages. "You are wrong if you think there is anything. Please go," the clerk concludes, "and you would have made all much easier."

"You don't realize," the Traveler says. He lowers himself against the clerk on the bed and with an easy gesture holds him. The clerk snaffles and sighs. Why not? "You misunderstand even yourself."

The clerk feels arms gathering around him, the hot, uneven whisk of brow against brow as the faces meet, and in that instant the clerk's control breaks to dependence and he begins—consider this, gentlefolk!—to cry. "Oh, my!" he says. "Oh, my God!" And he utters other similar reactions as his body begins to move in the ancient, winding motions. He brings down the sheet under which the clerk lies naked, seeks with his hand. "Please let me," the Traveler suggests, "please let me do this. There is nothing wrong with desire; it is only the warping that leads to destruction."

The clerk closes his eyes. He drifts at once into a far space divorced of sensation. In this space it is easy to allow the Traveler to proceed. His touch of insistence is like a wandering fly's crawl to the clerk. The Traveler's hands clamber over the body; the clerk allows them that majesty. After all, he is not personally culpable. We are now talking of someone else.

The Traveler heaves and groans; he penetrates as quickly and insistently as that fly might invade an ear, and the clerk permits this, too. No fissure at the entrance as is so often the case with Antonio. He does not split me—I mean the clerk—open; the Traveler (we are talking about someone else; I have nothing to do with this), instead, he closes up. The clerk regards this with detached interest. He feels to be at a great remove. The energy of the motions heightens; the Traveler groans and bucks behind. Rear entry. Invisible that way, he begins to whisper words of love, meanwhile twisting hair. The clerk closes his eyes once again and sees him radiant, an arc of light shrouding.

The Traveler comes. I hear—I mean the clerk hears; I have nothing to do with this—the faint whine and sputter of release. Otherwise, no sensation. No sensation. He falls away. The clerk digs his little heels into parting and stares at the ceiling as he rolls. Now, in the aftermath of emission, the face of the Traveler is cold, hard, driven to stone. Only the faint beating of those eyelids indicates that only months ago, moments ago, he reared over as if he felt that I, inert receptacle, could share his life.

The clerk knows that it is finished, and to the degree that he knows this the Traveler and he have become one. One.

X

At the final interview it was determined that the sexual fantasies of the subject were not granted, but the deeper sexual fantasies *were* granted, and the condition of the subject as a result of this may indicate that the Institute has no business going beyond its position as stated in the mandates.

The interviewer would also like to take this occasion —this report, that is to say—to resign from the Institute. This is an irrevocable decision, I believe.

XI

All is spiritless with the clerk the next morning when however spiritless he wends himself into the offices. On the access staircase, an assistance case who may or may not have been the woman the clerk remembers as threatening him some days ago looks at him profoundly and then with a giggle hurls him into the wall.

"I knew," she says, "I knew that you folks meant nothing; we can do anything to you, beat the shit out of you," and then she departs, leaving the clerk severely disturbed and agitated, although he does not, does not retaliate. Indeed, the woman may be right, although the clerk has not investigated the issue to sufficient death.

On the balcony, signals of the ceremony still remain. Posters and flyers and reproductions that the custodial staff have neglected to remove dot the walls. They mean nothing to the clerk. They have lost the power to touch.

He now hangs up his jacket in the staff area and then walks to a window where he looks out upon the city for a long, quiet time, meditating all of the events of the week and where they will take him. He tries to induce some feeling by tearing out scenes from those recollections and making posters of them himself—the Traveler panting, Antonio weeping, the assistance case shouting. Circuitry is dead and disassembled, however. Nothing happens. He should have expected nothing else, of course; it has been this way for many years.

At length, the clerk senses a presence behind him. He turns and sees Antonio and the Traveler together, their hands clutched, looking at him with expectation. In the joining of those hands he sees all that he needs and turns back from them, faces the window, looks out past the rim of the city to the brown fields of the enclosure. He feels a tap on his shoulder, however. So much for disassociation.

Antonio says, "We wanted to tell you . . . "

"I know."

"I tried," the Traveler says encouragingly, "but . . . "

"I understand that, too," the clerk says. He moves from them, gracefully opening up space between them and the window. "It does not matter. Nothing matters."

"Do you give permission, then?" Antonio says. His face is like a young boy.

"I have no permission to give."

"Leave him," the Traveler says, "just leave him alone."

"Do that."

"I know how you feel."

"I do not feel. I feel nothing."

"I know that," the Traveler says, this small shapeless man showing an authority never before suspected. Insistently, he leads Antonio away. It must be love that has given him this strength, the clerk sentimentally concludes.

He watches them disappear together. Perhaps he is envious. More likely not. Moment by moment, he will connect the devices of his life and resume the day: he knows this, but it is not without reluctance that he leaves the small ground that has been staked out and moves away from the colors of the city beneath.

Antonio will have left, he concludes, by the time he returns.

He should feel pain at this.

He does not.

He feels nothing.

XII

"I want to build cities. I want to love women. I want to enter the Institute and become a part of myself."

XIII

The clerk lies like a bloodstain in the bed, sopping. He lets the night overtake him.

XIV

He hurled himself into the girl of that summer—he moved into her so deeply that he could not tell if it was flight or discovery. He fucked. He came. He felt.

XV

In these months that pass he sees Antonio and the Traveler together and they seem happy. They looked at him with the careful, measuring eyes of strangers and he does not speak to them. If he spoke, it would be in a language that they did not understand. He does not want to hurt them. He can salvage that much.

XVI

"I will enter the Institute and become a part of myself."

XVII

In March, at the first brush of spring, death whisks at him with a groan in the heart and as he falls to the stones, breaking, what spills from him is the first that he has felt in over thirty years . . . and the explosion is so great that he seizes the lover death with a roar of need and mounting, mounting, rides him like a stallion through all the mad halls of forever.

THOSE WONDERFUL YEARS

I know a man who believes, really believes, that the Government continues to sanction hallucinogens and narcotics traffic because it wishes to keep the most potentially revolutionary youth in a condition not of nihilistic activity but of escape. This man, who I happen to feel is a rational and intelligent individual, thinks that all of the anti-drug literature, narcotics squads, operations interceptions and prison penalties are public relations cover to keep hidden the real purposes of the autocrats and technicians.

I have no reason to think this is so. Drugs are dangerous, even to those who would manipulate others by their use. There is another commodity much less expensive, more palatable, with easier access to the minds and hearts of our youth that would, ultimately, have the same counter-revolutionary effects as narcotics with none of the complications.

Published in yet another of the all-original hardcover anthologies that have glutted the field in recent years (*Star Science Fiction,* what hast thee wrought?), this story attracted no notice whatsoever. Perhaps this is for the best.

THOSE WONDERFUL YEARS

I

Listening to the great sounds of '63, pouring like fruit from the transistors, the engine on high, pulling me irresistibly toward that simpler and more reasonable time of my life. *All is love/stars above/know the tune/I lost so soon,* Cosmo and the Pearls, got it together in '61, got the sounds right the following year, hit it to the top with "Moonsong" in that golden year of the assassination, and then it all fell apart as so many lives have fallen apart during the '60s: drugs, divorce, abandonment, flight, hatred and Cosmo himself died in a fountain in Las Vegas—or was it a pool?—in '69; must have been around that time, maybe a year later. Does not matter. Old Cosmo was finished by the mid-sixties; the whole sound that he exemplified, the tender lyrics that he probed, overtaken by harsher jolts, but ramming the Buick at high speed down the expressway it is '63 again and Cosmo is young, all of us are younger and I let the apples and oranges of that music bounce over me, humming only a little at the rhythm parts. On the expressway I whirr past other aspects of the past: cars from the early '60s assault me from oncoming lanes, yield to me on the right and in the chrome, the strange, bent, archaic shapes of the '60s I know my history again and again revealed. "Moonsong" ends on a diminished seventh, or maybe it is merely a hanging chord (I know absolutely nothing about music other than how it affects me), and the radio is still; then there is a commercial for the Wonder Wheel chain of superior foodstuffs in the metropolitan area and without transition from '66 comes the sound of the Troopers singing "Darkness of Love." Sixty-six was a good year, too; although not as critical in many aspects as '63, still it is a period worth remembering. The Troopers help me remember. Locked to the sound, a little pivot wheel of memory, I soar through all the spaces of the expressway and into the impenetrable not-to-be-known future. The vaginal canal of the future, parting its thick lips for me gently as I snaffle along in pursuit of my destiny.

II

Outside the building containing Elvira's single-girl's apartment I wedge the car into a space, remove the key (cutting off Tom and the Four Gees in "Sweet Delight," a pure pear plucked from the tree of '54, a little before my time, but no matter) and sit behind the wheel for a moment, meditating. I am a little early for our date, which happens quite often, but then, too, I am in no hurry to see Elvira, preferring always to cherish the memories gathered through our times together than to go into the difficult business of creating new ones. (The past is fixed, the present incomprehensible, the future without control; I must remember this.) Already Elvira is an artifact to me; I can see her at times as I will in '81, putting another car through its expressway maneuvers, listening to the music from '74, which will bring back to me, in the immutability of a teardrop, the picture of Elvira as she looked to me during that summer. Her breasts already seem to have the glaze of embalming fluid, her mouth tastes like mucilage; it is not Elvira who I am kissing so much as the Elvira who I will remember. It is difficult to explain this. It is difficult to explain this, but I will try: Elvira and our relationship are to be a golden oldie of the early '80s. Thinking this and other muddled thoughts I step briskly from the car, move through stones and into the lobby of the building where I see she has already come down to wait for me, a handbag slung over her shoulder, a tight and aggressive expression across her eyes and cheeks. I know that I will have to suppress memories of Elvira's agression in order to be truly moved by her years hence. "We must make a decision," she says, grasping my arm between wrist and elbow, in the vicinity of the ulna, and applying modest pressure. "We cannot go on this way. Tonight we must solve our relationship."

"I am not prepared to make any decisions, Elvira," I say, submitting to her grasp. In ordinary life I am a claims examiner for a large insurance company that has, partly because of me, one of the lowest payout rates in the business, a statistic that they do not advertise. In that capacity I must do a great deal of writing and checking, but fortunately this is with the *right* hand and not with the left, which feels Elvira's pressure. Resultantly, I do not protest at being greeted by her in this way but try to take a lower key. Cosmo and the Pearls, according to the newspaper stories at the time of their success, are supposed to have met on an unemployment line in the Bronx, New York, but I do not believe this. I discard most public biographies as lies and, trusting nothing, believe that the truth can be found only in what Cosmo does to me. A little snatch of "Moonsong" buzzes through my head like an indolent fly, and I do not slap at it; I listen. *Lost so soon/all I loved/like the stars above.* Above, above. "We will have to take it as it comes, Elvira," I add, liking the sound of her name. *El-vi-ra;* it carries wthin it the characteristic sound of the '70s, posturing and yet somehow childlike, which will surely characterize this decade in the years that lie ahead.

"No," she says, tightening her grasp on the arm, leading me toward the one voluminous couch which, in shades of orange and yellow, dominates the lobby of her residence, "it cannot be. You've equivocated too much. I can't waste these important years of my life on someone who doesn't even know his identity!" She raises a fist to her face, dabs at her eyes. "And besides that, I sometimes think that you don't even really want me," she says, "that when you're with me you've already thinking about how you'll remember me. I tell you, this is no way for a relationship to function. I have a great deal to offer you, but it must be within the terms of the present. You've got to be here with me *now.*"

"You don't understand, Elvira," I say, guiding her to the couch, gently easing down, and at last her terrible grip eases and I run a fervid hand over my joint, relocating the source of circulation and bringing the blood to a clear surge yet again. "The past is fixed, the present incomprehensible, the future without control. If we repudiate our past, well, then, what are we? And if we do not cherish the past, that only immutable part of us, well, then, Elvira, what will we make of the present and the future?" But even as I am saying this I feel the hopelessness of the argument overwhelm me. Her little face is set tight, her little breasts jut with argumentation; if I touched her body my hands would recoil, I am sure, with a metallic spang. She does not understand. Slowly I disengage myself from her, stand, walk back through the lobby, gesticulating.

"I'm not ready to make a commitment," I say. "How can we know where we're going until we know where we've been? You've got to understand history; otherwise, the sheer accumulation of data overwhelms," and so on and so forth. Now I am beyond the doors themselves, the cool, dense glaze of air hitting me, ruffling my cheeks, and still Elvira sits on the couch, unmoving, her hands closeting her pocketbook, her eyes fixed straight ahead. She seems to be speaking, but I cannot hear a word she is saying. She mouths polysyllables; I concentrate, but all is beyond me. "I'm sorry," I say, "truly sorry." And walking back to the car I feel a fine, true instant of regret; I could come back to her, vault against her on the couch and confess my sin—that dark, unspeakable stain that radiates from the heart through all the tendrils of the body, that stain that begins in loss and ends in acceptance, but what good would it do me? Or her? No, our relationship is obviously finished. I restore myself to the seat cushions of my car, hurriedly start the motor and drive away, the radio, caught in the gears, booming.

The Four Knights, '59, "The Tears of Your Heart." Fifty-nine was a year of great transition, just as this has been; everything hurt in '59. I let the music run over me like blood and, for an instant, it is that year again and I, twenty years old, am trying to come to terms with matters that I do not even remember. In retrospect I glimpse Elvira; she remains on the couch, she is sunk on the couch like stone: already a perfect artifact nestled in mucilage, on display for the *tourista* of recollection which, in little fibers, I shall send on their way in all of the years to come.

III

A man with all of his limbs torn off by an automobile accident was denied compensation when I was able to establish through delicate interviewing and piecing together of evidence that the accident was self-caused and therefore not covered under the terms of his particular policy. For this I was given praise by my supervisor and a small bonus, but I cannot get over an unreasonable feeling of guilt, even now, as if somehow it would have been better if I had falsified the interviews and documentation and allowed the quadruple amputee to slip a false claim through the company.

IV

A Festival of Revival is held at the large municipal auditorium and I attend. All of the great performers of the '50s, excepting only those who have died or have gone on to better things, are there: the Chryslers and the Flyers, Lightnin' Joe and the Band, the Little Black Saddle, Tony Annunzio. Seated in the third-row orchestra, surrounded by stolid citizenry who have carried forward the menacing expressions of their youth and little else, I am stunned again by the energy of that decade, its fervor and wildness, the way in which it anticipated and sowed the seeds of so much else to come, but I am also humbled because in a critical way I have come such a short distance from that time; my responses to the Little Black Saddle are as they were when I was thirteen, no difference. This is no Festival of Changes. Of course, the '60s were even more significant than the '50s; I must remember that, and that is to take nothing away from the '40s, which prefigured both of these decades, to say nothing of the '70s, fast receding from us and likely to be remembered as the most moving decade of all. Tony Annunzio takes off his jacket and tie to sing his final numbers, just as he did in the old days, and I am shocked at how round he has become, although, of course, my memories of him are unreliable. His great hit, "Broken Chain of Circumstance," is the finale of the show, and while standing in tribute with the rest of the audience, I find myself thinking of Elvira. If only we had been able to share this moment together! But she declined my invitation, of course, hanging up the phone on me nastily, but not before saying that in her opinion my unusual attachment to certain elements of the past only showed a childish inability to face the future.

How could I have explained to her that the past *is* the future? And what difference would it have made, the spotlight on Tony Annunzio winking off, the house lights surging on and all five thousand of us rose as one to cheer the voice of his generation, and Tony, standing on the bare stage to take those cheers with the same grace and offhandedness with which, more than twenty years ago, he bowed to us at the old Orpheus, now the *new* Orpheus, also the site of many great revivals?

V

Coming home I find Elvira lying naked in my bed, the covers below her waist, her eyes bright with malice. Try as she may, it seems that she simply cannot leave me alone. I know the feeling well, although I have never had it with Elvira. "I'll tell you about the nostalgia craze and your golden oldies," she says with a mad wink. "I've been thinking this through carefully, and now I'll tell you the truth." She is thirty-one years old, attractive but not exceptional, and from the beginning of our relationship she might have regarded me as her last chance. This has led to much bitterness in the breakup.

"Let me tell you what I think it is," she says, her voice wavering, her little breasts shaking, the nipples pursed as if for a kiss. "The nostalgia craze—this constant digging up of the past for people like you who can't face the future—it's all a Government plot. It comes from the Capitol. They're manipulating everything by digging up the past so that people aren't able to bridge the distance between the present and the future. They think that they can keep people from seeing what's really been *done* to them if they feed them the past like a drug to keep on reminding them of what they used to be. They're going to keep us all locked in the past so that we won't really ever see what's going on *now,* but I won't fall for it, and I

won't let *you* fall for it." She leaps from the bed, breasts
shaking, and seizes me around the neck, gathers me in.
"Please," she says, "you must face your life, you must
face what you've become and where you're going; you
can't live in the past." Moving her body like a lever
against mine, bone to bone, flesh to flesh, and for all of
my embarrassment and rage it is difficult to suppress desire—Elvira and I always did have a good sexual relationship; I have saved certain memories of it and bring them
out now one by one in privacy to masturbate—but suppress desire I do, hurling her from me.

"Don't you ever say that," I say to her. "The past is
immutable, the past is strong and beautiful—the past is
the only thing we have ever known," and resist as she
may, I convey her shrieking from bed to wall to door,
pausing to guide her fallen clothes with little kicks toward
the exit. At the door, I pull the knob with enormous speed
and strength and then throw her, weeping, into the hall,
kicking her clothes after her. "Get out of here, get out of
my life, get out of my way," I say to her, and not bother-
ing to gauge the effect that these words have had, I slam
the door closed and lock it, turn my back to it trembling
and then stride toward the radio.

Turning it on to the station of the golden forever,
I hope that I will find some music of the '60s that will gal-
vanize me with energy and help me find emotional equivalent in events of the past, but something is wrong with
the radio; the dial is somehow set toward the only station
in the area that plays current hits, and in palpitation and
dread I find myself listening to the Number Two maker
on the charts, something about "Meanies and Beanies,"
the tune confusingly disordered to me.

It is too much. I simply cannot cope with it; not this
on top of Elvira. I sit on the bed wracked with sobs for a
while, whimpering like a dog against the strange music,
and then in the hall I hear the softest and strangest of
noises, as if Elvira had somehow found a key and was in-
sinuating herself within . . . and then, as the music goes
on. I look up to find that not only she, but also the quadruple amputee who I serviced, have somehow managed to

get into the room and are singing along with the radio; there is a tumbling, I shriek like wind out the other end and from a far distance hear "Meanies and Beanies" for what it always was—an artifact of the forgotten decade, as the '90s overtake me in sound and the amputee and El-vira roll against one another on the floor, their defeat accomplished as the smooth, dense wax of the embalmer pours from the tubes of the radio to cover them like lava on volcanic ash.

Introduction to
ON ICE

On Ice is a very rough story, so intensely written that it pains me to read it. It was written for, and rejected by, an anthology of short S-F on the subject of sex, and on the basis that it was "too harsh." I remain mad at the editor, whose name I will not divulge unless bribed. Like television, it seems that much of category writing (more in the mystery magazines than in my field, but S-F has the problem, too) is not supposed to be about what it is really about, but rather . . . well, you know, about something else. This is an S-F story about sex. I thought—still think —the idea is to drive themes to the limit if you have any respect for yourself, your craft and your field, and that is what was done here.

Naturally, it had very few markets available after the intended one had been rejected, and I was very happy to sell it to Ted White, editor of *Amazing,* who showed courage in taking it and to whom I owe a reasonable debt, if not refund, of the (minimal) sale fee.

On Ice, published in the January 1973 issue, is probably the most controversial story that magazine has ever published. Letters were violent for months afterward, and one correspondent, condemning it ("Malzberg is just trying to shock, but it's a hack plot and a hack treatment just using dirty words and a dirty subject"), noted that his S-F society was going to have a panel discussion on the story the very next Sunday.

Panel discussion?

On a *story* about sex?

They were going to discuss this story and sex, that is, for an *afternoon?* That was how things were going in that S-F society?

At that moment I knew that *On Ice* was not a fiction but, to steal a phrase from another description of another story a long time ago, "a literal transcription of reality."

ON ICE

I do it to my mother as I have always wanted (what else was there, ever?), and it is extraordinary, absolutely extraordinary: I did not know the old bitch had so much blood in her. "Give it to me, son!" she shrieks, her wrinkled, freckled hands beating frantically around my neckline, her thighs urging me into a deeper pace, and I give her everything that I've got, yards and yards of it, or so it seems at the time, my prick uncoiling like a rope within her and I shoot deep into the murky abscess of my mother's cunt the load I have held back for decades, the load I have always carried within me . . . and my sobs and shrieks could be mistaken for agony, for she holds me against her and murmurs comfort, soothes me, advises me to be calm. "I don't have to be calm, you bitch!" I shout then, rising from her, the weapon of my necessity still shrieking hard to the touch as I stuff it away. "I have a perfect right to do everything I want to do, and you can't touch me; you can't even understand me!" This, although a perfectly justified complaint and an old one, sounds somewhat thin under the circumstances, and so I go away from there quite hurriedly, seeking a different direction, and once again they pull me to the surface.

"I'm sure you found that fascinating," the girl at the desk says to me on the way out. "I can always tell, that's my job, and I can see from your face that you really enjoyed that. When may I schedule your next appointment?" She takes a card and holds a pen, looks at me expectantly and some aspect of taunting in her eyes makes me want to shout at her, brutalize her, tell her that whatever my condition may be she has no right . . . but then I remember that I am at the Clinic, and the Clinic is impersonal, and that once again I am stumbling into the old

116

habit of personal referent, so I tell her that she can make two more appointments and give her the money in advance as always and stagger out the door, as they say, a free man, purged for the t me being of these old resentments and obsessions, only mildly interested in the weather and situations outside, so absorbed am I in my sense of release. Free, free! . . . But I will be at the Clinic tomorrow.

Going under, I hold onto my desires until the last moment, meditating, then tell the technician who I want to do it to and how. I whisper it into the receiver like a horrid confidence, which perhaps it is, although I long since thought that I had purged shame, and then the drugs boom and ripple, overtaking me, and I am fully under and this time I do it to the receptionist, the receptionist at the Clinic. Naked, she lies under me, dreadful passions sifting and shimmering through her cheekbones, and then her mouth opens and she whispers the inexpressible. I lower myself slowly into her as if from a great height and let her work me over patiently, lovingly, feeling her smooth tongue wind its way in and out of my tortured prick as I consider her helplessness, my dominance, her submission. "You think you're so superior to us," I say, talking, inexhaustibly talking as she works on me with bovine competence, "seeing us come in and out, knowing what's in our heads, making the appointments for us or setting the tapes, but let me tell you this—you have nothing to hold over us, because who's paying the bills? Huh, who's paying the bills, you bitch? People like *me,* that's right, and anyway, I'm keeping my antisocial tendencies completely under check, thanks to this, which is more than you can say." And at just that moment I feel the come rising and billowing, try to disengage to stick it within her, but too late, too late . . . and so I come into the receptionist's mouth, drained dry of the last drop, and her eyes close to the force of my come, then they open, and with a look of perfect contentment she swallows everything. Everything and then releases me. Hovering over her, I see at last her helplessness, know that I have got her exactly where she always wanted to be, but before I can take advantage I feel myself rising, rising, and try as I can to hold onto the scene, it is too late and I surface gasping, the last image of the receptionist in the dream superimposed upon the look on her face as I leave, and as I make two more appointments she can surely tell from the look of me exactly what has been going on and what use I have made of her, but it is too late, there is nothing that she can do, and as I leave I cast her one wink from the door, which breaks through the mask, and she gives me a look of perfect astonishment which, mingled with my own satisfaction, serves to get me through the afternoon.

In the mandatory monthly before the next treatment, the therapist says that he is disturbed by certain aspects of my behavior. "You're not getting along quite as we had hoped," the therapist, a bland, rosy little man, says. Under the law the treatments, as I understand, can be given only in the guise of "therapy," but sometimes it is very hard, even so, to remain patient. "It's none of your business," I say. "I'm paying the price; I'm paying what you ask. Your responsibility stops there."

"Oh, no," the therapist says with patent shock and the slightest intimation of a lisp; we have gone this way before. "You know that this isn't the aim at all; the treatments are a *temporary* application. We use them therapeutically, and they are not in any way to be an end in themselves. Why, that," he says, "that would be *addictive,* if we weren't moving toward therapeutic goals, don't you see? And we just aren't very satisfied; I'm afraid that the new monitors show some very distressing things. You're beginning to incorporate people from your present, ongoing life in the treatment, and that isn't what we wanted at all."

"Just leave me alone," I say. Under statute the mandatory monthlies last half an hour and are supposed to deal with "progress" and "goals"; this is bad enough, but what is even worse is that they are considered as "appointments" as well, and we must pay for them at the same rate as for use of the machines. It is all part of the same insane swindle, of course, but there is nowhere else to go—one can hardly cross the street; the Institute, as its advertising makes quite clear, has every patent on the device. Nevertheless, the mandatories are impossible; I have heard rumors of subjects who bribed their therapists into silence and others who attacked them physically without retaliation, but the treatments are too important to me (I will admit this) to take risks, and so I have tried to take the tactic of patient listening without response. "I have nothing to say."

"But that's the point," the therapist says, his eyebrows rising, the lisp more important, "this withdrawal of yours, this refusal to recognize that you may have a serious problem. Now, the monitors indicate that instead of combing your past life and using the treatment mostly as a purgative, you're beginning to indulge yourself in fantasies not only with people from the present but with some of the institutional staff, now . . . "

"I'm paying. I'm paying the price. I'm meeting all of your fee schedules, and, furthermore, I pay by return mail, which is more than most of the others can . . . "

"Oh, come now," he says, "you don't think that the motives of the Institute are purely mercenary; that's the kind of thinking pattern we want to break. You regard everything in purely exploitative terms. We want to *help,* we want to see you *grow,* we want to see you *overcome* these psychic deficiencies. . . ."

"Enough," I say, "enough, enough!" And I rise from the chair, zooming, as if in intercourse, to great height and control. "I won't listen to this anymore. I can do anything I want to do because I can pay the price, and, furthermore, I'm not hurting anyone, and, furthermore, the only interest you people have is in the *money,* so you leave me alone now; it's time for my treatment in just five minutes and I demand that you send me there. If not," I say, leaning over the little therapist, moving forehead to forehead against him, "if not, I'll stop all the treatments, because you and I both know that I don't need them, and think of all the money you'll lose. Three appointments a week, five hundred dollars a week, twenty-five thousand a *year*: can you let that go?" And I feint a punch at him; he pushes the chair back, loses control, his little legs pump and skitter and he goes rolling across the room, colliding with a *clank!* against the wall, and quickly I am on top of him, seizing his thin shoulders and shouting, "You know you can't; now don't give me any of that therapeutic nonsense, don't give me any of that shit—either sign the paper and send me through or I'm finished!" And his eyes roll in his head, his eyes dance and glaze, his delicate forehead furrows and mumbling, muttering, he picks himself up from the chair by handhold, staggers across the room to his desk, signs the paper and gives it to me. Authorizes twelve more treatments, one more month. "You're making a mistake," he whines, a tiny forefinger subtly moving toward his nostril to pick and squeeze, but now, my purpose accomplished, I am insulated from him again and so I only laugh: laugh and laugh at the ignorant therapist and spring from the room toward the release of the corridors and the machine that I know will always await me.

I think of a cousin who teased and taunted me to coitus interruptus, I think of my father whose sallow cheeks I have always wanted to bugger, but they bore me: I have been there before, and if I have not I can always get there toward familiar ends. Instead, I whisper a more exciting order to the technician as the levers in the helmet close down and then I do it to the therapist: dream that I am standing over his naked form in a room hung with whips and garrots; in the midst of all this armament I order him to kneel, turning from me, and as he does so I seize a dull sword from its pocket on the wall and begin to beat him over the shoulders: the blood runs, his shoulders shake, he begins to cry, opening himself to vulnerability and pain, and as he does so I mount him violently from behind, an *aaah!* of surprise and delight pouring from him, and so I do it to him then, mounted, riding him, holding the sword. "You son-of-a-bitch," I say, "I can do anything I want for the rest of my life because I inherited

this money and this wonderful process has been invented
and there is nothing, absolutely *nothing,* that will stop me
from doing what I want to do." And he says, "Yes, all
right, you can. Please, don't hurt me, just get it over with."
And I get it over with: savage and quick strokes pouring
into him, pouring into the receptionist, pouring into my
mother, holding on to myself at the summit and screaming
with epiphany, enough insight and power here to get me
through at least two more days before the next session,
and I know in my heart as I lift myself off him that this
has been the best ever, the best to date, new territory
opened up and to explore and that the treatment, like my
own soul and possibilities, is endless, infinite. "Free!" I
shout to the technician as I surface. "Free!" I shout to the
receptionist as I leave. "Free, free, free!" I call to a young
girl on the street, pausing to seize her by the shoulders
and stare into her face so that I will have her features
memorized for the next session when (I decide with my
new sense of release) I will surely possess her.

Introduction to
REVOLUTION

There are some stories—among them this one—about which little or nothing can be said and which thus open the way to extraneous comments and opinions that would otherwise be impossible to get into print. As replacement for a preface to this story, then, a few such random comments/opinions that could have been stated nowhere else and which, for that matter, will never be stated again:

a). The S-F criticism of Damon Knight and James Blish in *In Search of Wonder* and *Issue/More Issues at Hand* (Advent Publishers, Chicago) is a wonder of infinite richness and should be investigated by anyone who cares more about this genre than as passage through a Greyhound continental trek. Both are critics of major dimension, albeit frustrated, since serious criticism and S-F strike most of its readers as antithetical. The criticisms of A. J. Budrys (1965–71 *Galaxy*, and not collected to date; someone please take note) are at a similarly exalted level, although perhaps too rooted in the pain of the embittered serious writer of this genre to be totally comprehensible to a large readership. It is my opinion that in almost three hundred thousand words of criticism Budrys made exactly one error of judgment . . . and that came from a failure of the heart, not intellect.

b). The best modern writer of modern S-F is Robert Silverberg. Thomas M. Disch, Brian Aldiss, J. G. Ballard and Frederik Pohl run very close behind. The best modern writer of non-modern S-F (which is not necessarily an inferior form) is James H. Schmitz, with Poul Anderson running a close second. The best modern writer of anything is, as of this writing, Robert Silverberg.

c). Except for the three gentlemen mentioned in *a*, and for intermittent columns by Joanna Russ in *The Magazine of Fantasy and Science Fiction,* the general (mass audience) S-F markets have never had, and do not now have, a developed body of criticism. This must change if the field is to grow.

d). The worst modern writer of modern S-F has never published . . . but if the markets continue to proliferate, he/she surely will.

REVOLUTION

Now they want to control our minds. It is not enough that all of our activities are monitored, that our thoughts are screened so that there is nothing we can think that is not instantly accessible to them, that our lives are dictated wholly by the Masters. Now they want to dictate the thoughts themselves. They will filter into our brains, via the electrodes, exactly what we are allowed to think at any time and will order our judgments. There is no end to their arrogance and repression. All of this came through in their latest directive dated 5/12/96. Some of it is couched in bureaucratic language, but their intention is obvious. They will leave us nothing. The Masters will leave us nothing. I go to the Bureau to complain.

"Listen here," I say at the main screening desk, showing the receptionist the directive, "you can't do this to us. We're allowed to hold on to some of our individuality. What right do you have to do this? None that I can see. There have got to be some limits."

"One moment," the receptionist says. She is a robot, I know, like all of the personnel at the Bureau, but were I not aware of this I would take her for human. There is a high gloss to her features, a spindly fullness to her upper torso that makes me want to reach and grasp . . . but I am in control of my impulses. No Bureau directives are needed to warn me against lust. "You cannot file a complaint without proper identification. Where is your identification card?"

"I destroyed it," I say. I feel a surge of pride at this; it is my first defiance of the Bureau. In truth, I did not destroy my papers but have them well hidden in my home under a pile of clothing, which is almost the same thing. Only I could find them. The Bureau's detectives would not know where to look.

"Impossible," the receptionist says. She suffuses, her skin becoming mottled and her torso inflates. Momentarily she seems indecisive and then her color returns to normal. "I cannot take your complaint," she says, "until you produce proper identification. I have now checked with my supervisor and this is policy."

"I insist," I say, "I insist upon making my complaint known." I lean across the desk, make a threatening gesture. Although I am only fifteen years old, I am large for my age and have a commanding physical presence, or so I have been told. They cannot send me a directive announcing that they will control my mind without some kind of struggle. I take pride in this. I take pride in my determination. "Get me your supervisor," I say.

The receptionist squeaks with dread and presses a lever. Behind her desk a panel swings open and another much larger robot enters, this one modeled upon the male. It simulates anger. "Now, what is this?" it says, striding forward.

"This juvenile threatened me," the receptionist says. Behind a palm, she seems now to be smiling. "Under procedure it was necessary . . ."

"All right," the male robot says, "come with me." An arm snaps out, I feel enormous pressure around my collar and then, in the grasp of this robot, I am pulled behind the desk and into the area closed off by the panel. It is a small room with two chairs and a desk. I am pushed down into one of the chairs in a position facing outward; as this happens I get a glance of amused faces looking at me from the reception area, some of them waving. There had been a very long line. The panels close, lights coming on and I am alone with the robot who assaulted me.

"What is this?" it says. "Why are you making threats against the receptionist? Don't you understand the function of the Bureau? Don't you know the penalties?"

"You can't do this," I say, coming right back at the device. The directive is still in my hand and I show it. "You can't get away with something like this. I came in here to protest. These are individual liberties you're taking away."

"You fool," the robot said, "you misunderstand completely." Nevertheless, it becomes seated, looking at me with what I suppose is curiosity, rubbing its palms. "No one has protested," it says. "That directive is two weeks old and no one yet has come to the Bureau. Now, why of all times . . ."

"It took me a while to get up the courage. You can't do this to us. You already have cameras on us all the time telling you where we are and scanners reading our minds so you know everything we think, but when you start to control our very *thoughts* . . ."

"You fool," the robot says again, "you poor fool. Fourteen years old . . ."

"I'm fifteen. I'm going to be fifteen next week, so I'm as good as fifteen."

"You poor child," the robot says, and now it no longer seems angry, merely distressed. "Don't you know where you are? Don't you know what this is?"

"Yes," I say, "this is the world, the world that you've made for us, one controlled by a Bureau that reads thoughts and tells you what to do and knows what you're doing all the time so that it could check, a world where the Bureau now wants to tell you what to *think,* and I won't live this way anymore. I can't stand it. I have a lot of friends who listen to me and who think the way that I do, and if you don't stop this on your own," I say and pause, then get ready to make the ultimate threat of which I am capable, only hoping that it is the truth, "if you don't stop this, we're going to have a revolution. We'll overthrow you. We'll overthrow the Bureau!" I shout, and now the words are out and I have said them and there is nothing more I can say and, strangely relaxed, I lean back. But it is not only relaxation; part of it is shame. I am ashamed of myself for having lost control and for having shown the Bureau's robot that that control can break. This is not the way to deal with them. The real revolution must be underneath, I have been told.

"Oh, my," the robot says, "oh, my, you'll overthrow the Bureau. If only you would. If only *someone* would."

It stands and extends a hand. "Come," it says, "come to the window. I want to show you something."

Still holding the directive, I stand and take the hand, allow myself to be moved to that space. There is a strange warmth to the hand of the creature, and for reasons I do not understand I am moved. Also, I am not quite sure why I followed the order to stand so readily, but I decide that it must have something to do with the controlling of my thoughts. Already that is being put into action. Already they can make me do whatever they want me to do, make me think what they will.

"Look," the robot says, showing me the world outside the window. We are at a slight incline in this Bureau office, on a little hillside surrounded by bone, and it is possible to look down here upon the old city, the dust and ash and little white shapes in the distance that I used to think were bone until I learned of mirages. "Look at that. Do you see that?"

"Yes," I say, my eyes being tugged upward by another of the disturbances in the sky; now birds are wheeling in the gray light, squawking to one another, and here, behind them, come the meteors again. They fall around us, some of them hitting the window so hard that I can feel the collision, although the windows and walls of the Bureau are very strong. "Yes, I see that. I've seen it all my life. So what? So what do you want to show me? You still have no right to control my mind."

"Oh, my," the robot says, "oh, my God." And it is unusual to hear one of the robots mentioning *God,* that supposedly is no part of their program, but it is stranger than that to see one of the robots weeping, but this robot is weeping and more meteors hit the pavement, the little

REVOLUTION 127

white clumps in the distance that look like bone shimmering and dancing through the haze like little spears, ash spewing up from the old city in the wake of the meteor winds, the directive flapping in my hand, my thoughts already controlled, the robot weeping, the city sinking, the Bureau standing. . . .

Introduction to
UPS AND DOWNS

Ups and Downs was written for an anthology of S-F stories about sex (*not* the one that rejected *On Ice;* that was the inferior a.o.s.s.a.s. that year) and is satisfactorily crazy in a characteristic manner. Certainly the presumption of a woman left aboard a spaceship by the benevolent NASA to accompany its first voyager on his long trip to Mars is no more absurd than the idea of a trip to Mars or a NASA is. No? Ask any eighteenth-century aristocrat.

It would be nice to make a few such remarks about this union of sex and science fiction in terms of fourteen all-new, all-original, never-before-published stories by the masters, but I find myself no less at a loss for words than the editor of that volume who had no blurbs. "Sex has a great future and so does science fiction"? No, that does not quite ring. "Science fiction has been characterized throughout most of its history as either not being about sex at all, or being about sex only in the most juvenile and simpering fashion; here at last, as we move toward maturity in this taboo-shattering anthology . . ."? No, again. One cannot instruct simpering juveniles to be daring and emerge with the work of unsimpering adults. Most of our writers, including so many of the contributors to that anthology, cannot write sex (or science fiction too well, for that matter). Why should they? After spending forty years breeding rats to be all black, can we change carrots and order them to henceforth breed white?

Still, to repeat, *Up and Downs* is satisfactorily crazy. Maurice Girodias, who knows more about sex-in-literature (if not sex-in-S-F) than anyone alive, read it in manuscript and said that he didn't have the slightest idea what I thought I was doing . . . which meant that it repaid in kind a debt that I have owed the good Monsieur for many years.

UPS AND DOWNS

"There's a long way between declining and death."
                              —Isaac Bashevis Singer

I

The great ship lifts, the engines cry, we are on our way to Mars. Oblivious of this new sense of destiny, I close my eyes and fuck the woman.

II

Oh, God, can she do it! Who would have expected this generosity, in and out of the program? Sliding against, plunging and ponderosity, feeling all of her slip at cross-purposes, then the engagement . . . and nipple in mouth, knee to thigh, I begin heavily to copulate, the sperm boiling in the precise tubes and vesicles of my body just as the fuel informs these mighty engines. Just as these engines lift almost casually but with enormous purpose toward Mars. We are heading in that way now, just the two of us and those eternal machines. "Isn't it wonderful," I say to her almost offhandedly in the middle of our struggles, "that we're finally on the way? Originally, you should know, the Mars Project was slated for 1976, and it was only an unusual series of delays and offsetting political maneuvers that set it back two decades in time. Nevertheless, here we are. Better late than never. Not only the early bird worms," I add, swooping down and upon her, and she says, "Yes, it is, it's the most remarkable fact in the whole history of the world." But even as she says this

129

quietly, whimpering from need, I can tell that she is just making conversation and that her real interest is in fucking. She is a good woman, obviously, cooperative, willing: a dead spot of accommodation carried deep within her so that even in the center of lust she will try to meet her partner . . . and thinking this gives rise to an absent rush of tenderness. The tenderness turns toward insistence, something meaner and darker then, and before I can gauge how close in I have come . . . I am letting loose. Overwhelmed by orgasm, I pour into her before she is ready. Levers smash, input regulates and I tear into her like the ship in the night.

It is good.

After a time, I roll from her, or she from me (who can tell the difference, such is our blending), and she says, "Well, now, really, that was quite interesting, wasn't it? There's nothing I like better than a little spot of fucking now and then to break up routine. But now I am afraid that you must go about your business, Jules Fishman, and meanwhile I will go about mine."

Mumbling, I agree. I am always stupid in the aftermath of intercourse. I cannot help it; this is not a deliberate selection, nor is the strange Britishism of her speech something that I can apprehend. I lift myself from her sighing and seek out my space gear, willing as always to get about the work of this ship, checking out the docks, shining down the brass, giving the ship all the dedication I have as it moves toward Mars at a corrected rate of eighty miles per second to penetrate the exciting and always entertaining mystery of the fourth planet from the sun, the vital and asymmetrical red planet.

III

I am an astronaut. As you have discovered, I am named Jules Fishman. The image of that name, hanging before me now and then at weak moments, loose and flopping, scales and gills distended, embarrasses me only a little, for I do not look like a fish. I look like a spaceman. I am, in fact, the most competent spaceman in the whole of these new United States, and for that reason I have been assigned as sole occupant of this first ship toward Mars.

I *know* that I am the most qualified because all of the tests have said so, and the tests as developed by the agency over a period of four decades are, from all sources, very precise and never lie about anything. My IQ is 195; my blood pressure at rest 115/50. Gross physical abnormalities are non-existent; functional psychoses are contraindicted. A slight tendency toward tachycardia has been observed under situations of great stress, but it is compensated for by three grains of sulfanamide and expressions of comfort. My physical profile is negative. I can fuck and come within ten seconds, and then, again, I have learned to extend a fuck for hours, easing myself into that slow, oozing penetration of skin beyond skin that is the essence of satisfaction. It all depends.

Everything depends.

Concentrate upon Mars; no talk of fucking now. Here in this Presidential election year of 1996 we need (I have been told) the successful voyage in order to placate the present political fix and make possible the re-election of the incumbent, and, apolitically speaking, I will do what I can. I seek to penetrate the mystery of the Von Allen belt, thus adding another stirring and eventual chapter to the continuing story of Man's conquest of space.

IV

I wonder how they managed to smuggle a woman, let alone one this attractive, into the capsule. (A certain kind of woman has been known to fixate upon astronauts and even technicians, but most of them, alas, are dogs: not this one.) It was a considerate gesture of theirs, a wonderful, thoughtful stroke, but she was not on the list of approved and accredited materials that I myself vetted with a pen three weeks ago, and I can only conclude that on some very high or low level of the space bureaucracy a busy but mad clerk took it upon himself to satisfy all of my unspoken needs.

Ah, I can see this clerk: his glasses shine in the spiteful fluorescence of his dingy office at the center as he takes the forms and draws them to his breasts. "Let's take care of this," my friend the clerk says in a whining peep, and as he says this, he adjusts his seat, sweats and makes the requisition. One woman, brunette if you will, twenty-seven or twenty-eight years old, large breasts, small waist, full hips and thighs, a calm and sweet intelligence with the ability to moisten rapidly to any touch of her little secret places. Pass the paper. "This will keep the bugger happy, keep old Jules Fishman in the pink; anything for the best of all our boys," the clerk burbles, then marks the requisition PRIORITY AND TOP SECRET. This moves it quickly through routine clearance to the supply crew itself (anything for the best of all our boys), and the next day—I can see this, too, unfortunately—the clerk suffers a heart attack and dies in his furnished room, overcome by the excitement and anticipation of the coming conquest of Mars.

I could, I would, touch this clerk, brother, friend, whisper to him of the needful ease he has given me, even radio through a message of thanks in code . . . but it is too late for this. Services were quickly arranged under the terms of his Orthodox Judaism and he was cremated within twenty-four hours. His ashes seem to whisk past me invisibly in this craft, penetrating the tubes of my nose. Still, a small price: what a legacy the clerk has left!

Somewhere in the anterior spaces of the ship I can hear her now. She is moving (I count on this), moving through all the small emptinesses of the ship, squirreling past the computers, the motors, the whistle of the life-support system, perhaps now leaning against one of the layers of padding in which eventually I will make my triumphant entrance upon Mars itself, inhaling deeply of those glistening and metallic odors of space, thinking of the sex we have had while I proceed on the vigorous and essential tasks involved in conquering Mars. She is a beautiful woman, soft and then hard against me, her breasts a consummation I have only suspected behind the clothing of certain women in certain postures . . . I wish that I knew her name.

Next time around, surely, I will ask her name. We will have much time with one another because the voyage to Mars will take six weeks' subjective time, and I want to fully explore with her during these weeks the possibilities and ramifications of a mature and serious relationship.

But first I must get her name. This would stand to reason. Beginnings, beginnings. But there are no flowers on this ship.

V

Mars is the eighth largest, the second smallest, planet of our solar system. Mercury is smaller, but since it is closest to the Sun, it would have to generate a certain slimness and nervous energy, and thus does not count in this history. It is red Mars, red as death or blood, leading our ancient sages and philosophers to refer to it as the planet of war . . . but it is also green and brown, brown and green in streaked passages of illumination that I can spot through this excellent small-range telescope that they have given to amuse me.

Looking at Mars against the panels, watching it rise and veer, I know that I will never understand another planet quite as profoundly as this—not even Earth, on which, as I am quite convinced, I was born and lived my first forty-one years.

I am forty-one years old. On the third day of the Martian conquest, by superb coincidence, I shall be forty-two, celebrating that day while voyaging here and there in the little landing craft, jouncing merrily through the dunes in search of treasure to ornament my new chronology. Forty-two and seeking pearls! I think that I was talking about something else. Mars is orbited by two satellites.

Two Moons in opposed orbit circle Mars. "Do you know that?" I ask the woman, who is spending the observation time beside me. "Are you aware of that, dear?" Sooner or later I must get her name; this is ridiculous. "Deimos and Phobos are their names. They are two small satellites that probably move through machinery."

"Fascinating," she says and protrudes an arm around my waist. "That's really interesting; the things you'll pick up on this ship." My cock, meanwhile, is busy, busy and light as air in my utilitarian, close-fitting space pants, but I refuse to show her in any way that I am respondent. Rather, I keep my mind on the question of astronautical referent. Astronautics are the key to the age-old dream of space; all the rest must fall into gear beyond this. "Tell me more about those two satellites of Mars; I'm truly interested." I think I see her breasts. Her breasts come halfway out of the strapless evening gown that she has now put on. It may seem peculiar that a woman on this spacecraft is wearing a strapless evening gown, but then, again, a century ago a journey to Mars would have been no more preposterous.

Technological progress is geometric. Always increasing. In 1900 the post-industrial period was ushered in. By 1915 the assembly line had been schematized. In 1922 several million automobiles were sold and Harding did not feel very well at all. In 1938 the first baseball game was televised, a night contest between the Reds and ever-popular Dodgers. In 1945 Dresden was bombed. In 1950 Korea was bombed. In 1955 the Cadillac grew fins. In 1963 a President was killed. Everything accelerates . . . except the timeless need of Jules Fishman, which remains as its single urgent level, never to be affected by machinery or the manipulations of bureaucrats.

"You must tell me about Damon and Pythias," she says. She touches my cheek. "You're not paying attention to me; your eyes are wandering with the look of eagles."

"Deimos and Phobos. You seem to have it confused. Damon and Pythias were mythological friends."

"Deimos and Phobos, then. If you will. They're such cute names. Who made them up?" I feel her box, sly and dangerous pressing against my buttocks through the fabric of the dress. Her hands drift across my neck like moths, flutter at my forehead. "Tell me everything."

I am distracted by my need for her. Surely this is not normal behavior: we have had sex only a few hours before and yet I have toward her the curiosity and galloping excess of a young demented adolescent. Sometime later, while setting the locks and switches, I will have to think about this. "They are believed to be artificial, these satellites," I assure her, resolved to keep my mind on business. "Not natural heavenly bodies such as our own humble Moon or say, Ganymede, the largest satellite of Jupiter, but, instead, machinery that was installed by the Martians themselves, an ancient and now extinct race of wondrous technological facility. This is the latest and most advanced thinking on the subject, at any rate."

"And now," she says dully, "and now they are all dead. The Martians." She is a sensitive woman, I already know this, and regret for the dead Martians drags her arm down my back. "How terrible for them, then. To create two artificial Moons that could live forever and then die." She is a little affected. "How horrible for them."

"We have no way, none of us, of knowing that it was horrible. All of this happened millions of years ago, It may have been exactly what they wanted, a very sophisticated race. Regardless, these two satellites remain circling, which is no small accomplishment for them."

"No small accomplishment," she says. "I knew you would say that." She grabs and twists at my cock and it surges within her hands. Even through layers of cloth I feel its whimper. "You're ready," she says harshly into an ear, biting. "You're ready to fuck."

Obviously she is not a scientifically oriented girl; either that or the onset of passion blocks off her intellectual faculties. I do not stand in judgment, having at this moment the same problem of thickening, of stupidity moving out through the vesicles to obliterate my more detached viewpoint. Jules Fishman is the most qualified astronaut in all of these United States to make the first voyage to Mars: all available polls and proof demonstrate this;

nevertheless, all that Jules Fishman can conceive of at this moment is fucking.

"Do you want to?" I say. "Do you really want to do it again?"

"Do what, you idiot?" she says affectionately.

"Fuck," I say, encircling her, carrying her back in a tumble toward sheer metal, layers and layers of tubing falling away from us as I bear her to the floor. "You must want sex; otherwise, you wouldn't be leading me on like this. I can tell. I've been out with lots of women; despite the fact that I'm unmarried, I have experience."

"You never know," she says, "now you never really know about things like that." And she opens her mouth to receive me. I put my tongue inside that mouth, it feels like wire, wire invading all the spaces around her tongue and teeth and knifing her that way I feel myself jutting, trying to prod. I reach for her evening gown and one breast tears free, the nipple winking. I encircle. "You want me," she says, and this is an assurance, "you really want me again."

"Yes, I do," I say, "yes, indeed, I want you." And I begin to tear at her. Here we are on the way to Mars and hundreds of tasks left undone, all of the ship to survey and a crucial mission in the bargain, and yet, and yet I can think of nothing but screwing. I wonder if the psychologists and neurophysicists were aware of this limitation.

"Go on," she says, "go on, baby, it's all right, all right." And, undistracted, I rear against her. Her gown dissolves, she is naked underneath, my own clothes dissolve and as the ship fires toward Mars I feel myself merge, and once again the ancient rocking begins.

I think of the clerk, that clerk who has so thoughtfully requisitioned this woman: that clerk, my brother, and he is dead and we will not meet; never will I be able to render him proper thanks. All of it a mystery as I boil down the alleys and out the other part of her . . .

. . . crying.

VI

Perhaps I am dreaming some of this. But which part would it be? The woman or the ship?

VII

It comprises an enormous responsibility to be the first human being destined for Mars; it comprises a debt to mankind that somehow I will try to repay through a careful diary that will be expanded into a set of memoirs that I hope will be salable to the very best markets. The first step in this log is to keep notation of all my activities, to prove that I have observed the rules of the voyage and will perform all of the necessary tasks.

Sexual obsession then will be kept in place. After this second and most recent fuck (which in obscure ways I found distasteful; coming up against myself in orgasm, battering against that familiar wall) my desire is reduced, patience heightened and I am moving beyond entrapment to a kind of control. The woman will not disturb me as I work over this long. She has gone to her own quarters, which she states are at the opposite end of the ship, secure from the monitors and the dangerous infrared of space. For the moment, then, I am alone, keeping these notes in order, performing necessary tasks.

Radiometers signal orders; the computers, in response to inquiry, indicate that all is well. Simple maintenance and life functions continue undisturbed; therefore, I am free to concentrate as always upon that most important element . . . which is the human.

The human element! This counts on the first journey to Mars, or so I was informed by the Chief of Bureau shortly before embarkation. The Chief of Bureau is named Milton Oppenheim, and he is forty-nine years old, half a generation older than the whimsical Fishman, but extraordinarily well preserved, a handsome man with streaks of obsession running in and out of his conversation and a total dedication to the vision of space.

"Remember, Colonel Fishman," the highly formal Oppenheim advised me at one of the last briefings, "the human element is the key to this. It is not machinery that we are sending to Mars now, but a person, a human being. This mission can be successful only if it is controlled by you. We have made mistakes in previous aspects of the program—I am the very first to grant that—but now it is 1996, a Presidential election year, and our mistakes are in the past. We are ready to fulfill our responsibilities to that human element. You—and you alone—will be in control of the craft, as you know. The computers will chart your voyage, they will guide the ship, but you can, at any time, through an automatic override, cancel them out and assume control. The ship will not be monitored and you need make none of those unfortunate broadcasts from space that gave some of our missions of the seventies an . . . uh . . . rather bad name. You are superbly qualified and have been prepared to chart your destiny on and off the craft. No one will look in on you; this is your mission. You understand this?"

"Yes," I said, "I understand all of this. The human element. An absence of monitors. Telecasts contraindicted," I say, meanwhile casting quick glances all up and down the offices of Milton Oppenheim, the very distinguished Chief of Bureau with whom I am sorry to say I had spent very little time up until this briefing. Perhaps it was policy to keep me lower down on the chain of command; perhaps it was a matter of individual calculation. "You say you are interested in the human element."

"Exactly. Exactly, right now. If we had wanted machinery to conquer Mars, we would have sent out another of the robot probes, but it is critical that we send a man. Critical in 1996. You are aware of that, aren't you, Colonel? There is a specific institutional need to land a man on Mars this time. The pressures come from outside of this agency."

"Oh, yes, indeed," I said, "oh, yes," thinking idly of the question of sex on the voyage, because two months of ship time and two weeks on the surface is quite a span, indeed, and Fishman, God bless him, is neither celibate nor abstinent, but a happy, normally unmarried American male of forty-one years (going on forty-two; remember that at all times) who counts upon his sex not twice or thrice, but a full four or five times a week, depending upon the weather, the phases of the Moon, the various extensions of his psyche. Would the ship, despite promises, be monitored, and would masturbation be detected? "I'll do the best I can for all of you. . . ." I wanted to raise this important question with the Bureau Chief, but I was not quite prepared to do so because . . . well, what might he have thought?

"What about masturbation?" I wanted to ask. "Is this a plausible activity, or will the sensors pick up the notations of energy, the raised heartbeat, the flutterings of eyelids, the sudden congestion of my organ and beam all of it back to Earth to be decoded to a stain of guilt. You'd better tip me off right now on this, because otherwise I plan to jerk off, and I wouldn't want to do anything to embarrass the agency," I wanted to point out to Oppenheim . . . but it was just impossible to raise to the Chief such personal material, particularly since the question of the human element had already been discussed. "I'll do the best I can," I said again, then turned to leave the room, hoping for some leap, some murmur of comprehension from Oppenheim that would indicate his extreme sensitivity to questions so that he would have been able to pick up on all of this to give advice . . . but no word from him. Stoicism, picking at papers, a distracted handshake. I left him.

I did not know that they planned to put a woman aboard, or I would never have even considered the issue.

But then the woman was a private decision of the clerk; he did all of this on his own, and talking this over with Oppenheim would have brought to his attention the complex violation of code that this constituted, and, therefore, she would have been canceled. Angry men would have prowled the corridors of the ship before launch to comb her out. This would have been an enormous loss, inasmuch as her companionship is so important to me; she will throw me a good fuck now and then, and, furthermore, it is too much to ask even of the highly trained Jules Fishman that he make tracks to Mars alone. He/I cannot stand up to the emotional burdens. The woman will ease all of this for Fishman and me, although it is to be admitted that so far she has not proven a sparkling conversationalist and our relationship has proved a little circular.

VIII

Forty-one years and never married. Few astronauts have a background of this sort. It is unusual in the program. Still, I was assured throughout that if the tests picked a bachelor, then a bachelor it would be. "It will not be held against you in any way," the psychiatrist said. His name is or was William Franks, and, other than a small beard and a certain density around the eyes, he has no physical peculiarities of any sort, exactly like the redoubtable Jules Fishman, or so we would like to think. "In fact, I admit that we were not ultimately disappointed in this result of the testing program. That you are unmarried is to our benefit. You may not have . . . uh . . . some of the certain emotional ties that a married man might feel and therefore can function coolly and dispassionately on the mission at hand."

The project is tenanted by men like William Franks, solemn men with dense eyes and delicate twitches of their hands as if they were gripping the controls of a capsule. But, then again, few wear beards. "We have decided that some of the difficulties in past missions might have stemmed from using men who were too preoccupied by their marital or family situations to devote their fullest attention to the job, and, therefore, we have decided— decided in consultation with the administration—that it is an excellent idea to have a single man. You have no plans to get married before then, do you? I didn't think you would; we're fairly conversant with your personal life, as you might guess, and we didn't see any indication, but, then again, one never knows. You people work quickly." He leered at me. I do admit this.

William Franks. Franks is my psychiatrist, Oppenheim my administrator. These two, along with so many of the others, have devoted their time, their talents, their energies and risk to just one end: that I might stand against the bulkhead of this ship, listening to the heave of the engines as I consider Mars. It is humbling. It is a vastness. It is a mystery. All of these things and many others I consider as the ship winds its way toward Mars. We have not been in flight for twelve hours and already I have found it one of the most truly memorable experiences of my life.

My life.

IX

Wandering through the ship, checking the readouts on the binaries for proper confirmation—nothing is ever amiss—I find her huddled and quiet, solemn and young now, leaning against one of the evacuation chambers, plucking at her hair with absent, tender caresses that fill me with pity for this child glimpsed: she is suffering. I seek to divert her with pleasantries. "Tell me," I say, advancing upon her quietly and with grace, not to frighten, never to frighten, "please tell me about yourself. Tell me your name, your life, your dreams."

"Tell me," I say, becoming more urgent, "of your childhood and what you did when you first saw that you were a woman. Let me know what excites you the most, what music touches you, how you run in a field with flowers. Let me know all this, for truly I cannot stand another mystery. Mars is impenetrable enough: I want to know you; I want to have a relationship." I am panting.

She says nothing. Her nails wink against the fluorescence and she touches her hair again, more gently. Her breasts heave; she is touched.

"I want to know," I say, "everything of you. We're going to Mars together. The only humans in our history of the world on flight to Mars and already we have made love, have scraped against one another, will know this again through spaces of the voyage." This sentimentality appalls me; I try to move into a more businesslike context. "My name is Jules Fishman," I say. "I am forty-one years old; soon I will be forty-two. When I was in my early twenties I owned a 1969 Cadillac with stereo equipment, and nothing before or since gave me as much pleasure as that car, although it was dying on me. When I was younger than that I went to the seashore and crushed the life out of frogs. Then I walked into the water up to my ankles. I had a conflict with my father that was resolved only by his death. Mother was a different issue. These are some of the small facts about me, but there are larger ones. I am not a limited man; I possess the highest qualifications. Now it is your turn. Tell me something of yourself."

"No," she says, "not yet. You don't understand, it isn't time for that yet." And she leans against the evacuation vault. Her legs flex, her face raises and I see the open spaces of her throat against the good, harsh, black sweater she has put on, below that a belt and slacks, things on her ankles, all of it offered to me, skewered open like ripe meat. "We have to wait, but if you want," she says slowly (and do I detect reluctantly?), "if you really want, you may have your way with me again." And she raises her arms. "I don't care, you can fuck me anytime, if only you're careful of my body."

"But you're the one who doesn't understand," I say. I hold ground. "It isn't only a matter of sex. Sex is important—it's vital; otherwise, why would the clerk have given me a woman? But there is the matter of contact as well —contact and knowledge, and how can we have that if I don't know who you are?"

"That's your problem."

"I want to feel that we are possessing one another in the most personal and specific sense, and in order to do that I must know something of you."

All babble. Meanwhile, throughout this, I am moving

against her more deeply, that fool's need beginning to stir
once more, the idiot's gift coming through the chambers
of self, and there is nothing I can do to stop it. Am I
insatiable? She smiles, drops that smile from ear to cheekbone and I feel the imprint of her mouth glowing fiercely,
a stain as she wrenches fully against me.

"Don't worry," she says, "none of this matters, and
you don't need any personal information. That's your own
socioeconomic problem showing through. Sex—*that's*
what you really want. And it's what I'm here to provide
you, and you want it again, you madman, you do, you
do," she says, her arms gripping, sucking me in, and even
though I am clothed I feel that familiar, shocking contact
of penetration, then the oozing slide that is already so
characteristic of this woman (I shall dream it), and struggling, we fall to the deck in front of the evacuation vault
while she licks my face all over like an animal and puts
her hands behind to remove her clothing. How quickly
it falls away! It is unusual how speedily she can undress,
but no time to contemplate; as time accelerates, so does
my prick, my prick, technology and time accelerating together, the prick looming forward to prod, and, miracu-
lously unclothed (I scramble to push it away from the
vault; it would be embarrassing if it fell into the cam-
bers), I batter at her, miss the right space as I have been
known to do and then, finally succeeding, plunge into her
and begin rapidly to fuck while with one careful eye still
open I stare through a space of the vault where I think
I see the veins of wire or, then again, it may be space
I am staring into, and the universe hung to dangle on
various props and poles, created for just this occasion.
Anything is possible. Many of the instructions were not
particularly explicit, and Mars, along with the Moon and
other planets, may be merely pasted on the shelf of the
sky, all of it fraudulent, but a necessary myth. Certain
ancient mystics, I have been told, believed that things
were constructed in that way.

"See" she is saying, "told told told you that you only
wanted to fuck, you animal, you," she says, pressing me
in. Her breasts are at the level of my eyes and I blink

at them, the nipples shrouded against that closure, popping against an eyeball, moving with marvelous flexibility to confront nose and mouth. I suck at them while frantically pumping and am rewarded at once: in a stroke I culminate inside her while she wipes a palm across my forehead, looking down at me, meditating, considering.

I have sensed no hint of her orgasm. She has not come. I cannot make her come.

"You see, now," she says compassionately, her voice uninflected, "it was sex all the time. That was all you wanted." This infuriates me. I want to strike out at her for the bitterness of what she has said, but I am weakened, weakened. Women taking it all away from you as always . . . and I can manage only a pat against her forehead, which she interprets as a caress. She takes my hand and strokes it, puts it against her breasts.

"Don't worry about a thing," she says, her nipple throbbing evenly in hand, "all of this will be answered in time, and none of it matters until it is, don't you realize? None of your questions, your curiosity, shadow-play, instructions from the outside—conclusions that you have been taught to respect but which mean nothing.

"All that matters is what happens between the two of us now, *here,* on *this* ship, and from that everything will follow." Her voice is like a machine. Listening to her I nod, fatigue tearing at my psyche with small, tight fingers, and then I fall, fall, fall against her.

Really, I am quite tired. It is too much to undertake at one stroke, this understanding, and it is also true: comprehension will come or it will never, but there now is nothing that I can disentangle from this woman lying underneath me, nothing but the sense of her flesh, which is already known.

"You must tell," I say, nevertheless, "you just can't do this to me; you must tell me your name, why you are here," I add. "I'm entitled to know who you are: all of this could be a hallucination, some of it might be a dream," I say, curling to sleep then against her. And her tolerant, wise smile in the aftermath of sex carries me to darkness.

In the dream as I lie swaddling her, bereft for the moment of questions 'and secure in the knowledge of loss, in that dream the ship, like a heartbeat, carries me to Mars and to the mystery of blood that that planet holds deep in its sac, that sac orbited by Deimos and Phobos—which, unfortunately, I have not yet been able to satisfactorily explain to her. If she understood those spheres she might tell me everything, and now I am sleeping, no, this is impossible, but I am falling asleep, this is possible now, I am sleeping deeply: she holds me as I wind myself into her, holding, holding, holding; what a good person she must be.

X

Later, when I awaken, she is gone and my mind is literally filled with mathematics:

The apogee of Mars is 36.8 percent when considered from an angle of 12 degrees. The zenith of that planet is 46.2 of the angle when tilted. The square root of two is 1.414 and pi remains 22/7, incontrovertible.

The first landing upon the Moon was accomplished on 7/20/69 by an astronaut of thirty-eight years who subsequently left the program to go into private industry. And the initial probe of Mars, proving that there was no life other than the vegetative, was in 1956. Later probes verified this further, although it is still believed by mystics that Mars is populated by sentientoaliens who will greet me at the dock and enjoy me for breakfast. My own birthday was 8/16/54, a good year for births and deaths since it was otherwise so uneventful, although it was not thought likely at the time that this would be the case. My pulse rate at rest is fifty-six, and I was fourteenth in a class of one hundred fifty-seven at the Academy before enrolling in the program. My mind is a glaze of figures.

My body is stiff.

Stiffness, stiffness: I roll from shoulders to hips, pivoting, and then stagger upright like that first primordial ape, feeling the aching that moves in tubers from the groin both up and down, the aching composed of both sex and its absence, spreading like a mold through the body; and, looking then through a porthole, I spy Mars. It is bearing atop me. Mars is gathering dimension in that view-screen; in just a while it will overtake, but now, in this poised moment before it has fully seized the ship, I can peek up and around it and in small patches of dark I can see the asteroids. I think it is the asteroids I see. My cock aches, my body aches: I have been ill-used.

It is kind of them to have considerately assigned a woman to accompany me on this first expedition to Mars, but it is a mystery as well and one with which, as I now consider this, I might have dispensed. I spend several hours then, anyway, looking through the spaces of the ship for the woman, but she is nowhere to be found and within hours, so intense my disillusion, I have forgotten the shape of her and the touch. Only her smell lingers, blowing dead quiet through the support system, but not through the smell can I evoke her . . . nor through anything.

I scratch myself, thinking spaceman's thoughts of Mars, and I wonder if the infrared of dangerous space will destroy my gonads. For all I know . . . this is my last fucking.

Introduction to
BEARING WITNESS

Bearing Witness is *Track Two* in reverse . . . that is, if *Track Two* is the journal of a disbelieving Christ, *Bearing Witness* might be the notes of a believing one who just happened not to be who he thought he was. Like *Chronicles of a Comer* (a work not included here), it points out that anything approaching apocalyptic acceptance would be regarded today as lunatic, would in fact *be* lunatic. This is not an original insight—I seem to recall starting a novel on or around my fifteenth birthday, making this point only slightly more earnestly—but in science fiction Dada, naturalism, stream-of-consciousness and headlining, all techniques of the literary novel of the 1920s have been seized upon recently as if they were remarkable, controversial innovations . . . so why should not this?

Any irony detected here has nothing to do with the subject itself, which is quite serious, and with the conclusion that I take to be extraordinarily accurate.

BEARING WITNESS

I

Definitely, the time has come around again. Mighty convulsions and armies are heard of in the East; in other parts dislocation increases. Earthquakes cleave the cities, turning them to rubble, and in the cloud of the atomic tests the curve of the great snake of Apocalypse may be seen. He is coming. He is risen again. On that day all shall be as one and His name shall be heard from the mountains. I am overtaken by stomach trouble and nervous tics, further evidence that all is breaking down in preparation for His mighty return.

II

"That is interesting," the Monsignor says to me. He is a tall, unhappy man in his mid-fifties who smokes incessantly, and it has taken me six months to obtain this appointment with him. The parish priest turned me over to the priest in another district, and that priest, although interested, felt that he did not possess the proper authority to go into the question. The matter was bucked up to the bishop, who sat on it for some time and then referred me to the Monsignor. The Monsignor, however, had been involved in a reapportionment of the school district and was forced to cancel all appointments for some time. At last I have been allowed to see him. All in all, I have been offered no more than ten minutes. The Monsignor is very busy. "Of course," the Monsignor adds after a pause, putting out the cigarette and lighting another, "we tend to be involved in more temporal issues. If, as you say, the time of the second coming is nearly at hand, it will occur without any assistance from me. Eh?" He leans forward, pats my hand distressingly, withdraws and looks absently at the ceiling, fondling the cigarette. "I'm impressed by your fervor," he murmurs.

"It is very much at hand," I assure him. "Within the very near future He will indeed come again. I have made detailed referents from the Book of Daniel and it will be within a matter of months . . . perhaps days."

"Very well," the Monsignor says. "Of course, there are many conflicting interpretations of Daniel. But that is neither here nor there. I am moved by your testimony. Unfortunately, I have so many things on my mind with the re-allocation of the district and the problem of funding the high school . . ."

"You don't understand," I say. For the first time, my control lapses. I resist an impulse to lean forward and shake the nervous Monsignor violently by the lapels of his business suit. (In this relatively liberal district, I understand, the clergy tries to Pass Among the People.) "I need help. I need to prepare myself for the Apocalypse. I need counseling, advice, instructions for prayer. If you people won't help me, who will?"

The Monsignor pales. Then again, he may not pale at all; it may be only a peculiarity of my own vision (I react badly under stress), and he remains fixed in position. "As I say," he points out, "I'm delighted by your expression of faith. More people like you are needed in these irreligious times; nevertheless, we have no *assurance* of the Second Coming, and it is something, in any event, very much out of our hands." He inclines his head. "We will all be vulnerable on Judgment Day," he says. "Meanwhile, we must deal in the world. Have you discussed this with your own priest?"

"I was referred . . ."

"I understand that. Nevertheless, I think you would do better at the immediate level. Perhaps you can be given some texts. A concordance is very useful and the commentaries of Augustine . . ."

"You still don't understand," I say. "I'm not even Catholic. I came to you because you're the apocalyptic religion and I thought that you could give me some help. But if you won't . . ."

"I'm really sorry," the Monsignor says. He lights another cigarette, puts it in the ashtray against the one that is already smoldering. "There has been a terrible mistake. I'm perfectly willing to talk to anyone, but my time has been very pressed recently, you see, and . . ." He kicks a leg under his desk, then I hear a buzzing faintly down the corridors. While the Monsignor folds his hands under his chin and stares at me with vague terror, his secretary comes quietly into the office and advises me that my time is up. "Yes," the Monsignor says, "I had forgotten, but your time is up. I had gotten so absorbed . . ."

"You'll learn!" I say, standing, shaking, brandishing a fist. It occurs to me that I may be impressing him as a religious fanatic. "You, too, will stand naked at the moment of judgment, and it will be entered against your name that you could not help me."

"That will be enough," the secretary says. Religious fanatics, it appears, are not welcome in these offices. He seizes me firmly by the elbow and conducts me across the lip of the office. "You see, we just don't have the time," the secretary murmurs, and propels me down the corridor.

Turning, I see the Monsignor frozen at his desk. His face inclines toward me, his features blur and then I see his lips appear to move. It seems as if he is trying to tell me something, but before I can get the gist of it the door is closed, apparently by the wind, and with the secretary's hand in my back, I am pushed onto the street. He closes the door.

Wind assaults me. In the wind it seems I hear the sound of trumpets.

III

Confused, I wander along the streets. A beggar pushes himself against me, demands money threateningly. I hand him a dollar bill and his features crumple. "Blessed," he says, "you are blessed, sir. Surely you are a creature of God to give an old man such a gift." He puts away his knife and hurries on.

In that moment I see everything—how it has come to this and what that small and terrible act of communion means. I push myself through the crowds, seeking a high place. The hood of a 1976 Fleetwood Brougham, stalled in traffic, seems to beckon. I clamber upon it, feeling only a slight knifing at the knees, a faint strain against the breastbone and then coolness. I stand, wavering, then find my balance and look out upon the street with certainty.

Hundreds are gathered. They look at me with astonishment and some with the beginning of respect in their eyes. I sense this and sense as well how they attend to me. I raise my hand and point to the nearest of them, feeling trumpets like flowers falling around me.

"I am Risen," I say.

Introduction to
AT THE INSTITUTE

Several of the pieces in this book bear a common device
—*On Ice, At the Institute, Going Down, The Battered-Earth Syndrome*—that was introduced to science fiction
by Peter Phillips in 1947 in his rather famous *Dreams
Are Sacred*, and which I am not done with yet. It deals
with the palpability of dreams, with dreams as an existential device that not only comment upon but can be
equated with reality . . . and how the manipulation of the
one may have effects upon the other.

Necessarily, this theme is not unknown to literary fiction and indeed has been one of the prime concerns of
the new surrealists (Barth, Barthelme) during the last
decade. The difference between S-F and literary fiction is
that what is metaphor in the one is device in the other—
that is, Phillips's protagonist had an actual electronic
means of entering the dream-life of the man he was assigned to bring out of catatonia, and the protagonists of
my stories are subjected to literal machines that impose
literal—pre-selected—fantasies upon them.

This is terrifying because it is quite real and scientific
research is well on the way to indicating that the specific
stimulation of specific areas of the brain can produce pre-ordained results. (They have already quite sophisticatedly
mapped the brain.) Thirst can be generated by one pressure point, sexual desire by another, specific periods
of childhood with yet a third . . . it does not seem unreasonable that within a few generations the technicians of
these times will have made the soft sciences hard, will
have converted psychiatry into an exact science.

Of course, humanity is unalterably perverse, a conclusion that occurred to Freud and which is built deep into
his vision, but which most of his descendants have never
understood, lacking any novelistic sense of irony as Freud
did not. (Skinnerian psychology is not only repudiated be-

haviorism, it is Freudianism without a sense of humor, which is to say that it can be as dangerous as misapplied Freudianism.) We may map the brain, as Flannery O'Connor might have said, but never the blood . . . and in the blood the technicians may see mirrored only their unspeakable craft, their demonic solution.

———◆———

AT THE INSTITUTE

I

"I want to kill people," I say to the interviewer. "I want to chew them up and spit them out. I want to make them hurt bad, worse than they've ever hurt in their lives, and then empty them. That," I say, "that is what I want. No more. No other."

There is a pause. The interviewer leans back in his chair and looks for a while out the window, then turns and leans back, the seat clattering. "I see," he says. There is no accusation in his voice. I did not think there would be. The Institute is dispassionate. Impersonal. All of that I know from the preparatory materials. "I see."

"I want to kill. I want to meet them in dark, strange places and show them the knife, see the fear in their eyes and then . . ."

The interviewer waves me off. He seems impatient, the investigation process having been completed. "I understand," he says. "Of course, you realize that there's no place for a person with those tendencies in our society. We have emerged from centuries of brutality and neglect only in recent decades by attacking root causes. Your desires are not shameful, but we cannot accommodate them. You know that."

"Yes," I say. I have been well briefed. There is no way to lie to the interviewers successfully, and I have come to the room resolved then to tell them the truth, but somehow I was not prepared for disapprobation. "It isn't my fault. I didn't want to be this way. It just happened. I have dreams. . . ."

"I know," the interviewer says. He looks out the window again; I wonder what he sees in the courtyard and have a quick apprehension of blood, bones, skulls and corpses lying against the stones, one of the familiar seizures. I close my eyes against this and force the images away. "We're going to have to treat you."

"Yes," I say. "I know of the treatments."

"There is no alternative." The interviewer sighs, he stands, he places his palms flat on the high desk and nods toward the door. Behind me I hear attendants entering. I wait for the touch of their hands, thinking of the many ways in which I would like to kill the interviewer.

"Take him," the interviewer says, "take and treat him."

II

The helmet comes down on me; I feel the electrodes wink home and then I am taken far from the surgical table on which they have placed me and am somewhere else. Before me, in the long, gray corridor, I see my father for the first time in fifteen years. I am told that he died painfully in an industrial accident but did not know him well enough at that time to care. "Here," my father says, handing me a gun secreted in his palm. "Here it is, son. Kill me."

"I don't want to kill you."

"Yes you do," my father says. He is very frail, looks just as he might have on the morning that the big crane took him. "That's what you told the interviewer, wasn't it? That you wanted to kill people. That you wanted to hurt them bad. Here's your chance." I feel the steel against my fingers; he seems to wink. "Go on," he says, "do it."

"I can't," I say, nevertheless raising the gun. "You died fifteen years ago. This is a dream."

"Of course it's a dream, but it's a true dream, son, and

only to help you. Come on," my father, dead fifteen years, says, "get it out of your system. Go on. Kill me." He giggles. "Bet you don't have the guts."

"Don't make me."

"You never did have the guts; none of you would-be murderers ever do. All you do is talk." He advances upon me. "All right, you whelp," he says, "give me the gun."

"No," I say, backing away from him, "no, I won't." I look down at this gray against my palm, feel the power. "Don't make me."

"Yes you will," he says. His voice is wheedling, yet smug. "Of course you will. You don't have the guts, you see. I knew you never did. I know your type."

I feel the rage. It moves up several levels and comes out of me in slow, churning waves. "You bastard," I say, "you can't do this to me." I raise the gun, point it toward his neck. "Stop," I say, but he does not stop. I pull the trigger, feel flame, the gun skitters in my hand. He falls, torn open.

I look at him.

III

When the helmet comes off I feel cold and for a moment too weak to open my eyes; I do, however, and look up to see the interviewer as if from a great distance. "You killed," he says, and I sense sadness. "You killed him."

"It was only the simulator," I say, "and I had no choice. He taunted me. He begged me to do it. He . . ."

"Do you still want to kill?"

I look up at the interrogator anl he looks down at me, and for a moment I say nothing, thinking of this. One cannot lie to the interviewers; this has been made very clear. Then again, the treatment is supposed to be unbearable. I had heard only vague rumors of it, but I suspect that it can get worse than this. "I don't know," I say. "Sometimes. But, then again . . ."

"Death is permanent," the interviewer says. "Do you know that?"

"Yes."

"I do not think that you truly understand yet the permanence of death."

"I don't know. I said, I don't . . ."

"Enough," the interviewer says, cutting me off. He nods toward the technician, who nods back and guides the helmet toward me again. "He is not ready yet. Give him more treatment."

IV

This time I dream that I am in bed with a woman who has betrayed me. I am deeply in love with this woman—whose name I do not know and who I cannot place, except by emotion—and yet the sense of her betrayal comes off her skin; I sniff apprehension in her hair and find that I cannot bear to touch her. "You cheated," I say to her, turning in bed. "You were with someone else."

"Yes," she says quietly after an instant, a woman incapable of lies. "I'm sorry. I didn't mean to; it just happened. It will never happen again."

"I could kill you," I say. "I could kill you for this."

"Please," she says, turning to me, catching my shoulder to lean over and show me her eyes full of pain, "please don't talk that way. You know I didn't want . . . "

"You cannot do this to me—it isn't fair, it isn't right, you don't have the means . . . "

"All right," she says, shaking her head and moving away, lying back on the pillow, "if that's what it means to you, if you cannot understand . . . then kill me. I don't care."

I know that this is only a posture—she is a very pretty woman and full of the instinct for life—but the sight of her throat open before me on the pillow, the naked and vulnerable throat pulsing its life away near my lips, inflames me, and suddenly I find that I am grasping and choking her. "You bitch," I shriek, "you can't do this to me, you've got to understand, I'm a killer, a killer, I cannot control myself," and she cyanoses under me, her face turning blue, her body thrashing. Death runs through her in small quivers and snatches; I squeeze her throat feeling death rise against me and she falls away in sections, screaming. Her eyes move open; death looks at me from those eyes.

I look at death.

V

"I'm sorry," I say to the interviewer when the helmet comes off. "I tried not to. I didn't want to, but she taunted me and finally . . . "

"Enough," the interviewer says, shaking his head. "You killed. You killed again."

"I didn't want to," I say, "don't you understand? I don't want to be a murderer. It just turns out . . . "

"Your father," he says, "and then a woman you loved. You are very determined. Do you know how few there are who kill through the second stage?"

"Please," I say. Even pinned by constraints I force motion, try to show the interviewer the sincerity of my position. "I wouldn't have killed this time if she hadn't forced me. It was against my will. It was . . . "

"You're going to have to go to the third stage," the interviewer says. "Very few people need the third stage, and fewer still fail that. But I must warn you that if you do, we will have no choice."

"I don't want to kill," I say again. "It isn't my fault, nothing is my fault, all of them have done it to me, pushed me, baited me, compelled me. It's their doing! I'm a victim!"

"The third stage," the interviewer says, and the helmet comes down and I dream again and no way, no way to resist it. They are cruel but practical. Kind but vicious. Scientific but righteous. Sympathetic but damned.

VI

I look at myself in the small enclosure of the dream. I have lived with myself for twenty-one years but have never known or seen this face as I do now. How ruined it seems! Small lines cut across it and lead toward darkness. Corrupt. I am irretrievably corrupt. "Please," the face says, "please don't kill me."

"I have to," I say, "it's for your own good."

"No," the face says. It is babbling. "Please, no."

"But it must be," I say reasonably. "I must kill you for your sake. You're a murderer in a society that will no longer tolerate murderers. They have been detected at the source and trained out of their impulses. If they will not take training they are obliterated." I am very reasonable—as reasonable as the interviewer. I raise my hands to the face.

"Oh, God," the face says, "please, no. I'm *you,* don't you know that? I'm *you!* How can you kill your*self?*" The face babbles on in this manner; but I am purified, I am seized by mission, and no less purposeful than the interviewer himself, and I advance upon the face. "You must die," I say, "because you're too dangerous and the treatments have proved how dangerous you are and you are incurable and it is irrevocable." And, saying this, I leap upon the face that is myself and, digging my nails in, I . . .

VII

Well, I awaken and there is the interviewer and there are the technicians and all of them are looking at me and I do not know what their expressions mean. "Did I pass the third stage?" I ask. "Did I pass it? I had to kill myself, you know, I was just too dangerous. I accept the fact of my danger and accept the necessity for its elimination; doesn't that count for something? It ought to count for something, you know. I mean, isn't that the purpose of the third stage: to see if I have the will to will it out of myself?" Blabbering and babbling just like the face in the dream, and as I look up at them I see finally what the third stage has meant and what it has tested and what they have done to me, and this knowledge is absolutely too much for me; I cannot take it and back away, losing toehold and then falling; I fall and fall a long time, but the faces are always there pursuing me down that well, and for all I know I am falling yet and still waiting to learn if they will kill me or whether I have passed the third stage. Or both. Or neither.

Introduction to
MAKING IT THROUGH

Another of the direct-commission stories, I was offered a choice here: a piece on either biology or religion. Since it would take an ironist greater than this writer to point out that they were one and the same, I selected biology—with Yom Kippur approaching I knew that soon enough I would have plenty of religion—and fusing a good degree of hard background in psychiatry with customary paranoiac approach I emerged with the following, which the editor loved and which started a career in writing for him which, three years, fifty-one stories and two and a half novels later, shows no signs of flagging. (See the May 1974 issue of *Analog*, containing other thoughts on this editor.)

This might be a good place to point out that I come by my background in the softer sciences legitimately and by inheritance: as an undergraduate major in Sociology, as an employee of the New York State Department of Mental Hygiene and as the nephew of the man who was, for thirty years, its chief statistician and the author of several landmark works in the field of identifying, mapping and defining by socioeconomic strata and ethnic affiliation the types of mental illness.

Dr. Benjamin and Barry N. . . . . I am convinced that two hundred years from now the two Malzbergs will have fused in card catalogues and in the dim consciousness of the few specialists still interested in reading. "Malzberg?" a specialist will say. "Oh, yes, you mean the fellow who wrote about mental illness. Right. Novels and statistical abstracts, am I right? Published by Albany and Random House. He sure knew a lot about craziness, all right . . . but that stuff never sells." My uncle died on 4/12/75. I miss him.

MAKING IT THROUGH

I

"Back to Ganymede," the Captain says somewhat drunkenly, his eyes rotating unevenly within their mad orbit, "back to the base. We must tell them what has happened to us. Lord save us from the sons of bitches, my mind is reeling. Sa, sa, sa." And he takes a concealed knife from a bulkhead, lurches toward me. I slap the knife from his quivering hand with careless ease, drop him to the panels with a blow and do what I can to lash him with ropes. Unquestionably he has gone mad. This does not fill me with panic so much as a querulous nostalgia: now as never before I remember the Captain as he was in his sane periods, and he was everything a Captain should be: stolid, efficient, sexually repressed. Now it is all different.

The arthopods of Jupiter have gotten to him, exactly as rumored. Malevolent, mysterious, they have brought their strange powers to bear upon him and the Captain has crumpled. My own resistance level seems to be somewhat higher, but then, on the other hand, one never knows.

II

The arthopods of Jupiter, the best scientific informants have advised us, possess a secret and pervasive weapon of enormous range and total penetration: they break down the amino acids upon contact to produce all of the classic symptoms of the archaic disease, schizophrenia. Three exploratory flights have gone and returned with their crew totally insane: now it is our chance. We have been given further shielding, deliberate instructions, drug therapy, tests for resistance. It is hoped that these preparations will make our mission successful and we will be able to conquer the dread arthopods of Jupiter and claim that planet, as so many others, for mankind. All that we have to do is to settle in orbit and use the incendiary devices prepared for us. All life on Jupiter will perish under atomic bombardment and the way to the planet will lie clearly before us. Utilize one simple control and that will be the end of the arthopods, the only suspected sentient life on Jupiter. We need, we have been advised, the living space. Yet, despite all these preparations, the Captain's sanity has already collapsed and my own is preserved only by this careful set of notes that I will keep straight through. I will keep them straight through. One simple control is all I have to push.

III

"Double up for comfort," the mad Captain sings, now lashed to the floor. "They could have sent us one by one at less risk and expense, but they have a crew so that no one can trust anyone else. To report on each other. A crew of two for me and you," the Captain murmurs and makes a series of fishlike struggles against the bindings, gives that up and motions me to him with a demented wink. "Listen here," he says, "you know they're all out to get us—the administrators, the colony, everyone. How can we tell the aliens from the enemies? Turn around and go back there. Use the explosives on them. That's a direct order, you son-of-a-bitch," he says and caresses my cheekbone with a careful finger. I feel a suspicion of sexual response; I have become very attached to the Captain. "No," I say, *"no,"* and I leave his side, remembering the dread persuasiveness of the paranoid-schizophrenic: his ability to conjure a reality that matches his own construct. We will be within orbit in a matter of hours; I must retain control just long enough to use the

devices and destroy the arthopods. Then I, too, may have
the pleasure of going mad if I wish.

IV

The ray of the arthopods, we have been told, is their
only defensive mechanism. They are a shy, stupid race,
somewhat less intelligent than horses who graze amidst
the gases of Jupiter and routinely emit this ray as a skunk
might emit odor, with no more sensibility. We need not be
concerned about their elimination. Jupiter is a fertile
world and we need the space. Schizophrenia is reversible,
although the kind of schizophrenia that the arthopods induce has not responded to any treatment so far.

V

The Captain evinces the blunted effect and ideas of reference common to chronic undifferentiated schizophrenia.
"Look here," he says to me with stunning persuasiveness,
marred only slightly by the indignity of his position, "I'm
not insane. *You* are. I'm the Captain and far more biolog-
ically resistant to the ray. You've gone insane and
are showing a paranoid reaction. This is not a mission of
destruction. Please listen to me. We are on a mission of
investigation—to study the arthopods, who are a highly
intelligent race, if a slightly clumsy one, and to make
overtures of accommodation to them. These atomic devices we carry are only for self-defense. You have become
the schizophrenic, paranoid type and believe that we must
destroy the arthopods and with the muscularity of the demented have overpowered me before I could protect myself. Please listen to me. Please release me and go to your
room. I will turn the flight around and we will return. I
will take no retaliatory action against you. You are a sick
man. You have a terrible disease."

"No," I say with the impassivity necessary to confront
the schizoid, "you are wrong. You have gone mad and I

retain a wedge on sanity. We are to wipe out the arthopods and you are cunningly trying to turn it the other way. I will not listen to you anymore. Twenty minutes now before we slide into orbit and then I will press the button. I will wipe the buggers out of the solar system because they are evil."

"No, you have it wrong," the Captain says, now whimpering a bit, his control evading him. "You are quite mad. I am sane. Please release me."

"No," I say. "This mission will succeed. I will not be deterred. I am more resistant."

And so on and so forth, our discussion, querulous and bitter by turns, continuing as we approach the point of orbit. It will not be much longer now. Not much longer. "Surely we deserve the solar system," I say. "That's the least I can ask for our trouble getting this far."

VI

To steel myself and retain my perspective, I inscribe the six forms of the old disease schizophrenia: hebephrenic, simple type, catatonic, paranoid, chronic undifferentiated and schizo-affective. Catatonic is the deadliest, chronic undifferentiated the most insidious, schizo-affective the sanest. They are caused by imbalances in the blood system in turn caused by faulty adrenals, a discovery made by Folsom in 2009 that brought about effective drug therapy that wholly wiped this scourge from mankind by 2035. We are no longer a schizoid race. We have made great advances over these centuries. Our goals are perfectly reasonable: they involve the conquest of the universe.

VII

"Please," the Captain says to me as we slide into orbit, "please think about this; don't you recognize your own symptomology?" But it is entirely too late for that. I silence the lunatic with a single threatening gesture and then I press the button, fondling it only slightly, the lovely button so resilient in its dimensions and I see the fire, the brilliant arcing fire that shows the bombs glancing off atmosphere into immediate connection, and just as I do so, as I accomplish the desired, I feel my will and rigidity collapse like scaffolding, and from that instant I am as mad as the Captain. I am as mad as the Captain. Feel myself choked by sobs, remorse, pain, guilt, anguish, because I have destroyed the arthopods: the lovely, lovely arthopods, that through their great gift wanted to bring back the sanity we had lost hundreds of years ago and I too stupid to see it. Beside me, still bound, the Captain is mumbling of defense mechanisms; I do not want to think of defense mechanisms but only of the arthopods, those wise and saddened creatures who now (perhaps I am dreaming this) lie as ash beneath us while our little ship, on full automatic, speeds back toward Ganymede to give the joyful news.

TAPPING OUT

This, for an Avon anthology of original S-F concerning and aimed for children, raises the question as to whether there is any such thing as "juvenile" S-F, a subgenre of a genre that restricts its audience even more closely. There evidently is, at least in fact—note Andre Norton and the phenomenal works by Robert A. Heinlein in the 1950s, both aimed for children—and this leads to the depressing conclusion that "juvenile" S-F may have a much wider audience and influence than "adult" S-F, because most children (who read at all) will pass through science fiction at one stage or another, whereas only a tiny fraction of adult readers read in the field. We are thus confronted by the potential of a literature to influence far beyond the potential of the larger literature from which it is drawn. In practical terms, it means that we need our best writers and editors working in the juvenile field . . . but then, we *have,* historically, and it hasn't helped us to hold the audience, most of it beyond adolescence.

Is that because "juvenile" S-F is superior in quality to the nominally adult stuff? Let's think about that for a while. . . .

———◆———

TAPPING OUT

I

The machine is merciful. I must remember that. The process, although painful, is essentially kind and leads only to the most reasonable of ends. Deep in the drugs, sensors link, I descend and at the end of that flight find my father. He is pretty much as I remembered him, although somewhat older and with a thin taint of incompetence oozing from him; incompetence and fear. This is the way it should have been.

"No," he says, gesturing, "you cannot do that." We are having another one of our meaningless arguments about my career or my late hours or perhaps, simply, about our inability to bear one another. The issues are not important. "I will not permit it," he says, backing up a step and teetering against the wall of our living room, "not at all."

"Yes you will," I say, coming right to the point. "Yes you will; you will allow me to do that because I am more important than you and I am not afraid of you and your whole life is worthless, anyway." And with surpassing ease I lean forward, close the gap between us (I seem to be moving through gelatin) and begin to throttle him by his wizened neck. "I can do anything I want to do because I am no longer afraid," I say, and my father says, "Ulp," then dissolves underneath me to the floor and he gasps, "Yes, you're right, I'm sorry," and flaps helplessly beneath me and I feel the strength, the strength and the triumph building: I have at last conquered my father, and as I take in my first breath of power, watching him struggle below, I begin to feel better—better than I have in months, anyhow—but before I can truly appreciate and enjoy this I am yanked away at growing speed, move far away from there and surface, as always, to the technicians who lean over with gloved fingers to take the leads away. I feel electrodes imploding within and at some pity in the technicians' gestures shame as well.

Nonetheless, I sense that I am progressing.

II

At the new session with my doctor we agree that I have made strides and am showing a new maturity and am well on my way to a full discharge from the Institute; nevertheless, he warns me that I must take nothing for granted. "The process is risky, still experimental," he says. "In the fantasies you are assuming a far more purposeful role in relation to these authority figures, but too much cannot be taken for granted. The test will come when you must live in the world again—whether you will be able to carry over the reconstructed to the real." *Reconstructed to the real.* My therapist is a birdlike man with displaced eyes who insists upon talking to me in this way. We have never had what might be called a relationship. "You are becoming far more dominant in these fantasies," he says, "and this is all to the good, but transfer is vital. You are only seventeen years old, however, and there is much promise. A younger person such as yourself has more of a chance. Later on, one rigidifies."

One rigidifies. It is really impossible to take my therapist seriously; nevertheless, our sessions are mandatory. There is no use of the machine—they have explained to me—unless the "discussions" with the therapist continue, and it is the machine that will make me well. I will come out of here in due course and live my life with gentle power.

The first thing in my new life I will do is to tell my father how I hate him. Then I will say the same to my mother, and after that—how I look forward to it!—I will take care of all the others.

III

At the next process, locked in the sensors again, I reconstruct a girl who I barely remember who once turned me down for a date. In this reconstruction I launch myself upon her like a bird and have my way with her without resistance: at the end she cries my name and I pitch over the edge to find myself once again throttling my father.

IV

"You have got to modify your responses," the therapist says. He looks slightly worried, but on the other hand it may be only a gastric disturbance: I refuse to be sensitive to him. "The point of the process is re-enactment, not indulgence. We want you to be able to review your relationships—the relationships you have had, I mean to say—in light of what you should have done, but we do not believe in impossible aggression." He shakes his head, considers certain records before him that presumably contain the content of my activities under the machine. I really did not expect these to be secret, but it is somewhat dismaying to realize that everything I have done under the privacy of the sensors is, in a sense, public record. "This is very expensive treatment," my therapist says vaguely. "You are costing your parents a great deal of money. I tell you this frankly so that you will treat the opportunity with the respect it deserves. You are here not to indulge yourself but to get well. If you do not cooperate and use the process in the way it is intended, you are abusing it." He taps his desk, looks at the wall, turns back to me. "You have a schizoid condition," he says. "I know you know that. You have a chance for a complete cure, but you must cooperate and do better."

I promise him that I will, looking at his blotched, shrunken neck and thinking of other things.

V

"You must cooperate and do better," my therapist says in the sensors, and I say, "Go to hell, Jack," and fling myself upon him, screaming: attempt to choke the life out of him. He is much livelier than my father and it is difficult, but at length I succeed. It feels good to have killed my therapist and I am enjoying the various sensations of power and fulfillment, but before I can truly luxuriate I feel myself being yanked to the surface rudely; I struggle like a fish in sand, and when I come to myself I am lying on the table under wires, as always, and the technicians are looking at me in a terribly unfriendly fashion. I wonder if I have displeased them.

VI

My father comes to visit me and after a while says that he has talked to my therapist and the therapist says that I am not doing very well. I have not responded to treatment. Further treatment is contraindicted and I am being discharged. I will be sent to the state hospital tomorrow for more conventional treatment and of course my father is sorry; nevertheless, it appears to be my fault. According to reports my father has heard, I have never cooperated.

I do what I always did with my father in difficult moments: I collapse against him and beg forgiveness, but all the time behind my closed eyes I see the images of how in the machine I killed him, and knowing this, knowing that I have done it, I know that I will never truly be the same again. Nor will I be different. Schizoid condition, the therapist said. I am seventeen years old.

Introduction to
CLOSED SICILIAN

The literature of S-F stories on chess is neither long nor honorable—there have been a few, and two novels by Poul Anderson and John Brunner—with the exception of a piece called *Von Goom's Gambit,* but that is not to say that a man cannot try. I *had* to try; I had spent the better part of the better days of one of the poorer summers riveted to the transcription of certain events occurring in Iceland, and I was damned if *all* of this was going down the drain. (The writer, although member of the legion unemployed, has one slight advantage: anything is material, everything therefore deductible.) *Closed Sicilian* came out with pristine sincerity and clarity; never had persona and situation seemed to mesh so perfectly, and it went off and sold to its first market without a hitch, illustrating as could nothing else the sublime *correctness* of its narrator . . . he does indeed rule the universe. . . .

Later, with similar facility, the short story converted itself into a novel (*Tactics of Conquest,* Pyramid, 1973). The assurance of the narrator is a wonder; it carried its originator helpless before it and left me wishing that I had been a chess player. "But this is an old fantasy—wishing that I had been something else, that is to say; all writers have fantasies, most of them verging toward sports or manual labor. As for me, I would rather be a good chess player than a writer, assuming roughly equal income, but what I would *really* rather be, revealed herein for the very first time, is a first-desk violinist with a major symphony orchestra, playing on the audience side and giving kindly lessons to local prodigies at enormous, confiscatory fees in my free time to fill out the salary. I am a *lousy* violinist and have not, for that matter, really played the instrument in several years, but, then again, I know a lot of lousy writers on the best-seller lists, and

the St. Louis Symphony would suit me. . . . Could anyone help me out?)

I wanted this introduction to be a speculation on why
it is hard to write good chess fiction, but I got sidetracked,
probably profitably. There is not much good chess fiction
because chess and literature are two different transmuta-
tions of reality and cannot be imposed upon one another,
I guess. Most stories fail because literary intent or necessity outweighs the primacy of the game. If this one fails,
it would do so, at least, for the opposite reason.

I forgot to note the one great work of literature on
chess we do have and which solves the problems—
Nabokov's *The Luzhon Defence.*

CLOSED SICILIAN

1. P-K4

He *would* open with his standard King's Pawn, looking
to transpose into the Ruy Lopez at the earliest opportunity, and I have known this in dreams as in study for
most of my life, yet I cannot transcend the thrill of mingled terror and anticipation with which, nevertheless, I
react to his first move. Sitting across from me in perfect
repose, his suddenly alien eyebrows curl into the faintest
and most tremulous posture of inquiry as his eyes flick
beyond me and with studied disinterest to the audience
of nine hundred million around and below us. Due to the
high ethics of the match and the scrupulous efforts that
I have conducted throughout to force the spectators to
conform to the code of play, they do not react to his gaze,
nor do they murmur. Seated with my back to them, facing
the bleak panels of this high-walled room in which we
play, I am able to bring my utmost concentration to the

board and thus my line of sight descends and my opponent, at this moment, no longer exists.

We are playing for the fate of the Universe. Previously we have played for the fate of the world, the worlds, the Solar System, the Milky Way, the Galaxy and the known Cosmos, but due to an apparent series of close defeats I have suffered due to the clever manipulations of the Overlords, the stakes have been progressively raised from one match to the next, and from this final confrontation there can be no appeal. I am not concerned. My game is in perfect order; I have spent eight months with my miniature chessboard and the Blue Book of my opponent's games preparing myself for this last great test. Several times I have forced postponents due to feigned illness or displeasure with the match conditions in order that I might have every opportunity to bring my studies to fruition. Pausing only for food and sleep, a couple of errant comminglings with terrestrial females who I have had sent to my quarters, I have dedicated myself utterly to the comprehension of my opponent's weaknesses and the development of strategic lines of attack that involve much original thought. I cannot fail the Universe in this last and most conclusive of all our tests, and now I know that essential control has passed into me. I feel small surges of power radiating through my bearded and distinguished frame; I feel a little tremor of my opponent's weakness intersect my own synapses and pass through them quickly. He has been greedy and should have cashed in on the Galaxy. But now he will pay by losing all.

I sit in perfect serenity, and when I have used up the time I have allotted myself on the clock, I make my response:

1. P-K4

Originally, my opponent and I did not seem fated for such great and meaningful confrontation. We were born within months of one another, spent our early years being raised in the same complex, discovered chess together and passed many pleasant years solving the mysteries of the game. As youths, we did not otherwise neglect more routine pastimes; we went out with the same girls, progressed with them sexually at about the same rate, shared classes and areas of subject interest—chemistry and textiles, as I recall, although it is hard to remember this far back; since I became involved in this, my early life has become so dim—and in fact became chess professionals on the same day, meeting all of the qualifications of the League and receiving our initial assignments. Only then, in fact, did our paths diverge; my opponent went to Brooklyn to become a promising newcomer on a team that needed shoring up badly, whereas I went to Bismarck, North Dakota, Ganymede, where I led the team in my first season to a tie for third place in the satellite division. Who was to have known when we were innocent lads growing up together in the towers that it would be he because of his fatal weakness to fall into the hands of the malevolent X'Thi, scourge and enemy of all humanity, whereas I, no xenophobe but loyal to my heritage from the beginning, would become the last bulwark of defense against occupation of the Universe by these terrible aliens? Who would have known? . . . But as my opponent himself said in one of the authorized interviews before the match (I have cooperated in these myself to build up the gate), *the ways of life are strange* and now I have succeeded in blockading the King's Pawn and cramping his position as early as his second move. What now, then? I look at him with a careful, triumphant smile and stand, take myself hurriedly backstage where refreshing snacks and fruit juices are available to us at all times by the courtesy of the Earth Federation and the X'Thi Congress, one of the few areas in which these deadly enemies have shown cooperation. Soon enough, there will be no need for further concessions:

2. Q-B3

When I return, having had a cruller and a small nourishing handful of Jovian lice, the aspect of the stage has subtly altered; the lighting has changed; my opponent is leaning backward, hands on knees, with a contented expression on his face; and small darting tadpoles of light draw me irresistibly to fixate upon the board. He has pushed his Queen peremptorily, a characteristic that he has evinced in several previous games, but it is one of those critical weaknesses upon which I have concentrated in my studies, and I am prepared now to punish him terribly for it.

My opponent has always had this tendency to develop his major pieces too rapidly. On Nulla, in the Solar Championships of 2256, who can forget that famous game in which he prematurely wedged open his Rook file with an unsound sacrifice and then, doubling his Rooks through additional sacrifices on the twelfth move, proceeded to dismember the hapless Wojewscking in the finals? Yet, all along, as the Blue Book reveals, Wojewscking could have averted the disaster through playing his Queen's Bishop to the seventh rank (now undefended because of the sacrifices) and castling. Well, there is no way of explaining such things; Wojewscking was playing in the uncongenial gravity of Uranus, whereas my opponent had prepared himself for the Championship by residing on that unhappy planet for three Earth weeks prior to the opening. It does not matter; Wojewscking's disaster only made my opponent more attractive to the vicious and malevolent X'Thi when they came into known space in 2271 and sought a proper turncoat who would help them to enact their dreadful schemes. Under the illusion that they had possession of the best chess player in the Federation, they allowed my opponent to play for progressively higher stakes, and now they will lose the Universe.

Looking at him in the strange lighting, I see that he is both smaller and older than I remembered him to be, and I feel a flare of pity instantly canceled by cold resolve. I am a man of some personal limitations and minor neurotic traits, but when I play chess, as it has been noted, I become steel, and there will be no remorse for my opponent, that traitor now, simply because he is aging and destroyed by pressure:

2. QN-QB3

The aim is to develop my minor pieces quickly while he falls into the lure of launching an early, unsound attack. "Just imagine," I remember saying to him in the projects of our youth, oh, so many years ago when we were playing yet another of our casual games, "what would it be like if we could play chess for the fate of the Universe? Wouldn't it make more sense than fighting wars or things? We could be the two best players in the world and countries could choose up sides, and that way one game or a series could settle everything."

"But if we were playing for the fate of the Universe, it would be more than just the world and countries and people then, wouldn't it?" my opponent said, demonstrating even then, at the age of twelve or thirteen, that treacherous cunning with which, years later, he would leap into the hands of the ugly and tormenting X'Thi when they offered to resolve all differences by playing off the worlds. "But of course I don't think chess could ever be that important," he added, pushing his Knight's Pawn to the seventh rank and forcing a checkmate, which I could have easily avoided if I had not felt pity for his youth, his abandonment, his unhappy upbringing in the Projects and had wanted to give him a gift in the form of a small crushing defeat.

It is a long way from that to this, but I am entrapped by no such feelings of pity or mystery today. Let it be said and be done: I deliberately threw the matches for the world, the worlds, the Solar System, the Milky Way, the known Galaxy in order to force this final confrontation. I knew that, spurred on by their greed and thoughts of an easy victory, the X'Thi would accept our proposals for continued games, upping the stakes, and I have been merely waiting for this great opportunity to toy with them and crush them:

3. B-B4

Continuing his unsound attack by posting the King's Bishop at an unsafe square. The normal continuation in the Ruy Lopez would be *B-B5,* but he has a weakness for variations of this sort and now will pay for them dearly.

The X'Thi are corrupt, deadly, vicious and evil, and are prefigured in detail by *The Revelations of St. John the Divine,* which talk about that great Snake that in the last days will appear to battle Mankind at Apocalypse. Actually, the X'Thi do not look like snakes; they are, in fact, rather pleasantly humanoid in appearance, but no matter of that; the tempter and the Final War would have to come in the guise of the familiar. (Note the Book of Job.) I have a minor interest in Bible lore, which is one of my few areas of relaxation outside of my lifelong dedication to the art and lore of Caissa. Clearly, what my opponent and I are now contending is the last and great battle between the forces of light and darkness that will usher in the divine era of the Second Coming, but this enormous obligation does not cause me to tighten with pressure (I feed upon it), but instead makes me relaxed and easeful. Not only are my skills superior to his despite the apparent record of successive defeats; my cause is essentially righteous, whereas his, of course, is that of Satan. It is always unwise to open a Queen prematurely when fighting for the cause of Satan.

The murmurs of the spectators, evenly divided by fiat between humanity and X'Thi, the combined political leaders of all the separate worlds, that is, admitted by invitation only, rise slightly and billow toward me as I prepare my first and devastating combination:

3.   QN-R4

Threatening the Bishop and unleashing a devastating attack upon the Queen side. My opponent seems to pale and puts a hand indelicately to his mouth as he leans forward, the implications of the move and his terrible error with the Bishop already clear to him. For an instant, just an instant, I want to reach across the board and take his hand, take it as I might have in the old days and say, "Listen, it's all right, don't be unhappy, don't take it personally, it really doesn't matter that much at all, and it's no reflection on you as a person if you lose a game of chess," but this would be preposterous since everything depends upon this game of chess, and if he loses (as now he must), the X'Thi would surely draw and quarter him before winking out of our Universe forever. "It's pointless, it has nothing to do with the situation, relax, take comfort," I want to say to him, but this is surely insane since the situation is climactic and irrevocable.

What has happened to me simply enough is that I am being assaulted by feelings of sentiment on the precipice of my immortal victory. I would not put it beyond the cunning and tormenting X'Thi to have contrived this themselves by manipulation of certain devices within the chair, the hall, the lighting, which can change my brain waves and interfere with normal psychic functioning. It was for this reason that I insisted that security in the hall be so tight and that the fruit juices and snacks be prepared and tasted by my own staff before their emplacement backstage, but I always knew that, given the final test, my will would be stronger than theirs and that none of their terrible devices could affect me.

They do not affect me now. I lean back in my chair, feeling a slight, cramping pressure within the bowels diminish, feeling all sentiment depart, and look out toward the audience for the first time; blue haze in the darkness, wisps of smoke, the soft purring of the atmospheric reservoirs that maintain the segregated sections of the hall at the proper balance for the two races. "Well," I say to him, then turning back, his face like an egg caught between two lights, his features crazed and crayoned, weaving insubstantially against that bleak shell, "what are you going to do now, eh? What are you going to do now, you traitorous son-of-a-bitch?" And then I take from my inside pocket one of the foul cigars I have brought for just this occasion and, extracting matches, light it deliberately in front of him, pouring out smoke, extinguishing the match, making him gasp as plumes of gray waft toward the great dome. Lasker was famous for tactics of this sort in 1924, but it is not 1924; it is more than three centuries later and here I am yet, and now humanity, the seed of Abraham, will overtake the Universe and I am glad, glad, for I know my name will be legion.

"My friend," my opponent gasps, "my old friend, this is too terrible," and incredibly, leaves his chair to reach toward me in a mad embrace and I dodge it only at the last instant (I abhor physical contact of any sort now) and with a shudder, revolve my chair, leap out of it. "My old friend," he says again, "this cannot be," but he subsides; the features seemed washed and muddled by some fluid; he returns to his chair and ponders the board silently, chin in his hand.

Suddenly it is all too much for me—the signals must have become displaced, and it is he, not I, who is undone by sentiment—and I hurry backstage again, seeking the soothing fruit juices and the knowledge that when I return he will have made the evasive move with the Bishop, losing a full tempo, to demonstrate his irrevocable loss:

4. QxP Mate

When I do return I see him before I see the board, and he is weeping. For a moment I want to embrace him then, if only in a kind of comfort, but the years of discipline and denial are too ingrained, the task too enormous, to allow me such failure, and so I take my chair and look at the board then to consider the best way in which I can continue to crush him.

Introduction to
LINKAGE

The conceptual premise upon which *Linkage* rests is one that has been worked through perhaps as obsessively as any of my themes; it occurs in at least four S-F novels (*Herovit's World, Beyond Apollo, Overlay, Gather in the Hall of the Planets*) and innumerable short stories; perhaps it is time to quit: granted that S-F and S-F writing sit upon paranoid, meglomaniacal, solipsistic visions, *do these visions have literal truth, or are they merely neurotic and in extreme cases psychotic?* Can they be taken seriously as serious probings of possible futures of humanity, or are they merely conventional power fantasies for conventionally disturbed adolescents and adolescents at heart?

Well, are they? The one single critical spike upon which category science fiction has been impaled by literary critics (those who deign to notice us at all) has been precisely this: that we are writing only grandiose versions of the fantasies of disturbed juveniles and therefore are not subject to the kind of serious questions of form and content with which realistic/surrealistic modern or historical literature can be probed.

It can be and has been pointed out in reply that the question of audience motivations or psychic symbols is less important than the question of veracity . . . that is, these plots bear the seeds of some potential and literal truth . . . but still left is the matter of literacy and technique, and most science fiction falls so far from conventional standards here that the temptation to attack at the level of neuroses is, perhaps, overwhelming. I have hardly been able to resist it myself.

Linkage, quite short and perhaps too slight, manages to raise and examine the issue in barely fifteen hundred words and leaves it at dead center, awaiting the reader's response. Is Freem crazy or isn't he? Is he imagining all this or not? Does he have extraordinary powers or does he need help?

Well, literary critics, how about this for an answer? Just for your consideration of course: *how about both?*

———◆———

LINKAGE

My name is Donald Alan Freem. I am eight years old. I can do anything with the power of my mind. I can make people say what I want them to say; make them perform actions that I have predetermined. I have always had this gift.

Because of my power, people fear me. They know that I can control them and take away their free will, and this terrifies them because they wish to hold to their pitiful illusions of freedom. Resultantly, I have been institutionalized since the age of five with the full consent of my parents and at the expense of the society that traps me.

I am not concerned. This institution cannot control the power I have. My mind sweeps and soars, moves far beyond their pitiable effort to entrap me. I can do anything I want. It will always be this way.

"You must face reality, Donald," Dr. Nevins says to me at our weekly session. "If you do not face reality you will live this way all your life, and I do not want it to be this way. You are very young, you are highly intelligent, you are malleable. We believe in your ability to break this. But you must help us."

I recline on the chair, look at the round, disturbed face of Dr. Nevins, then out the window to the grounds where some of my peer group are playing mindlessly with a ball. "I made you say that," I point out. "You said that because I ordered you to say it."

"Donald, you can no longer function this way. We must make progress. . . ."

"I knew that you would say that. I sent through an order from my mind telling your mind to say 'we must make progress.' Everything that you do is because I make you do it."

Dr. Nevins slams down a palm on his desk, stands awkwardly. This is the way in which our interviews usually terminate. "I don't want to lose patience," he says, "but you're not cooperating. You're not even trying. . . ."

"I knew that you would say that. I knew it before you did, and I made you hit your hand on the desk. You are afraid of me," I say, "but there's no need to be frightened. I would never do anything bad to you. I would never make people hurt themselves."

Dr. Nevins exhales, puffs his cheeks, shakes his head. "We'll discuss this again next time, Donald," he says. "You're going to have to think about these things. . . ."

"I wanted you to say that," I pointed out and, with Dr. Nevins, stand, send orders from my mind for him to open the door for me and send me out with a small flush of rage, sending red sprinkles through his clear cheeks. He does so. I leave. At the end of the corridor I disperse a message for him to slam the door, which he does with a metallic clang.

I did not develop the powers of my mind. They came to me full blown. I cannot remember a time, even when I was very young, when I could not make people do what I want. When I was six years old I was visited by an alien with whom I had a long discussion. The alien told me that I was the first of a super race, the first human being with my abilities, and that he had been sent back from the future to investigate and to guard my health. He promised me that my powers would breed true and that when I was an adult I would be able to reproduce with a female who would bear children like me. Tens of thousands of years in the future, my descendants would be the dominant race of the planet and would have, with their great powers, long since conquered the stars and invented time machines. One of these machines was being employed as a means for one of their scientists to come back and check on me—measure my progress and assure me that, in the long run, all of my difficulties would work out. "You will be kept in the institution for a long time," the alien said, "but, eventually, during adolescence, you will finally learn to lie and conceal your powers from them. You will say that you realize you control nothing and no one, and they will release you as 'cured.' Quietly, then, you will sow your seed and so on."

"I don't want to lie to them," I told the alien. "I'm proud of my powers and I know that it infuriates them when I brag, but I see no reason why I should have to treat these inferiors with any courtesy." Perhaps I did not put it quite that way. I was only six. In the last two years I have learned to read well and have been able to express myself in a far more sophisticated fashion. Probably I merely told the alien that I would do exactly what I wanted and he and no one else could stop me. At six I was very grandiose, but I have calmed down somewhat since then. I say and feel the same things but have learned to take a little of the edge off them.

"I will be back occasionally to check on your progress," the alien told me, "but, essentially, you have to live your own life." I have lived my own life. The alien has returned only once so far for a very brief discussion. I accept the fact that I am on my own.

Dr. Nevins loses his temper and says something about giving me more "injections" and "needles" and "drugs" if I do not cooperate with him, and for the first time he truly angers me. I tell him about the alien and the pact he made with me about my future. It takes me a long time, and when I am finished Dr. Nevins shakes his head with a pleased expression and finally says, "I'm very pleased, Donald. At last you're opening up to me."

"I made you say that."

"I'm beginning to see the fantasies that are at the root of your condition. Now we can begin to work. You've enabled us to make a start. I'm grateful."

"I ordered you to say 'grateful.' Anything I tell you to say you will say."

"Yes," Dr. Nevins says, patting me, and leading me to the door, "this is very helpful, Donald." And he ends our interview so rapidly that I realize I have not had a chance to make it finish the way I ordered. This is the first time it has ever happened, and I am somewhat disconcerted. I remind myself that even Dr. Nevins has a kind of cunning and must be watched.

The alien comes to see me that night and tells me that he is extremely disturbed. I can sense his agitation. "You shouldn't have told them about me," he says. "That was not very smart, Donald. You could upset all of our calculations, the whole projected future. Now they will concentrate on exactly those elements that are most central."

"I don't care," I say, "besides, I made you say that."

"No, Donald. This is very serious business. This was supposed to be our secret. I am very upset."

"I wanted you to be upset. I did something to your mind to make you upset."

"They will focus on specifics, Donald, and may even convince you that this is a fantasy. You may upset the whole track of time."

"I want to upset the whole track of time," I say. "The track of time is anything I want. I think that I'll get rid of you." And I do something to him with my consciousness and with a roar the alien vanishes; he was never there in the first place, as a matter of fact. I never knew of any aliens, and quite weakly it occurs to me that all these years Dr. Nevins has only been trying to help me, and I owe him nothing less than my assistance. The two of us, perhaps, can work this out together, and I am beginning to find it very boring to have things turn out exactly the way I make them. The other way would be more exciting. I will let them do what they want for a while.

Introduction to

INTRODUCTION TO THE SECOND EDITION

The issue here is very close to the one raised in *Linkage* (perhaps you should go back and look at the introduction to that story: thank you very much), except that here the terrain is not that of the S-F fantasy, but the murder mystery, a genre that strikes me as several degrees crazier and somewhat dumber than S-F overall, but with a better class of readership and with a far better public relations approach. Here at last the genres merge and the great question is put: Is he crazy, or is he merely doing the will of others?

Here at least, and for once, Malzberg offers an answer not subject to editorial interpretation, and for this reason he is not entirely pleased with the story. The editor who originally published it must have been; he said, "If the field of S-F, and, for that matter, the world, has a conscience, then the name of that conscience is Barry N. Malzberg," a clear·signal for a sophisticated readership —confronted by any writer or politician represented to be the conscience of his generation—to grab its money and run. The opinion of the editor is not that of your humble proprietor, who, like Herovit, can barely manage his own affairs; unlike Herovit, he will not try to run the world.

———◆———

INTRODUCTION TO THE SECOND EDITION

This is the third time that I will murder my mother. The first two times were not entirely satisfactory but brought me, regardless, toward the more central material: one of these go-rounds I will surely get it. "You lousy bitch," I say, raising the knife, "you ruined everything. My whole attitudes toward sex were entirely warped for thirty-eight years by your pointless moralizing. Also, you insisted that I get a fifty-cent allowance when my three best friends were all taking more than a dollar. I'll never forgive you for that. Never!" I say this, and in the midst of her protests and shrieks I, drive the knife straight toward her heart and part her like a fish, watch with some limited satisfaction while she collapses to the floor. "Grrll," she says, dwindles and vanishes. They have made great progress with the simulacrums but still have difficulty in mimicking human speech.

"So much for that," I say, sheathing the knife and placing it back in its proper place on the table, turning away from her and toward the exit before my timespan is ended and the lights collapse on me. (I find this very embarrassing.) Behind me I hear the sound of the Sweepers; before me I hear the sound of the machinery taking coins, but my business is done for the day. I push straight ahead, past the crowds, and there on the street I merge with the others and am gone. Still damaged, still cursed, the taint of my mother lying crosswise against my heart until I realize again, gasping in the open air, how they have always cheated me and how yet I will be back tomorrow.

For the fourteenth time I allow my father to kill me. I have killed him only eight times myself; there is some vague imbalance here, but it is not to be corrected and only barely understood. "This is for you," he says, standing before me terrific and powerful, the man that I have not seen thus for thirty-three years, stripped to the waist, the prematurely gray hairs of his chest winking at me in the dangerous life, "this is for ruining your mother's figure, turning that gay, small girl into gloom and disaster, sowing the seeds of disunion in our marriage, locking me into my miserable job, ruining my life. I don't have to take this anymore," he says almost conversationally and raises the gun; he fires the gun, I feel the bullet in my intestine and with a grateful moan fall to the floor, dying for him as I have always wanted. Spaces contract, sounds diffuse and I come to myself in the Recovery Room where an old attendant who looks strangely like an uncle leans over and asks me in a whisper if I want to go again. "A bargain rate," he says, "another death for half-price, or you can take a kill for only three-quarters. Wouldn't you like to kill?" he says with a horrid wink, and I tear the helmet from my head and stumble from the table, leaving quite rapidly, although some tug of responsibility makes me turn at the door and say politely, "No, I don't want to get hooked on this; I'll take it within limits." Infinitely compassionate, infinitely tender, the old attendant nods and I push my way into the street, gasping in the open air, knowing how they have always cheated me and how yet I will be back tomorrow.

For kicks I elect to kill an old girl friend. I have not seen her in fifteen years; now, as I last remember her, she stands before me, naked to the waist, pathos and lust intertwined in her features, her delicate hands cupping her breasts as last she did. "You can if you want to," she says with great sadness, "but I'll never have any respect for you as long as I live if you think I'm so cheap." And I administer poison: shovel the vial between her lips and administer it in choking draughts. She falls with a gasp, her limbs coming open and I am seized by need—a mad necessity comes over me and I collapse on the floor to mount her—but before I can do anything her body retracts, retracts very quickly and attendants seize me by the shoulders. "Not here," they say. "You know perfectly well that that isn't part of your contract," and with great speed and force they usher me through the hallways and toss me past bystanders into the street; gasping in the open air I know that they have cheated me again and yet I will be back tomorrow.

I am told that my contract has expired and am offered a new series of treatments at a higher rate. "That's impossible," I say, "you're extorting money from me, and besides, I don't need the process at all; I'm perfectly free." And they say to me, "If that's so, don't renew; go into the street." And suddenly I realize that I am not free and I do not want to go into the street, so I renew for twenty-five more treatments at three times the per-treatment cost, which it was when I began, and they thank me and dismiss me and I say, "When will I be free? It doesn't seem to *work;* when will I be purged of these needs, as you promised?" And they rub their hands and shake their heads, say vaguely that there is no way of telling, but the rate of purgation in the long run is very favorable, and besides, the treatments in themselves are catharotic, and I go gasping into the street feeling that they have cheated me again and yet I will be back tomorrow.

I allow my mother to kill me. It is the culmination of an old grudge; it has to do with my poor eating habits and sloppy table mannerisms. "I'm sorry, sorry, but this is necessary," she says, and then cuts me ear to ear with a knife and I fall dying and yet ascending, moving toward consciousness, and my mother leans toward me: her face has the calmness and certainty of a very young girl and, "Yes," she says, "Yes, yes, yes," and falls toward me; I seize her from affirmation and something goes wrong with the cortical blocks: something is not quite right, she becomes my father, and then again she becomes my girl friend; becomes my uncle and herself again, passing through various stages, skin slipping and sliding, features riven under my gaze and I say, "What is this, what is this?" And I begin to shout from panic, but before too long attendants come and cancel out everything and take me to a quiet room where they talk to me briefly. The process is still new, they say. The process is not perfect, they say. The process is still liable to errors, technological failures, mechanical breakdown in the cerebral implants. It means nothing, they assure me; everything will work out as it always has, and to ease my feelings they offer me an additional fifteen treatments on my contract at only three-fifths cost. I take them gratefully, accept the bargain, accept their assurances that I am a pioneer and leap singing to the street, knowing that what they have given could have been in no other way, and for all the tomorrows, as long as my income and the process holds, I will repeat, I will repeat, I will repeat.

Introduction to
TRIAL OF THE BLOOD

"Write Dracula's diary," the editor who commissioned this said, "and I'll pay a hundred and thirty dollars for three thousand words plus a pro-rata share of the royalties."

How could I resist? Not the money, of course (the money means nothing; like all serious artists, I am in it solely for the pleasure of the work), but the attempt to reconstruct the persona of one of the most famous characters in horror literature from the inside out would hardly pass this way again. The story was done quickly and got me one of my few kind words from *Publishers Weekly*, a journal that has not seen eyeball-to-eyeball with me on many occasions, but which I nevertheless revere. It even comes together in a fashion not inconsistent with the novel and makes a kind of sense: this may be the way the Count would have seen it.

Of course, this story partakes, as does so much literature, of the fallacy of transcription . . . of the conceit that individuals who do most of the world's splendid work cannot wait but to hobble to their journals in the evening to put all of it down. This would only be so if the people who did the work of the world were writers, which most of them are not . . . or if writers did the work of the world, which is even more ridiculous. It is, of course, that basic conceit without which fiction of any kind could hardly exist, founded as it is upon an understood desire to transcribe or one (if you are writing third-person) to rationalize a lot . . . characteristics that do not obsess most of our politicians, alas.

But this leads to an even more considerable thought: fiction—all fiction as we know it—may be an untruth since it considers and articulates events as *they would be seen by writers*. Writers write, surely . . . but is it possible that they write of and for themselves and merely project their characteristics upon characters? If this is so, the argument against fiction is compelling. Best to get to Toynbee, Arthur Schlesinger, Jr., or Malcolm Muggeridge posthaste, or, at least, to those distinguished proponents of the new journalism, Tom Wolfe, Seymour Krim, Norman Mailer. . . . *They* are telling the truth. Aren't they?

TRIAL OF THE BLOOD

June 16: I think *this:* it was not cruelty that drove but rather an excess of feeling, a need to touch, to burst through the barriers to create something else and to know, then, the naked, vulnerable human heart. I do believe this: I am not a cruel man. I derive no emotional satisfaction from what I have been forced to do; I am seized by *regret* and *remorse* at almost all the worst moments . . . and yet, to what point? I must go on. I do the necessary as do we all. And now, my power at last deserting, I confront what has happened and know that it could have been no other way.

Out into the tangled landscape again this evening, prowling the corridors of this ruined country: dead kings and warriors glinting at me through the forest, the broken paths, leaping and stumbling through this abandoned country that will (I do see this) some day be overtaken by machinery that will break the landscape to shreds, into an isolated house that I had marked upon my sheets as a marginal possibility months ago (now exhausted, I have come to marginality) and into the bedrooms, passing through the locks with old cunning among the sleepers. An old man, old woman, another old man, old man . . . age, senescence, dust, death, and at the end of the hallway one last bedroom where the virgin slept. I know she must have been a virgin. In my mind at least all of them are untouched: no one knows better than I, or will ever, their corruption, the rotting of the flesh, the unspeakable pleasures that even the most innocent of them have shriekingly indulged . . . but in the cool, gray abcesses of the mind all is purity. I saw her. She saw me, her eyes fluttering to connection. We looked upon one another. She stroked a hand against her mouth like a butterfly. "No," she said, "no." I spread my cloak apart so that she could see me, her eyes terrified, glazed with knowledge. My reputation, you see, has gotten around. I fell atop her without preamble and sank—ah, *sank!*—my teeth into her neck, feeling the smooth pearl of the skin part. She thrashed against me like a fish. I held her down easily with my weight. I put in my tongue. I drank.

And drank of her until the white of skin that had blended with the sheet faded to gray, her struggles, dying, locked her body rigid against mine and then, finally, finally I pulled away from her, shaking, and left that room. Breath to the corridors, quiet singing of the wind against the shutters.

I wept. Remorse, gentlemen, has me in its clutches. But what can I do? Considering the situation—and I am sure that you will in your ponderous gravity—assessing and understanding all . . . what could I have done?

At sleep I possessed her again and in the dream her blood was a sea and I dove, singing.

June 17: A man of means, a man of substance, moderate nobility coursing through these veins, earldoms and fiefs clamoring in the background generations past . . . yes, I am not an ordinary assassin, not the casual beast, but a murderer of some distinction and to be understood only in this way. Writing these notes, leaning over my desk, supporting the weight of my collapsing frame—I do not sleep well—I feel a sense of power of resonance, and maybe it is this that takes me to these notes, because I cannot be ignored. I cannot be allowed to pass: I must leave some small legacy of explanation that will finally render my position clear; it is unfair that I have done *so much,* and yet what will be remembered (if any is) is merely atrocity.

The landscape runs with blood and terror. Houses are boarded up, the constabulary continue their hopeless search for what they describe as a *fiend* . . . and of intention nothing is known at all. Fear has beaten understanding.

I am not a fiend, but a man of substance, moderate nobility coursing through these veins. . . .

"I did this," I wanted to say over her body last night, "I did this for love, for necessity, for the connection. I did it because I wanted to take your blood and body unto me in the most ancient and sacramental of all the rituals; I wanted to possess you utterly and make your flesh whole. For love, for love, that was all I wanted!" I could have shouted but her blood had run out over the sheets in little anguished droplets, her body had broken on the bed like an hourglass and nothing to say then, only flee the room, flee that damned house of breath, run through that landscape like a loon and finally to this ruined, cluttered castle itself, the specters of ancient earldom staggering through, and I know that whatever I do and however I try, no one will ever understand but the word *fiend*. Only in these notes can I make it clear; I will continue this journal; I have a certain alacrity with the language, smattering of education, bit of literacy, am pleased with this means of expression, and if I can only, only get it down straight. . . .

I feel the urge coming over me again.

June 18: Further and further in my adventures; now I must go miles from this castle to conduct my intricate business. The surrounding populace is terrified, chains, bolts, guards, fires, all-night watches by the citizenry in the wake of the girl's funeral this morning, an event that the entire village, I am led to believe, attended. . . . It is more and more difficult to continue these tasks that I thought at the beginning reasonably controlled, carefully attended, would sustain me until the need had passed. But the need has *not* passed; I must admit this: the taste of blood has bought the blood's rising, and now I cannot

sleep or think for the thought of *blood*. . . . Will there
ever be an end to this? Miles from the castle in this morning's dawn, leaping the weeds like a dog, I felt a dread
depression for the first time: how long can I go on this
way? And if the fear spreads as it is seeming to, throughout the country, will I be reduced to waylaying travelers
in the fields? This is a very tricky business. I do not
know; I bounded and sniffed, fired with desire and then,
as if in a dream, saw in the weeds a child sleeping. I advanced upon the child slowly, slowly, saw as it turned
that it was a young boy and for one stumbling instant
considered: I have never before attacked a child, and it
was with a feeling of ominousness, of a line crossed never
to be traversed over again, that I fell upon the boy in the
bushes and attached my mouth to his, then biting, biting
down, taking the neck in that familiar spot, smaller and
more fervent than I had ever known it, and, sinking the
teeth in, heard that recollected shriek as never before, a
high, pitiful whine, and I could, oh, God, have still
stopped them and fled—the boy was uninjured but
shocked; he never would have caught me—but I could
not *stop*. The first taste of blood pricked up the hairs of
the scalp like insects and the hunger was uncontrollable;
I savaged him violently and, oh, what dreams he must
have had then, rising from sleep to death and falling back
then upon the grass as I drained him.

Now, strangely at ease, my head and mouth buzzing
with sticky memories, I look out from the window to
see two men approaching the door downstairs. Local officials. They are pounding on the door. They wish to see
me.

I wipe my mouth again and inspect it in the glass, then
go down to greet them. Part of me, part of me—I admit
this—wants discovery because it will allow me to make
my explanations to the world, but another, more intelligent part, that wants to live for blood another day, does
not. They stand now cautiously, still serfs in the presence
of the fiefdom their hands apologetically clasped as they
wait for response . . . and I know that I will have no
trouble with these.

June 19: I could not sleep. After the interview I resolved to be cautious for some days, allow the terror to
subside, but at midnight I sat in the bed, all fibers trembling, and knew that I must drink again. The constabulary
are confused, there are no clues, I had no difficulty in
getting rid of my two visitors, already sunk by class differences into a pool of trepidation: yes, I have heard of
these horrible events, gentleman; who has not heard of
them? Yes, I am entirely dismayed; no, I have myself
observed nothing amiss in the neighborhood; yes, I am
taking protective measures; no, I have no idea of who the
assailant might be; yes, I will cooperate fully with any de-
veloping investigation; no, there are no clues. No clues,
no ideas, no assistance, gentleman: I am sorry! And they
took their leave of the premises as, I regret to say, some
of my victims have taken leave of their senses, quickly,
gracelessly, shambling off the terrain. And now I sit
hunched over these notes like a snail, knowing—*knowing*
—that all wise counsel would lead me to *desist* for a few
days—Few days! Few *weeks* is more like it—until the investigation has collapsed into false evidence or futility or
until some hapless peasant has been brought in and
charged with the crimes: I should stop! Lie low! Solder
my forces together! But I cannot, and I know that before the sun has come, I will go a-hunting again.

I know that what I have done, what I seek to do, comes
not from cruel or cold impulses, but from love—*love!*
—of all humanity, a desire as I have already said, I think
(I never review these entries after I have written them;
the moment to be seized is the next, and the past is but
a dream), for connection, blending, a fusion of forces, but
I am gravely misunderstood; throughout the countryside
my motives have never been approbated, but they have
been ignored, and my two visitors spoke of "atrocities"
with lowered eyes, referring delicately to certain "wounds
about the neck and facial features" that marked the assailant as a "madman," and how I wanted to cry unto
them *no madman but one who would turn the ancient
ritual to fresh necessity* but said nothing of the sort, of
course, sitting quietly, rubbing nobleman's fingers into a

palm, tapping a foot on the floor and giving quick little twitching nods of assent so that they would believe in my own horror of these crimes. In part I want to be caught and to confess, this is true, but I do *not* want to confess and be caught; if they can have me I will tell them all, but cannot myself into their hands willingly commit. And now the need is strong within me; the need growing like seed within the vitals and I can barely hold this pen any longer; I must go upon the fields like a hound and *show* them that I am no fiend, but destined for the purposes of love.

June 20: Now I think of torture. Blood is weak liquid; it will not serve indefinitely, and what I am beginning to understand is that my error in taking my victims might have been the absence of confrontation: one shuddering gasp in the night, one thrust of the mouth, shrieks, whines and death following, but that singing instant in which they would see me and *understand* what is being done to them and *why* has been lacking. There must be something darker and stronger; I must bind them and bring them to awareness.

I do not know what is happening to me. I fear that I am losing control, and yet the thoughts of torture would strike one more as a *gaining* of control, would they not? A supersedence, sense of motion, accession to a higher mountain of purpose, and yet six decaying generations of vanished nobility yet admonish and hold me back. Is it *right,* Count? They seem to want to know. Do you really think that these are acts of nobility? Have you considered your forebears and your *history?* I cannot rip these little threads of advisement from my consciousness; they run through and around like bright ribbons, and yet I know now that until I do so I will never be free. Must go on, I must go on, then, if I am to plant that seed of love that will flower and in two hundreds years will cover the continent in its fields of yellow and red, blazing.

Not to talk upon what happened in the moors last night. Never to talk about it. That is a closed incident. That is *finished*. I will not think of it and instead will meditate upon the antique and honorable history of torture which, as we know, has been used by the best governments throughout all of the ages, for the betterment of men and the continued ascension toward their goals. Can a man be less than his governments? Or must he, rather, strive ever to be more?

June 21: Curiously spiritless today; able to accomplish nothing. A feeling of sea change, movement toward another level, uninterested in blood, no thoughts of the cords of the neck snapping as incline the head toward the perpetrator. No thoughts of any kind; moving underwater like an unformed creature of the depths, heading toward another shoal.

Constabulary by today, on another routine visit, they told me deferentially. Pressure from the capital now to solve the mystery; panicky reports from the provinces are upsetting the balance of the country. Any further ideas? No. Any strangers in the neighborhood? No. Have I lived in this castle for all of my life alone as is rumored? No; not for all of my life, but it has indeed been for a very long time. Any living relatives? Gentlemen, not even any *dead* relatives. Thank you, thank you. Fools: fools. If all that my quest has accomplished is to bring officials like these to stumbling, apologetic search, then I have accomplished nothing. *Nothing.*

Too depressed to go on. Everything changing. Tomorrow, a new purpose, I feel.

June 22: That business on the moors, feeling his body break and open under mine, the blood *leaping* at me, choking, drowning in it, an agressive dying, that, and his whimpers not horrified but somehow placative. Realized then, still realizing, that this cannot continue; that the taking of their blood was never the answer. But I said— I *said*—I will not write or think of this anymore, and I will not. I will not. A closed incident.

Still spiritless, but a feeling of gathered energy. Large events in the offing; a sensation of having passed the last barriers. In dreams my fate was never so stricken, my consequences so large: I sat at my mother's bosom and drank and drank of her, the infant's thoughts as aimless as a fly buzzing on paper, locked to her uncomprehending of destiny, but all of that, all of that is now and eternally departed. There is no return of any sort; panels fall like eggs at the bowels of this rotting castle and my misery tonight is so great that were they to appear at the gates again, I would deliver myself unto them quickly, dumbly, the gallows a beckoning ring beyond.

June 23: Young, another young girl, coming to, conscious, terrified now, looking frantically for escape, still trying to measure the situation, the bright bruise on her forehead where I had struck her to unconsciousness exploding with blood, looking, looking, then trying to move and screaming as she saw that she was bound. Hands bound, feet bound, trussed together, loop within loop, lying in the cellar like a fowl. *"Kyrie eleison,"* she said, but liturgy means nothing to me. I showed her the knife. I bounced the light from the knife into her eyes and she gasped with strain; I saw that she might faint and yanked her chin around to face me, putting the knife against her cheek so that she would stay in the valley of the sane. "Listen to me," I said, "now, listen to me." And once again I opened my cloak so that she would confront me. "This is me," I said, "do you understand that? It's me! *Don't turn away!"*

"Oh, my God. My God. . . ."

"God will not save you now; neither will he take you. Only the anti-Christ will have your soul when I am done, but not yet, not yet. Do you know why you are here?"

"Help me. Please help me. . . ."

"No help," I said, *"no help!"* She would not listen. None of them ever listened. This is the horror of it: even at this moment, when all is done, *none of them are listening.* "I'm going to torture and kill you," I said, "but I want to tell you why." She inhaled and seemed about to faint again; I had to use the knife. It opened up a small wedge in her cheek. *"I want to tell you why."*

"Help me," she said again, mindlessly, "help me." Stupidity, fear, loss, the savage waste of it all. Yet one must go on. Whatever one makes of it: *one must go on,* there being no alternative to any of this but the grave. Her head rolled to the side, her eyes staring like a corpse, tongue protruding from the panic, but I knew then that she was listening.

"Hear me," I said, "hear why I am doing this; one of you, somehow, must listen." Perhaps I was somewhat out of control. My mental state throughout these recent months, and now accelerating in some unknown way, has been precarious. "I wanted to know love. I wanted to change the face of the time. I wanted to carry a message and burn that message deep into the heart of this continent: that we must truly know one another and whether that knowledge is known through pain or lust, connection or fury, it must be known—we must break through to a level of feeling we have never had before, because it is this and only this that separates us from the beasts, and if we do not have it, well, then we shall surely die." She squawked in place, held by the bonds. "And death," I said, "death is as nothing to the pain of ignorance; to know our humanity is to cherish eternity." And saying this, saying no more, I brought the knife down upon and through her, spreading her like a rack of meat and then . . .

And then enough. I cannot bear to continue; these notes shriek to me; the pen itself feels like a knife in the hands and cannot continue. Her blood, when I was finished, tasted stale and weak against my lips, no longer the ingestion of vitality but a drinking in of the death, and illness overcame me; in revulsion I vomited and then dropped the knife, staggered from the basement and came up here to this high turret where with the laughter of all ancestors around me, mad and rising laughter, I went to these notes, but I simply cannot continue; I cannot continue, gentlemen, for I know now that I have failed.

And will somehow have to dispose of her now.

June 24: Odors wafting up from the basement and something must be done, but I cannot do it. I cannot summon the energy to move her, although if I do not move her, I will not be able to save myself. Have sat at this desk all day, watching the light and the dark, moving in slow convulsions of moods but can do nothing: not eat, not drink, not even relieve myself. A feeling that all is ending.

June 25: The house stinks, the boards rot; I should put her in a sack and drag her upon the moors, and yet, yet I still cannot. Search parties in the fields. I can see them from the distance and the temptation is awful, it is absolute, to go outside and beckon them into the castle. "Here she is," I would say, "I killed her; just take her out of the basement and do with me what you will." And it would be over, but what then? What then? I cannot even find the energy now to contemplate my own outcome.

June 26: The castle stinks, these rooms stink, I stink myself, my own flesh oozing corruption. It is impossible that the stain of implication does not waft through the air for a square of ten miles, so awful is it here. In the distance I see the two officials at last; they are moving toward this castle at a good speed and behind them is a party of men, ten or twenty in number it must be, hard to tell, do not know, deference is no longer their gait, detachment no longer their duty, but instead they seem impelled by urgency, and in only a minute or so they will be at the door and this time I know they will not knock.

I could still flee. There is time yet; hurl myself into my robes and scuttle out the back way, make haste across the fields and by dawn bribe my way by carriage to the capital and into anonymity. I could blend for fifty years into the capital and no one would ever be the wiser, and it is tempting, quite tempting: after all, I do not want to burn anymore, alas, than any of my victims.

But I will not do it. I know this. I do not have the energy to flee. I will remain at this desk until the shouts have coursed their way from ground level to the stairs and then like blood in an artery run their way up here. I will sit at this desk completing these pitiful notes (which can never be completed) that have attempted to explain so much and have, I know, explained so little, I will sit and sit, the pool of odors coming over me, and at last they will open the door and seize me in a grasp like iron, my presence the implication, and as I bare my neck to them, waiting for that bite of salvation that will free me at last of these wretched and timeless burdens, I know that I will hang frozen in the air for a long, long time, the knowledge at last pulsing through me that for me, at least, that Bite will never come . . . and that I will have to face the consequences of my mortality.

Introduction to
GETTING AROUND

The name of the game, at least in the literature (which
is not to say that it has totally overtaken the middle
classes; wait a generation, or six months, anyhow), is
polymorphous-perverse; sexuality not harnessed or narrowed, but extended toward new activities or combina-
tions in the name of liberation. Who is to say that this is
wrong? Only iconoclastic types like myself might still hold
that variety comes from delimitation, just as great art
comes from compression . . . and they'd merely be talking out of envy. Clearly, if we are entering the era where
everyone will have a college degree, no one will have to
know how to read, everyone will make a hundred thou a
year and no one will be able to get a tankful of gas . . .
we are similarly entering the era of liberation in which
everyone will be liberated and no one will be able to do
much of anything.

My old friend, the commissioning editor, asked for the
"ultimate story of perverse sexuality," in search of this
one. I do not myself believe in ultimates—if everything
is an ultimate, then standards collapse; if everyone
is somebody, then no one's anybody—but they make
packaging easier and also convince publishers that they
know what they are doing . . . not another anthology, but
an "ultimate." Like the search for the apocalyptic orgasm
that will make further orgasms unnecessary, the quest for
ultimates will go on . . . at four cents, sometimes even
five cents, a word, against pro-rata royalty share, of
course.

GETTING AROUND

—I would very much like to have sex with you and think that we've reached that point of our relationship where it's become inevitable.

—So do I.

—But before we begin, I'm afraid I have a confession to make, and no getting around it. You see, I have no penis.

—Oh.

—Yes, I was born that way.

—Well, that's nothing to be so terribly ashamed of. Medical science is doing wonderful things nowadays; progress is being made in many areas. Perhaps you could . . .

—Oh, you're right about medical science. Until three years ago I had no arms and legs; six months ago I had no vocal cords. They're putting me together step by step, as you can see. But they haven't tackled the penis problem yet. They say I'm not ready for that yet. Maybe in a little while. . . .

—Oh, I'm sure they will! Doctors are *so* wonderful!

—In the meantime, I can offer you oral sex, manual sex, polymorphous, perverse sex . . . oh, many things. I hope that will be satisfactory.

—It sounds wonderful.

—I'm so glad that I told you this rather than having you discover it on your own.

—I'm glad, too. You mean you were born without arms, legs and vocal cords?

—Yes.

—You must have had a very unhappy childhood.

—Oh, no. You see, I didn't have a brain, either.

—Now I'm excited. I'm *really* excited.

—Let's go to the bedroom.

II

Dear Lucinda: I know that this letter will do me no good and that writing you in this way is an infantile gesture and yet, somehow, I cannot control myself even though at this moment I hear your calm, reasonable voice saying as you look at me out of those penetrating eyes, "Herbert, you're making a very bad mistake. Herbert, you're an emotional fool." And so I am, Lucinda, I am an emotional fool; but nevertheless, looking at you across the room at the Intermix again last night, seeing you in the arms of others, your body open and sprawling before them (as it had opened and sprawled before *me* at the Intermix before), I could not, somehow—and this must be faced squarely, so I will face it—could not somehow escape strong feelings of *jealousy* and *desire,* because I wanted you very much, Lucinda, and was hurt to know that since I was not in your assigned group last night I could not have you.

I know better than you do the pointlessness of these feelings and how more than anything else they must work against the *spirit* of the Intermix, which is liberation through exposition to various levels of contact and partner (I can quote this jargon even better than you might think, being, as you know, a copywriter), but nevertheless, I feel impelled to give you these feelings straight out because one of the other lessons of the Intermix is the *freeness and openness* between persons as a result of the experience, and how can I be free and open with you, my beloved Lucinda, if I sit upon this well of feeling that was opened by seeing you held by others whose delight I could not share since I was not last night a member of your activity group?

Well, this is no way for you to answer this, Lucinda, no way whatsoever; what has to be faced as well (and even in my misery I counsel my own openness and hence will face it) is that you are not terribly bright, my dear: an impulsive being who lives very close to your emotional surfaces and their immediate response, you lack the capacity for *pain,* which I feel, Lucinda, and doubtless have very little idea of what I am talking about.

But just this, then, saying just this: looking at you across the room, held by another (I do not recall her name; a pleasant, heavy, suffering girl who lives on the lower western section of the city, I believe, and who I have seen a few times at Intermix, although never so intimately), I felt pain the dimensions of which I will not explain to you and the rising of an ancient, almost absent desire, something that I thought did not exist anymore; it was the desire to have you exclusively for my own in some world where Intermix did not exist and where we could lie on fields, say, green fields inhabited by grass and sheep, and we would hold one another and roll on that grass, overcome by the evil design of possession, and in this world, where Intermix did not exist, I would not have to share you, and in my unseemly need for you this image cajoled me over the edge, and before I quite knew what had happened I had dumped into this pleasant, heavy girl a vast, suffering load drawn from me not into *her,* but into some image of *you;* I know that there is no hope for me, Lucinda, I know that there is no hope whatsoever, but I found myself unable to stay away from this letter, and if only I can gain the courage I will drop it through the delivery chute and what will you say, what will you *say* when you read it? No, I cannot go on this way; "Herbert, you are a fool." I hear your admonition now, and saying no more, knowing that I am indeed a fool, I will only instead dispose of this and . . .

III

Notes for Orientation Lecture (copyright, (c), 1981; unauthorized use or duplication strictly prohibited):

a) Post-technological era; shift of culture toward consumption-orientation.

b) Love ideal as culture lag; love ideal linked to

pre-consumption culture in which *denial* was celebrated.

c) Need for new ethic in post-technological, consumption-oriented culture. More in tune with times.

d) Goal-oriented behavorism. History, *cf* Skinner.

e) Historical roots of Intermix: Encounter, group sex as primitive efforts. Lack of systematization.

f) The need to systematize as the key to post-technological relationships and thinking.

g) Huber, 1975, and the Code of Intermix. The history of Huber, early defeats, misunderstandings, hostility as evidences of culture lag.

h) The heroism of Huber, fight against establishment, Skinnerian ideal versus Freudian cant. How it prevailed.

i) Establishment of the Institute, the acceptance of Intermix.

j) Early versions of Intermix: homosexuality, multiple sexual behavior, animal perversions. Superseded in the search for the heterosexual ethic.

k) The establishment of the heterosexual ethic.

l) Present success of Intermix, acceptance of the Institute, Intermix as goal-directed behavior, as healthful and super-cession of neuroses. Etc.

m) Possible future of Intermix. Eastern cultures, pre-technological cultures, polygamous cultures, the adaptation of the code.

n) Intermix and religion.

IV

—I feel so terribly awkward.

—Just relax.

—You see, it's my very first time here; previously I . . .

—There must be a first time for everyone. Just relax.

—I was a monogamist for many years until my wife and I had a misunderstanding. . . .

—You had a wife? How amusing.

—That's how I feel about it.

—What a strange sect! I knew you looked terribly quaint when you came through the door.

—Well, yes, yes. I make no excuses, of course; it's all completely my own fault.

—Come here, you strange little man.

—I'm a little frightened and nervous. But I *am* responding. There! Can't you see I'm responding?

—Of course you are. I always knew you would.

—I'm glad that they gave me a specialist for my first time.

—Well, of course. Yes, you can do that. Ah! Do it more, more, more.

—My wife always liked that, too. She said . . .

—Don't say anything about your wife! You must not mention your wife! Do you want to ruin everything?

—No, of course not.

—Then concentrate on the present. In Intermix you live in present time. Intermix destroys the past and future and uses the ingredients in the timeless present. That is the theory. There! You're doing much better.

—Thank you.

—You'll do even better than that if you'll just close your eyes.

V

Dear Lucinda: Last night, although it has been several weeks, perhaps I am thinking of months, since you switched from the group and I last saw you I found myself thinking of you again and, try as I could to combat that image, that sudden, shrieking, poisonous image of you that rose before my eyes like a sheet, staring at me bland and expressionless, eyes dense with knowledge, try as I could to combat that image, as I said, I found myself hopelessly battering at it, moving my way as if on a staircase of feeling higher and higher against you, and at the moment of climax with a partner I cannot even remember now (how dark glows my sin!), it was into you I came, into you, blessed Lucinda, and now I know truly that I

am damned, for after the session I did not as proper render full explanation and appreciation to my partner (s),
but instead rushed from the Intermix in awkward haste
and silence, stumbling down corridors, your face shrieking
its way through my being as I came back to these rooms,
and even at this moment I cannot forget you; I cannot
eliminate this feeling; I know now that it is too late for
me, and realizing that if I were to mail this letter (I have
never mailed you any of my letters), sure destruction
would result for the two of us, I want you to know that I
am destroying this and then will take the capsules that
will end my life.

Oh Lucinda, Lucinda, it was never to be, but I will say
it and be damned, say it and know the vengeance of Huber through a thousand centuries of afterlife, say it and
then end: we should have been monogamous and I should
have should have should have had you alone, but I
know . . .

VI

—I see that you've received your penis.

—Yes, I got it just today; isn't it beautiful? And
it's guaranteed to work without fail ninety-nine times out
of a hundred or they'll fix it free. Forever.

—Oh, I'm so pleased for you! Are you complete now?

—Except for a few last touch-ups and details. They're
going to put feeling in next Thursday.

Introduction to
TRACK TWO

Track Two is a reverent and doctrinal story, in my opinion: the journal of Christ—I want to explain this—as it might have been written if he had not known of or believed in his divinity—but it wasn't reverent or doctrinal enough for the religious anthology in which it was supposed to appear, and I therefore sold it to *Amazing*, which through the years has been, along with its sister publication, *Fantastic,* one of the more tolerant and receptive of markets to my most ambitious work and which has published for the first time a lot of stories that otherwise might not have found an audience.

So it is often in science fiction—the best later work of C. M. Kornbluth appeared in the penny-a-word S-F magazines; Phillip Jose Farmer, that great innovator, was forced to do his work in *Startling* or *Thrilling Wonder* because the three-cent-a-word markets were afraid of him—and so it always will be. Robert Silverberg recalls one major market in the '50s as "wanting only to say positive things," and another as "wanting to say nothing at all," and this was one of the reasons why he got out of the field almost entirely for six or seven years. The ambition and topical courage of an S-F magazine appears to be in direct inverse relation to the size of its audience, which is unfortunate . . . but which at least makes the life of a penny-a-word editor gratifying, as I know from my own experience. (There is a great deal of very good stuff floating around; as editor of *Amazing Stories* myself back in 1968, I routinely saw ten to fifteen manuscripts a month by recognized professionals better than anything published in *Analog,* or for that matter, *Playboy*.) And these restrictions do not apply to the original S-F anthologies, another stab of optimism.

In fact, the magazines (except for *Analog* and *F & S F*) are dying and the original anthologies flourishing, I believe, for precisely this reason.

———◆———

TRACK TWO

Track One: "Don't be ridiculous," he says, poised on the cross, looking down where a group of the mercenaries now appear to be casting lots over his vestments. Or something of that nature; very hard to tell from this aspect. "None of this is happening."

"You'd better believe it's happening," the man on his right said, "it's happening right now. How long do you think we have? An hour? Two hours? I say less than that." The man on his left mumbles in agreement.

He had almost forgotten about the two thieves. Silly of them, really; they had been up here all the time with him, flanking him on this damnable mountain, muttering to one another the vague complaints and curses of their profession intermingled with occasional screams of real pain . . . and he had managed to shut them out of his consciousness completely until reminded. Really quite foolish of him. On the other hand, certainly he has an excuse. None of this is happening. All of it is a dream. The two thieves are no more real than the crowds down there milling around, watching the soldiers gambling for his clothing, no more real than the pain of the nails or the blasted heat itself. None of it exists.

"Don't you understand?" he says, quite reasonably he thinks under all these circumstances. "None of this exists. I'm merely having a nightmare. As is well known, the kingdom was established and I, the Son of Man, reigned forever and ever, just as predicted in the testaments. Of course, there was a little bit of difficulty winning the people over to my point of view, and you know the pharisees were very protective of their position, of course, but that was all to be expected. Actually, things went off without a hitch if I say so myself; it all worked out pretty well, although now and then I do have these terrible nightmares about how it might have been if I hadn't been able to prevail, and they sometimes have quite a real aspect. Like now. I'm dreaming that I'm being crucified."

"You aren't dreaming, friend," the thief to his left says, and, "This is no dream at all, pal," points out the one on his right, and swinging his head from side to side, seeing the faces of the two, some aspect of the sun comes into those faces, they refract the light, the light bounces off his eyes, then comes into a clear, thin beam that penetrates his consciousness, welds him into position, and it occurs to him for the first time that this is really going on for quite a while and he is not waking up and it is really time that he should be waking up, but . . .

Track Two: "It's not my responsibility," Pilate says. He is a small, nervous man with a habit of rubbing his palms together as if he were trying to clean them. "No, sir, it is not my responsibility at all; I'm not in a position to decide what to do." He winks, or at least seems to wink at the soldier escort, but it is only a nervous tic, for in the next moment all amiability passes from Pilate's face and confusion replaces it. "I have nothing against the man," he says. "I'm in no position to make a decision about this one way or the other. What do you want me to do?"

People surrounding him point out that they would like to see him executed. This discomforts him but he manages to fix Pilate through this with a poignant gaze that locks their eyes together and he thinks then that he is making some kind of connection. He knows that Pilate is not a bad person; actually, he is merely a minor political functionary who has been placed in a very difficult position. "Are you the King of the Jews?" Pilate asks. There seems to be sympathy in his tone.

He shakes his head. Really, there is nothing to say;

whatever comes out he will sound like a fool. If he says that he is not, then he will be taken for a madman; but if he says that he is, he will be adjudged doubly mad, and in any event, what happens to him will have nothing to do with his answer. "Well," Pilate says, shrugging, "I suggest that we put it up to a public opinion poll. Ask them outside if they want him back. There's a thief we've got in custody named Barabbas; put it to them this way: they can either have this Barabbas or they can have him. One or the other. That's fair, isn't it?" The escort seems to think that this is fair. Soldiers depart, heading toward the courtyard, and for just a moment he and Pilate are alone except for the three sullen men who hold his chains almost tentatively. "You've got to understand," Pilate says, "that I'm in a very difficult position here." He rubs his hands again, then seems to wring them out. "I have nothing against you, it's just a question of the politics here, and I'm not equipped to deal with them. Actually, I don't know the first thing about the situation."

"It's perfectly all right," he says. "This is just a dream, this never happened, and I assure you that you haven't a thing to worry about. Actually, I'm imagining all this. They never brought me into Rome."

"Well," Pilate says with a burbling little laugh, "well, well, *well,* I certainly hope *so.* It would be pretty awful if things like this were really happening, wouldn't it? What a refreshing attitude—that this is all a dream and so on. Well," he says with another wringing gesture, then gives a light little hope, "I'm just glad that you understand my point of view here." He looks up, across him, and the escort is coming back. "Yes," he says, "what have they decided?"

"They want Barabbas," someone says.

"Ah," says Pilate with a little sigh. "Well, that's certainly unfortunate, but Barabbas is an excellent man and has a fine career ahead of him, I am sure. He's very well thought of in certain circles. Give them Barabbas," he says, and then turning to him, says, "You see, it was a perfectly fair choice, I can't be blamed, and anyway, maybe you're right, maybe this is all a dream." And he turns then, waddles toward the courtyard, the chains suddenly seize him and he is being dragged away, but this is quite impossible; he came into Jerusalem riding an ass, but after that everything was entirely different. This is not real, it should stop, but . . .

Track Three: "I can't do a thing for you," he says to the woman gently. He is trying not to unsettle her further; really, the woman seems radically disturbed. "I'm sorry that you lost your husband and I'm sure that he's a wonderful man, but I cannot raise the dead from the tomb, not even your Lazarus."

"But that's ridiculous," she says, raising her arms, closing the ground between them. Now he has the feeling that the audience has expanded; the woman knows how to play to a crowd and he puts down a sudden, bitter flare of rage at her; it is really not fair to him. "The reports were quite definite from the provinces: you turn loaves and fishes and wine from themselves, you multiply objects, you heal people . . ."

"I'm afraid that the reports are incorrect," he says. "I'm really nothing but a simple carpenter from Galilee who turned to the rabbinate a few months ago because I felt a calling. You know how these stories from the provinces can be exaggerated. Actually, I don't perform miracles; the miracles are within ourselves. . . ."

"You're a liar," the woman says. Her face has become constricted; she gestures toward the gravestone. "I know that you can raise him. You can bring my husband back. Bring him back! Bring Lazarus back!"

"I'm sorry, madam," he says gently, "you misunderstand the nature of miracles; miracles occur within ourselves a thousand times a day, and even to the least of us, the very act of living, loving, drawing breath, knowing God is miraculous, and we should praise God and ourselves for having that capacity, but as far as this . . ."

She reaches out and grasps him. Her fingers bend into his wrist like wire. "You're a liar," she says, "you don't *want* to raise him. If you did, you would." She swallows, then her face breaks and she is crying. "You just don't want to," she says. "It's not that you can't, it's that you don't want to. I'll give you money, I swear, I'll . . . "

"Madam," he says softly, "madam, you misunderstand." But the crowd has moved closer, the air is suddenly sweltering, there is a feeling of vast pressure and closure and he sees that the situation is about to turn ugly. There is no way that he can prove to them at this point that the reports about him are entirely false. "I'm sorry," he says, "I'm truly sorry, I mean it." And he waits for this scene, like the others, to dissolve; having said what he had to say, he waits for it to go away and the crowd comes in closer. Some of them are cursing, the crowd comes in much closer, it is really time that this dissolved, but . . .

Track Four: He is on the desert in his thirty-eighth day. "You know, I really don't want any of this. I'd much rather go back to carpentry if it were all the same," he says to Satan, with whom he has become quite intimate during this period; the old angel is the enemy, of course, but this does not preclude honest affection, even an understanding of shared travail.

"I know," Satan says. His voice is sad. "I've had the same feeling. It's not easy taking on this burden."

"I'm going to be terribly misunderstood and in the end I'll probably be put to death."

"That is very likely."

"And the question of resurrection is a very chancy one. I mean it may well happen, but I'm thirty-one years old now, and what does resurrection have to do with me? I wanted to lead a simple life."

"We all do," Satan says, sadly again. "That is all we ever wanted, all of us."

"Probably the only way that I'll be able to get through it most of the time is to make believe that it isn't happening. I'll have to deny the sense of my own mission." He kicks at some sand, discouraged. "It's disgusting," he says, "it's really quite disgusting."

"It is," Satan says, "but what's the alternative? You have to do what must be done. I've had the same problem for a long time."

"I'll probably go through a lot of things and not even accept the reality. I'll say that it's all a dream." He blinks against the sun, inhales the dry, beaten odors of the desert. "Still," he says, "some good will come of it, I hope."

"Oh, I hope so," Satan says mildly. "I certainly hope so. It's been difficult for me for a long time, you know, being alone."

"At least," he says, looking at Satan directly in an honest and appealing way, "at least even if we fight we can agree at some level to be friends, can't we?"

"Oh, yes, indeed," Satan says quietly. "Oh, very definitely. I would hope so."

"Well, then," he says, "well then. . . ." It is the thirty-eighth day and he needs a day and a half to get back, so all in all matters can no longer be postponed. He has gotten to this point: there is really nothing else to say. "Well, then," he says again and extends his arm with a friendly smile, Satan smiling back at him, the sky closing in on the two of them like a blanket, "shall we wrestle, then?"

"Indeed," says Satan, and slowly, slowly they mesh. At the first touch of the enemy's arm he is amazed at his strength, but as the match begins he knows that his strength is at least equal, and as the afternoon goes on he feels Satan begin to weaken. By nightfall he will be on the road back home. They will be waiting for him there. He will have to tell them all about this.

THE BATTERED-EARTH SYNDROME

The title of this piece was given me by Virginia Kidd (agent, editor and writer, and a good example of all three), who said that it had been haunting her for years: could I write a story utilizing it? I did the best I could.

The story appears in an anthology nominally on the theme of "ecology," actually about the end of the world; an anthology that contains twenty stories, an essay and a couple of poems about how we will surely do it to ourselves within one generation or three by fire or flood, pestilence or disease, overpop or famine, all of it written with that grim earnestness characteristic of science fiction when it is determined to Save the World. (The opposite side of this coin, of course, is scatology; as everyone knows, scratch a pornographer and find a preacher.) I cannot imagine how such a collection could be commercially viable, but apparently it is. Twenty stories about how the world will end may be just what the market needs at this point in time.

———◆———

THE BATTERED-EARTH SYNDROME

Sixty-Seventh Dream Festival: Down 46, the engine on high, the cylinders lurching power, beer cans trailing from the windows, and what in hell is that son-of-a-bitch in the old Cad up ahead trying to do to us? With a scream Nick cuts him off, pulling into lane then to move to the top of the tach and in the rearview we can see the Cad wobble, shriek, leave the road in plumes and dust. "Fuck him," Nick says, tossing a beer can out high; we see it twinkle and then fall against a motel sign. "Fuck all of *you*." Speed increases; we roll.

Laughing, tumbling, moving against one another in the back. Margo and Junior; Mickey and me. Nick alone in the front because he can only drive in solitary. *Hamburger Hurrah, Jack's Best Buys,* the *Hostess Motel,* the empty field in the distance on which the cars are stacked, stacked and stacked, burning in their haze . . . and I feel Mickey's breast under my palm, lean down to knife her with a kiss while Margo and Junior struggle—Are they really struggling? What is going on here?—and Nick rocks the car, back and forth we scoot on the lanes of 46, tremors shooting up through my ass, which increases the need; I reach for Mickey, clamber against her and at just that moment the old Cad reappears, or I think it is the old Cad, swinging out to overtake and then cutting in front and Nick, cursing, has no choice except to brake; the car screams, we all scream and go piling off the road with a jounce and clank, rolling free then across the fields and smashing with a whine into the office of the *Hostess Motel,* cheap rooms at bargain rates, transients always welcome and everything becomes bloody and confused; I fall to the seat of the car, fall past the office of the Hostess Motel, Mickey wheezing all the way, hostess herself greeting us from under an impacted bumper and, oh, goddamn it . . .

II

Sixty-Seventh Dream Festival: Coming against the wind we see the deer for the first time, poised on a ridge, blinking. Nick pokes me, hoists his rifle. "Let's get the son-of-a-bitch right now," he says and lifts the rifle. I lift my rifle, center in on the animal. "No," Nick says, "this is mine, first kill," and I lower my rifle; Nick always has first shot: Nick always drives the car. Nick always gets first crack at the ass and none of this is fair, but on the other hand, this is the way it was assigned. "Watch this," Nick says, giggling, and pulls the trigger, the deer falls, the deer opens like a bloody sack in the distance, rivers of its thin blood pouring down the ridge and the ridge becomes 46 and 46 is filled with traffic; here we are standing on the goddamned highway, cars tearing past us, the blood still coating stone, Nick giggling with panic. "They had no right, no right to do this," he says. "It isn't fair; they can't switch on us like this all the time." But too late for this nonsense; here comes a diesel and the diesel is bearing down on us, beer cans pouring from the windows and I try to brace myself for the impact, but, Jesus Christ . . .

III

Interim: "How long have you felt this way?" the short thing asks me. I would gesture to answer, but being bound as usual find it almost impossible to reply. "Tell me," the short thing says, "tell me everything from the beginning. You are being unresponsive, you know. You are being highly unresponsive."

"Go to hell," I say, which is the only reasonable statement under the circumstances, goddamn them, "leave me alone." Nick is also in the room, although I cannot see him from my particular angle of vision. He is, however, moaning and cursing throughout his own interrogation. I cannot hear the questions but I can hear his answers. Nick has not yet learned, may never learn, how to deal with them.

"You must understand," the short thing says, "that you have suffered a terrible injury, something in your own background that causes you to strike out . . . "

"Go to hell," I say. "Screw you. Drop dead. Leave me alone," and so on and so forth, struggling all the way but keeping my cool because, unlike Nick, I have learned that the situation can be managed if you *do not show temper.*

"To strike out repeatedly," the interrogator says, "and you have not yet learned; you understand that until you learn we must repeat and repeat the process. . . ."

"Oh, fuck off," I say and thrash around a bit, Nick

screams in the background, the short thing leans toward
me, simpering, fitting down the lenses again, and before I
have a chance to set myself it all begins again, but nevertheless . . .

IV

Sixty-Eighth Dream Festival: In the city I take the
short route to center, me driving this time, Nick in the
back, grinning. Gun in my back pocket, ready for use.
Never come into the city without a gun. "Take 'em over,"
Nick says, "we're going to take them over."

Cut right at the river. Now I can see the water itself;
brown it lies before us, small objects dipping and cresting
in the oily filth: cigarette cartons, prophylactics, the scent
of dead animals, a drowned car whose hood peeps up
shyly, its chrome ornamentation covered with insects.
Something floundering in the water, but I will not investigate.

"Used to be pure," Nick says, "at least that's what I
hear." And he laughs; Nick is always laughing: through
fair and foul, in whatever circumstances, that laugh carries us through. (We do everything together.) Kill the
engine. To our left, way down on the docks, we hear
screams as bodies are unloaded into the water. "Two hundred years ago it was clean," Nick says. "Wonder what
happened to it?"

"Who knows?"

"Going to take over the city," Nick murmurs. "Going
to take over this thing. Let me out." He leans against his
door, it heaves open, he staggers to the ground and wan-
ders toward the river. I get out and follow him at a distance, touching my gun. This is Nick's idea; I would not
interfere. Dream-festivals alternate, or in any event this
is the rumor. Nick looks over the river, small shapes bobbing in there as we come closer, swaddled in murk. "Look
at it," he says, "look at this." He unzips his fly and pisses
in the river.

"Good," I say, "good, good." And I try to do the same,

but when I make the attempt something has happened to
my urethra, or perhaps it is only tension I am talking
about; I am unable to release water and stand there
pinned against the river, foul wind rising and against my
eyes, the wind bringing tears as I lock there unable to
finish, Nick smirking at me and this one goes on for a
long time, too goddamned long by far and how much of
this can I take and oh goddamn them all . . .

V

Later we prowl the city looking for a Kill, but there is
no one at large in the city; they have heard the reports
and are locked in. Up and down the blocks we drive, the
motor whimpering, the car squeaking, and finally pull
to the side against a gutted building in which mad dogs,
held by chains, bark. There is a CONDEMNED sign on the
building and underneath it writing saying that the area
will be renewed, but I am more interested by the dogs,
who scream in human voices. "Big buggers," Nick says.
Chewing gum now and taking out his guns, he shoots the
dogs. One, two, three, flopping in the stillness. "They're
going to renew this," Nick says, moving from the car to
ease a foot between railings and kick at the carcasses.
"Wonder what it's going to be like?"

"Beautiful. It will be beautiful."

"Renewal," Nick says, "renew everything." And he
puts a few more bullets into the corpses, they shake, the
CONDEMNED sign falls to the walk with a clang, and as
Nick and I turn toward one another to face this new situation I see something in his eyes and he sees something
in mine and it must be the same thing because I realize
that we have nothing left in the world to do and where
the hell is the car and how did we get here and what are
they doing to us and what is this supposed to prove and
anyway . . .

VI

"Measures," the short thing says, "we must take measures. You are not responding. You fail to show insight. We are becoming impatient."

"What do you want?" I say. "What do you want of us?"

"We want you to understand. We want you to realize the source of your acts. We want to change lives, incorporate understanding, help, you know. . . ."

"I don't need any of it, Jack," I say and close my eyes. "Get lost with your insights and understanding, because this is our life and we are the future, and that is exactly the way that everything is supposed to be."

"You don't realize," the short thing says. It is gibbering. Although I find it impossible to deduce expressions from the alienness, I can sense that it has lost control of the situation, or so fears. "You are not even trying. We've never had anything like this. Your responses are totally blocked; you will not even accept the reality of what you have created. We want to help you, but . . . "

"But *what?*" I ask. I turn for the first time to look for Nick, but he is not there, which is unusual; this is my first solitary situation. "Don't do me no favors."

"But you won't be helped. You won't even accept empirical verification. Never before have we had . . . "

"Where is he? Where is Nick?"

"Your friend," the short thing says, "your friend is not here anymore. He was unable to make adjustments."

"You mean you cracked him?"

"We will not talk about your friend. We will talk only about you. Your situation . . . "

"You broke his mind," I say bitterly. "You broke Nick. You and your damned dream festivals. Those aren't dream festivals. . . ."

"We will not discuss this. We will fixate upon your own situation—your need to strike out, your need to abuse. Don't you realize? The environment is not discreet; it is bound to you. You are your world. And, furthermore . . . "

It is babbling. The short thing is babbling. I stand, I throw off the shackles (they were only a state of mind) and confront it whole.

"I'm not afraid anymore," I say. "There's nothing you can do with my mind."

"You don't understand. It is only your mind that exists; only your mind that . . . "

"You can't touch me. I can do everything I want to do. You broke Nick, but I'm stronger than him and you'll never break me."

"Punish," the short thing says, "the urge to brutalize. The uncontrollable urge, why, my God, you people are . . . " It stops, seems to gain some control. "Stop this," it says in a harsher tone. "This will get you nowhere."

"Yes it will."

"You will simply re-enact over and again impulses that you can never purge. You will destroy . . . "

"Free," I say. "I'm free." I back away from the thing and will myself from the room. This is the way that it is done. There are no doors in their rooms. Ever. Nor rooms in their dream festivals. The room flickers, I depart.

"You fool," the thing says behind me, "you brutal *fool.*" But it's too late for any of that. Now I am gone and like Nick I will learn to piss in the river.

VII

Sixty-Ninth Dream Festival: I lie in emptiness, the sands absorb me. In the dream I have then, *Hamburger Hurrah, Jack's Best Buys* and the *Hostess Motel* are burning, but I do not feel the flame; I am encased in ice and everything moves away slowly and then more quickly and I wait to come out of this dream festival as I have come out of all the others and I wait and I wait and I wait and oh Jesus Christ now, goddamnit, I was just trying to shape the thing up and I wait and I wait . . .

Introduction to
NETWORK

This story as a reasonable projection of the future city at the time it was written (December of 1971) may turn out to be a wrong guess, which would be happy news to the few urbanites among us (I am no longer one) who believe that it is possible to live, with children, in a decent and dignified way in the great metropolitan centers.

What may have undercut this well-informed guess is the so-called energy crunch, which, as I write this—February, 1974—has already appeared to have reversed the urban-suburban flight, keeping people in the cities during weekends, bringing city life at night to life again, leading many suburbanites to consider a return to the city for lack of commuting fuel, and so on. Indeed, the energy crunch has had substantial side-effects, not all of them dire: families who despise one another are saved indefinitely from the necessity to visit at distances of more than ten miles round-trip. "Forgot to get the tank filled on Friday, Mom, and I have two gallons left until Tuesday to get the kids to the hospital if they should fracture an arm. Sorry. I'll call you next week." This need not be tragic. Also, adolescents will be able to get down to the desired business at hand without wasting hours and gallons in the ritual preliminaries of cruising. As one born at the darkest end of the 1930s and raised toward maturity during the happy and free era of the 1950s, I can only applaud this. It *does* seem to be a little better for the kids, cynics like myself notwithstanding, and if it's better for them it will be better for all of us, someday.

This leads a long way from *Network,* which is quite a savage story, written, incidentally, partially in tribute to that remarkable (if remarkably uneven) writer, Harlan Ellison.

NETWORK

Sitting in the enclosure of the Institute, *Death and Disorder 104,* watching on film the great events of the past, now darkly receded from us. Zapruder frame 333 *et seq.,* old Kennedy getting his brains blown through, a clear, rosy halo surrounding the skull for one tricky instant, then collapse, mortality, apotheosis. Kennedy II holding onto himself on the floor of the kitchen, Williams and Connell knocked off the speaker's stand during the Jubilation of '93, locked in parody of homosexual embrace by the grenade: falling, falling. Watts making the changes again, the colors of Chicago in the '70s, switch again to close-up on Hendrickson's mouth as Hayes blows his fusion away. Color and more color, the sound billowing around us, four hundred (survey course) in the tight room, Jigger's knee prodding against mine. I prod back, think emptily of connection, of taking him by the hand, leading him from this room and somewhere in one of the cubicles to the rear, grasping and grasping him again, making all of our own changes as the film rolls and the band plays on. But no time for lust, not in *Death and Disorder 104*; now Wallace grabs his stomach in the shopping center, melting all passions away to the stones and the lights go on, the film snaffles off. Jigger and I, we blink our eyes by the stabs of light, stab at them, murmur, look at the floor. Through the megaphones, the lecture begins.

"Commonalities," the voice of a man now dead, taped ten years ago, says to us through all the sides of the room, "commonalities, common denominator, root causes to be sunken out. For what do we see here? What underlay, what link?" Jigger and I wink at one another, touch hands in the pause. "All of this," the speakers say, "occurred in the cities. Urbanopolis, agglomeration, cultural flux and

223

flow and lag, all known and known again in those great
population centers which, in the mid-part of the twentieth
century, became base mode of existence for upward of
seventy percent of all tenants of the country. Do you understand this?"

There are rasps on the tape, mumbles and grumbles
of response throughout the room. Intervals for answer are
an archaic feature of the tape and are certainly laugh-
able, but on the other hand, *Death and Disorder 104* has
a well-deserved reputation as being one of the easiest
electives available within the second-year context of the
Institute, and Jigger and I, as we have put up with so
many other things, can put up with the issue of inadequate tapes.

"Solution, so long staring authorities in their collective
faces, the rising alienation and violence in a direct correlation with the incidence of the urban centers and the
compression of their population, finally became apparent
to them through a series of discoveries and researches too
complicated to be passed over lightly and which will be
significant subject matter of this course. Authorities, seeing this solution at last, were first hesitant to seize the
moment, then hastened themselves along that course so
long ordained embarrassed, but now picking up the time.
The *death and disorder problem was the urbaniza-
tion problem.* By solving first the one, the other could be
solved. By eliminating the symptom, one could control
the disease. And so," the speaker concludes, the voice,
unmodulated, shrieking by flutters into a whine, "so then
in its elegance was the period of dispersion commenced,
and from that period the flowering of the culture we now
enjoy as well as the creation of the Institute to maintain
continued vigilance."

Film again: the Network seen from a great height, fifty
miles or more, swaddled in its vapors, its outlines vaguely
perceived jagged, cutting like sores through the overcast.
Southway, Easto, Northing, Westfield, pan in, straight
zooming drop into the banks of Westfield, cans drifting
in the oiled waters, scattering through the pilings. Intercut
with Zapruder again, split-screen technique and then out

with the high sound of music in the distance. Richly does *104* deserve its reputation. Not thirty minutes into the first class of the first session, the speaker says, "Orientation concluded. Early dismiss. Follow your reading lists and report tomorrow." And the lights go on, discovering us in the hall again, Jigger and I knee to knee, tapping fingers together, while in other rows couples and threes in-similar embarrassing positions pull themselves apart reluctantly. Time to get back to quarters.

"Time to get back to quarters," Jigger says. He looks at me and winks; I feel the stirrings again. We have thirty minutes' free time until *Containment and Jurisdiction 19;* time enough. It is time enough.

"Time enough," I say, and Jigger laughs.

Gut course.

II

I dream that I am lying near the pilings of Westo, watching the sun collapse into the water across, arms behind my head, knees pointed to the sky, Jigger behind me and close. In my ear I hear the voice of a Supervisor. "What are you doing here?" he says. "Don't you realize that the Network is off-limits to all but approved personnel and suitably protected research teams from the Institute? How did you get here? Don't you realize that you could get killed? We cannot take the responsibility."

"Cannot take the responsibility!" Jigger gurgles. "Cannot take the responsibility!" I shout, and leaping into the breach we yank pilings from their root and with much abandonment beat the Supervisor around the face and arms, laughing. "Brutes!" he screams. "Disgusting brutes. You've become as bad as *them;* you've become one of the gangs!" And this fills us with great excitement and glee; we beat him harder. Deep in Westo, under the collapsed sun, laughing with the strangeness of it all, Jigger and me, we beat the Supervisor into the dust of Network, and it is as if with him we are beating the Institute itself, the whole stupid Institute with its *Death and Disorder* and *Contain-*

ment and Jurisdiction and *Basic Lethal Processes* themselves, and, oh, my, oh, my, the pleasure of this! But then I awake from that strangled doze to find that our thirty minutes and more have passed and it is time for Jigger and me, however reluctantly, to heave our way to class, and although this is only the first week of our sophomore year, I am stunned by the bleakness of it all, and within me, like a tiny mad animal, an idea formulates and beats away with its little claws: there must be a way out of this and we will find it or Jigger is not Jigger and I am not his forever on all the shores of Westo.

III

At night I propose the idea at Commons and he is interested. "Yes," he says, his eyes narrowing to the Jigger slant, "yes, yes, indeed, but there is much to be done." He puts down his fork, calculates. "We'll need a car. We'll need to cover our time. We'll need to find a way past the Barriers. We'll need firearms and explosives and gas when they crawl out to attack us." His eyes weave merrily under his bleak forehead. "But let's do it," he says. "Won't it be something? Field research and contact." He pats me on the hand. "It's the right idea."

It is the right idea. I have always had the right ideas; even when I am wrong, the formulations are basic. Life in the Institute is pleasant and dull, dull and pleasant, contained and simple; it gives us nothing that will not add to our knowledge, but on the other hand, we are given nothing as well that can test that knowledge. Now it is time for breakout, field research, extrapolation, an understanding of those elements for which we are being conditioned and that someday we must control. From the abandoned armory on the far side of the grounds I find a gasoline car in running condition; past the curfew hour I risk discovery by tinkering with it, bringing it to operative status and filling it with contraband fuel from the secret pump that Jigger and I discovered by the athletic grounds in our freshman year. Barrier check we will simply have to negotiate on our own; no other preparations can be made. From some awesome cache that he will not reveal, Jigger produces: one antique pistol, five hand grenades and two handfuls of poison capsules. "In case we are captured by the savages," he says, winking, "and find it necessary to do the deed."

"Don't be ridiculous," I say, feeling a tickle of horror. Jigger has a baroque sense of humor; sometimes I do not fully understand him. "We'll be perfectly safe. They're shy of outsiders and keep to themselves. Their feuds are internal; you know that."

"No, I don't know that," Jigger says grimly, flipping me a handful of the capsules; they scatter like little insects and I have to scramble to pick them up one by one from the floor and under furniture: disastrous consequences if they were discovered on room check. "I know only that we've been *taught* that. But there is a difference between what they *want* us to know and what actually *exists,* and that is what we are going to find out. Unless," he says and pauses, "unless, of course, you've changed your mind and don't want to go."

"I want to go."

"The savages may seize your brain and destroy your mind."

"Don't be silly."

"They may pass upon us the oaths of their tribes and torture us to death."

"Nothing will happen."

"Bands of them may encircle the car and approach with rifles, screaming."

"Enough," I say, "enough." And Jigger is laughing, I am laughing, both of us are laughing in that room and then clutching one another, and that is enough discussion for one night; and the next, the very next, right after the last class and before the weekend hiatus, we leave the Institute to begin our journey into the Network. We will be missed and there will be inquiries and on Monday surely there will be retribution, but we are not concerned. We will bring back first-hand reports. We are not the first. This has happened before. Boys, they will be reminded then, *boys will be boys*. Even in this year of 2019, the human spirit is imperishable. . . .

We will remind them.

IV

So Jigger and me, Friday night, we go into the Network. The car snaffles at the road like a beast in search of water, dangling its mufflers like dugs, but then remembers its heritage and begins to settle into a droning, incessant forty, moving us toward the ruined skyline. Jigger sits an uneasy distance from me, working on the ups and downs while I apply myself to the brakes, the steering, the accelerator, half-remembered pages of exposition from the manual opening themselves up to me as I ease the car through the dangerous roads now vacant, the lights probing like insects through the dark. We are quite alone, twelve miles of road from the Institute to the checking gate, at that gate a young guard, strangely smooth cat with grief-stricken eyes, holding up a hand like a display in an old poster. The stopping is unusual; we know from our informal knowledge of procedure that the checkpoints are not applied severely these days. There is so little traffic, after all, into the Network. The underlying philosophy, as it has been often expressed, is that anyone who wants to go in there deserves exactly what he gets, but every time you decide that the policies and procedures definitely do not apply, they will pull a reverse, proving that rambles in the dormitories of the Institute are not complete conditioning for the lives of us nowadays. Jigger spreads against the door as we stop, putting his feet on the upholstery, illustrating the distance between us to the guard with slow circles of his hand. Homosex is accepted; the purges and convulsions of the last century are long gone . . . but outside the borders of the Institute, moving into the Barrier, it is best to be circumspect. "You'd better forget it," the guard says, his gaze nervous and transfixed, locked far above our level, weaving out the sky. "Things are battering tonight." Despite the fact that he holds a carbine, he looks ineffective. The patrols are largely staffed by inadequates—we know that from our sociology instruction; nevertheless, it is dismaying to see this demonstrated. Some facts would better remain abstractions. "Down on Southway, they are bulldozing."

"No problem," says Jigger with infinite calm, and I understand once again why I feel for him so deeply; he can manipulate situations as never I could. "We'll skirt Southway; we got other thoughts."

"Westerly not too good, either," the guard says, his voice dull and flat. Strictly speaking, access to the Network cannot be denied any non-felon; the purpose of the Barriers is to keep the lumpen *out* . . . and to harass Jigger and me on our way in. I recount this to myself: I whisper and remember. Looking at the guard more deeply, I can see that he is terrified. Patrolling the out-limits of Network is no promising job for the flunkies from the Institute who end up here. I shudder, caution myself to apply hard to studies. "Northing, no reports."

"Screw the travelogue," Jigger says, "we are going in, man. We are from the Institute and will make our own alliances." He pats my knee below the level of the guard's vision, winks. Everything *up*.

The guard shrugs. In this shrug I can see the shift of his mood; now fear becomes detachment. If we want to kill ourselves, he thinks, this is our survival problem and not his. He is covered under all the rules of Barrier Service by issuing warning. His eyes clear; he is a mirror without resonance. "Institute," he grumbles, "Institute chappies. Well, now, I don't really give a damn, then. Give it in. There's no blockade; you've got your warnings now. How are things in the place these days?"

"Pleasant and dull," Jigger says, "dull and pleasant. Just the way it should be always." He touches the accelerator, the car moans, he puts it into gear and we hit out flat, the Barrier just clearing the way as we stumble through. "Southway, Northing, Westerly, screw them all," Jigger says, and we roll, screaming across the waters.

Jigger breaks out another of the uppers he has brought for the party and slips one into his mouth. "How about

Easto?" he says, balancing the wheel with a knee, leaning out the window simultaneously to leave a trail of spit for the guard. "Or should we just go center and see what drags?"

"Don't care," I say, "don't care." I touch my own gun in an inside pocket, wondering what might have happened if the guard had balked us. Impossible, of course . . . they have no right to stop entry. The Institute draws fear from them like sweat. Nevertheless, nevertheless . . . would I have shot him?

Don't know. May never know. He would have opened under the clout like a greenhouse filled with decayed flowers, falling and bleeding in little petals down the uniform. Good thoughts for a trip into the Network. The tab hits; I feel a jolt of connection, then acceptance as the feelings spread. Like flowers. I reach out my hand to Jigger for another.

"Pot luck," I say, and he laughs, I laugh, he yanks the car onto a "down" ramp and *whap!* we are in Northing.

V

Easto, Westerley, Southway, Northing. Northing, we understand, is the most dangerous of them all, due to the natural advantages of terrain. Attached to the mainland, it sprouts hundreds of secret pathways to the outside, all of which must be covered by Barriers, but new access is constantly being found and, resultantly, Northing is the bloodiest of them all. The bands scoot, laying down their direction like little fibers, now and then coming straight upstate to be found wandering and exterminated fifty or a hundred miles from their source. Northing, in other words, is the central way out and demands the closest control. Consequently, it maintains the highest level of tension.

Still, Northing has open space and patches of unsettled land arcing down from the fields upstate, natural advantages of terrain not given to, say, Southway. For that reason I am fonder of it than the other sections. Also, Northing is an undeclared area, open to all bands, unlike Westerley and Easto, which are formally at war and hence usually ripped by gases. Southway, which we are told has the riots tonight, is oddly the only section without distinct characteristics of its own. It borrows Northway's landscape, the meanness of Easto, the gaseous aroma of Westerley . . . but fails to blend them in a new way. This, in fact, might be the reason for the riots. Lacking any natural advantages, Southway's bands have to make it on sheer toughness.

Stay out of Southway, then. Northing is tough enough for two sophomores from the Institute making only their second trip into Network. (And the first cannot count; we came in with supervisors in armored trucks for formal reconnaissance, the areas swept clean for us. This second is really the first. Humility must overtake me.)

"Look," Jigger says, the car still rolling, pointing. We move through a dense, gutted area; the high smell of the air, darkness in all but that spilling from our headlights. Initially I see nothing, but then, following Jigger's point, I see that there is indeed activity. Forms scuttle; whisk of shape, the sound of crackling. Bands are on the move tonight. Or maybe it is only free-lance—a dangerous thing to be here, always—having a look at a strange car.

"Take them in," Jigger says. "Let's go." His hands embrace the wheel, we roll to quiet, Jigger's rasp now the only sound in the car. "They're coming now," he says, rolling his forehead against the windshield. "I can sense. I know how they prowl." He is excited and happy.

Not so, me. "Maybe we should move," I say, feeling for the first time (the guard does not count) the Network fear. It is one thing at the Institute to plan the trip and hear the stories, another to be at rest on a street in Northing, waiting for the unknown to close. I am not ashamed of this fear, although surprised; once again I have not been able to judge the context of my true feelings, even with Jigger (who does not feel) beside me. "We can make a reconnaissance sweep."

"Nonsense," Jigger says. He works out another tab, passes it to me. "Stop quivering. No delay this time; this is what we wanted, right, on the probe?" Right; he is right. He chews, ingests, meditates, considers, all in a trice while the sounds leap on us. "We'll get the bastards."

Now there are forms around the car, two of them, possibly three: a man and a girl, something indeterminate, lurking behind them. Probably the cover. I see their faces as they move in and they are the faces of Network as I have always imagined them: implacable, staring, ageless. They are not the same as we. We can never understand them and yet the Institute forces us to accept the point: these are people. People live here.

Jigger rolls down his window and the forms circle to that side. The man leads. Now I can see that the third is not hiding at all but merely the smallest and slowest of the three, possibly a child, scuttling to the rear. Jigger gives me a wink and then leans out the window, saying nothing, waiting. Waiting.

"Please," the man says to him.

"Please *what?*" Jigger says.

"You're from the outside, aren't you? I can tell."

"Yes," Jigger says. "We are from outside." His jaws move as he ingests the tab; his hands skirt his jacket, touching the gun. "Who are you? Tell us. What are your names? What are your plans? What is it like to live here?"

"Please," the man says again. Now, close to us, his face is no longer ageless; it becomes a child in the overtaking pain. Network is a difficult place for all. "Get us out of here."

"Yes," the woman says, moving beside, touching his arm. "We've been waiting all season for someone to come. Please, now, take us out."

She is not pretty, although I can see that I might give her a fuck or three if inclined that way and under the right circumstances. Heterosex is a mystery that someday I must explore. (I conceal these thoughts from Jigger, however.) She backs away from Jigger's side of the car, comes toward mine and I remember old warnings from the Institute about their technique of encirclement. Probes for the bands. I touch my own gun while at the same time I roll down the window for confrontation, thus risk-

ing all. We look at one another and in her face I see myself.

"We can hide in the trunk," she says. "Just past the
border and we'll get out. Get us through the Barriers, I
beg of you."

"Let you into this car?" I say. I fondle the upholstery
respectfully. "You really think we'd let you in here?"

"You came to see the Network," the man says hoarsely
to Jigger, poking in an elbow. "Now and then there are
people like you who come in to see—to see how we live,
to learn from our systems. So take us out with you and
we can give you much information. We know all the secrets of Network. We'll tell you many things."

Jigger nods, sucks away at a fingernail. "You must,"
the woman says to me. The thing that is a child moves
behind her and, hidden now, whimpers. I am keyed up
and prepared for this.

I take out my gun and, holding it firmly, show it to the
woman. "See this?" I say. "It works. Get away. Get away,
now."

Jigger takes his gun and levels. The man retreats from
the window. "Oh, no," he says, "this is impossible." There
is no surprise, however, in his voice. "I don't believe it,"
he says, sounding as if he does.

"Nothing's impossible," Jigger says, "not in the Network. Haven't you studied the forms? Don't you know?
Free fire zone." He pulls the trigger.

The man falls from us, moaning. There is a wet sound
as he hits the turf of Northing and then the moans stop.
The woman tries to dive through the window, her hand
outstretched for my gun, but geometrics do not permit
this, of course, and she merely clouts her forehead, claps
at it. "Are you crazy?" she says. "You must be. You're
crazy." I shoot her.

She falls away as the man did, although not nearly so
quickly, giving up her handhold on the car in small
chunks and pieces, but when she is finally out of my line
of sight, the child is still there, whimpering, reaching.
"Please," it says. All of them, their weapons taken away,

ask so nicely. *"Please."* In five years or less, this one, too, would be ready for the bands.

So I shoot it. I shoot the thing, Jigger laughs, spins the gun and shoots it as well; then we point our guns to the ground and empty them into whatever is below. Bullets spang off the car; groans reach up toward us.

We roll up the windows, put away the guns and stare at one another. Jigger looks the same, but I suspect that it has been his first Kill as well. There are whole areas of our lives, despite the closeness, that we have agreed not to discuss. It does not matter. A Kill is a Kill; all the feeling comes after the fact of it.

"Bastards," he says, wiping the windshield clear with a sleeve. "All of them are bastards."

"Let's go, anyway."

"I hate them. They're vermin." He trembles; I cannot tell in the darkness if he is crying. "Had to do it, you see," Jigger says. "Otherwise, it would have been us."

"I know that. Let's get out of here."

"Where?" he says. "I don't like this. I don't want to suck them out anymore. Waiting and shooting, it's not for me."

"Let's see the riots in Southway."

"I had to do it. They wanted to get out the Barrier; they would have escaped upstate and started killing citizens."

"Let's go to Southway," I say again, very slowly. "We can see the riots in Southway with the windows up. No shooting unless shot at this time."

"What if we can't handle it?" Jigger says with a little more firmness. "Then what?"

"We can handle it," I say, examining the new assurance within me. I am filled with the glow of the first Kill which, unlike Jigger's, has strengthened me. *You are never the same person.* "We can handle anything now."

"Not in all of Network," Jigger says. "Remember, we're still sophomores." But he starts the car and drives; he says no more, holding the wheel tightly and looking down the roads. Although the tabs have kept him down I can sense his panic, and this makes me proud, because until this moment I thought that he had been the stronger in our relationship. With this secret discovered, changes will be made and things will get better, better; we shift in accord.

"Anywhere," I say, "anywhere we can handle it." And we pick up the highway quickly again, almost no traffic because of the warnings and hit dead toward the sea, toward Southing. Looking into the river I think briefly of the three of Network we have killed and of the horror we have saved them and citizens together; that small and deadly purification brought through the grace and cunning of the Institute to the Network this night.

VI

Through Westerley and out the other side, the highway, gray like a dream, unrolling before us. We have not talked for half an hour, being occupied with memory, with images of the Kill. In *Death and Disorder* now I remember we were told that this first Kill might change our lives; that one could not go simply into the Network but had to undergo some kind of metaphysical re-alteration at the understanding that *these people were not human* and that unless this truth were internalized Network might kill us all, but I did not—I will admit this—truly believe. The Institute provides us with a history of the Network: policies, procedures, attitudes, modus operandi, but the matter of true feeling is very private and personal. There was some word for this (they have a word for everything) and they called it *ethos*.

The Network as we understand it is almost a century and a half old, but it became fit for an Institute only in the 1970s. Matters accelerate. Twenty years more from that to this; the Institute formalized by need. Now the Network is closed to all but approved and weaponed travelers. Are Jigger and I approved? . . . a dark question, but it does not matter; certainly we have qualifications . . . and at this phase of thought I squeal in panic because the road has fallen away from us, literally fallen away, and we skitter through a hundred feet of stone into the outskirts of Southway, the car out of control; Jigger tabs and all screaming with fright as he works on the wheel and finally we plunge into an abutment and come to rest, the car ruined, stinking in a puddle of its residue. Jigger tries hopelessly to re-start and then sighs, releases the wheel. "Finished," he says, his voice wavering. "We're finished now."

"Don't panic," I say. I will control and test various surfaces of the body, finding that I am not injured. "It does no good. We're in control of this as long as we stay in control of it; remember that."

"How the shit are we going to get out of here?"

"Somehow," I say. "We'll find a way. I realize that Jigger is indeed younger—only a couple of months, but still significant until one has reached the twenties at least. He is a child despite all of his attitudes and deeply shaken by the Kill yet, and knowing this increases my calm, knowing that I must function for the two of us. I am the stronger.

"All we have to do is get to checkpoint," I say. "We have our full credentials, and once we get there we'll be shielded in the Barrier until we're picked up." I do not mention the disciplinary measures likely to be invoked by the Institute because of our unauthorized absence. I will have to deal with this later. "There's nothing to it," I say.

"How are we going to get to checkpoint? We're ten miles down, maybe fifteen. I tell you, we're trapped!"

"We're ten miles from *Northing* checkpoint. But there are others, I think," I say, courses in Network geography, freshman survey, wheeling before me in clots of color. "The Westerley checkpoint should be only a little way from here. It's on the tip of Southway."

"We'll never make it," Jigger says positively. "I tell you, we'll never make any Barriers." He kicks, groans, pushes on his door until it saws open and then stumbles to the pavement. "Never, never, never make it through. Why did we come in? It was stupid."

I push on my own door. It yields and I come through slowly, joining him on the pavement before the hood. Little ropes of steam curl from their concealment, flickers of

pain in my legs and belly, but I do not feel seriously at
bay. "Yes we will," I say. "We're on the docks; all that
we have to do is walk. They never come this far out; no
meat. We'll walk it through." I examine the terrain
keenly, my institutional preparations assisting. Dead animals, what might be a human corpse or two lying near the
waterline, the shapes of what might have been automobiles scattered around the pillars. Artifacts, frozen already
in time and quiet, quiet. Too far north, apparently, for
the rioters; too far west to be part of Westerley, as I have
said. "They must have wrecked the highway," I point out.
"Sooner or later that was bound to happen. We'll report
it when we get back, anonymously if you want, and
they'll seal off the area for the time being."

"They wrecked the highway to trap us!" Jigger whines.
"That was their plan from the beginning, to suck us into
the cage." In truth his nervousness and fear are now becoming disgusting, although I remind myself yet again
that he is only eighteen. Eighteen, four months and five
days. "They'll pick us off like cats if we move. I can hear
them watching and waiting; they're in the water now."
He goes inside his jacket, removes the gun again. "But
I'll take some of you with me, anyway!" he screams.

"Now, stop it," I say. "Just stop it." I hit him on the
shoulder in a special way between us, not sufficient to
paralyze, but enough to make him whimper and he stops
flailing. I know all the parts of his body like my own.
"Help me," he says, then, in a voice like the ones
we heard in Northing: "Someone, please, you've got to
help."

"I'll help," I say, "I'll get us through," although my impulse right now is to abandon Jigger where we stand, on
the rim of Southway and let him deal for himself. The
Kill has changed my blood and his; I know that something between us is now finished. The impulse to leave is
easily understood, but it would be regretted soon enough
. . . for his lone, staggering form would soon bring the
bands upon him, and for the bands, then, a straight line,
an easy search, from he to me. I take his uninjured shoul-

der. "Come on," I say, "we're going to stick to the waterline."

And past, then, all of the decaying matter on the river,
past the hulks of rotting ships and all of the corpses we
pick our way, Jigger and I, pick our way through
the odors, striving for the Westerley checkpoint . . . which
I am not sure, despite my reassurances, does exist. All of
this has happened so quickly that for the moment I do not
think of the riots, or at least the possibility of riots, which
had so terrified the young guard and the rioters then come
upon us so quickly, with such efficiency and attention,
that there is not even time for me, at least, to panic. "Oh,
my God," Jigger says, "now we're finished."

VII

Backed against the fence holding off the river, Jigger
and I are being closed off by a band from Westerley. I
know they are Westerley, for they wear the insignia of the
area, the logicon of the *W,* and it now comes back to me
that the Westerley bands are the most dangerous of all
because their terrain makes it necessary for them to nav-
igate on water as well, and this water knowledge has enabled them to voyage out of their territory as the other
bands, even those of Northing, cannot: the Westerleys
can strike at Northing, hit Southway a devastating blow
and then, still circling, come in on Easto . . . there are ten
or twelve of them this time. These are not the ageless like
the older tenants of Northing, but rather more definable
as being of our age or even, impossibly, a little younger.
"Stop there!" says the one in front who must be the
leader. (They go in a simple pack-and-point formation.)
"We want to talk."

"God," Jigger says. He is twelve years old. "God,
God," trying to reach inside for the gun, but it is with his
injured arm and he stops in the motion stupidly, gasping
with pain. "Oh, my God."

"Stop it, you fool," I whisper. "We emptied them out
on the ground, don't you remember? Don't show it

to them; they'll kill us for it on the spot. Stand your ground."

"We were going to refill them," he says. "Oh, my God, we were going to *refill;* why didn't we? Just a simple thing; I can't stand this anymore. I'm so afraid. Run, please run me, oh, please. . . ."

Repellent. I level it off inside my skull; turn his shrieks into babble . . . willing him to leave. It is terrible to know that Jigger, who I have so admired, was, after all, the lesser of us, but it makes no difference as well, not in terms of the urgent and rising situation that I must confront. *Some will grow from the Kill,* I remember, *and others will die from it.* The litany of the Institute.

"Shut up," I say to Jigger then and strike him in the mouth.

The leader watches this, laughs and then reaches inside a pocket to show us his own gun, a shape that I grasp, even in the darkness. "That's enough, you," he says, "citizen scum. Root in place!" Breaking on the *place,* his voice is that of one even younger than we, not that this will bring us mercy. The lumpen are full grown at twelve, deadly and quick, most virulent in their late teens . . . and few of them live beyond thirty. Jigger roots in place, breath pouring from his mouth and cautiously, cautiously, I put my hands at sides, risking a glance toward the river. It is impossible that this can happen and I know better, yet I cannot dodge the hope that the Institute has somehow kept a benign watch on us and a full patrol in reconnaissance is waiting for rescue after we have learned our lesson. The lesson: never to go into the Network without protection. Surely the Institute, which has invested so much in us, could not abandon us now: not in terms of the cost of our training, the knowledge we have gained of Network as the result of our unauthorized visit. We are too precious to risk, I think . . . and come back into focus, hearing Jigger's voice again.

"Please," he is saying, "please don't hurt me. It was all his idea; deal with him," he says, gesturing to me. "He took us in here." And so on and so forth and I must strike him yet again, this time in the plexus and so hard that he prances whispering into the mud and stays down. So quietly he lies; I hope that he is in fact unconscious. The leader looks at me, knowing that I am the stronger, and winks.

"What do you want?" he says quietly. "Why are you here?"

"We didn't mean to be. We're looking for the Westerley checkpoint."

"There's no Westerley checkpoint," he says. "We blew that out a long time ago. Don't you reason? Sightseers," he says and looks behind him, motioning for the band to close in. "Suburban sight-seeing scum."

"No," I say quickly, "you don't understand. It isn't like that at all. We didn't come just to look, we had means, we . . . "

"Thrills. You came in for thrills, just like the others we mop up. See the Network, get a jolt, but you always get a little more than you hope for, don't you? This is *our* Southway, citizen, and *no* sightseers come in here without us giving permission and guiding them, and you have no permission at all."

"Please," I say. Now I sound like Jigger. I move and stumble over my fallen friend, losing balance and collapsing into the mud, feeling the repellent ooze up my wrists and ankles as the band circles. "You're wrong; we came to help you. To learn about you. To learn about the Network." I can hold back nothing; it is my only hope. "We're from the Institute."

"What institute?" one of the band cries. "What are you talking about?" And then other voices pick this up and soon five or ten or twenty (oh, my God, I cannot count them) are shouting "what institute?" as Jigger tries to crawl away in his unconsciousness and I try to recover my own balance in the mud but cannot, cannot, cannot negotiate the grounds of Westerley (being out of my element) and flop helplessly.

"Save him," the leader says quietly, tossing something into the river. "I want to deal with him later, have some fun with him. The other one, mop up. Institute! We'll institute a little something, won't we, men? I want him saved for later . . . but don't be too careful."

"The Institute!" I shout, trying to get out the words, but they come over me then in a pack like the gases of Network itself, and I must hawk and gasp to speak, trying to get out the words that will save me, but they close over me like a shroud and those words only a whimper that Jigger (who does not need to know) can hear: *"The Institute for Urban Control."*

And then, good Lord, I fall into Westerley.

A DELIGHTFUL COMEDIC PREMISE

This story was written about a year after *Herovit's World;* it might be called a distillation, and, uh, compression of the themes of that novel. The editor, who had indeed commissioned the piece, sighed over what he called the throwing away of two perfectly good and original themes for stories he would like to publish, but he took the piece, anyway. I never minded throwing away ideas, no matter how attractive: the act of professional writing has nothing to do with ideas, but structure and articulation, and every good professional will tell you that he has infinitely more ideas than he will ever be able to use through the full range of his work. I throw away two valid ideas here; three stories in this collection are built around the same one. So it is. Fiction is not a consistent business.

Incidentally, and as long as I have mentioned *Herovit's World*, has anyone noticed that the book owes a clear conceptual debt to Wilfrid Sheed's second novel, *The Hack?* Sheed is a remarkable novelist, overvalued as a critic, who, in *The Hack* and *The Blacking Factory,* wrote two of the most valuable works of the decade.

———◆———

A DELIGHTFUL COMEDIC PREMISE

Dear Mr. Malzberg:

I wonder if you'd be interested in writing for us—on a semicommissioned basis, of course—a funny short story or novelette. Although the majority of your work, at least the work that I have read, is characterized by a certain gloom, a blackness, a rather despairing view of the world, I am told by people who represent themselves to be friends of yours that you have, in private, a delightful sense of humor that overrides your melancholia and makes you quite popular at small parties. I am sure you would agree that science fiction, at least at present, has all the despair and blackness that it or my readers can stand, and if you could come in with a light-hearted story, we would not only be happy to publish it, but it might start you on a brand-new career. From these same friends I am given to understand that you are almost thirty-four years of age, and surely you must agree that despair is harder and harder to sustain when you move into a period of your life where it becomes personally imminent; in other words, you are moving now into the Heart Attack Zone.

Dear Mr. Ferman:

Thank you very much for your letter and for your interest in obtaining from me a light-hearted story. It so happens that you and my friends have discovered what I like to think of as My Secret . . . that I am not a despairing man at all, but rather one with a delicious if somewhat perverse sense of humor, who sees the comedy in the human condition and only turns out the black stuff because it is now fashionable, and the word rates, at all lengths, must be sustained.

I have had in mind for some time writing a story about a man—let me call him Jack—who is able to re-evoke the sights and sounds of the 1950s in such a concrete and viable fashion that he is actually able to *take* people back into the past, both individually and in small tourist groups. (This idea is not completely original; Jack Finney used it in *Time and Again*, and of course this chestnut has been romping or, I should say, dropping around the field for forty years, but hear me out.) The trouble with Jack is that he is not able to re-evoke the more fashionable and memorable aspects of the 1950s, those that are so much in demand in our increasingly perilous and confusing times, but instead can recover only the failures, the not-quite-successes, the aspects-that-never-made-it. Thus, he can take himself and companions not to Ebbets Field, say, where the great Dodger teams of the 1950s were losing with magnificence and stolid grace, but to Shibe Park in Philadelphia, home of the Athletics and Phillies, where on a Tuesday afternoon a desultory crowd of four thousand might be present to watch senile managers fall asleep in the dugout or hapless rookies fail once again to hit the rising curve. He cannot, in short, recapture the Winners but only the Losers: the campaign speeches of Estes Kefauver, recordings by the Bell Sisters and Guy Mitchell, the rambling confessions of minor actors before the McCarthy screening committee that they once were Communists and would appreciate the opportunity to get before the full committee and press to make a more definite statement.

Jack is infuriated by this and no wonder; he is the custodian of a unique and possibly highly marketable talent —people increasingly love the past, and a guided tour through it as opposed to records, tapes and rambling reminiscences would be enormously exciting to them—but he cannot for the life of him get to what he calls the Real Stuff, the more commercial and lovable aspects of that cuddly decade. Every time that he thinks he has recaptured Yankee Stadium in his mind and sweeps back in time to revisit it, he finds himself at Wrigley Field in Chicago where Wayne Terwilliger, now playing first base, misses a foul pop and runs straight into the stands. What can he do? What can he do about this reckless and uncontrollable talent of his, which in its sheerest perversity simply will not remit to his commands? (It is a subconscious ability, you see; if he becomes self-conscious, it leaves him entirely.) Jack is enraged. He has cold sweats, flashes of gloom and hysteria. (I forgot to say that he is a failed advertising copywriter, now working in Cleveland on display advertising mostly for the Shaker Heights district. He needs money and approbation. His marriage, his *second* marriage, is falling apart. All of this will give the plot substance and humanity, to say nothing of warm twitches of insight.) He *knows* that he is onto something big, and yet his clownish talent, all big feet and wide ears, mocks him.

He takes his problem to a psychiatrist. The psychiatrist takes some convincing, but after being taken into the offices of *Cosmos* science fiction to see the editor rejecting submissions at a penny a word, he believes everything. He says he will help Jack. This psychiatrist, who I will call Dr. Mandleman, fires all of his patients and enters into a campaign to help Jack recover the more popular and marketable aspects of the '50s. He, too, sees the Big Money. He moves in with Jack. A psychiatrist in his own home: together they go over the top-forty charts of that era, call up retired members of the New York football Giants, pore through old Congressional Records in which McCarthy is again and again thunderously denounced by two liberal representatives. . . .

Do you see the possibilities? I envision this as being somewhere around 1,500 words but could expand or contract it to whatever you desire. I am very busy as always, but I could make room in my schedule for this project, particularly if you could see fit to give a small down payment. Would fifty dollars seem excessive? I look forward to word from you.

Dear Mr. Malzberg:

I believe that you have utterly misunderstood my letter and the nature of the assignment piece.

There is nothing *funny* in a fantasy about a man who can recapture only the ugly or forgotten elements of the past. Rather, this is a bitter satire on the present that you have projected, based upon your statement that "people love their past," with the implication that they find the future intolerable. What is funny about *that?* What is funny about failure, too? What is funny about the Philadelphia Athletics of the early 1950s with their ninety-four-year-old manager? Rather, you seem to be on the way to constructing another of your horrid metaphors for present and future, incompetence presided over by senescence.

This idea will absolutely not work, not at least within the context of a delightful comedic premise, and as you know, we are well inventoried with work by you and others that will depress people. I cannot and will not pay fifty dollars in front for depressing stuff like this.

Perhaps you will want to take another shot at this.

Dear Mr. Ferman:

Thanks for your letter. I am truly sorry that you fail to see the humor in failure or in the forgettable aspects of the past—people, I think, must learn to laugh at their foibles—but I bow to your judgment.

Might I suggest another idea that has been in mind for some time. I would like to write a story of a telepath—let me call him John—who is able to establish direct psionic links with the minds, if one can call them "minds," of the thoroughbreds running every afternoon, except for Sundays and three months a year at Aqueduct and Belmont race tracks in Queens, New York. John's psionic faculties work at a range of fifty yards; he is able to press his nose against the wire gate separating paddock from customers and actually get *inside* the minds of the horses. Dim thoughts like little shoots of grass press upon his own brain; he is able to determine the mental state and mood of the horses as in turn they parade by him. (Horses, of course, do not verbalize; John must deduce those moods subverbally.)

Obviously, John is up to something. He is a mind reader; he should, through the use of this talent, be able to get some line on the outcome of a race by knowing which horses feel well, which horses' thoughts are clouded by the possibility of soporifics, which other horses' minds show vast energy because of the probable induction of stimulants. Surely he should be able to narrow the field down to two or three horses, anyway, that *feel good* and, by spreading his bets around these in proportion to the odds, assure himself of a good living.

(I should have said somewhat earlier on, but, as you know, I am very weak at formal outlines; John's talents are restricted to the reading of the minds of *animals;* he cannot for the life of him screen the thoughts of a fellow human. If he could, of course, he would simply check out the trainers and jockeys, but it is a perverse and limited talent, and John must make the best of what God has given him, as must we all—for instance, I outline poorly.)

The trouble is that John finds there to be no true correlation between the prerace mood or thoughts of horses and the eventual outcome. Horses that feel *well* do not necessarily win, and those horses from which John has picked up the most depressing and suicidal emanations have been known to win. It is not a simple reversal; if it were, John would be able to make his bets on the basis of reverse correlation and do quite well this way; rather, what it seems to be is entirely *random*. Like so much of life, the prerace meditations of horses appear to have no relationship to the outcome; rather, motives and consequence are fractured, split, entirely torn apart; and this insight, which finally comes upon John after the seventh race at Aqueduct on June 12, 1974, when he has lost fifty-five dollars, drives him quite mad; his soul is split, his mind shattered; he runs frantically through the sparse crowds (it is a Tuesday, and you know what OTB has done to racetrack attendance, anyway) shouting, screaming, bellowing his rage to the heavens. "There's no connection!" he will scream. "Nothing makes sense, nothing connects, there is no reason at all!" And several burly Pinkertons, made sullen by rules that require them to wear jackets and ties at all times, even on this first hot day of the year, seize him quite roughly and drag him into the monstrous computer room housing the equipment of the American Totalisor Company; there a sinister track executive, his eyes glowing with cunning and evil, will say, "Why don't you guys ever learn?" (He is a metaphor for the Devil, you see; I assure you that this will be properly planted, and the story itself will be an *allegory*.) And, coming close to John, he will raise a hand shaped like a talon, he will bring it upon John, he will . . .

I propose this story to be 25,000 words in length, a cover story, in fact. (You and Ronald Walotsky will see the possibilities here, and Walotsky, I assure you, draws horses very well.) Although I am quite busy, the successful author of fifteen stories in this field, two of the novels published in *hardcover,* I could make time in my increasingly heavy schedule to get the story to you within twelve hours of your letter signifying outline approval. I think that an advance in this case of fifty dollars would be quite reasonable and look forward to hearing from you by return mail, holding off in the meantime from plunging into my next series of novels which, of course, are already under lucrative contract.

Dear Mr. Malzberg:

We're not getting anywhere.

What in God's name is *funny* about a man who perceives "motives and consequences to be entirely fractured . . . torn apart?" Our readers, let me assure you, have enough troubles of their own; they are already quite aware of this, or do not *want* to be aware of it. Our readers, an intelligent and literate group of people numbering into the multiple thousands, have long since understood that life is unfair and inequitable, and they are looking for entertainment, release, a little bit of *joy*.

Don't you understand that this commission was for a *funny* story? There is nothing funny about your proposal, nor do I see particular humor in an allegory that will make use of the appearance of the Devil.

Perhaps we should forget this whole thing. There are other writers I would rather have approached, and it was only at the insistence of your friends that I decided to give you a chance at this one. We are heavily inventoried, as I have already said, on the despairing stuff, but if in due course you would like to send me one of your characteristic stories, *on a purely speculative basis,* I will consider it as a routine submission.

Dear Mr. Ferman:

Please wait a minute or just a few minutes until you give me another chance to explain myself. I was sure that the two story ideas you have rejected, particularly the second, were quite funny; but editorial taste, as we professional writers know, is the prerogative of the editor; and if you *don't* see the humor, I can't show it to you, humor being a very rare and special thing. I am, however, momentarily between novels, waiting for the advance on the series contract to come through, and *would* be able to write you a story at this time; let me propose one final idea to you before you come to the wrong conclusion that I am not a funny writer and go elsewhere, to some wretched hack who does not have one quarter of the bubbling humor and winsomely comprehensive view of the foibles of the human condition that I do.

I would like to write a story about a science fiction writer, a highly successful science fiction writer, but one who nevertheless, because of certain limitations in the field and slow payment from editors, is forced to make do on an income of $3,483 a year (last year) from all of his writings and, despite the pride and delight of knowing that he is near or at the top of his field, finds getting along on such an income, particularly in the presence of a wife and family, rather difficult, his wife not understanding entirely (as she *should* understand) that science fiction is not an ultimately lucrative field for most of us but repays in satisfaction, in *great* satisfactions. This writer—who we shall call Barry—is possessed after a while by his fantasies; the partitions, in his case, between reality and fantasy have been sheared through by turmoil and economic stress, and he believes himself in many ways to be not only the creator but the receptacle of his ideas, ideas that possess him and stalk him through the night.

Barry is a gentle man, a man with a gracious sense of humor, a certain *je ne sais quoi* about him that makes him much celebrated at parties, a man whose occasionally sinister fictions serve only to mask his gay and joyous nature . . . but Barry is seized by his fantasies; people do not truly understand him; and now at last those aforementioned walls have crumpled: he takes himself to be not only the inventor but the *hero* of his plot ideas. Now he is in a capsule set on Venus fly-by looking out at the green planet while he strokes his diminutive genitals and thinks of home; now again he is an archetypical alien, far from home, trying to make convincing contact with humanity; now yet again he is a rocketship, an actual physical rocketship, a phallic object extended to great length and power, zooming through the heavens, penetrating the sky.

I'll do this at 1,500 words for five dollars down. Please let me hear from you.

Dear Mr. Malzberg:

This was a doomed idea from the start. I hope you won't take this personally, but you need help.

Dear Mr. Ferman:

My husband is at Aqueduct today, living in a motel by night, and says that he will be out of touch for at least a week, but I know he would have wanted me to acknowledge your letter, and as soon as he returns I assume he'll be in touch with you.

I assume also that in saying that he needs "help" you are referring to the fact that, as he told me, you were commissioning a story from him with money in front, and I hope that you can send us a check as soon as possible, without awaiting his return. He said something about a hundred or a thousand dollars, but we'll take fifty.

Joyce Malzberg

Introduction to
GERANIUMS

If Dore Previn wrote science fiction, she'd write it very much like Valerie King . . . a twenty-six-year-old emigré from the cultural subcondition of California who, given the usual mixture of luck and circumstance that must accompany talent, has a chance to be one of the truly valuable writers of the genre. She appears to be almost completely original and, like most of the originals, co-exists unhappily with her talent, which she sees mostly as making her life more unpleasant than it has any need to be.

Geraniums is Valerie's story with my ending—the ending was highly visible in the text of the piece, but like many newer writers she was not able to get hold of the subconscious in a death grip to see the implications of what the subconscious was chattering about—and a revision of the material so that it made reasonable inference of the ending. The style is almost completely hers; it has that hysterical edge that I have always associated with fallen Catholics or Californians. I think—being prejudiced —that it was the best story by far in the anthology in which it first appeared, an anthology that contained one of my own distinguished works, written uncollaboratively.

GERANIUMS

ROOTS: Dmitri was no one's fool. The world was going mad, but he wasn't. Not that way. He knew a geranium thief when he saw one. And there she was, sliding up the walk. God, they were cunning!

Cunning, cunning! It was hard enough to coax the plants along the asphalt, past the clay, without these constant thieving forays. The rectory was stone, he was earth (he thought of himself as brisk, mud-covered, perhaps, but always brisk), but how could you win? And there was the religious overlay, too. He had never thought he would end up among Catholics. Maybe the geranium thieves were demented and the cunning was something that he credited them with only because one wanted to see, *had* to see the enemy as personal. Nevertheless, in a eucalyptian crouch (the branches wavered) he shook with rage as he watched the bitch. All of them had the same gait: mince with the shopping bag dangling from an arm, the other free to deftly snatch a plant. They were pure evil; the rectory could have its snake. And yet, rage or not, he would stand in something close to anticipation (all right; he *identified*), watching the ritual of movement: the hand would shoot out between the fence grillwork and snip a stem or two, then the explosion of bloom. *Slam!* Into the bag backhand and then the mince again. Up the path and across the street. You had to admire them. They knew what they were doing.

This lady, he supposed, was a new one. Maybe not; their faces blurred like flowers. New or old, though, the thieves worked the same: limp, sweep, snatch, stagger . . . and then he saw her back as she moved sedately down the street. Her shoulders trembled. She was laughing at him.

Hilarion was no help. Father Hilarion thought the thing was delightful. "Geranium thieves!" the crazed old celibate would say, his eyes glazed with passion or holy water. "A parish of geranium thieves! Well, Dmitri, one must share blessings earthly as well as un———." And so forth. "What's so bad about a few miserable geraniums? It could be the roses!" He hated the man.

Dmitri saw Hilarion stumble from a side door and come toward him clasping a rosary; then, at the exact moment when he thought communion was about to be offered, Hilarion swung north and followed the geranium thief up the path. Dmitri turned on the sprinkler. From this new aspect Hilarion disappeared into shining mist, a rainbow, in the center of the rainbow a potted plant.

STAMEN: In the last two years dreams of his childhood had overtaken him. At the beginning it had only been once a week or less, the dreams interrupted by a heightened apperception of what was happening to him now, but the tempo had picked up: now they were coming almost all of the time, and in the dreams there was a succession of fat women in black dresses, talking to him inexhaustibly, lifting, sweeping, stirring and passing on advice in a language he could not understand. Isolated phrases—*humming; persist; consider the lilies*—would sweep in, connect, they would lapse into jargon and he would bolt from sleep, swearing. He could not understand what they were trying to tell him. Lying on his back, sheets to his knees, he would imagine himself to be looking not at the miserable gardener's ceiling but a wedge of pure sky, rain falling.

In the dreams his childhood accumulated. He had not been sensitive to it the first time around, but now it was all coming back, the ethos of it, so to speak, the realization that it had all somehow been quite painful. Obviously, he was going to get all of it back if only the women would open up and speak comprehensibly. The dreams, furthermore, had been coming on him recently during the days, stroking at him like wind in the dust of the garden. He found himself locked into recollection and came from it to see that time had passed, and once, through the window, he had seen Hilarion waving at him with the lazy strokes of a carnival wheel.

PISTIL: Dmitri had made sure to put the Empress of Russia in the center of the garden. Safe from the hands through the fence. The Empress of Russia was a miracle; the black-purple blooms had the texture of velvet. It proved that the apocalyptic Catholic were fools.

All of the thieves were after his Empress of Russia. Of course they were. But Dmitri, like the Apostle Paul, had drawn the line: some things were theirs and some were not. The ladies might snatch a geranium, but no more, not by vaulting the fence or a more subtle attack.

Shutting off the sprinkler, Hilarion down the path, Dmitri worked ten minutes or more, clearing a shallow basin beneath the tangerine tree, sneaking little glances now and then at the Empress. All right, he should have married or at least worked for a non-sectarian institution. It took him a while to realize that he was being watched.

He rose and looked at the lady. She was the same one who had been there before. Green pedal-pushers. No shopping bag this time. "Isn't that beautiful?" she said and pointed to the Empress. "Give me a snip. Just a little one off to the side where it won't show."

Dmitri went to the Empress, broke off a stem and, going to the fence, handed it to her. "It won't work," he said pointlessly. "Won't work at all."

"That's the only one I wanted," she said. She looked at him and she was one of the ladies in his dream and little insect eggs of understanding became larvae through him. Aristocracy. Of course! The stout ladies with their perpetual cleaning and lectures were part of fallen aristocracy. Like the Empress of Russia. Of course.

"Actually," the woman was saying, "I'm not a Catholic, unfortunately. We're Methodists, pretty lapsed, but Catholicism is so *persuasive*. Flowers from stone and all that."

"Get out of here," he said.

"Yes," she said, "yes." And she cupped the Empress and walked away. He put his hands on the fence and watched her.

PETAL: "You're handling this all wrong," Hilarion must have said to him. "If you can't bear to give away cuttings, why do so? Pretend you're deaf. Turn your back."

"They're evil."

"Evil," Hilarion might have pointed out, smoothing his robes, "does not have anything to do with flowers."

. . PISTIL: Later he must have returned to the basin. Late afternoon now. His digging had uncovered a gopher hole, and looking into that darkness, Dmitri had an insight: he dragged a hose to the basin and turned it on full force. Then he shoved the hose all the way into the hole. Water came out of the hose, turning the basin the colors of the rainbow. Never had he felt so much in control. The nozzle should go *all* the way into the hole, he thought ponderously; that way the gopher, if it was still there, would certainly drown. He slammed it in so deeply that the stream departed. Dmitri understood what the women in their black dresses had been trying to tell him. They had not liked the cheerless atmosphere; that was all. Something to brighten it up, perhaps, Dmitri? They had been talking about flowers.

A small and dark thing came out of the hole and bobbed in the water. Dmitri fainted or imagined that he did.

Hilarion was beside him, in full dress. "What's wrong?" he asked. He extended a hand, from the hand a flower. "Tell me, my son," he said. *Son.* Dmitri was fifty. More of their mysticism.

Dmitri looked up. Hilarion seemed to be of an enormous height, at a great distance, shuddering over him, hand extended. A gopher, the old fool was saying. Dmitri had caught a gopher. Wasn't that nice? It showed that the rectory had life in it.

He rose. He looked beyond Hilarion to the clusters of geraniums. The Empress blossoms were bruised and he became aware of a fine, spidery aching within his chest. God, he needed water.

He was pulled upward. The hose was taken from him. Waving, Dmitri opened his arms to the sun. He waited. In due time a hand would snake through the fence, draw him out like wire, and take him toward Ascension.

In the background, Hilarion seemed to be chanting the *Kyrie.* The old fool. They understood nothing. There were no mysteries. The world was a greenhouse.

Introduction to
CITY LIGHTS, CITY NIGHTS

This is another assassination piece; it reappears expanded as the opening section of the novel *The Destruction of the Temple* (POCKET BOOKS, 1974). Much of what is implicit or omitted entirely from the story becomes clear or clearer in the novel, but I was not even aware when I wrote this that it would *be* a novel: writing, which is for the most part a ghastly, boring procedure, offers little surprises now and then. (So do diseased women weeks after the fact; I am not trying to romanticize the profession. In fact, I advise everyone to stay away from it, and these days, as I look upon the mostly wasteland of writers younger than myself, I believe that they are. "More for me," my father would say when I would pass a second helping. "More for me," I say about the paucity of good science fiction novelists under thirty-five.)

Why am I so obsessed with the theme of political assassination? (And I am; appended is merely a partial list of novels and short stories utilizing the theme.) Well, these are difficult times and, of course, I was at Aqueduct racetrack in the borough of Queens, New York, on the afternoon of 11/22/63 to hear the initial announcements. This would induce a certain guilt to overlay the depression. Also, most of the works dealing with political assassination in its wake have either been dismal (*That Day* by Robie Macauley) or cheaply melodramatic (*One Day* by Wright Morrisor). Richard Condon's *The Manchurian Candidate* is superb commercial fiction but predates the assassination (for my generation it is always *the* assassination; for my daughters it will be *when they killed people a lot*) by some years. J. G. Ballard, a great writer, has done a serious body of post-assassination fiction, but as I said elsewhere, five years ago, and which I still hold to be self-evident, he is not an American and therefore does not count. That was no metaphor; that was my *life*.

In any event, here is how a part of the canon stands to date:

NOVELS	SHORT STORIES
The Destruction of the Temple (1974)	*The Ascension (Amazing,* 1969)
	Death to the Keeper (F & S-F, 1968)
Underlay (1974)	*Major Incitement to Riot (Fantastic,* 1969)
Overlay (1972)	
	Trashing (Infinity Five, 1973)
	Agony Column (EQMM, 1971)
	Overlooking (Amazing, 1974)
	By Right of Succession (Galaxy, 1971)
	Offertory & Resolution (Universe Day, 1971)

———◆———

CITY LIGHTS, CITY NIGHTS

I

Oswald shoots Kennedy again.

Kennedy, that idiot, has decided for some reason to do this take standing in the car. He falls heavily across Jacqueline, dislodging the roses, which collapse underneath, exploding petals on him, and Oswald, happy for this, anyway, throws the rifle down five stories from Municipal and leaves the window as I run out for the mop-up. The rifle is deflected by a third-floor balcony on Municipal and misses my ear by only inches, hitting me a terrific blow on the shoulder. Lumpen idiots. They really should know the geometry of this after all the time spent blocking. I fall to the ground in pain and rub the shoulder convulsively until the worst recedes. Perhaps I make slightly more of it than it really is. But they must be taught a lesson. Precautions prevail.

They gather around me quickly: Kennedy, Jacqueline, Johnson, Connally, the security forces. Even though the necessity is to stay in role, I can see fear hammering at the edges of the characterization. Sweat drips; they are frightened. Good. It is necessary that they show me the proper respect. After all, if I am going to perform the auditor's role over and over again, they should take care with my person. "Are you all right?" Kennedy asks. He runs his hand over his jacket, the other hand pumping away in a side pocket. Difficult to believe that he was dying only seconds ago. He has worked himself almost totally out of the role. Discipline. They must learn discipline.

"Get the hell back to the car!" I say on the ground, still rubbing the shoulder, then staggering upward. The sun is uncomfortable, the air binding. Manhattan makes a very poor Dallas; I must remind them of that. "What are you waiting for?" I say as they remain around me. "Get back to it."

"We were worried," Jacqueline says, running a hand across my forehead. The fat, stupid bitch; I cannot bear to be touched. How many times have I told her this? I only allowed her to play the role because she begged for it; this is the response I get. She is no actress. Kennedy is no actor. None of them, except for Oswald, has any conception of professionalism.

It is Oswald who joins us now. At a dead run from Municipal he comes toward me, feet clattering. He has seen the rifle; now he sees them gathered around me, the concern on their faces, the way that I am holding my shoulder, and he understands what has happened. He is a man of moderate sensitivity, unlike the rest of them, who are lumps. I do not really know what he is doing in this group, but it is probably unwise to speculate: at least he is around. Were it not for him, the re-enactments would be a complete fiasco.

"Are you all right?" he says, stopping some feet from me, backed off from the others, still locked into the role, which is good. He knows he should feel their repudiation, be in flight. At this moment, in fact, he should already be half a mile away, sprinting toward the police car. "I guess you're all right."

"I am," I say, turning from him now to face the others, who are already in scatter, anticipating. "Get on with it!" I shout. "Can't you do anything right? Don't you have any sense, any discipline, any professionalism?" The same old pointless rant. I am sick of hearing it myself, but at least it works. They shuffle back to the cars, the grounds, various positions. We are already three minutes behind schedule.

For a moment I think of canceling, telling them off and striking the set until the afternoon, but they have worked so hard up to this point that it is really not fair, and there are also certain notes given them the last time that I must reinforce in run-through or lose forever. The hell with it, then. "Let's go," I say, raising my hand, and they see me in the sun; they see me standing there, see the power coming from that hand, and the cars begin to move. Sirens start. Oswald is already gone; it is not impossible that he will retrieve all of the lost time. I pick my pad from the place where I had dropped it and, taking the pen from my pocket, continue my observations. Locked within directorial detachment again, it is as if none of this is happening now but has already happened a long time ago, in a Southwestern city, fifty-three years ago next Thursday, already frozen into artifact and how much longer can I put up with their incompetence?

II

Later, with Lara, I try to relax. She is the only one of the players whom I will call by her real name, even in these notes, which are supposed to be confidential and which are to be opened by the Outsiders only decades after the fact, 2050 or something like that; it is difficult to keep track of everything. Under the arrangements I am compelled to keep these notes; actually, I would rather not

bother. Lara played Mrs. Connally today; I have shifted
her to all of the feminine roles, even in an outrage once
to Jacqueline, but these enactments do not suit her quali-
ties, whatever they are. She becomes frozen at critical
times, postures aimlessly, sometimes lets her sentiments
overcome her to the point where she cannot function at
all. A bad actress, in short, although she has abilities of
another sort. "Don't you ever get tired of this?" she asks,
her head now leaned across my legs in a posture of relaxation, her hands rather aimlessly prodding my thighs,
slivers of sensation traveling to me that way, although I
am not to be moved by any of them. Even by her. They
suit limited purposes, is all. "I would think that you're
getting bored."

"I am not getting bored. I never get bored. It's work,
that's all it is. Don't worry about my feelings."

"All right," she says in a mollifying way, increasing the
rhythm of her stroking, as if this could affect me, "you
don't have to lose your temper. I was only asking."

"I did not lose my temper. I never lose my temper."

"I don't understand why you want to do this. I can see
everything else and what you might be trying to do, but
not what you're getting out of it. What could you possibly
have to gain from this, even in satisfaction?"

Lara is the most intelligent of them and the only one
with whom I can manage some informality, but she, too,
is disastrously stupid, like the rest, and I perceive, not for
the first time, the hopelessness of our relationship. "Stop
it," I say. "I don't want to discuss it anymore. It's work,
that's all it is, and when the day is over, one can go on to
other things. You're here at your own request, you know."
This is not a pleasant thing to say, but her incessant questioning disturbs me more at some times than at others and
the run-through today brought me to a point of understanding I had evaded before; it is really quite hopeless.
They will never be able to do it right, and we are moving
further from true effectiveness all the time. It is possible
that on the second run-through, no real preparations, just
a set of notes and a quick enactment after their initial
familiarization, they did as well as they ever can, and

from here on in it can only become worse, completely mechanical. Three more days here and out; it will all be over, but what have I learned? I will learn nothing; this is the tragedy. "Go," I say, inflamed by pique and other emotions. "If you have nothing else to say, just go."

"If you want," she says, lolling to the other side, picking herself away from me in one gesture and opening ground, "if you want me to, I will; it's your choice, you know. Why won't you ever talk to us? Why won't you answer my questions? Once I thought it was because you had your reasons, but now I'm beginning to be afraid that it's only because you have no answers. Do you really want me to go?"

I reach for her. My cardiovascular and sympathetic nervous systems have been immobilized previously, this being one of the requirements before entrance to the city, but I feel a distant, uncoiling response, more dependent upon memory than connection. "No," I say, "I don't want you to go."

Cunning, cunning, she retreats and holds herself before me with new assurance. "Then you must tell me," she says, "the real truth of why you are here and putting us through these performances. No one Outside even knows that we exist anymore, and yet you come here for these rehearsals. You must tell . . . "

"No," I say, getting to my feet, stalking from her in one motion, "no, there is no more. You must go, Lara."

Stricken, she holds to place. "You must tell me. Otherwise I can't go on . . . "

"You will go on," I say. "You will go on as long as it is necessary and then further yet, because this is what I want you to do. When it is ended you will have your explanation, but not until then, and I will say no more."

"You think that you can control us," she says quietly. "You think that because you're from the Outside and we the lumpen of the city you can make us do anything you want because of your authority, but you don't. . . "

"And can't I?" I say, looking at her. An attractive girl but amorphous at the edges, filled with small shadings toward darkness and dead in the center as all of those left in the city are. She cannot touch me; it means nothing. "Can't I?" I ask again.

She looks at the ground, shakes her head, says nothing. Rumble of stones above; sympathetic collapse of great structures in the distance. The city is falling always as we work through our rituals. Now, leading her from the small enclosed place in the Battery where we have been, I can see the destruction again. Animals whisk invisibly through the park; I feel her hatred as if strung through me by fine wires filled with explosives and the scent of gasoline.

"Yes, I can," I say, answering my question, and so deep am I in the speculation this sets off when I say it that I do not notice when Lara leaves . . . if she has left. If she is still beside me it makes no difference; I am wrapped in directional contemplation.

III

I did not think it would be this complex. I envisioned it as a simple process, an assemblage of lumpen glad to cooperate with a director from the Outside (because, by inference, it might be the only escape of their own), a few rehearsals, logistics, geometry, line readings and blocking adjustments here and there, and then the crews would be summoned, do the filming in one take and that would be the end of it. I would be out of this accursed place, and on tape would repose my masterpiece or, if not my masterpiece, certainly an interesting idea strikingly put together. Auditors could hardly fail to see the originality of it and would give high marks for audacity if not execution. A grisly historical event—it has been one of my minor interests for some time now—re-enacted and brought back to the sense of its original grubbiness by a cast of lumpen playing in the landscape of the city! Yes, it would have all worked out if it had only been that simple. The griminess, the incongruity, the sheer *incompetence* surrounding those bizarre events that become part of our common (unknown) history would have been fully reconstituted through my process, and the insights thus gained would have raised the popular awareness considerably or, if not that, at least the awareness of the Committee through which all projects of this nature must go in partial fulfillment of, etcetera. But the simplicity of my vision has always been contradicted by an overwhelming breakdown in carry-through; I have had no luck is another way of putting it, or possibly the word I am scrambling for is "foresight," and it never occurred to me, somehow, that the lumpen would—most of them, anyway—be dismally untalented, some of them barely able to read the lines of the scripts, let alone play them with conviction.

I should have known it! I know I should have known it, but one tends to romanticize, at least in the abstract, these lumpen, just as all stricken creatures must be romanticized by intellectual types such as myself: sturdy survivors of an era, urban artifacts, lone hangers-on, exiles in torment and so on. Who knew what veins of conviction and energy I would tap? And so on. . . . But what I did not see (until it confronted me in all of its wondrous and forthright simplicity) was that the lumpen were what they were for good reason; only a tenth of them at best are in the city by choice, the remainder either there by relationship or in penalty or for reasons of idiocy (what else could voluntary election of the city be?), and the five to ten years that is the average time spent here has brutalized them all, even the least of them, to the level of little more than pigs who after rooting around in bad grounds for years would not even recognize good hydroponics when they sniffed it. By these terms Lara is *in reductio* as well; my feelings for her are barely more elevated than for any of the others (it is only the instinct for lust that kindled my interest, the desire to function despite the circuitry that blocks this), and what she says to me, stripped of emotional content, comes down to the same complaints that I have heard from all the others: weak snufflings of resentment disguised as regret, and beyond that, stupefying incomprehension. I cannot stand it anymore. All of them are getting worse.

Worse: they are not even at the level where I had them two days ago and now time is almost over. Like it or not, the technicians will be in tomorrow for the taping and the show will then be struck. Oswald simpering, Kennedy effeminate, Connally palsied and with strange attacks of temper that cause his face to suffuse as he forgets his lines. I refuse to call them by names any other than these; they exist to me only in terms of the roles they have been assigned—or would so exist if things were going satisfactorily—and will not be dignified by any other term. They are lumpen, Lara as well, and the worst of them, because she has the presumption to think that she understood me.

Miserably: it is going miserably. Oswald levels the rifle, narrows down the sight, and even from this distance I imagine that I can see the lines of involvement working small crosses and hatch marks across his face—the bad actor's method of working himself into a role only through grief or rage recollected—but even as Kennedy huddles in the car, moving darkly toward Jacqueline, a little clot on the cushioning now, burrowing himself into an angle for the shot, I see that it will not work; the synchronization is off. And to compound the disaster, the old car leading the motorcade must throw a piston or something; it comes to a stop with a scream and from that car leap the Secret Service detail, cursing. They make hand signals that the motorcade is to stop, but the cars behind do not see them or see them quickly enough, and the cars pile upon one another with a series of dull thuds, only their extreme low speed giving a certain comic intensity to the performance. Kennedy sways out of the car wiping his forehead, the agents surround him, Jacqueline holds an elbow. From this distance I see Lara, the only one of them with professional discipline, still at rest quietly in the car, her hands folded, locked in the role. She is waiting for the motorcade to resume. The others are gesturing at one another, talking in progressively louder voices, and Oswald disappears from the window to run clattering down flights of the Municipal to join them. The run-through has been ruined. They do not even look at me as

I come toward them gesticulating, ranting, slapping the notes in my hands. I am not sure of this but have a certain intimation of laughter, as if all the time they cooperated with me only unwillingly and are now free to show their contempt.

It is the end, the end of it; my last reserve of containment is emptied as I come toward them and I realize—from long knowledge—that I am on the verge of a serious loss of control, something that I should be unable to risk in this context, but it is too late to talk quietly to myself in reasonable tones, small whispers of assurance. "Goddamn it!" I scream at them. "Goddamn you all! Can't you do anything right? Don't any of you understand what's going on here? I can't stand it; I can't stand this anymore. We had only three days to get this thing right, and now you've ruined everything! Dogs, pigs! You deserve to be in the city! Once I took pity on you, but that was before I came to know what you are! You are incompetent; there is nothing you can do in terms of your lives because you are incapable of running them!" And so on and so forth. . . . I am really quite out of control and it is pointless to abuse the lumpen so, because their condition alone is retribution and abuse means nothing. I know this. Nevertheless, I cannot stop. "Three days to get a simple scene staged and taped and you've ruined it all!" I shout. "You've ruined everything."

I realize that I am not being entirely fair, because the lumpen have ruined nothing for themselves—their lives are already entirely ruined—but only for me, the director, the scheduling, the necessities. Nevertheless, I cannot control myself, flinging my notes now to the gound, where the winds of the Battery promptly whisk in to scatter them on the ruined clumps of earth. "How," I say, "how am I ever going to get anywhere with this?"

"It isn't our fault," Kennedy says. His eyes are persuasive, at least to me; I still accept him in the role. "Nobody here wanted to do this. We offered our services as a favor to you. We've done the best we can."

"That's right," says Connally. Texan, diffident, he slides a hand into a pocket, looks at me with tormented little eyes. "You made us do this. We had nothing to do with it at all."

"We're doing the best we can," Kennedy says. "We have no idea what you want. It's up to you to tell us."

"Right," Connally says, "that's right. If you don't like what we're doing it's not our fault, but yours, because we didn't want to do it in the first place."

"They're both right," Johnson says, striding over to us. Of all the principals he is the most poorly cast, being a dwarfish man with stiff hands, and no talent for gesture at all, but the first directorial impulse is often the correct one, or at least so I was taught in the final seminars, and I was convinced that he would be able to work his way through the part. I was wrong about him, however. I was wrong about all of them.

"I was wrong about all of you," I say. Frustration makes me rash; momentarily at least I must forget where I am, the nature of the people with whom I am dealing. "You're all worthless," I say, "all of you. You pity yourselves and work on your small resentments and hatreds and blame everybody because you're not on the Outside and they call you lumpen, but the fact is that you are lumpen, nothing else but that, and you all deserve to be here. Every one of you. You've made your lives and you have no right to complain about everything because it's all your fault. You disgust me," I say. I am shaking. "All of you disgust me."

Lara is out of her car now, touching me on the elbow, and in that touch I feel quivering. "Please," she says to the rest of them. I do not know what she is talking about. "He's not in his right mind. He's very young and there's so much he doesn't understand. He doesn't even know what he's saying. Please leave him alone."

"Leave me alone?" I say, not comprehending. "Why should they leave me alone? They've ruined everything for the taping; why should they desert me?"

"You don't realize," Lara says to me, "what's going on here. You don't understand him," she says to the others. "Please now, let me talk to him. I'm sure that I can make him see if you'll only give me time."

But it is too late for this, and finally I become aware of what is going on. They close about me now: Johnson, Kennedy, Connally, the Secret Service agents. Even Oswald, with a demented look settling into his features, has joined them, and I feel the press of bodies, the beginning of enclosure; scent a high, penetrating smell that can only come from my own glands. I feel their pressure against me. "Now, stop this," I say. "This is ridiculous. It's only a play, a re-enactment, a simple run-through for researching purposes, and if you don't see that . . . "

"We see," Oswald says to me. "We see what we need to see." And their hands are on me now. I feel the dread contact of bodies, the actual sense of connection filling me with a revulsion as pure as I have ever known, the *reality* of those bodies, and then I feel myself taken away from there in a struggling kind of fashion, but past the first struggles I can do nothing whatsoever.

"Lara," I cry, "Lara, tell them to stop this. It's impossible. They can't do it to me, and anyway, when the crews come in and see this . . . "

"Our laws," someone says, "are not your laws, here in the city." And then I see where they are taking me. Doors open, I am thrust into a smaller area, a rising stench confronts me, old metal and gates swing open and I am escorted within.

The old Tombs. "I can't do anything," Lara says, "it's all your own fault." My head strikes a bar, I stagger, fall and see no more for a while.

When I return to myself, I am incarcerated.

IV

In the cell, I soon realize that it is useless to struggle and hunch myself against a wall, knees drawn up in a fetal position, staring, listlessly I suppose, although I am mercifully unaware of my own facial expressions, at the small sprays and dots of light that scatter through the one barred window too high otherwise to provide me perspective. In a corner opposite are a cup of water, a few slices of bread, pure food from the city, only slightly marred by dirt, and I suppose that I should make the effort to have some, not only because I must keep my strength up, but because in leaving this they are showing obvious consideration of which I ought, by right, to partake. But it is too much of an effort to readjust myself and go over to that opposite corner, some ten to fifteen feet from here; much easier to simply sprawl and let the impressions overtake me. It is quiet in what remains of the Tombs, quiet and isolated and a good place to do some thinking if one were interested in thought; never a contemplative type, I prefer to leave the impressions subvocal. It was insane to come into the city.

Insane to come into the city from which most of us have been trained from the beginning to flee, crazier yet to involve the lumpen in a project of this type—how could they understand it—but where else was I likely to find cheaply the participants necessary for the project? Professional actors would have been necessary Outside, actors and space, and I did not have the means to hire. The lumpen were known to be submissive, and would not my quickly acquired cast think that cooperation in the project might be a means of making their way into the Outside? Nor did I ever mislead them; I made no promises. Simply enough, I did not calculate for their strangeness, stupidity and violence, and this makes me a fool.

Lara appears at the gate and, putting her hands on the bars, leans inward, alone. "Are you all right?" she asks. From this aspect she seems more attractive than I have ever seen her, but I know their irretrievable corruption now and am not tempted by feeling.

"Leave me alone," I say, "or get me out of here. Nothing else."

"Please," she says, "you must listen to me. You never listened."

"I have nothing to say."

"Please," she says. Is she weeping? "They are very angry. They feel that you have used and manipulated them and they plan to do terrible things. . . ."

"The crews are coming from Outside," I say. "They

should be here within a matter of hours now, and when they see what has happened there will be terrible retribution. I am perfectly willing to wait a few hours. Your prisons mean nothing."

"No one will come. They will turn them back at the docks."

"Then they will circle and come in from the uptown side. You are a fool, Lara."

"No," she says, "you are a fool. I do not even know your name. You never told me your name."

"It doesn't matter."

"You never told me your name or what you planned or what we were supposed to do and now it's too late. You are the one who is a fool." She leans toward me, instinctively trying to put her head against mine but, of course, the bars stop her. Who is in jail? Who is really in jail? "I think I can get you out of here," she says, "but you'll have to make the escape on your own. I can't help you any further."

"I need no escape. It is they who will have to escape when it is seen what has been done to me."

"Oh, you fool," she says, releasing her grip on the bars and fluttering her hands like the wings of a fowl, moving away from me. "Oh, you fool, you fool. You don't understand anything at all, do you?" And I hear footsteps and the footsteps are upon us and lumpen come into the corridor and seize Lara, drag her away, leaving the hall very quiet again. In the distance I hear sounds. Then the door down the corridor opens and they come again; I see Oswald, Kennedy, Connally, other faces I do not know, peering incuriously at me through the bars, their faces bland, as if healed over from pain, only the eyes dark and alive in those faces, the hands raised like a network to guide me through. And without necessity to hear what they say, I stand, bracing myself against a wall, feeling the stone moving against my shoulder blades and buttocks, or then again the wall is stolid, unshaken, and it is I who am trembling upon it like an insect.

"Come," one of them says to me, and I come. Through

the corridors of the Tombs, like deep roots from a plant sprawling through the earth, and onto the steps, where I see others gathered to await me.

I would fall gratefully but am held by arms before, arms behind. "Now," one of them says, and I am led toward the motorcade.

V

I do not like the lumpen: I hate and fear them. But in how many dreams did they move before me, those forms clotted by darkness, shadows against the sprawl of the abandoned city? "We are your history," they have whispered to me in those dreams. "We are what all of you have been and yet could be if you were not part of the city." And I do not know if it was tenderness or mockery, but those faces broke open softly, feeling coming out of the planes of those faces like blood, and in those dreams I must have answered, saying, "Yes, it is true. Yes, you are our history, but there must be more to it than that, something that I can extract." And they laughed then as lumpen often do in their silly, abandoned fashion and said, "There is nothing you can extract. There is nothing you can learn. We have nothing to say to you, no mysteries to impart, we are mute as stones." And so on and so forth. What intense dialogues I had with them in these dreams! Why, I must have been obsessed with them for years, and in terms of that, it made a great deal of sense when it came time for the project in partial fulfillment of, etcetera, made a great deal of sense to go back to the city itself and confront them in the real. Because if I could use them, could make them part of the project, then— was it as simple as that?—they would be wrenched free of history and import and would become merely actors in my own staging, which was their only function and certainly a far more reasonable way in which to confront the lumpen problem. Wasn't it? How did I ever end in this situation?

"Let me do this," I said to the Committee in gravity

assembled after I had made the presentation, "and I can bring back to you a genuine reconstruction of an important historical event. What we have forgotten, living on the Outside, is the genuine grubbiness of most of these tragedies. They did not occur in high places among the cleanly assembled but were in fact stumbling events enacted by people very much like the lumpen. I can show you this. I can show you something understandable and important that you have yet avoided. Besides, it is going to be fifty-three years since the assassination a few months from now, and in terms of the new calendar this is an important anniversary. You can franchise the tapes. Not only will I profit but the Academy as well."

Oh, how they mumbled and grumbled, stumbled and rumbled. "The dangers," the Committee said, "and the known instability of this class of people, and then again, really, how much control can it be said that you will exert over them? They are a violent, unstable class of people; it is a condition of their environment. And furthermore, you would have to sign a full waiver of release not only for yourself but for the crews."

"The crews are no problem," I assured the Committee. "We can use for personnel those who are already on the verge of exile." I must have smiled at them then. "This will assure their total cooperation."

"Of course," the Committee said. They—he, it—inspected fingernails, looked over the small room in which the orals were conducted and then, putting hands on the table, stood ponderously. "Let us think about it," the Committee said, "and we'll let you know. An interesting project, an interesting idea, but minor, we think. Essentially minor. Of course, you have made the sensational aspects of it quite clear to us, but it is not merely *sensationalism* that we seek from a major in the histories; rather, there must be a certain depth, and the idea seems lacking, rather . . ."

"But remember," I said, rather hoarsely perhaps (I am at times more aware of the tones and tenor of my voice, the sense of my gestures, than the normal person; an extraordinary sensitivity must be the explanation), "the lumpen. They will be playing the roles, and the majestic irony, the complexity of the fact that these figures and events are being reconstructed by the filthiest, dirtiest, grubbiest, most dangerous, malevolent, degraded and diseased segments we know. . . ." Choking, I was quite unable to go on. The filthiness of the lumpen has always filled me with excitement. It must have something to do with that obsession to which I have already frankly referred. "It will be a fine project," I finished, rubbing my hands. "A fine project, an excellent project, and the tapes will be priceless and become the property of the Academy."

"Well, that is thoughtful," the Committee rumbled and stumbled and grumbled and bumbled and mumbled and went on its ponderous way, leaving me with a promise for decision in the imminent future, and in due course permission came down and I journeyed into the city alone and unarmed (because I had no physical fear of them) to put together my cast for rehearsals, with the crews to come in independently three days later, and everything was to work out splendidly, a remarkable project. And then the rehearsals fell into some difficulty and they would not listen to me when I gave them orders and the blocking became unstuck and the line readings broke down and I had to tell them what they were because this was the only way to shock them into compliance and then they turned upon me and threw me in a cell and then took me out of the cell and . . .

How did I ever get into this?

VI

I find myself thrust into the third car of the motorcade. Roses all around me; Lara to the left. It is going too quickly for detached observation; the car begins to move. Lara, to my left, sits frozen, hands clasped, looking ahead; in her blank cheeks I can see no reason, no accessibility. They step away from me; the car moves somewhat more quickly. Sea breezes off the Battery waft the smell of fish into my nostrils; I wonder what Kennedy smelled on that day almost fifty-three years ago. Strange, strange, I have never felt so close to him.

"What is going on?" I ask Lara. And again, "What is going on?" And she turns toward me then, her eyes round and open, her mouth sagging. She clutches roses, spills them like blood drops from her hands, and I see in the slackness of feature that all along I must have misjudged her. She, too, is lumpen. From the beginning, I was surrounded by them. I thought that I was the director and all the time it was they who . . .

The sun comes against my eyes; I squint, raise a hand in a blocking gesture and I feel the increased acceleration of the car pressing me firmly into the cushions. Amazing that they were able to get this old fleet of archaic vehicles running again somehow; high marks for their animal cunning and ingenuity. I feel increasing speed. "What is this?" I say. "This is entirely wrong. This is not the way it was supposed to be. I am the director. I do not belong in here."

"Quiet," Lara says. "Stay quiet. And keep down. Get down now!" And the rising thread of her voice loops me, causes me to look up at the twinkling sun, at Municipal above me. There is someone in a window of Municipal; I can see the barrel of the rifle moving and retreating through the aperture. "Oh, my God," Lara says, "you fool." And I dive then, beginning to understand what has happened, but as I do so it is with hopelessness, because I know that it is already too late and I should have done the diving three seconds or maybe it was three months ago. I feel the impact like a horde of bees around my scalp; it does not hurt very badly.

"The crews!" she cries. "Where are the crews?" And I look up again, trying to sight them. The crews are here at last. They will gauge the situation in an instant and rush in to save me from these barbarians. But then, as I do indeed see them, just coming into view on their slow-moving vehicles at the rim of the Battery, telescopes fixed and pointing at me . . . Well, as I see them, I see everything at last, and it is really too much for me. I cannot deal with it. I cannot begin to deal with it. *Why me?* I ask, but no point in pleading. I see the answer. *Why not?* something else says. *Why not you, indeed? It could, after all, have been anyone.*

I dive toward the floorboards of the car, hoping that they will support me against impact, and as I do so, in mid-gesture, I feel the second hit, the real one, tearing in through the side of my neck. It must be the windpipe. My breath is cut off; I flutter like a fish against the cushions and then collapse in Lara's lap, groaning. Everything goes away from me. I feel her hands. *It could have been anyone.*

"The crews, my God, the crews! They've shot my husband!" she screams, and this is really the last thing I hear, at least the last during this disgrace, but as I drown in my own series of explosions, I think what it might be like to have confronted the Committee with my knowledge of their treachery . . . and to explain to them that it could have been worked out even more easily and at less expense.

The *randomness* of it all.

Is this why they allow the lumpen to live?

Introduction to
CULTURE LOCK

Homosexuality is coming into the mainstream of acknowledged human affairs, and I am all for this; it is too late, but it is time, and I can see only one deleterious effect: we are going to lose, in a generation or two, the homosexual subculture that rests on unfortunate guilt, self-loathing, exclusion and the insight of those who have truly fused their personal condition with that of the external world to construct what under my definition is art.

If the homosexual no longer feels shame in his condition—and why should he?—the literature born in repression, full of irony and levels of meaning, will also be lost. I can think of no one who this will hurt as much as the isolation and self-loathing of most of the homosexual culture *has* hurt, and therefore let it go willingly.

This story—the editor commissioning asked for a "highly condemnatory study of homosexuality"—is an example of what will be lost. Good riddance to it . . . it is not, all of this literature, worth the shame or the doubt of a single adolescent. Bad life may be a pre-condition to good art . . . but it is not; I assure the world at large, it is never worth it.

CULTURE LOCK

I

Friday is make-it. George and Fred and Karl and Miller and Kenny and me in George's apartment on the thirty-sixth floor of the project. Kenny is the complication; since we have taken up together, last Wednesday, a week ago, I have been thinking about make-it night with a mixture

275

of fear and doubt. Should we stay away? Should we pass
up the session? I know without asking him that Kenny
does not want to go, that what he feels building between
us, etcetera, is important enough to take us out of the circle. Nevertheless, the forms must hold. If we do not come,
there will be questions raised about the absence, and the
tenuous solidarity of the group itself may be menaced.
What will happen between Kenny and myself will happen, exclusive of make-its. I explain this to him. Quietly,
sullenly, he nods. We go into the elevator and to George's
apartment, the two of us by our entrance already showing
them everything they need to know.

Leers, winks, shouts of greeting as we blend into the
circle. It is understood in that first moment what is going
on between Kenny and me. Shouted remarks from Miller, brusque mutterings from George, who, as the host
this night, must spread all of his favors equally. Fred
winks. Only Karl stays away, showing his comprehension
in the one bleak look we exchange. Not too many months
ago, it might have been the same between Karl and me.
He is bitter. Perhaps not. Perhaps I am merely projecting
my own embarrassment upon him. It does not matter. I
remind myself of this, clutching Kenny's hands before the
lights go out; nothing matters.

Darkening. Music rises from the center; the make-it
has begun. "Remember," George says ritually as we huddle together, "remember the principles." Since he is the
host this week it is necessary that he make the statements;
his resentment and boredom, however, come through,
even under the first haze of the hit. "The principle of
blending," George says, "the principle of accommodation.
The principle of sharing and that of connection. Brothers
all, one to one and then together for the greater good."
His breath is already ragged, uneven. Our clothes come
off. "For the city," George says, "for the city and thus for
the country. All together. All blending."

This is one of the problems of the make-it, the posturing and formality with which, I think, none of us agree.
Nevertheless, we must go through it. A tradition handed
down to us by forebears. Who are we to reason why and

so on? In the darkness, I feel Karl's hand on my knee and the drugs lift, they vault. He says something foul into my ear.

"No," I say, moving from him, "no, no," trying to dive into Kenny's body, but in the darkness the shapes have become rearranged and I cannot find him. I feel pressure, the first tugs of entrance and then the oozing, familiar slide of Karl's entrance as he buries himself in me, the first time in many months. "No," I say again, but in a whimpering way. He has made me the woman. Karl has always made women of his partners; this is why it never could have been worked out.

"It's make-it," Karl says, moving on top of me, "it's make-it and you cannot deny. You'll have your slut later." And I feel his moments of accession then, submit to him slowly, small bits and pieces of myself yielding to Karl, and then the old fire, however unwillingly, rises. "You tramp," Karl says, slamming himself into me, and under the drugs, in the darkness, I feel my whimpers turn toward submission and at last, however reluctantly, to lust as he overtakes me.

At his peak I reach blindly, hoping that I will touch Kenny, but my fingers squirrel emptily against the surfaces of George's rug, and it is only lint and dust that my palms gather as Karl works his will.

II

In the morning, in my apartment, the drugs still dissipating from my system, he turns to me in the bed, his face open and pained, and hurtles himself against me, not for connection but for comfort. I gather him against me, which is all that I can do, feel his moans against my shoulder, accept his need, which is all that I can do. He is trembling, dependent; he will always be a woman, which is, possibly, his primal attraction for me, although already, in just the eighth day of our serious relationship, he is already becoming burdensome. "Why?" he is saying to me. "Why must this be? I don't understand it. Why can't we just be together? Why can't people just live? Why do we have to go to the make-its and trade off like that? It's evil, I tell you. It isn't the way that it should be." And, twenty-three years old, he begins to sob.

I pat his neck, absently. "No choice," I say, and, "This is the way it must be," and, "We still have each other, don't we?" The aimless platitudes that, for Kenny, are as close as he can come to knowledge, and at last he quiets. Without lust I hold him, shroud him with my body.

At length he sleeps, unbonded from the drug-panic at last, and I ease from the bed, relieve myself and then walk to the window where I look out upon the city for a long time, willing my mind toward blankness and acceptance as it is stated in the principles. Dust sifts upward, light down, light shimmers and glimmers through the one hundred stories of the project, grouped upon one another like bodies grappling at a make-it. At a far distance I think that I can see the limits and beyond that still, a hint of fire, but this must be only fatigue and I block out the illusion, going back then to the bed.

Kenny lies there open-mouthed, his face a child's face, his chest moving easily, helpless against my gaze. I could mount him like a stallion and have my way; I could strangle him in his sleep and no one would know the difference; I could stagger with him toward the window and throw him down forty-seven stories of project to let him burst upon the pavement and no one could stop me. He is completely at my will; I could do anything to him that I wanted, and this, then, must be part of the excitement. Standing by the bed, looking upon him, I find that my fists are clenching and unclenching in the old rhythm of masturbation, but I do not do it.

Instead I crawl beside him on the bed, carefully so as not to wreck his sleep, and roll against him, and then for a while I myself sleep, the sounds and odors of the city combating dreams for a while for attention and then disappearing at last in an oily and satisfying enclosure that I must know as rest.

III

In the morning again, but later, Kenny and I arise and leave my room quietly, journey down the forty-seven flights of the project and take a long walk around the winding paths, ending at last at the gates beyond which lies the river. Hand in hand we look at the river for a long time, talking quietly of arrangements, plans, possibilities. By some unphrased understanding, we have agreed not to mention the make-it again, not this day, maybe not for several days. We decide that the time has come in our relationship where Kenny will vacate his apartment on the fifty-sixth and move in with me, at least on a temporary basis. After that, who knows? We will see where the relationship goes. His fingers against my palm begin to excite me; I rub the small of his back, feeling the slow beat of him radiating. "Will it work?" Kenny says. "Will it work between us?" He has already told me that at the beginning of his relationships he is sentimental, hoping for permanence, hoping that this one at last will grant him stability. *It's only later that I become a bitch,* he has warned me, *when I realize that I will never find that stability, and then you will hate me.* But that is a good way off, weeks at least or perhaps months until my relationship with Kenny becomes sour and embittered, and even though I can see the patterns coalescing faintly, like the shapes of dead animals in the river, they do not concern me now.

"Yes," I say, "yes; it will work between us." Looking at the river, thinking of the city, all of the city seeming to overtake me now on this late and strange morning, my body still aching from Karl's penetration but yearning toward this new lover by my side. "It's got to work," I say. "I promise that it will work." Thinking of the city and how we have come to survive in it and how wrong, how wrong all of the sociologists and analysts of forty years ago were, because the patterns that they detected as the sickness of the city were, indeed, only those of health; it was the accommodation that they saw, but locked into their culture as we are not, they did not understand the cure for the illness, but, instead, gave it a different name.

"I know it will work," I say quietly, testing the firmness of his rectum with a delicate finger, feeling the gentle pulsations from that flower as all unconscious it wraps itself around me, and then he slumps against me and I gather him in, my lover, my friend.

"I don't think," he says then, "I don't think that I could stand it if it went wrong again. I've been hurt so much. Last night at the make-it, when George came into me I thought . . ."

"Quiet," I say, putting a hand against his lips, "quiet. We agreed we wouldn't talk about the make-it. That's a long way off. We don't even have to think about it for six days." And he laughs, gently at first, then harder, the bursts of his laughter carrying him into my arms, my arms taking him in, little whiffs and smells of the river compounding my excitement, and right there, against the gates, with all the project looking down—And who could care if they were? Who could care?—we have at each other, the clothes falling away, our bodies joining, the lifting and the joining together, and *"Oh!* he cries at the climax. *"Oh, Bert, I never thought it could be this way!"* He is twenty-three years old, I am twenty-eight, but it is not a matter of ages. There are things I understand all too well that will never touch him, and it is this, his frailty, his accessibility to pain, that more than anything else must thrust me over and I dissolve into him, groaning and beating against the gate, against the river, the project revolving slowly above us as we thrash together on the ground.

At length we separate, but hands interlocked, we walk back toward the project to make the transfer of quarters in perfect silence and understanding. The make-it is far behind us. And it will be six days more until we must test our partnership again.

IV

At the beginning with Karl, in the second week or the third, it must have been, we, too, came down to the river; oh, this must have been months ago, six or seven at least, Karl now being as dead to me and distant as the spaces of the countryside I forsook to return to the city, but at that time what was building with Karl seemed significant, or then again maybe it was not, maybe nothing was significant, and we stood against the gates looking upon the river, just as I had with Kenny this day, and he turned to me then, dropping his hand, and looking at me, he said, "Bert, we're sick. We're sick and we're totally insane. Bert, do you see what's become of us just so that we could survive? Is it worth it? Is it worth it?" And there was nothing to say to him, there was never anything to say to Karl in any of these moods, and so I let it pass, I the submissive one then, leaning against the gate, letting my posture go slack, and at this impression of vulnerability (how he always made me the woman!) Karl came upon me then and gathered me in. "I didn't mean to hurt you," he said. "I didn't want to hurt you. Forget I said it. Forget everything. Just let me hold you." And so on and so forth. "We aren't sick," he said. "It's just a dream, a dream of the city, and so it will pass." And against the gate then we did the necessary, but it was never as good as the way it was going to be later with Kenny (I believe this; I must believe this), and as I rolled under him, eyes fixed way above the project on the damp and obtrusive sky, eyes rolling in the spasms of the approaching orgasm, I told myself even then that it was temporary with Karl, a way station, and that at the very next make-it I would have to keep my eyes open for someone else, someone who would reconstitute me at the level of health I deserved, and this is how I met Kenny, Kenny, who had not been mine in other than a casual way as part of the group for three full years, and I knew then, looking at the sky, just as I know now, embracing my lover yet again in an ecstasy of connection, that the city is good and the city is merciful because it has given us, in its justice and wisdom, the opportunity to do without penalty exactly all of those things that we must in order to bear it.

Introduction to
AS IN A VISION APPREHENDED

Although by no stretch of the definition am I a practicing Jew, I am a darkly believing one and feel that within the rather scatological husk of the man is imprisoned the ranting soul of a nineteenth-century Chasidic rabbi. Why, if this is the case, I have almost never approached the Judaic theme in my fiction is something of which I am not entirely sure. I always intended to . . . it's just that it's been done so well (although not, interestingly, in S-F; Jack Dann's ten-story collection, *Wandering Stars*, contains about the only explicitly Judaic fiction the field has had) that there seemed little enough to add.

As in a Vision, written instead of going to the shopping center on Memorial Day, 1972, is, perhaps, the only treatment of the Chasidic Judaic theme that I will ever do; it is a little heavy-handed (utilizing deliberately certain formal "folklore" devices that I. B. Singer does so much better; the influence is there) and more than a shade self-conscious, but it appears to *work,* which is what a story must do or it is nothing, and the point, turning upon its apparent thematic basis, as is characteristic of so much of my work (hence the comparisons to Kornbluth), is almost original.

It would be a lifetime to partially investigate the wisdom and traditions of the Judaic faith and way of life, and now and then I wish that I had. Oh, well, my aunt always used to say that I should become a rabbi.

Which I did in a sense, of course—do not misunderstand me. This is my pulpit.

———◆———

AS IN A VISION APPREHENDED

Mottel was possessed and through the fourth week the demon overwhelmed him so that he could do nothing but lie on his bed and moan of the vision, call for the Rabbi to help him. But the doctors having given up, the Rabbi had already come there on the morning of this day and could do nothing. It was a case, he suggested, for the darker sects; perhaps a mystic could help. There was said to be in the countryside . . .

"I see," Mottel had gasped to the Rabbi, "I see a vision of death and burning, such burning as we have never known before. I see men led off to be murdered for nothing but that they are of our people; I see their women and children being taken with them and murder committed as it never has been before in the history of the world; not by knife but by machine. I see millions in line to be slaughtered, some of them filled with knowledge but most of them dumb as cattle, innocent of their burden, and in the midst of these flames I see armies; armies such as there have never been, sweeping and looting and pillaging their way through all the villages and over the oceans as well. Oh, it is terrible; I tell you I cannot stand it anymore, I was not meant to see this, I was not meant to know such things; you must help me, Rabbi," Mottel cried and lay back on his bed. But the possession was so fierce, of course, that by the early afternoon he had forgotten that the Rabbi had come and was begging for his presence again. His relatives held a meeting in the parlor, then, when the Rabbi had left in despair, trying not to listen to the moans and screams coming from the back, trying to talk over the matter of Mottel's possession reasonably, for they were all, even to the cousins, reasonable or so, at that time, did they think.

"I will have nothing of witchcraft," Mottel's wife Rachel said. She was a tall woman with fierce eyes who could not stop the movement of her hands, but for twenty years she had served Mottel well and borne him three children, and in his right mind he was devoted to her. "I say it is a dream, a passing fever, and he will be well again if we leave him alone. I want nothing of the soothsayers."

"The Rabbi himself says that it is a dybbuk," her brother Jacob said quietly, and the other brothers agreed as did her eldest son Isaac, a boy of seventeen years who it was felt was likewise entitled now to sit in upon the conference. "If it is indeed a dybbuk, a possession, and we do nothing," Jacob said, "then we take upon ourselves not only the responsibility for this man but the damage that the demon may do all of us, for it is well known that a dybbuk, once uncaged, can lodge in one soul or the other, and we expose all of ourselves to risk."

"It is merely a sickness; it will pass as have all the others," Rachel said desperately, and at that moment the screams and whimpers of the anguished man in the bedroom, adjacent became so loud that all of them, Rachel leading, raced into the bedroom where Mottel could be seen dimly in the shadows, rising from the bed and trying to balance himself against a wall. "Darkness such as we have never known," Mottel cried, "the next century is filled with death, a legacy of death not only for the Jews but for all peoples of the world, and I tell you they must be warned, warned of the next century before it happens to us. I have seen it all clearly. Do you hear me?" he screamed, facing them, his beard matted with a week of neglect, the skin of his face pale and yet luminescent against this beard. "You have got to help me; you must assist me from this bed so that I can spread the warning, the warning of this terrible darkness, it is coming. . . ." And reaching toward them in an ecstasy of rage, the sick man lost his balance and toppled gracelessly to the floor, still talking. Jacob and the others lifted him groaning to the bed where Mottel lay sobbing on his back for a moment and then put his palms against his eyes. "I see it," Mottel said, "I see it, and I cannot stand it anymore."

"All right, then," Rachel said quietly as they looked upon her. Although women had no true authority under the codes and the final decision was not hers to make, the others looked toward her, instinctively reaching toward one another as if to witness a judgment. "If you know of one of the mystics who will come, get him to come. He has been sick for weeks now; he cannot stand to suffer any longer." And she left the room then, unable to look upon her husband, and who could blame her? Mottel had driven and repaired all of the carriages of the village, a strong, vigorous, righteous man not yet forty; now he lay before them like one dying of old age, spent and broken, images of bone protruding from his face. For possession consumes not only the soul as is well understood, but the flesh itself; arcing its way through the flesh as it does to get to the souls of the righteous and wicked alike, whose names, through all of the centuries of possession, are legion.

In the countryside surrounding this village there lived a fallen Rabbi whose name was Felix and who had not been seen in the village by any but a few merchants for many years. There were rumors that Felix had once had a large and vital congregation that had fallen, one by one, upon paths of wickedness, and Felix had cursed them at a Rosh Hashanah service and had told them that such as they were not only to be left out of the Book of Life but were indeed holding the sword against other names in their greed and spite. There were other rumors that no such thing had happened; Felix had never had a congregation, but after years of wandering in search of truth had been jailed by the authorities as a threatening influence and released as the result of a purge only many years later, shattered in his faculties by the imprisonment. And there were stories as well that Felix was neither an itinerant nor a Rabbi at all, but one who had merely, to create an air of mystery and protection around himself, created all of the rumors and actually was a purposeless man, little more than a beggar, who could not partake of the community. But it was to Felix that they came in search of a mystic, for they knew of no one else who might even know of the lost texts of darkness, and this was a time of great persecution in the country of the village, during which many good and wise men who the authorities thought had forbidden knowledge or otherwise displeased them were jailed, some of the fortunate for exile, others for worse outcome. They told Felix, one by one and then confirming one another, of Mottel's possession, and Felix, who was very old, heard them out quietly. "It is a case of possession; that is right," he said when they were finished, "but I do not know if there is anything I can do."

"A dybbuk can be exorcised," Jacob said. "We know of this; we know that the demon that enters can also be taken away, but we know nothing of this. . . ."

"No one knows of possession," Felix said. "It is a mystery so enormous that who knows more knows less. Nevertheless, I have heard of Mottel; even here in this isolated spot in which I live I have heard of him, his warmth and his goodness, and it is an evil thing that a man like this should be seized by a demon."

"Will you try to help him, then?" Jacob said.

"You do not understand," Felix said gently, flicking some dust from the bare earth on which he was sitting, looking absently in a strange way down the far distance, his glance passing from their faces to the sky and then back to the earth. "You do not understand the means of possession or what it entails. A seizure is caused by a demon, but the motive of that demon—his means of entrance or his true purpose—is not to be defined in the languages we speak. There are lesser texts that can give us some of the clues to this, but in the Torah itself there is not a word, and even the Talmud speaks endlessly only of the ramifications of justice. The justice that we know does not address the demon, and the penalties for mingling with these forces are terrible." Felix stood, a large man even in his age, his body crooked, to look down upon them. "I am an ignorant man," he said, "a man of just enough learning of this matter to have fear, and I want to tell you that we know nothing—nothing whatsoever."

"You will not help us, then," the son Isaac said. "You will not help my father, even though the Rabbi himself says that there is nothing to be done and we must search for a mystic."

"You could see a doctor," Felix said. "I am sure that in this countryside there is a doctor who could administer to him in such a way that the demon, all unaware, might be coaxed out. You do not know. You do not know what you ask."

"We have tried doctors," Isaac said. "We have tried doctors who have sent us to the Rabbi, and now the Rabbi has said that the cure is beyond him and you say it as well. Is my father then to die?" He looked at Felix in a level way, and in his eyes Felix must have seen not only the son Isaac, but the reflection or mirror of his father within those eyes, and his body caved in further.

"You do not know what you ask," he said. "Possession is something beyond our means, and the penalty for a false exorcism is more terrible than the demon itself. Once in Belgrade," Felix said, and then his voice broke and for a moment he could not go on. "Once in Belgrade," he said finally, "there was a young woman, a girl, really, who was taken in this manner and I volunteered my services because at that time I thought that the common mysteries could be solved, and when I came to her and performed the rituals . . . " Again Felix was unable to continue; he raised his hand to his eyes finally and rubbed them for a while, mechanically, like a man using a piece of linen to burnish copper. "All right," he said, "I will try. I am a ruined man and my soul already a ghost; no demon would inhabit me, for I would provide nothing. I will try," he said, "I will try."

And before the old man could change his mind, so filled with dread and wonder were they that they fell upon him and escorted him at once back to Mottel's house where the cries of the patient could now be heard upon the open air, emerging from the chimney like thin strands of smoke. "Darkness, darkness," the strands were saying, "all is darkness." And Rachel, as she saw them, came from the house in torment, racing toward them with her clothes disheveled.

"He is worse," she cried. "He will not stop screaming. He will not rest and I cannot hold him down in the bed. He says that he is going to the capital to deliver a message to the world before it is too late, that he will tell them to kill themselves before the next century can happen, and I can do nothing, nothing with him!" And at that moment Mottel, too, dressed in strange clothes as if for an unknown ceremony, emerged from the house and stumbled toward them. His *tallis* was wrapped around him in disarray, his belt swung loosely, but in his left hand he carried the whip with which he always went on journeys.

"Get out of my way," he said, looking neither to them nor the distance, but as if directing his gaze to some strange, undiscovered part of himself, "get out of my way, all of you. It is too late. It is too late for any of this. I must go to the capital at once." The fever, deeper within him, had turned his skin orange now and had mapped out strange lines upon his face. "I will tell them what lies in wait for the world," he said, "and since the capital is full of men strong enough to have tormented me all my life, they will be able to deal with this. The century will turn soon, but it will not turn at all if strong men don't take measures. Get out of my way."

"Get out of his way," Felix said quietly, and they broke in front of Mottel; Mottel walked through them as if they were sand, and quietly Felix followed at a couple of paces, motioning behind him that they were to be left alone. "I'm a Rabbi," Felix said as Mottel stumbled past his cart, ignoring it, and onto the roadway, five hundred kilometers from the capital. "Would you like to talk to me?"

"I remember speaking to a Rabbi before. I think that

I spoke to a Rabbi. It means nothing. I do not want your comforts. I want to deliver my message."

"I have no comforts," Felix said, falling into stride beside the possessed man, adjusting his step so that the two of them shambled along in unison. "I have no prayers. I seek only to help you. What do you see?"

"You know what I see!" Mottel shrieked, his voice becoming loud again, the demon flatting out his vowels and stretching the consonants so that Mottel talked like one mad. "I see death, darkness, machinery, disease, brutality and at the end of it murder: murder of three generations of our people, murder of millions of others, the engines of darkness closing in upon that century . . . "

"But it is 1878," Felix said, "twenty-two years at least before this next century? What can we know of it or it of us? What does it have to do with us?"

"I cannot bear it! I see the machines . . . "

"But by the beginning of the next century," Felix said persuasively, putting a tentative hand upon Mottel's prayer shawl, and bringing him to a halt, "by the beginning of the next century, my friend, you will be an old man if you survive at all, and I will most certainly be dead; your son will be your age and almost all of your friends old or dead as well. What does the next century have to do with you or me or any of them standing behind? They do not know, as we do not know, if we will live to see tomorrow. The government and disease are everywhere; so is uncertainty. It is enough to live for the moment. . . ."

"Yes," Mottel said, collapsing upon his limps and sitting unmoving in the roadway, "we are all dogs, living for the moment; that is what our tradition and what our government has taught us, but by living for the moment we are standing in watch for the greater peril and I cannot move. I can no longer move; I am very weak. Will you help me? Will you assist me to my feet?"

"You cannot get to the capital," Felix said, squatting beside him. "The capital is a month's journey even by cart, and you will never get there." He held Mottel's hands, felt the softness and withering of the flesh, the beat of the demon inside. "You cannot deliver the message," he said, "and if you did, no one would listen."

"Then *you,* Rabbi," Mottel said, and with a demon's strength, gathered himself to seize and press the old man's hands, "you deliver the message. Take it there, take it on the road: tell them what I see. If you are a Rabbi, a man of wisdom, even the authorities will listen to you. They will hear what you have to say before they turn their armies upon you."

"I will not live into the next century," Felix said quietly, and remembering dimly certain ancient rites and rituals, pressed his mouth against Mottel's ear and whispered the Third Oath of Release, calling the demon toward him. "What do I care of the next century when I do not know if I will survive this night?"

"You must, Rabbi," Mottel said, "you must think of the next century; our people have never thought of the next moment, that is their tragedy, but I tell you . . . " And at that moment, responding to the Oath in a way that it never could have understood had it been given breath, the demon sprang from Mottel's soul and with a knifing twist, deep into that of Felix, who, in the saying of the Oath, had left himself open as he had never done that time long ago in Belgrade. Felix screamed once and then fell before Mottel in the dirt, gasping.

"The engines," he moaned, "the engines, oh, my God, the *engineering* of it," but he could say no more. He was a much older and less vigorous man than Mottel (who the demon had almost destroyed), and with no other sound he fell over to the earth like a carving, lying still at Mottel's feet.

Behind him, Mottel could hear his relatives shouting as they, having witnessed the scene, ran toward him; ahead of him, Mottel, in his weakness and released delirium, thought that he could see the capital itself hanging heavily in the sky like overripe fruit, but what he thought and saw most of all lay before him in the dying old man, and even as he leaned forward to try, one last time, to get the sense of it, it dwindled and perished before him, leaving Mottel alone then, waiting for all of them to come upon him and the moment went on forever.

Introduction to
FORM IN REMISSION

The editor of the anthology in which this piece appeared wrote a fifteen-word blurb that killed the story . . . gave the ending away.

I've heard of such things happening—science fiction magazine illustrators do this all the time—but it had never happened to *me,* and I did not realize how truly infuriating it could be. Not to overrate the piece that is three pages long and not to be confused with major work . . . but it has a point to make, sets it up carefully (and not predictably, I believe), makes it elegantly and quits, which is what the short-short story is all about. All of this was undercut for me in a sentence.

It's not fair, but the story has another chance here, and my introduction is too skilled to give away the ending, to be sure. In fact, it is hellishly subtle.

FORM IN REMISSION

Gentlemen:

Well, you can imagine my shock and horror to wake in my own humble bed in this strident but serviceable collection of furnished rooms I call my home to find that lying beside me was some kind of loathsome *insect* the size of a man with strange greenish scales and deep peering eyes all over its body, eyes covered no less by little black *eyelids* that winked and fluttered at me; you can imagine my increasing fright at this *thing,* which I find almost impossible to describe because I cannot still completely forget that first emotional reaction, addressed me in a perfectly normal if somewhat bleating and effeminate tone of voice. "Well, Frederick," it said to me, "this is what your life has become; this is what you have made of your life and I am very much afraid that you are going to have to accept me."

The *reasonableness* of the creature! Well, there is no way that I can set down these bizarre reminiscences so that you will believe me; let us face the truth, gentlemen, *I* am ready to face the truth: this letter that you will receive tomorrow evening at the Bureau in my best estimate can only strike you as *insane* and as the ravings of a *madman,* no matter what tone I adopt, but when you understand that all of this is in the context of my *irrevocable resignation* from the Bureau and all of its devices, you will, I know, at least read on. Compelling and horrid fascination will drive you through these brief pages; if nothing else, I was an excellent if overly compulsive clerk and can ill be spared. You will want to know the reasons, and to the best of my ability this letter will contain the reasons, whether you *like them or not.* You may mail me my final check, including accrued vacation benefits, overtime and sick leave to the address given below, that address being my mother's; in due course I hope she will arrange to get it to me, but you cannot send it to my own address because *the insect will not leave me,* not for a moment, and I could hardly appear in the lobby before the dismal lineup of mailboxes in such a condition without inciting disastrous events. So far I have been making my way passably through the order and delivery of food and drink over the telephone, shielding the insect with my body as I open the chained door just enough to take in the boxes and pay in cash, but I do not know if this will continue indefinitely, and some of the delivery boys look at me strangely indeed. Fortunately, this neighborhood in which I live will tolerate almost any kind of individual insanity as long as it is self-confined and also I have long had a reputation here as being a little "strange," so it is possible that I will be able to carry the situation for a while. Perhaps not. It is out of my hands. The *insect* will make that decision.

I am talking, however, of that morning four days ago when I woke up with it lying matter-of-factly beside me; the evolving circumstances here need not concern you. "Frederick," it continued, "you have lived an ugly, cruel, useless and purposeless life and have therefore brought me upon yourself. There is no one else to blame. In fact, Frederick, *I am your life*," the insect said and reached out tendrils to massage and stroke me.

Oh, the horror of it! That clear, ringing, cold touch in the gray spaces of my bed, little patches and snatches of sunlight spotting the floor but leaving us in essential gloom. I again say that I cannot describe this, nor is there any reason why I should; certain sensations, gentlemen, cannot be communicated. I tried to rear from the bed but felt myself still locked within that clasp, the creature regarding me from its various abscesses with deadly calm. "You can, of course, never get rid of me," it said. "I am going to be with you until the end of your life. Nevertheless, we can do this pleasantly or unpleasantly. I suggest that you accept the situation; you have no alternative."

At last I was able to tear free from the bed and took up a posture against the wall, clinging to it as if for support. The creature lay in the bed, its protuberant surfaces moving unevenly, regarding me without expression I could understand. For the first time then I noted the odor coming from the thing; an odor of mingled exhalation and sweat, foul, moist, corrupt, moving upward in circles from the bed and overtaking the room. My disgust turned to urgency and I felt myself seized and heaving, made my way to the bathroom then, where, for a very long time, I poised solitary over the bowl. Finally, able to stand, seeing that I was alone, I made my way over to the basin, gazed in the mirror at the ordinary, humorless, poignant face of Frederick Walker, assistant chief claims clerk, division of the Bureau, and seeing the serenity and limpidity of those eyes was able to convince myself that it must have been a dream, a fit, a wish of some sort: the creature did not exist, I had imagined all of this, and that upon returning to the outer room to find it empty and sterile I would make arrangements at once to put myself in the hands of a competent doctor for aid.

For too long, I was able to admit to myself, I had refused to admit certain facts of my life: the neurasthenia, the loneliness, the failure of human contact, that dim hatred of my mother that had made me fear contact with all women . . . and found this admission therapeutic; I would obtain medical treatment, I would lay bare the facts of my life; it was not too late at forty-three or beyond to make a fresh start. So thinking I came back to the bedroom where the creature had shifted its position to a chair where it sat, awful little legs curled in upon one another, waving in the breezes of the air, looking at me. The odor was, if possible, stronger and more penetrating. If I did not take some measures at once it would fill the whole building to the sixteenth story, and where would I be then when at last an investigation was made? I found a spray cleaner and worked it through the air, hoping all the time that the creature might prove to be fatally allergic. It made no move from the chair, however, continuing to regard me in its sad and solemn way, the cleaner at least working the corruption out of the air so that my apartment smelled no more ominously than a public urinal. At last there were no more tasks to do; I had to face it, I did face it, from the distance across the room. My horror had to some degree abated; there is nothing, gentlemen, nothing the unconquerable human spirit cannot confront if it is accustomed. "Please," I said to the thing, "please tell me why you cannot leave. You *must* leave; I cannot bear this."

"I am sorry, Frederick," the insect said, "but I cannot. For the rest of your life I will have to stay beside you; there is the possibility of another assignment or return after your death, but that cannot be considered at this time. You will have to accept me. You will have to accept this. For neither of us is there any escape."

"But, why?" I said, feeling myself beginning to gather for retching again but forcing it down with an effort of will. (And now four days later, gentlemen, I do not retch at all and have accepted the situation, but you must accept my resignation without protest and forward my check to my mother's address immediately because *any frustration could set me off again.*) "Why are you here? What has happened? Why are you with me? This is hell."

"No, Frederick, no," the thing said sadly and moved in the chair; the odor wafted to me again and for the first time I understood then that the creature's revulsion was as great as my own, that it was filled with horror, that it was maintaining its own control only through access to energies I could not grasp. "No, Frederick," it said, "you're not in hell.

"I'm in hell."

Introduction to
OPENING FIRE

Traditional science-fictional portraits of "the aliens" (who we will surely someday meet) divide into two streams: the aliens as malevolent, brutish pillagers of our Way Of Life, and the aliens as benign, benevolent, fatherly (or motherly) individuals who will surely help us change our ways, or, at the least, keep us in quarantine for our own and their sakes. It could be said, and probably has been, that these views are opposite sides of the child's reactions toward his parents in middle-class culture, but I never pointed this out.

There is a divergent and iconoclastic stream hinted at in a few stories of the '50s and elaborated on in my own work that the aliens may be neither brutish nor benign, but simply incompetent . . . hapless bureaucrats at the bottom levels of civil service trying to keep themselves in the good graces of headquarters while fulfilling mission requirements according to policies and procedures. I like this better.

However you take it, there *are* aliens, and someday we are going to meet them. As Fred Pohl says, "First contact is a reasonable event somewhere in the future of the human race."

If this is so, it is going to provide an important role to a personality type now not in the highest repute, as the following makes clear. In fact, that personality type may prove to be absolutely necessary to our continued survival. Perhaps the best or worst thing that one could say about *Opening Fire* is that the late John W. Campbell, if he had been able to get past the rather murky style, would have absolutely agreed with the premise.

OPENING FIRE

During the training sessions we were instructed that the aliens were kind and the aliens were benevolent and the aliens were a race of creatures whose motives were as sensible as our own and who must be approached in a spirit of mutual confidence. The aliens, who are known as the V'raquai, because that is as close as our language can reach the sounds of their own, were benign creatures and our contacts would be carried out in accord and harmony because they were no less spiritual and rational than we. We were taught all this about the V'raquai, the twenty of us in the training sessions, because it was very important, we were told, that we purge all xenophobia, bigotry and hatred from our systems *before* the contacts began.

Our instructors were reasonable, rational, benign, pleasant men with degrees in psychology and advanced rank in the services and it was impossible not to pay them honor. Nevertheless, I hate and fear the V'raquai and am revolted by them spiritually and physically to the depths of my being, and when I saw the films of their civilization brought into the Institute I wanted to attack the screen with my hands, so deep was the disgust.

I hate them and fear them and have ignored every lesson of the Institute and nevertheless hear that I am on the voyage, bound to meet the V'raquai on an edge of the spiral nebulae where the first discussions of our mutual self-interest will be held. And I have not concealed my hatred from any of them.

II

I am on the voyage despite my failure to respond to the training sessions because in the opinion of the senior staff I represent a valid point of view that is deserving and must be represented during these initial contacts. Xenophobia—the human instinct toward hatred of all forms of life different from its own—is part of the history of mankind and has enabled us at many stages of our development to survive, by force of sheer hatred or suspicion, forces that might destroy us. If man was not innately xenophobic he might not have developed the technology that enabled him to voyage among the stars where he first intercepted the ships of the V'raquai. Even though contacts with this alien race can prove mutually beneficial and all of our relations to date have been cordial, it is still the opinion of the senior staff that it might be better to have at least one dedicated xenophobe aboard in order to test the reactions of the crew and function as a standard against which the aliens' behavior may be measured. It is felt that the xenophobe will function as an early warning system in the event that the V'raquai make potentially menacing gestures, and it is also theorized that if the confidence of the xenophobe is won by the creatures, then the rest of the crew has nothing whatsoever to fear.

And that is why, despite the fact that I have failed the psychological profile, the Markson Index of toleration, the Zalo Charts of bigotry and various other measures of suitability, I am occupying quarters on this ship. "Bigotry has a long if dishonorable history in the race," our group head advised us on passage day, "and in view of its persistence it might be wise to give it a voice on this crew, if not precisely a position of honor."

III

I have a voice on this crew, if not precisely a position of honor. I am more aware than the others might think of how I am regarded, that mixture of pity and contempt with which all my activities are greeted, that bemused and sometimes concentrated hostility that attends most of my routine appearances. My presence, my role on this flight, is regarded by the remainder of the crew as somehow shameful—as if I were a filthy little secret that was being carried, helter-skelter at the speed of light, to the edges of the Crab Nebula—and at the same time, however, they are not completely able to repudiate me. How often, scurrying down these corridors, struggling over my papers, looking over the carefully assembled still-albums and tapes of the V'raquai statesmen, have I seen the eyes of a crew member passing over mine and then locking with a sudden acuity of perception as that light of hatred I emit at all times beams off something in the observer, and coughing, he must turn from me to speed forth on his duties.

IV

I take the words of the group head seriously and have never had any reason to doubt my feelings or, even, to re-evaluate them. Bigotry, hatred, xenophobia, hostility, the revulsion for all forms differing is built deep into our personalities. We are a suspicious race by natural selection; generations of predators have had their shot at us. If it were not for bigotry we would have all been eaten; the hatred of different life forms persists, in a milder and somewhat chastened form now as prejudice against other subgroups of mankind not analogous to one's own. It may be lamentable, but so was the use of saber-toothed tigers for stewing meat. Our hatred has taken us far; it is the price we must pay for our dominance. I know that the V'raquai, no less than any of the other races of the past, are antithetical to our own and if granted an equal opportunity would destroy us and this is why I hate them and my hatred is pure and cleansing and when I actually meet with them it will be reinforced and I will slowly parcel out my hatred to the members of the crew, converting them to my cause, and there will come a time, a natural, inevitable time when we will have to take the V'raquai by surprise and overpower and overthrow them and I will lead the revolt because of my natural force.

They will know that I have always been right. They will acknowledge me as their leader.

V

In loose orbit at the nebulae, I catch my first actual glimpse of the V'raquai. One of their crewmen enters hurriedly in full gear for quick conference with our technical forces, something to do with atmospheric conditions in the conference room and the general schedule of the dialogue. The V'raquai is clad in full space armor since our atmosphere would kill them instantly. They subsist, we are told, in an ammonia and nitrogen environment. Under the dull, alien metal of the gear I can catch a hint of scales, ooze, corruption, odors and inconspicuous as I am trying to be in the rear of the room, checking through my tables (my official post on the expedition is as mathematician), I find myself seized by retching and must leave.

VI

Agreements are reached during the conferences which, of course, I do not attend. Only the captain, his political advisors and the senior sociologists are permitted to meet in the room with the four V'raquai who appear to comprise their own bargaining committee. The V'raquai will give us access to formulas, mysterious metals, cures for wasting diseases, a hint of the direction research must take for immortality. We will furnish them with grenades, incendiaries, bombs, leveling materials, the technological means for waging war, in short, against another race who is nameless but appears to be fighting them for dominance within their own solar system. This other race is implacably vicious and, the V'raquai assure our representatives, will have no dealings of any sort with civilized cultures. The talks go well. Tentative accords are reached for countersignature by the Premier and his advisors and plans for the next meeting are set. During these days I drift on the edges of the conference like most of the other crew members, getting occasional glimpses of the aliens as they make their strange and mysterious way to and from our ship. The environment on their own ship, they have explained, could not safely be adapted to humans. On the final day of the conference I am summoned to the quarters of the captain where I am greeted by him and one of the senior sociologists. A faint trail of the aliens' odor comes off them and their walls, causing my face to constrict with revulsion, but I try to conceal my feelings. Proximity to the V'raquai and the glimpses of them I have caught have not decreased my hatred. Sometimes I have felt myself seized by the dangerous urge to grab weaponry from the walls and kill them all. I could almost do this before the unthinking crew could stop me. But I have restrained myself. I am here, as I have been reminded by the Institute, merely as a checking device. I am not to perpetuate action.

"The talks have gone well," the captain says to me without preamble. "Now all is signed and we are finished."

"The talks have gone very well," the senior sociologist says. "They will change the course of future generations. We are highly satisfied and have so already advised headquarters." He seems uncomfortable as if he does not really want to be here or even question the uses of our discussion, but he holds himself in place nevertheless. It occurs to me that the senior sociologist, in his way, is as xenophobic as I, although in his case he thinks he had reasons. I have never sought explanations, which explains, I was told, my unique value.

"However," the captain says, "under the procedures we were handed, we must at this time call you in and ask you: do you still hate the V'raquai as much as ever? Or have your feelins of hatred been reduced?"

"I hate them as much as ever," I say. "I do not trust them. They revolt me and they will destroy us. They are a cowardly, treacherous race and they have scales. No thing with scales may be trusted."

"This is pointless," says the senior sociologist, "pointless and embarrassing. How can you solicit . . . "

"It must be done," the captain says quite sharply, causing the sociologist to mumble. "Under the statutes."

"I still say . . . "

"Quiet! You still think they will destroy us," the captain says to me quietly, "and you do not trust them."

"I am repelled by them," I say quietly. "If I were not under the partial block of the drugs administered before the voyage, I would kill them myself. They breathe ammonia, have scales, speak treacherously, tell us nothing of themselves and I think they itch all the time, too. Dirty, poisonous creatures; how can any human sit with them?"

"I am sorry," the captain says awkwardly, after a pause, "I am truly sorry that you feel this way."

"No you're not, or you would listen . . . "

"Truly sorry," the captain says, and the cast of his face changes; it shudders, it pulses, it shows something alien of its own under the mask of the human features. "Nevertheless, it must be done."

He stands, goes to the door on the other side of the room, behind his desk, opens it. In the door stand two of the V'raquai in their garb, holding weaponry. "You heard," he says to them.

"We heard," one of them says.

"It wasn't my doing," the captain says, "you have to understand that we were instructed . . . "

"Of course," says the V'raquai. "Of course." He walks into the room determinedly, leading the other by a few spaces, pushes the senior sociologist from his path and closes the ground between us. I smell the rank odor coming from the creature, I feel my pain and its power. The senior sociologist gibbers in fury and then quiets as the captain steps to his side. He leans over, whispers, seems to be comforting. The two stand in frieze.

"You realize," says the treacherous V'raquai, lifting its weapon, "that you've given us no choice at all." I see the barrel of the weapon, see its opening then as the fire begins, "but really, there can be no progress between our races and no vanquishment of our terrible enemies until those like you are eliminated."

I feel the flame parting my back, tearing me open, vault ascension, then a feeling of departure as the filthy, evil bastard deposits its load of hatred upon me and then stalks from the room leading the others toward a new era of prosperity and interstellar accord. Dying at the hands of Others, then, as somehow I knew it must always be: and this then is why I hated them so.

Introduction to
RUNNING AROUND

Is it possible that there remains one last spate of energy, no matter how slight, in the exhausted, done-to-death time-paradox theme? Subject of at least twenty novels and two hundred short stories over the last couple of decades, is there *any* way of approaching it without reiterating all of the work of the past, which has worked more out of this theme perhaps than it ever had to offer in the first place?

I don't think so, although *Running Around* is certainly a competent enough work-through (so was David Gerrold's time-machine novel, *The Man Who Folded Himself,* published in 1973 as "the last word" in the genre), but the choice was not mine; the story was commissioned by an editor who wanted a "time-travel story," and who is Malzberg to dispute his editors? Grumbling, I did it, asking myself throughout questions summarized in the first paragraph, and although the story is not an award-winner, I do believe I have an answer.

The turnover in commercial, genre writing among readers is close to ninety percent in four years . . . in other words, studies have shown that ninety percent of people reading, say, *Galaxy* today, were not readers of the magazine four years ago. In this sense it means that for all but the few thousand collectors, enthusiasts and professionals the field literally has no history; destroying said history at the rate of two and a half times a decade, a rate that even the government of the United States could not equal.

Because the turnover is so complete, because the field has no history, it means that virtually no given work or body of work will survive to succeeding generations of the readership, far less "finish off" a given area. No matter what you do, ten years from now you (or your heirs) will be dealing with an audience that will act or react precisely as if you had not done it at all. This is reasonably discouraging. It functions as one explanation—there are many others—to why so many of our Big Names are ex-writers and drunks in the bargain.

Still—I speak from experience—the sex market is even worse. Work there turns over every four *days*.

———◆———

RUNNING AROUND

I travel back in time seventy years to the bucolic and gentle year of 1903, where I meet my grandfather as a young man and kill him with a .32-caliber Smith & Wesson revolver. By so doing, of course, I assume that I have settled the difficulties of the instant situation, but when I return in my self-invented, secret time machine— I work in a laboratory in the cellar and refuse to patent any of my devices since I believe that modern corporations are irretrievably corrupt and will steal anything—I find my wife in her accustomed position in the living room, her arms folded, a bitter expression on her face.

"Now, we won't have any of that," she says, referring to my travels in time, with which, of course, she is familiar. (I would not have her misconstruing my jaunts as adulterous quests or expeditions to the bar, and thus keep her abreast of my findings. "There are the same bills to pay, the oilman is knocking down the door, the credit bureau has called three times this afternoon, and I'm tired of lying and this has got to come to an end. Edgar, you must face your responsibilities."

Edgar. My name is Edgar. My wife's name, on the other hand, is Betty, and in a moment of passion some years ago I dragged myself, to my infinite regret, from my laboratory to court and marry her. We have two children, Richard and Helen, fraternal twins, eight years old. This was a dreadful mistake. Not the children, I mean—children are inevitable in any marriage. The marriage itself was a dreadful mistake. Inventing a time-travel machine had been my hobby, and I should have left it at that. But the flesh is as infinitely destructive as it is cunning.

"Well?" my wife Betty says to me. "What do you intend to do about this now?"

"Fix it up right," I say and return to the machine, which is a delicate cubicle, man-sized—or woman-sized, rather—about five-feet six-inches in height, three feet all around, just suitable for traveling if I wedge myself within. I turn the dials to *1933* and hastily go back in time.

"Fix it up right," I repeat to the bland inner surfaces of the machine. I have tried to furnish it in a somewhat homelike way with pictures of my family and two covers ripped from old pulp magazines, but it is difficult to dress up any cubicle five-feet six-inches in height and three feet all around. I ignore the pictures and instead absorb the sensations of traveling back in time, one year to three seconds, forty years, one hundred and twenty seconds or two minutes, that is to say. Travel in time is essentially uneventful; I think of it as being something like making love to my wife, Betty—an impenetrable surge of moments during which very little seems to happen until there is an eviction—but do not wish to be cruel to her. "I've got to solve this situation," I add.

What I have had in mind, of course, is to eliminate myself painlessly. Bills, obligations, job troubles (I have a very mundane civil service position, but there has been reordering in the department and I am on the verge of losing my probationary status), marital woes, the general depression and fatigue of being a citizen of the twentieth century have overwhelmed me, and what I want to do is to end it all in a way so final that it will have never happened at all. Killing one's grandfather is the classic means of doing this, according to the science fiction stories I have read, but it does not seem to have worked; therefore, I will have to kill my father, instead. Surely if I get rid of the old man—for whom I have always had a distant affection; I wish to emphasize that there is nothing personal in this and that parricide or grandparricide gives me no emotional satisfaction whatsoever—in 1933, four years before he met my mother, let alone married her, I will cancel out the fact of myself, to say nothing of my wife, Betty (she would have met and married someone else) and my twin daughter and son. Likewise the creditors and the ugly leakage that has begun to appear in the basement as the result of my experiments.

The dial comes to rest on *1933* with a *click!* and hastily I power down, reset the controls and in a somewhat molelike way emerge from my cubicle, giving the pulp-magazine covers and portraits of my family in repose a last affectionate glance. I am at Broadway and Eighty-seventh Street forty years ago in what appears to be the late-afternoon rush hour, throngs of people passing me busily reading news of the bank closing, marvelous antique buses pouring fumes into the air and past my nostrils. No one appears to notice a blinking thirty-two-year-old man who has just emerged from a five-foot-six-inch cubicle, which cubicle instantly dwindles to the size of an apple and is picked up by this man to be inserted in his inner jacket pocket. As I recall, my father, before his marriage, lived with a friend in apartment 3-B at 149 West Eighty-seventh Street, and hastily I set out in that direction. It is convenient that the machine has dropped me so close to the destination; calibration for space in what I like to call (pardon my vanity) Edgar's Device is still inexact and I could as well have been at the intersection of Broadway and Wall, watching some rich panic on the stock exchange. Time is my specialty, it seems; I am loose and sloppy on the space issue, but the fact that I have been able to calibrate so exactly gives me a little surge of feeling; surely this is a good omen and proves that I am on the right track. Now, all that I will have to do is to hope that my father is in, kill him promptly and let events take their course.

I go into 149 West Eighty-seventh Street unnoticed by passersby and two police who are inspecting a fire hydrant gone mad from the economic disorder of 1933 to hurl torrents of rusty water down the pastoral aspect of Eighty-seventh Street of forty years ago, find my father's name listed in the vestibule and, pushing open the door—building access was easy in these times; the crime wave did not get really bad until after the war—sprint up the two flights to 3-B, knock on the door once and then, unbidden, walk in.

I find my father, much younger than I ever knew him, of course, standing in his undershirt by the window, looking out at the street and the accident of the fire hydrant. He turns toward me, his eyes blinking and full of light, and raises a hand in greeting. A merry man. I never knew him this way. He must have been quite a merry man, however, before he met my mother.

"Hello," he says, "how are you? I don't believe I know you, but that's perfectly all right. Maybe you're the man with the salt?"

He must be referring to some obscure forty-year-old grocery errand, but then again *salt* may have a peculiar local significance that escapes me. "No," I say in any event, "I'm not the man with the salt."

"Ah," he says, "that's a pity." He turns back toward the window. "If they don't seal that hydrant soon, New York's going to be underwater," he says, "and then I won't have to go to work tonight. Which, come to think of it, is all right with me."

As I recall, my father was a used-car salesman at this period of his life; a virginal used-car salesman, as a matter of fact, and according to testimony . . . but then again, and as Thomas Wolfe once said, who can know his father's face? And this is not my concern at the present time. The time to have established a relationship with my father was in 1947 or thereabouts, certainly not in 1933, eight years before I was born or, properly speaking, even in seed form. "You're never going to work again," I say and, reaching into my suit pocket (not the pocket with the dwindled time machine; the *other* pocket, the one with the .32-caliber Smith & Wesson), take out the pistol. "I'm going to kill you," I say to him matter-of-factly.

"That's ridiculous," he says, not turning from the window. "No one's going to kill me. This is 1933, it's modern times, and people just don't shoot strangers in their own apartments. People don't come off the street and kill strangers for no reason."

"You're not a stranger," I say. I feel a little pity for the old man, now so young and confused in his undershirt; it would have been nice if we had established some kind of relationship, I think, but, then again, we were never able to talk to one another (which is one of the reasons why I became neurotic and wound up in a mundane civil service job, piddling around with time-travel as a hobby instead of making a lot of money for myself), and this is no time to start. "I'm your son," I say nevertheless. "I've got to kill you."

"My son?" he says, turning, hands on hips. "I have no son, and besides, if I did he'd be a wee infant, not a big guy like yourself, about thirty-nine years of age, I'd say."

"I'm not thirty-nine," I say angrily, the gun shaking. Always, always the old man was able to get my goat. "I'm thirty-*two* and I'm unhappily married and work in a mundane civil service job with bills way over my head and I've decided to end it all by getting rid of you. It's all your fault."

His eyes widen, or perhaps in my excitement I think that they are widening when they are merely deepening. "You must be crazy," he says.

"I'm not crazy. I come from 1973, forty years from now. I was born in 1941, four years after you were married to a girl you won't even *meet* for four years, and frankly, you were a lousy parent, but I don't even want to get *into* that area now. All I know is that if I kill you now you'll never meet the girl or get married and have me, and that means I never will have been born to be in this lousy mess. It's not your fault," I say, leveling the gun. "I mean, there's nothing personal in this. Even if you had been a *good* father I'd still want to kill you. But we were never able to have a good relationship. Every time I tried to talk we got into these silly arguments about my shoes not being shined or why didn't I make something of myself in school, and I just can't get into all that stuff again. I'm sorry," I say and, concentrating hard, start to pull the trigger. It is really a very difficult and embarrassing thing, I have just discovered, to commit parricide. Grandparricide is easily possible—for one thing, I had never *met* my grandfather, who was dead years before I was born—but the father-son relationship is profound with, as they say, many Freudian overtones.

Thus, I am still concentrating on the effort of pulling the trigger and battling a deep sense of remorse when behind me there is a bang of the door and the two patrolmen whom I saw on the street enter the apartment purposefully. Skillfully they surround me, skillfully I am disarmed, skillfully I am manacled and placed in their custody. There is not even any time to reach for the apple-sized object in my left jacket pocket, much less to try and explain the situation to anyone. Before I quite know what has happened I am very much in the hands of the Depression police and being led gently enough down the stairs. "Don't worry about this one," one of the police calls upstairs to my astonished father, "we had reports that something like this might be going on in the neighborhood. You'll have to come down and give testimony later, maybe, but there's no reason for you to worry about anything like this." From two flights above, my father looks down at me open-mouthed and with some interest, but there is really very little that I could say to him—now more than ever we would have difficulty relating—and so I allow myself to pass from the building and into the street, where the Depression Era police walk me down to the corner, toward the precinct. It seems that, in these times of apple-selling and bank holidays, New York's finest do not have cars at their disposal, although then again they may be specially detailed foot patrolmen. The hydrant, I notice, is no longer gushing. It must all have been a blind to make their presence on the prospective murder scene natural and acceptable and I realize then that all along I have been outsmarted and that probably they were waiting for me.

"You must have had advance knowledge," I say, being half-lofted in their strong arms, my little feet scuttling delicately on the gray but pleasant pavement of old New York. "Someone must have told you that I was coming."

Cunningly I try to reach an arm inside my jacket to get the time machine, but they are far more cunning than I; the hand is slapped away, another hand inserts itself and deftly removes the machine. The patrolman to my right looks at it with a delighted expression. "And there's the evidence," he says. "We've got him cold."

"You'll pay every bill you owe, buddy," the other policeman advises. "You'll work hard and you'll meet your debts and be responsible to your family. If there's one thing I can't stand," he says with a trace of disgust, "it's seeing a man trying to avoid his responsibilities."

"How did you know?" I ask pointlessly as we whisk toward a stoplight. "Who told you?"

"We got a tip."

"I know you got a tip," I say rather desperately, "but around here who would know? Who could possibly *know?*"

"Never mind," the policeman holding the little machine says, "we have our methods. And we have our sources of information. Anyway, I think that you'd know this informant very well. She certainly knows *you,* friend, and is she mad!"

"She?"

"Her name is Betty," the patrolman on my left says amiably enough, "and if I were you, which fortunately I am not, I'd *never* want to go home again, which unfortunately you will have to, because we have too many mouths already to feed in 1933 and, whatever you think, it's better up the line."

"Betty," I say, "Betty." The conniving, rotten woman. And then a certain sense of absurdity overcomes me, or maybe it is a flash of the divine, and I look beyond the flat, high buildings of old New York to the sky of the Depression looming over us, and I laugh.

Introduction to
OVERLOOKING

Overlooking, written out of sinusitis and gloom Christmas
Day of 1972 is a good example (*Trashing,* not collected
here, is another) of a piece written without hard knowledge that proved to be a fairly accurate simulacrum of
events forthcoming . . . although the political comment
here is probably sufficiently subtle as to make this fact unknown even at this point.

Still—and the question is now asked specifically about
political fiction, i.e., fiction that attempts to make a political statement that will have a proselytizing effect—what
does it matter? Does the knowledge of anything forestall
its repeated occurrence? Or, to steal the phrase from
Robert Sheckley, is it really possible to learn from something we already know?

OVERLOOKING

Play it again, Sam. This time with a little passion, if you
please; watch the ethos and infuse the shades with light.
In that bucolic and paradoxical year of 1951 the Dodgers
are leading the Jints 10–0 in the bottom of the ninth of
their second playoff game for the National League championship; Labine is sailing right along and it looks bad for
the Jints, but there is, of course, always tomorrow, and
Bobby Thomson has been hot these last few weeks. Willie
Mays, too. Come back tomorrow and see if the Jints can
bring this one off. Across the bridge they are bowling and
drinking at Fitzsimmons Lanes across the street from
Ebbets Field; only a few unbelievers are clustered around
the twelve-inch television set, watching the Jints in their

last throes. Much fun at Fitzsimmons Lanes, although the Dodgers' collapse these past two months has worried a few of us.

Toots Shor is whooping it up again; flash-cut back across that bridge. I believe that it is Toots Shor I see, laughing and trading affectionate insults with the heavyweight champion of the world, the famous and extremely well-thought-of Jersey Joe Walcott. Way to go, Jersey Joe. Louis was a better man, but you finally caught him on the downswing and beat the hell out of him. Toots passes Jersey Joe a drink. *Shit,* says Jersey Joe, or at any rate I think I hear him say *shit;* the conditions in this room are so crowded and then, too, the sound splicing is awful, out of synchronization with the picture and often fading toward inaudibility, *can't do that, man, I'm in training.* Jersey Joe laughs, old Toots laughs; patrons and hangers-on in the area join in the laughter as well and the picture collapses; one moment I am grooving on the sights and sounds of Toots Shor's and the next, the very next, all has gone away on me and I am sitting in the darkness surrounded by unease and the first sounds of violence. The patrons, an unhappy lot, were pleased and diverted with the film just as was I, but now with their palliative gone the original mood has returned and the air, dark as it is, seems dense with the shapes of trouble. "Get that fucking thing on again!" someone screams and, "Yeah, I want it to be 1951 again!" a heavy bartender's voice shouts, and "You dirty bastards, give us our money back," some entrepreneur bellows, and all around me in the theater now, like moths descending to snaffle over my head begins the sound of feet pounding the floor, curses and boos, the cries and threats of the cheated who feel that they, no less than the tormented Jints, will have one last inning tomorrow. "We want Jersey Joe!" a woman shrieks and throws something at the blank screen. It must be an incendiary. The screen goes up in flames but still it stands inert before us.

It has the outline of a bad scene, a bad confrontation, indeed—if the projectionist cannot get things going immediately, he better have either an iron door or a quick trap-exit—and like all of these things the aspect of real danger as well; if the patrons cannot obtain satisfaction from management, they are as apt as not to turn upon one another. Either way, I want no part of it. Quickly I come from my seat, feeling the damp little deposit from my sweating buttocks part from me like a rapidly batted ball and head toward the place where I remember an exit as being; the spectators—grotesque, misplaced humps in the dark—do not notice me. The door swings open easily —but soon enough someone will think of locking them in —and I come quickly onto Fifth Avenue, blinking at the sudden onset of cold and the rapid emergence into the world which, for a short, tortured time, I have left. To return to the world so abruptly, without even the satisfaction of an ending to the film and the shuffling, companionable trip up the aisle with the audience as companions, to return to the world so abruptly as I say is unbearable, and the Fifth Avenue that I see is surely not the Fifth Avenue I have left but something grimmer, bleaker, intolerably more dangerous than I would have suspected because the world, as compared to the innocent times of 1951, which were reconstructed so briefly for me, seems irretrievably confusing and corrupt. I lean against a theater wall, teetering in the cold, looking with fright at the crowds that whisk by, the young girls particularly intimidating, looking so hard and cruel as compared to the gentle girls of 1951, most of whom saved their bodies for marriage or would have liked to.

A derelict approaches me, the insanity of 1962 stamped deeply into his eyes and brow, and says, "Give me a fucking quarter, you son-of-a-bitch."

I shrug. It is best not to antagonize derelicts; they are a new and far more dangerous breed than those of the past. "I can't," I say, "I don't have it."

"What do you mean, you don't have it?" he says. He shrugs and trembles inside his ill-fitting coat, wipes a fine tissue of discharge from under his nose with a forefinger. "You just came out of that fucking place there; I saw you, I had a watch. You've got a quarter."

"I can't," I say honestly, "I spent my last money to get

in there, but now the film has broken down and there's going to be a riot."

"Fucking Kennedy," the derelict says pointlessly, shifting to another topic with the thundering emotional lability for which they are so well known, "son-of-a-bitch is going to bomb Russia, and I can't even get a fucking *quarter*." He rubs his nose again, sniffs; I wonder idly if he is on drugs of some sort. Heroin seems to have become popular in the lower regions of the city during recent years and many tenants of Harlem have particularly been subject to the drug. "Dirty bastards," the derelict says, "all I want is a few dollars so I can get in there, see the films." He points to the theater entrance, the slow lights blinking out from the lobby. "Is that so bad? Get a little pleasure in our last moments?"

"It's no good," I say, moving away from him, "it's black and white, not color, and it's really just the quality of poor newsreels. Besides, the sound failed and I think that the tape itself has lapsed. There's going to be a riot in there soon. I just came out to get ahead of it."

"Not fair," the derelict says, rubbing his nose and blowing it frantically into his fingers, "don't care, don't care, I want it to be 1951 *again*. Don't I have a right? In 1951 I was twenty-eight years old; things didn't look so bad. Now what am I? Almost forty and picking up quarters while the fucker gets ready to bomb Moscow." He is weeping. "I can't take it anymore," he says, and sniveling within his coat, walks out of my life forever. I am left standing outside the theater, hands in my own pockets, shuddering against the cold while within I detect with a fine, attuned ear the first dim sounds of the enveloping riot. It is time to move on.

I move on. I do not want to be part of the crowd spillage; particularly if there are people inside there with incendiaries. MEMORY PALACE, the billboard outside says, BE 1951 AGAIN, and I feel a dim sense of outrage as I stalk through the wind; what memory palace? What 1951? It is 1962 and the films do not work; here, as in so many other things, they have lied to us. The process was never perfected; now it is something only for fools and indigents. Furthermore, after all the fine promises embodied within his inaugural address, the President seems insistent upon restoring to us whole all of the myths and cold war lies of the previous decade during which all of American foreign policy seemed to function only in terms of diabolism. It is disgusting. It is enough to spit. Really, there are great gaps in my own intellectual and academic background, but even I can see that American foreign policy, at least since 1917, has been founded upon an insane series of assumptions that have never been tested empirically or, for that matter, put up to the populace for any kind of a reckoning. They are merely there, slow-acting poison like the organic imbalance of the schizophrenic, undetectable, indecipherable, affecting everything, being affected by nothing. Memory palaces have nothing to do with it. The memory palaces were certainly a good idea from the government's point of view: keeping people in the past certainly made their recognition of the present less and kept them in line, but if the film is poor, if the sound synchronization is weak, if we cannot concentrate upon 1951 without being reminded of the unbearable 1962 and the other prisoners in that cellblock, what then is the point of it? I decide to think no more. I have fifty cents left in my pocket, enough to get me a Four Roses beer chaser, if I head far west enough. Perhaps two if business is slow and I ingratiate the bartender. Crisis situations always bring people closer together, and being on the brink of an atomic war certainly should make a boilermaker-on-the-house possible. Prostitutes in building alcoves proposition me in desultory fashion as I scoot westerly, but I do not acknowledge them or even slacken my step. Sexuality and stress do not mix for me, never have, and since the great depression of 1955 that drove the then-administration out of office, and on a less cosmic level cost me my career, I have been functionally impotent. Nothing wrong with me, the clinic doctor said, when after waiting months I finally got an appointment, everything in place but simply not working, like an appliance not plugged into a socket. Wait a bit; times will get better and then you should function again. In the meantime, get on along without it and don't unduly expose yourself to challenges. A common problem, more common than you think. All will work out. That was seven years ago and I still have not had an erection during the daytime, except vagrant boners upon awakening, dimly recollected nocturnal emissions. But I do not blame the clinic doctor; the advice was sound, and if things did not get better how was he to be blamed? Perfectly reasonable advice. The clinics themselves failed of funding and were ended in 1958. Sometimes I wonder what happened to that doctor.

At length I find myself in a Blarney Stone at Eighth Avenue and Forty-ninth Street, just one block south of the Garden but deserted tonight, of course; no events in the Garden for three years, other than political rallies. The Rangers were folded, I think, the Knicks still in the Sixty-ninth Regiment Armory. The dog show upstate; boxing exhibitions in the streets around the Garden all the time, of course, but the boxing represented by Jersey Joe Walcott, next to the last of the heavyweight world champions, simply does not exist anymore. Which, of course, does not bother me. A long time ago I seemed to have been trained in the botanical sciences.

The bartender gives me a Four Roses in a shot glass, no water, ice on the side, a small glass of beer. No seven-ounce chasers anymore; three ounces, take it or leave it. I take it, take both in two choking gulps that leave me momentarily discombobulated at the bar, soaring high and free beyond the reaches of the Madison Square Garden, but then I return to shove the coins across at him and look down the long, empty line of the bar toward the television set that is turned once again to one of the President's crisis speeches. "Another five cents, friend," the bartender says, and then as I look at him with a slow, dismayed come-to-realize (the Blarney Stone along with the rest of the world simply seems to have gotten away from me), he gestures with disgust and walks down the line holding the coins. He whispers something to the old other bartender down at the register and puts the coins away. *Fuck it,* I am sure he has said. *Fuck it,* I agree, and look up at the television. It hardly seems to matter. In his position I would have taken the fifty cents also.

The President has been introduced and is already speaking. The President of the United States is addressing the nation about further moves in the Cuba crisis. He must inform us that in the absence of agreement it is necessary to strike the missile sites at once, an agreement already withheld twenty-four hours from his ultimatum yesterday; he has had no choice but to order the Seventh Fleet and the President's Air Force to move in upon Havana and outlying provinces at once with heavy air strikes. Small-bore nuclears will be employed, but the civilian population will be protected to the extent that they now heed his warnings to disperse. If they do not disperse, it is their fault, for their leaders are being given two hours' notice to disperse. "A presence such as this within ninety miles of our borders is intolerable," the President says and strikes the table with his fist. He appears to be sweating. "We don't have to take this kind of stuff," he adds in a heavy whisper, and the camera, mercifully, backs off. "Thank you and good night," he concludes, as if finishing a horrid secret, and while his recorded theme is played the camera turns quickly to the Secretary of Information, who says that he would like to add to the President's remarks certain instructions to civilians. A nuclear strike by the enemy himself cannot be entirely discounted and we must be prepared for it, although the Secretary of Information hopes, of course, that the enemy will show awareness of the consequences of such action.

The bartenders go to the set, and leaning their hands on the high railing, look up at the set as if it were on an altar, surrounded by flowers and the dust of incense. They turn the volume up even higher so that they can get the word from the Secretary of Information. But suddenly disinterested I turn in upon myself, cave in upon myself, run my finger through the empty beer glass while an image from the memory palace extrudes itself against the fresher memory of what I have just seen, and everything, however perilously, at last begins to make sense, although in no way that the Secretary would appreciate.

I remember a brief clip of the President, then eleven years younger in that pastoral era of 1951; he was addressing a press conference and reminding us that Hiss, of course, would stop at nothing to save his neck. It was just a little clip, nothing much to it; the essential orientation of the film we saw was oriented toward sports, but suddenly, juxtaposing this against the speech of tonight, all comes clear and I see it as I see my finger roaming the inside of the glass. (Is this a symbolic frigging? I might ask the clinic doctor if he were still around.) The President is crazy. He was always crazy. He will be as crazy as this for as long as he lives, and his craziness is the world he has given us.

The thought is momentarily purgative but then it slips like a mask like all of these thoughts do and I realize that it is still 1962 and still the world and still the oncoming nuclear war and nothing to be done about it by any of us until it is over. And the equipment in the memory palace does not, did never, properly work. That was government for you.

Introduction to
TWENTY SIXTY-ONE

I've long been a fan of schizophrenia. Schizophrenia, before it moved west like the Brooklyn Dodgers, and became, thanks to the public relations efforts of Szasz and his disciples, the New Life-style, seemed to be the only human illness that was genuinely artful, which made a profound comment on its own terms and not through that hit-or-miss process of deduction/analysis that is all most of us have gained from the socialization process. *Twenty Sixty-One* was written out of that interest, and instead of being a cautionary tale—as most of my work might be characterized—it is rather a happy and upbeat statement, almost a summary of one way out of our dilemma. Properly applied, schizophrenia might save all of us yet.

My objection to Professor Szasz is that he feels schizophrenia is an equivalent, if different, form of sanity; he would rip down the walls of the institution and deny the segregation between the "well" and the "mentally ill." I do not quarrel with the compassion of his point of view, only its applicability. I'd rather keep the institutional walls *up*. I'd rather that the institutions remain and that we, all of us, visit them periodically, as in popular literature one might revisit a marital bed. From there might come restoration.

———◆———

TWENTY SIXTY-ONE

Bleuler said, "I think I'd better be switched to a mixed type."

"No chance," the technician said.

"I don't think you understand," Bleuler said a little

more earnestly. "The paranoid symptoms are fascinating, of course, and I wouldn't have given up this experience for anything, but I'm starting to become grandiose now and also to hallucinate, and this is highly disturbing."

"Live with it."

"Please," Bleuler said, rubbing his palms together, "you could at least hear me out. I'm trying to be reasonable about this." He cleared his throat and said rather ponderously, "I'm beginning to feel that I'm a Christ-figure instead of a mere humble alienist. Imagery of crucifixions and so on. So if you don't mind," he said, giving the technician a winning smile and brushing some lint from his shoulders backhandedly, "I think that the chronic undifferentiated syndrome would be much better for all of us now."

The technician grunted. He had a blunted effect—this came with the job, he supposed, but it was more than the job; hell, *everyone* had a bit of a blunted effect, nowadays —but this did not preclude his ability to make intelligent sense of the situation. He would make intelligent sense of the situation. "Explain yourself," he said, shifting in the chair, sneaking a look at the clock. In fifteen minutes or a little less, the session would be over, and that was worth looking forward to. He could stand anything knowing that he was almost out of this.

"It's like so," Bleuler said, leaning forward again. He was a small nervous man with a beard and piercing eyes, the beard false, of course, the eyes' brightness drug-induced; but in certain angles and aspects he looked exactly the way he should. "My name is Ernst Bleuler. I am an alienist and the discoverer of schizophrenia. Schizophrenia is a mental disorder literally derived from the Germanic root *chiz:* to break, to shatter, the breaking and shattering of the personality, that is to say, into its component parts so that they no longer coordinate, the emotions and the will. Before my own contribution, the disease was known as dementia praecox, dementia of the young, so-called because the disease was characteristically manifested in adolescence and highly misunderstood. I have been able to prove first of all that the condition is not limited to the young."

Bleuler was becoming excited, his limbs heaving now in the uncoordinated manner of schizoids under stress, the technician noted. "It is a clear, distinct mental illness often appearing in, but hardly limited to, the young," he said rather hysterically, "and it can be further divided into six subtypes, although of course they won't get into that stuff for years and years. At the present time I am a schizophrenic-paranoid type characterized classically by unsystematized delusions of persecution and a confusion of identity, but the syndrome has started to shift into megalomania." He rubbed his palms together, looked at them, winked spasmodically. "This is quite dangerous," he said.

"Is it, now?"

"Of course it is," Bleuler said. "Once the paranoia modulates into religious or political fantasies, the patient can become genuinely dangerous to himself and others. Reality contact may be severed."

"Is that so?"

"Of course it's so. So I think it's time to reverse the syndrome. I'd like to become a chronic undifferentiated."

"You said that," the technician said, "already. Nevertheless, you must understand the policies and procedures of the center, Dr. Bleuler. You were inducted into the paranoid syndrome," and here the technician took a folder from a desk drawer, looked through it quickly for verification, then left it open before him, "at your own request only two days ago and signed on for a full week. Five days more remain, that is to say. Alterations of the cycle are very difficult and medically dangerous. At this moment your circulatory system is literally awash with potent drugs; the reversal of their effects might even be more damaging. . . ."

"Enough," Bleuler said as if to someone in a corner of the room, "leave me alone now." And then he turned, leapt at the technician, seized him by the collar and closed distance. The technician felt the room wavering, saw Bleuler momentarily as a dwarf throttling him, and only through an effort of will was he able to break the hold by chopping frantically at a wrist. Bleuler receded, gasping. Schizoids were very strong; they could sustain a high degree of muscle tension. Also, they did not feel weather as the normals did. The technician looked at Bleuler, as the man now began to sob, and wondered, not for the first time, if working at the center was really worth it. A man could be killed by one of these lunatics. But, then again, there were the benefits.

"I'm sorry about that," Bleuler said, and with the characteristic emotional lability of the disease he indeed seemed to have changed from a threatening to a sorrowful condition. "I really am; I warned you that I wasn't right." He sobbed once convulsively, rubbed at his eyes. "The paranoid delusions are much stronger all the time, and of course the religious overlay would rationalize. As you can see, I'm being very objective about this. The intellectual hemisphere is walled off, intact. I could kill. You'd better give me some help."

The technician looked at the clock again. Now it was only ten minutes until session's end . . . but if something happened to Bleuler here, he might be tied up for hours filling reports, making a formal presentation, answering the queries of the supervisors. He was authorized to murder patients, of course, but bureaucratically speaking, he would have to answer for it. All in all, it was not worth it. It simply was not worth it. The hell with Bleuler. It was his risk.

He reached into another side of the desk and took out a small vial.

"I think that's the right idea," Bleuler said, his eyes emitting a feeble light. "Really, it's much easier to do it this way; I knew that you were lying about the dangers of reversal; it's just easier to let the reactions go on, but only to a point. I don't want to make difficulties for anyone; it's simply that my tolerance is low. . . ."

The technician quieted him by shoveling a pill directly into Bleuler's mouth. Bleuler brought his teeth down, just missing a finger, chewed it meditatively while the technician made an entry in the open case folder, initialed it and, closing the folder, put it away. He looked up to find Bleuler staring at him from a different face.

"My name is not Ernst Bleuler," he said.

"That's right," said the technician.

"I am someone else whose name is actually unimportant. I am forty-one years old, classification B-20 in the underclass."

"Correct. All correct."

"I have been suffering from schizophrenia, paranoid type, self-induced, and the concurrent delusion that I was Ernst Bleuler, originator of the name and modern definition of the disease. This is a common autocratic fantasy."

"Of course," the technician said. He stood.

"I've got a few problems, but nothing that I can't control. In fact," the man who was Bleuler said, standing with the technician and beginning to weep, "what I have now is merely a normal and terrible depressive reaction. I think I'll go home and kill myself."

"Not so bloody soon," the technician said. He moved toward a wall, his gestures animated for the first time since Bleuler had entered. The clock showed a few minutes left, but the hell with that; for all intents and purposes the interview was over right now. "You have something to do first."

"Do I?" the man who was Bleuler said. His face was as dull as if it had been scrubbed down.

"Of course there is," the technician said a little coaxingly. "Don't you remember?"

"Remember what?" the man said. His head lolled; he put a hand on a cheek as if to steady it. "I don't remember a thing. Don't tell me that you're going to force something on me, now. All my life I've been pushed around, and I just can't take it anymore. I'm entitled to be treated like a human being, don't you think?"

"It's quite simple," the technician said. "Don't cry." He took the man by the hand, led him, both staggering a little, to the other side of the desk and placed him like an object in the seat that the technician had occupied. Almost immediately the man who was Bleuler took on a little color and life. The energizing effects of the analytic role, and so on. Well, fuck that. The technician went to the other side of the desk, sat and leaned forward. There was a considerable pause.

Finally, the man who was Bleuler said as if reading the words off the wall, "Yes? What is it?"

"Ah," the technician said. "Well, then." He rubbed his hands together, looked down, looked up, checked the situation. The man would hold. He would definitely hold. "Doctor Bleuler," he said, "I'd like to be a catatonic now, if you don't mind. The schizo-effective symptoms are fascinating, of course, but I'm beginning to get delusions that I'm a technician and that this is an institution of some kind where people who cannot bear their lives switch off roles with the help of drugs and treat one another."

"Of course," Bleuler said. He backhanded some more lint. "Go on."

Introduction to
CLOSING THE DEAL

About this piece could be written an essay twice its length, but I think I will skip it. It comprises my first sale to *Analog* out of more than one hundred and thirty short stories sold in the genre, and twenty-four novels. It was not sold to John W. Campbell, who died suddenly on July 11, 1971, but to his successor, Ben Bova, and it is infuriating to some people that I, a writer who represents many stylistic and ideological positions that the post-1950s J. W. C. came to loathe, am not only now a part of the ongoing tradition of the forty-five-year history of this magazine . . . but won the first award for best S-F novel to be given in his name.

This essay, certainly, would not be about myself but about John W. Campbell, and I have gone on record in so many other places under other circumstances that to do so again here would be a redundancy. Campbell was the most important single figure in the history of our field; modern science fiction owes everything to the editor that J. W. C. was in the 1940s. His position froze in the early 1950s for many reasons—see a chapter of Donald Wollheim's Harper & Row book, *The Universe Makers,* for the best single analysis of J. W. C. ever made available—and his influence upon the field was reactionary for the last ten to fifteen years of his life, in my opinion, but this neither diminishes our debt to him nor the dimensions of his early accomplishment. Simply stated, science fiction, had it not been for J. W. C., would be a dead or embalmed genre with somewhat less of an audience than that of western fiction. Instead, it is becoming increasingly apparent that it is the American literature of the last third of the century.

Campbell and a lot of writers like myself could not work together, a loss that was at least mutual. His successor, faced with an almost insoluble problem—the need to

improve and open up the magazine while at the same
time holding on to the very loyal and specialized audience that J. W. C. had built up through thirty-three years,
an audience that comprised twice that and more of the
next best-selling S-F magazine—has done well and
brought *Analog* to life again, at least intermittently. It is
not easy to follow a huge figure who has made his very
field a living memorial; Ben Bova has done extraordinarily well.

I am proud to have finally published in *Analog:* I
wish that J. W. C. had not had to leave us all for this to
be the case. If property is theft, hard-core Campbellians
might say, then progress is destruction.

-----◆-----

CLOSING THE DEAL

"She flies," the father said, indicating the little girl dangling uncomfortably midway between a baroque chande-
lier and the rather mottled carpeting. "And she has for
more than five years. You can imagine that it gave us
quite a turn when we saw this *three*-year-old just swoop
up from her toys and begin to bat around the room, but
after a while you can become accustomed to almost anything. That's the human condition, am I right?" He spread
his hands and looked at the guest directly, gave a little
laugh. "Actually, she's a very sweet, unspoiled little child
and I've tried to give her a healthy, wholesome upbringing to make her take her gift in stride. *Never* in front of
anyone other than me without permission and *double
never* out of the house. All right, dear," he said, "our
guest has seen everything he needs, I'm sure. Come down
now."

The little girl bobbled near ceiling level. "I can turn
over in the air," she said to the guest. "I can do dips and
floats and even pirouettes. If I went to ballet school like

I wanted to I could do even the better stuff, but he won't let me."

"I'm sure he would," the guest said gently. He opened the loose-leaf binder on his knee, took a pen from his suit pocket and made a note. "You have a very kind and understanding father."

"I have a very kind and understanding father, but he won't let me go to ballet school and he won't even let me fly unless he wants to show me off," the girl said. "I don't think that's right, do you? Not letting someone do what they really do best except when *he* wants me to." She revolved slowly, drifted toward the floor headfirst, reversed herself clumsily near the prospective point of impact and landed, wobbling, on her feet. "I'll go and *watch* television," she said. "I know you want me out of the room now. He always wants to show me off and then throw me out."

"That's not necessary, Jessica," her father said uncomfortably, "and you know perfectly well . . . "

"But it's *true*," the girl said. She nodded at the guest. "Actually, I can't fly all the time." she said. "You ought to know the truth; I can't even do it every time I *want* to. Actually, it's a very tiring thing. No more than fifteen or twenty minutes and then I have to rest for a whole day." She walked to the door, as clumsy on her feet as in the air, attempted a curtsy and left, closing the door not too gently.

The guest and her father sat in the living room, looking at one another rather uneasily for a time. The clock banged out four syllables, or then again the guest thought that it might have been five; it was very hard to keep track of the sounds that were swallowed by carpeting, and then, too, this was a peculiar household. Nothing was quite as it seemed to be. Four or five, however; it was certainly late afternoon and he wanted to complete his business and go on his way.

Idly, the guest imagined a large, frosted cocktail glass before him, around him was a large roadhouse, quiet conversation. He could ask this man for a drink, of course. But that would only compromise their dealings.

A drink could cost him a hundred dollars in this living room. *I must get hold of myself,* the guest thought rather frantically. *This is only a job and I ought to be glad to have it, everything considered. Involvement, pressures are on the agency, not on me.* "Remarkable child," he said hoarsely, scribbling something else and then slamming the binder closed, reinserting pen in pocket. "Very intelligent for her age. Of course, extremely undeveloped, as both you and she know. Her management of distances . . ."

"Well," her father said, spreading his hands again, "I *have* tried. The fact that she has one remarkable talent doesn't excuse her, after all, from living in the world. She's in an accelerated program at school where they take her to be simply a bright, normal child, and I've also arranged for reading tutorials at home and music lessons twice a week. She's studying the violin, my *favorite* instrument. Frankly, the child has almost no ability, but the cultural background . . ."

"I understand," the guest said rather hurriedly. "You're doing an excellent job within the limits . . ."

"It isn't easy in a motherless household, you know. I've had to be both parents to Jessica, which would be difficult with even a *dull* child, and she has to be shielded and educated carefully." The man paused, wiped a hand across his streaming forehead. "It's really been quite difficult," he said. "I'm sure that my wife had her reasons for leaving me and I was right to insist upon custody and I'll concede, too, that it was a *relief* when she walked out, but all of this has descended on me and I've had very little help from the woman or anyone else, for that matter. She was always selfish and inconsiderate, her mother, and I think that the flying business was the last *straw* in a marriage that frankly was never very good." He paused again, eyes rolling meditatively. "But that's neither here nor there," he said, "and you're not over here to be burdened with my personal problems. The point is: what are you going to do? I brought you here for *your* proposal."

"Um," the guest said, "isn't the point though what *you*

want to do? What do you expect, sir? The organization that I represent, you understand, is an exceptionally co-operative one and never makes outright conditions. Rather, we're here to listen to what you think you might have had in mind."

Carefully, the guest put a hand into his jacket pocket and fumbled for a pack of cigarettes, extracted one, lit it hurriedly and then, in response to a long, poor glare from his host, put it out in a large, green ashtray at his elbow. Little foul emanations stabbed at him like vipers and he choked. "Sorry," he said. Sinus trouble again; nervous strain. Why did the caseload always turn out like this? By definition, parents of the psionically gifted, particu-larly the levitators and telepaths, seemed to be at least mildly insane. Maybe that was the biological secret: in-sanity transmuted itself to psionics in the second genera-tion. Or, then again, maybe levitators and telepaths *made* parents insane. That was a thought, although, unhappily, not a new one. He choked again. "I apologize," he said, motioning toward the cigarette, "I didn't realize that smoke offended . . . "

"I will not tolerate smoking here," his host said. "That woman smoked, all she *did* was smoke; it took me three years after she left to get the air cleared and the smell out of the house. Smoke also inhibits Jessica's levitation."

"It shouldn't," the guest said firmly. "There is no con-nection."

"But it does." The man leaned forward, almost fore-head to forehead now. "The time for amenities is past, don't you think?" he said. "And I know you're a busy, responsible man. Now, what I'd like to hear is your offer."

The guest sighed. "It isn't that easy."

"And why not?"

"Everybody, all of the people, think in terms of offers, simple all-inclusive figures. But there are so many other things involved: the terms, the conditions and, more im-portantly, the strength of the talent and the degree of its refinement. . . ."

"Flat offer," the man said, touching palms with himself. His face seemed tinted with sweat or excitement; he had to work on his forehead again. "All-inclusive. Everything. Full responsibility, full control. Live-in."

"You wouldn't even want to retain . . . "

"Nothing," the man said quickly. "I've done everything I can for my child. Now she ought to be in the hands of people who can really develop her. I want an all-inclusive offer for total control."

"No subsidiary? How about participation in the secondary rights: performing, options, a percentage . . . "

The man cleared his throat. "I'll take it all on the front end, as much as I can get," he said.

"Ah," the guest said. "Ah." He opened his notebook again, extracted the pen, thought for a moment and then quickly wrote down a figure on a fresh, blank sheet, tore it past the reinforcements and handed it to the man, who seized it. "That's really the best we can do," he said. "It's a nice little talent, but levitation is far more common than you might think, and Jessica is completely untrained. She'd have to be trained from the beginning; the first thing she would have to do is to *unlearn* levitation so that we could start her from the beginning without any bad habits. The child has no body control at all."

He closed the book, sighed. "People think that all we do is go to work," he said, "but there's more than you might think and the key issue is the training, which is incredibly complex and expensive. Believe me, I have seen many who would cost more to train than they would eventually return, like doing heavy repairs on old cars. Fortunately, Jessica does show some ability, very raw, but she might be third-string somewhere, and there's a need for this."

The man closed his mouth finally and handed back the paper. "This is ridiculous," he said slowly. "I mean, it's robbery. It's less than a quarter of what the child is worth. A true levitator! A natural talent! Any one of the other agencies would *double* this price. I don't care who I'd see there."

"Then I suggest you *go* to one of our competitors," the guest said quietly; he put his pen away for the second time, closed his book with a snap and stood. "I'm afraid that we do not misrepresent or pack our offers as our competitors do. Our policy is one figure, a fair offer, taking into account every aspect of the situation. If it's taken, fine, and if it's not we happily accept the loss, because a higher offer would have been unprofitable and thus self-deceiving. Our policy is built on rigorous fairness and the skills of its highly trained field staff; and now," he added, moving toward the door, "if you will excuse me, my working day is done."

"Now, wait a minute," the man said slowly, the words wrenched from him one by one like sobbing exhalations from a balloon. "I didn't say no. I mean, I didn't *flatly* say no. I mean, if that's really your policy, one offer, how was I to know that?" He touched the guest on the arm, trembling slightly, backed off at once. "I mean, I know your reputation," he said, "that you're honorable people."

"Thank you."

"But frankly, I *have* to get a little more than that."

"Try one of our competitors, then. You said they would do better."

"But I have to think of my *child,*" the man said quickly, almost hysterically. "Now, I mean to say, what's a few dollars more or less when it's your own child at issue; and I know that you'd get the best for her, make the best possible development."

"If we can."

"So maybe, well, let me put it this way, then." He placed the most delicate of hands on the guest's wrist again, this time letting it rest there. "Would there be maybe a ten-percent give in your position? On the upward arc, of course."

"Of course," the guest said, "of course upward, always upward. No one ever thinks downward, do they?"

He paused, sighed, looked at the man. "Levitation is a dime a dozen," he said. "We reject more levitators than we take. In its crude, unfocused state it's worthless except as a party trick. How many violinists are there for every concert master?" He paused again and then shrugged. "Look here," he said.

The guest put the binder under his arm, lifted his index

finger and as clumsily as Jessica moved upward two or three feet, dangled his feet, kicked for effect and then swam inexpertly through the air to his chair. Breathing unevenly he hung there for an instant, then released the field and dropped into the chair. The father watched this intently.

"You see?" the guest said, taking out a handkerchief and wiping his wet forehead. "And I'll never be anything more than a field investigator."

That hung in the air for a moment. The father seemed to dwindle within himself, dropped his gaze, looked at the floor thoughtfully. At length he lifted his head, looked at the guest again and very awkwardly rose from his own chair, hanging in the air tensely.

"All right," he said. "I see. I'll sign anything."

And so the negotiations ended. Another day; another dollar, the guest thought.

Introduction to
WHAT THE BOARD SAID

Another and perhaps the last in the immortal line of Malzberg Assassination Stories. A review (highly favorable) of Richard Condon's new novel *Winter Kills* appears in *The New York Times* on the day I write this, and that admirable writer is to be congratulated for having produced his best novel since the magnificent (if deliberately junky) *The Manchurian Candidate* . . . but let us remember, Condon and Lehmann-Haupt alike, who, in all the years while the heavy artillery was mumbling and grumbling in the back lines and being fed slowly with shot, was keeping the enemy occupied and off-balance at the front. Not many of us, folks; not many of us.*

———◆———

WHAT THE BOARD SAID

In Brooklyn I thought I saw the answer, touched it whole for a shimmering instant until a beggar, one of the thousands who infest the area near the landing stage, came upon me and slapped it away. In Tripoli the answer was there clear and shining, ready to be grasped, but my mind and heart scuttled off wildly after a whore who showed me with a crook of her finger yet another way home; in Jakarta I came upon it so close, so brilliantly near, that it would have been mine if I had only swung the door of consciousness to admit it, but I did not; I could not make

* Credit for the very first salvo that appeared in print goes, of course, to J. G. Ballard's *The Assassination of J.F.K. Considered as a Downhill Motor Race,* which, when first offered to market in 1965, was considered incomprehensible by every American editor to whom it was offered and wound up in *New Worlds.*

that last gesture, and it was then, friends, that it occurred to me for the first and perhaps only time that I did not *want* to find the answer, that I was as frightened of that conclusion as an ecclesiastic might be at the presence of his Host, and it was then as well that I realized I could not live a life of pursuit anymore—that I would have to come to grips with my problem.

So I returned to the board, passing through Jakarta, Tripoli, Brooklyn, Washington and other sites both visited and unvisited in my pursuit, all of my history returning I could say in little glimpses as I hopped from one stage to the next on the way to the meeting place, and when I appeared before them at last it was with the look of eagles: the aspect of a man who has seen many things, who has touched an overwhelming set of experiences and was, in many ways, beyond their simple stone comprehension. Standing before them straight and proud, this perception of distance in my eyes, I knew I cut a dashing picture before them, but there was some self-consciousness as well because I knew—oh, I am willing to admit this—that to a certain degree I had *contrived* to give this impression and was taking unfair advantage of their own tendency to be swayed.

The board has a tendency to snivel. This characteristic, one of which the board is itself aware, has been controlled but not eliminated in recent dialogues. Now as it saw me standing before it, it seemed to inflate with self-pity, or perhaps it was only confusion at my sophisticated and well-traveled aspect. Rubbing its hands uncomfortably, the board said, "Well, have you found the answer?"

"Yes, I have," I said, "and the answer is that there is no answer."

"I am sorry. I do not understand this sophistry."

"Don't be stupid," I said to the board, going to a sideboard and fetching myself a tall, glistening tumbler filled with whiskey. I drank it down, choking only slightly, then threw the tumbler to the floor, splintering it, and said, "I will clarify." The board twitched. "The answer is there, but it is in terms that cannot be embraced by human thought or speech. We have not yet evolved to a level where we can frame or state the answer, and therefore the mind rejects the task. So we must stop."

The board shook its old head. "That is ridiculous."

"It may be ridiculous," I said, "but it's the truth." Kicking the splintered pieces aside, I took another tumbler, filled it and drank more slowly, watching the board's pale complexion. In ill health and aged before its time, the board owes its continued survival only to the ministrations of full-time staff, including prayers of half the population of the globe. Even so, it is clearly failing; there are times when I must wonder if it will last out a night. "We must quit," I said.

"Never. The quest is what makes us human."

"Then we must make our humanity the acceptance of failure. The answer is beyond us. That's what *keeps* us human, knowing our failings. Have you ever considered that?"

"I really am sorry," the board said. "We were instructed that the answer was available, and you were selected from a list of highly qualified applicants to find it."

The board shifts between the first person and the collective so swiftly, sometimes within the course of a single sentence, that autism is suspected. This kind of emotional lability, failure of proper orientation for time, place or person, rapid swings in identity, is one of the symptoms of the truly insane. I know this. A schizoid break, a fracturing of the personality. Still, having said that, what is to be done? The board is a constant, an unchanging, part of our world, no less than the converter. One must get along as best as one can. "I'm sorry, too," I said and put down the second tumbler with a crash, cracking marble, "but I have nothing more to say. The answer is easily beyond our means; I have chased it through Jakarta, Tripoli, Brooklyn and a hundred other cities to ascertain this, and now the quest must be abandoned."

I turned to go from the great hall in a dusty corner of which the board sits near the sideboard but was called back by a cry so tormented and alien that it wrenched me around; it might have been a stricken animal or some massive rending of the walls themselves, and I turned to see the board weeping. "Do you mean it's over, then?" it said. "After a thousand years of struggle it has come to this?" It ran a splayed old hand across its forehead, placed an elbow on the table for support. It wept.

I was moved. How could I not be moved? One would have to be a monster not to have been touched by this vulnerability in the board that I had always thought of as more of a machine than a person. This recognition of its humanity quite unsettled me, but, then again, it could not in any way change my position or the validity of my insight. "I am sorry," I said gently. I touched the board's robe. "I wish that it could have been different. But we are not yet ready for the answer. Perhaps in another five million years we may find the language to apprehend and discuss, but not yet." And I turned to get out of there before sentiment fractured completely. I did not want to cry with the board. What good would that have done?

None of that for me, oh, no, none of it: I had come to deliver my message and to be done with that. I returned as quickly as possible to the stage and joined a long line of tourists shuffling toward the converter. There must have been at least two hundred before me of many ages and backgrounds, and as I took my place at the end it was with great bitterness. As rapidly as the converter worked, it would still be at least ten minutes until I reached my own place, and in the meantime anything could happen.

Anything. Breakdowns in this part of the continent were common. The converters were overloaded and a breakdown might even occur in transit, some hapless soul held in limbo while the technicians tried to restore the circuits and electron feed. Indications were likely that such malfunction would occur; the converter was never really constructed, I have learned, to handle more than fifty transmissions without pause—and here I was, two hundredth in line.

The trouble lies in culture lag; we are still trying to make devices accommodate us that represent a simpler level of technological necessity. Thirty-five billion are too much for the present converters. They should have been rewired and expanded years ago, but no one anticipated, no one cared, and now we are in serious trouble. (As one of those who was forward-looking and foresaw this situation years ago without being able to influence the administrators or the board itself, I am understandably bitter. Much would have been different if they had listened to me.)

In fact, the line had not moved at all since I had joined, and now behind me another forty or fifty had assembled. I could hear vague murmurs of impatience drifting from the front and the tourist directly ahead of me. A fat man who looked vaguely like the board itself, although younger, said, "We'll never get out of here."

"Yes we will," I said shortly. I try to discourage conversations. "Don't worry about it."

"I was supposed to be in Omaha by fourshift. Why couldn't they anticipate this?"

"They did," I said. "We'll just have to wait."

"I've *been* waiting. Waiting up and down the line. It's ridiculous."

His voice had been rising through this and had attracted an unpleasant attention around us; some intensity of gaze gave me the feeling that with nothing else really going on we were the focus of attention. "Please keep quiet," I said urgently, "you're creating a scene now."

"I want to. Maybe we'll get some action from the technicians if they realize that people won't just submit to this."

"The technicians are trying their best. Please keep quiet," I said. "Let's wait our turn and all will be well."

"You're just like the rest of them," the fat man said, "you're a passive fool. You'll put up with anything in the name of the converter. How well it works, how trustworthy the technicians are! Do you know what I'm going to do?" he said cunningly. The insane shift moods rapidly. The fat man was insane. Most of the people with whom I deal are crazy; it is a consequence of modern technology.

"No," I said, "I do not know what you're going to do." The man, I perceived, must have been drunk, or, then again, it might have been only my own relative inebriation, thick fumes wafting from his mouth or mine, the air, the heat, the noise, the impatience making me sick. "I don't know what you're going to do, and I don't want to know, either."

"I'm going to complain to the board," he said. "I'm going to march right into that hall and let it know what's going on here. He's around this area, isn't he? I don't have to put up with this; I'm a citizen. If the *board* knew what was going on it wouldn't stand for it. I'm going to tell it everything," he said. "I've been meaning to drop in on the board, anyway."

I raised a hand, blocking his attempts to break the line. "No," I said, "don't go to the board. Don't move."

"Who are you to say that?"

"It doesn't matter," I said, "it doesn't matter who I am." I found myself talking with desperate intensity, aware that we were now indeed the sheer focus of attention as far as I could see. Movement in the distance indicated that the conversation, the noise level, had reached the technicians themselves. Shortly they would come through to see what was going on and then it would be all over; I would have to tell them everything. "Just stop," I said again, "don't go to the board. The board cannot be seen."

"I know what it is," the fat man said, "*now* I know the secret. I anticipate everything you're going to say. The board doesn't exist, does it? There's no such thing. They just told us there's a board so that they'd have something to hold over us, something to frighten us with. Actually, there's no one in the great hall at all. *There's no one running the world.*"

I shook my head desperately. "Not so," I said, and then it came spilling out of me. I tried to hold back the words but could not. "The board does indeed exist, is a reality; I'm one of his special deputies and perform tasks for him. I've just completed an assignment and spoken to the board and I'm afraid given it a rather unpleasant shock, quite a tragic shock, as a matter of fact; it can't be seen now, can't absorb any more difficulties of this sort, is quite unsettled, in fact, and therefore . . . "

"You're mad," the fat man said and turned toward the line, spoke to the tourists. "This man is crazy, isn't he?" he said, and they nodded bleakly, solemnly, *yes.* I could tell that and then he was pushing past me, his body a blur. "All right," he said, "I'm going to see your damned board and give it even more of a nasty shock. I don't have to listen to this nonsense. If I can't get to Omaha by fourshift, someone has to take the responsibility, right? Someone runs the world, right?" And voices called *right* and he drove past me. I tried to block him, was pushed out of the way, appealed desperately to the crowd then, saying, "You can't let him go; can't you understand that? If you let him get to the board he'll kill the board with the shock of his presence, and then all of it will end." But they did not listen, they did not listen at all, in fact (I find this hard to believe, that I made no impression at all, but must accept the facts as I have stated them); they began to laugh and as I fell to the stones, feeling the ragged strip cut open my cheek, as the crowd passed me in pursuit of the madman heeding his cries to follow, it occurred to me that I had lied to the board, that all along, in fact, the answer had been there . . . had been there to be touched, had been in these damned cities, all of them, had been in *this* city . . . and if only I had found the language to speak, all would have been different.

But the failure of language had been my own. The answer could have been spoken. I had not, until then, known the words.

Lying there in Dallas I heard them tear the palace open.

Introduction to
UNCOUPLING

The best stylist pound-for-pound (I'd make him a light heavyweight) in the history of this field is probably Alfred Bester, and *Uncoupling* is a shameless pastiche, proving if further demonstration be needed, that I retain my ability to write in the style of any writer, living or dead, although I am not quite sure why I ever found this necessary.

Alfred Bester is distinctly living, sixty years old at this time and writing, after a long pause of years, at *Holiday,* at the top of his form. A partial novel of his, *The Molecular Men,* was presented to Ed Ferman and I in our capacity as dual editors of *Final Stage* (Charter House, 1974) about a year ago, and on this evidence, on this tribute to the will and spirit and fire and drive of Alfred Bester, I would say that this man's career, thirty-five years after his first published story, still lies ahead of him. Of no writer could more be said; someday, perhaps, it will be said of me.

Uncoupling was written shortly after I encountered the aforementioned *The Molecular Men* as a tribute to a writer who I greatly admire. If it works, it works on Bester's strengths; any weaknesses are my own.

UNCOUPLING

I came to the Towers fuming. The walk across town had bent my breath, shaken the substance, broken the spirit (too often I tend to think in expletives, but pardon: it is an old trait), but the flesh unmortified quivered, reaching for its own purposes. At the unoccupied desk I stood

there for a while, inhaling great mouthfuls of hydro-
genated O2 (one of the chief lures of the Towers is that it
offers an atmosphere of pure oxygen, no small thing in
these difficult, crumpling times) and screaming for service.
"Come here!" I shouted to the gleaming walls, the spick-
and-span corridors, the aerated passageways of the fluorescence. "I need attention. *Je bien attendu. Je desiree
a fornication.*"

An attendant appeared, neutered in flowing robes.
Everything in the Towers is done for effect; go one inch
under the surface and the substance disappears. Nevertheless, one must persevere. The world is plastic. The
world is corrupt. Still, in or out of it there is no alternative.

"Je suis au pardonne, monsieur," the attendant said
in execrable French. *"Je desire a' service mais je non
comprendre votre desiree. . . ."*

"Speak English!" I snarled, hitting the counter, a tall,
bitter man in my late thirties, the snakes of purpose wend-
ing their way through his shattered but wise features. (I
often tend to depersonalize, sometimes lapsing even into
the third person in my desperate attempts to scrape free
of the trap of self: *au pardonniere.*) "Speak English!"
the tall, bitter man shouted, his voice echoing through
the amplifiers in the walls of the Towers, and the attendant trembled, adjusted his/her robes more tightly about
himself/herself.

"Yes," he/her said. "I am here to help you, all of us
are here to help you, but you must understand, you must
simply understand that in order to achieve you must
modulate . . . "

"I will not modulate!" I screamed, slamming a bitter
fist into the gleaming and refractive surfaces of the desk.
"There is no need for modulation. I am entitled to service,
service and understanding—don't you clowns understand
this?—and furthermore," I added more quietly as sev-
ral threatening robot policemen, noiseless on their canisters, glided into the reception area holding cans of Mace
at ready, "anyway," I whispered to the attendant, the gen-
tlest and most winsome of expressions chasing all the

snakes from the panels of the features, "this is one of my prescribed days for heterosex and I want to make the most of it. Time is money, after all, money is the barter of existence and without time and money where would any of us be? I wish to engage in normative heterosex during this, my relaxative period." I perched an elbow on the desk, turned a non-threatening blink upon the attendant. "Pardon me for my haste," I added, *"pardonniere moi au mon haste, je suis* so needful."

The attendant foraged under the desk, produced a standard application form, passed it across to me. The robot policemen chattered to one another, their tentacles flicking in a consultative manner, and then as noiselessly as they emerged, withdrew, leaving the reception area blank and impermeable once again. I respect the means by which they maintain security here. Really, the Towers is in a difficult position, catering as it must to the full range of human desire and perversity, and if I were administering it, which I happily do not (the Government itself administers everything nowadays; the projections of the mid-1900s were absolutely correct), I would be even more forceful than they. People must learn to accept their condition. People must realize that in a world of poison, overpopulation and enormous international tensions, where five people occupy the space biology would have reserved for only one, tensions accumulate and the only way that the world can be prevented from complete destruction is a firm administrative hand at the top. People must fall into place. (I wrote my thesis on neo-Fascism and have in my cubicle a handy collection of whips that I am apt at jocular moments to lay merrily about myself and all visitors.)

"Fill out this form, sir," the attendant said to the tall, bitter fascist standing at the desk, "name, address, locality zone, authorization, desire and credit voucher." It gestured behind itself meaningfully to a small machine perched on a lower shelf. "We will then feed the application through into the bank and everything checking out satisfactorily . . . " It paused, cocked an eyebrow, looking surprisingly desirous in its pale, pink robes, its catatonic lack of affect. *"Je suis attendre,"* it said.

Hastily I filled out the form: name (irrelevant), age (I have already conceded this), housing (lower domicile in the Blood District), authorization (Condition F-51: Perversities and heterosex) and desire (fornicative). Credit information entered in. I passed the form hurriedly to the attendant, feeling the swift, cool slash of its fingers as it appropriated the form, sending renewed surges of desire through me. "I wonder," I said, leaning across the counter, "I wonder if you yourself might well be . . . uh . . . "

"That is impossible, sir," the attendant said. A modest blush seemed to steal over its features much as embitterment is known to tear over mine. "We are not available for any purpose other than reception, and in any case, you are here seeking heterosex; is that not correct?"

"That has nothing to do with it," the man said in a keening shriek, once again causing the canisters of invisible robot policemen to brush against the floor, "that has absolutely nothing to do with it, and furthermore . . . "

"Je suis ne heterosex pas," the attendant said and turned, fed the application into the machine that seized it angrily, yanking off strips of paper as it ingested. *"Je suis* neuter and therefore would not be satisfactory for your requirements."

"You do not understand," the man said. "In the Blood District we do not, we absolutely do *not,* put up with insubordination from functionaries." He put his hand against the concealed weapon at his belt. "It is insufferable for you to address me in this way. . . ."

Abruptly I stopped. The robot policemen were back in full force and also the lights in the Towers were beating now like little hearts: *wicker, wicker,* sending darts of greenish sensation into the deeper centers of the cerebrum. Abruptly I understood everything. Deprivation of heterosex in my program leads to an accumulation of tension: disassociation reaction, abusiveness to attendants, flickers of bad French. Disturbances of vision. Abrupt disassociation reaction, lapses into the third person. Understanding this, I felt a perilous calm being restored and was able to look at the attendant with neither fear nor desire. *"Je votre au pardonne,"* the bitter man said to the attendant, *"je suis tres excite."*

"Est rien, est maintenant rien," the attendant said, making a signal to the robot policemen. They had closed in on me during this latest insight and were now, twenty or fifty of them in their Government-issue and insigniaed uniforms, staring balefully. The nearest of them, apparently a supervisor, clapped its tungsten club from hand to hand meaningfully and turned its circuits to orange.

"Est rien," I said and reached a hand toward the supervisor, a hand of comity and understanding. I have always believed that man and machine can co-exist in a technocracy. My fascism has a certain overlay of perversity, but that perversity has never included fear or loathing toward machines. I get along with machines very well. Without them the world would have fallen into the sea long ago. Control. Absolute control.

"Est rien," the supervisor said in a metallic gurgle, and, retracting its club, spun away. Tentacles waved. The troops, having finished their consultation once again, disappeared. I shuddered with relaxation, realizing that my clothes were drenched and warned myself to bring no further disgrace. There are no tolerance levels for scenes in this world. Confrontation must be avoided at all costs. The world is five times overpopulated.

"You are adjudged competent for heterosex," the attendant said. The rosy blush had returned; now it seemed heightened and darkened by some information it had picked up on my printout, which was still whirring slyly out of the machine. All of my horrid little secrets being displayed to the attendant, but who am I to complain? With my newfound grip on sanity I smiled back implacably, imagining a daffodil in one corner of my jacket from which I might take absent sniffs. "According to the information you have not had heterosex for two months and therefore may engage in it freely. Your credit rating is also satisfactory."

Two months. Two months! Understanding lying under

me like a gray pool filled with the winking fish of knowledge, I plunged into that pool wholeheartedly, splashing
around, spouting little sprays of abysmal French while I
did so. Two months without heterosex! No wonder the
disassocation reaction was so advanced; no wonder that
not once, but twice, I had caused the robot policemen to
be summoned. "Two months!" I said. "But under the
medical profile entered in my twenty-third year I am to
engage in heterosex once a month. Once every month.
Recherche du las temps perdu. I must have forgotten to
make my obligatory last month. Of course," I confided to
the attendant, "I have been terribly busy." This happens
to be absolutely true. I have been engaged in a massive
research project on the induction of pain and my concentration has been fervid. Even food and drink evade me
when I get deeply into a project.

"You must have forgotten," the attendant agreed. Its
eyes became wistful as it put the printout into the
shredder and reluctantly demolished it. "But that's perfectly all right now. The Towers are here to serve you.
Your Government is here to serve you. You will be well
taken care of."

The tall man turned from the counter and found himself in the grip of another attendant, a somewhat burlier
one who put two incisive fingers into a forearm. "Just go
along," the attendant at the desk said, "and you will be
bien service, je vous assure."

"Certainly," the tall man said, feeling his balance momentarily flicker as the burly attendant made a seizing
jerk, then readjusting himself to new sights, new sounds as
he was carried beyond the swinging gates of the rear and
into the deeper mysteries of the Towers. "This must be a
very dull job for you," he said to the attendant, "conveying people from the reception desk into the fornication
rooms. Undoubtedly you must feel some resentment, too,
no? To realize that these people are engaging almost
routinely in acts that are permanently denied to you must
be quite painful, and, also, your job must be quite delim-
ited. But I don't mean to pry," the man finished, "I don't
mean to pry."

"Forget it," the attendant said, "my speech organs are engaged only for simple commands." And it carried me deeper into the corridors and hallways of the Towers: now I could see the various rooms on my right and left moving deeper into the Towers, the doors of the rooms open (why not? who would interfere?) in which however dimly I could see forms struggling, some in pairs, others in multiples, elaborate equipment, gleaming utensils, the cries and unwinding shrieks of copulation. Carried ever further I went past the section marked SADO-MASOCHISM into a somewhat lighter area stamped BESTIALITY in flickering letters, from which now and then from the doors (closed this time: certain things must be forever sacrosanct) I could hear vagrant moos and cackles, crow cries and the barking of dogs, squealing of pigs and the sound of milk cans toppling. Out of bestiality then and into an aseptic corridor in which the word HOMOSEX had been embroidered in swinging tapestry that hung in strands from the ceiling, the attendant's grip ever more devastating on my arm and well it might be since the tall man found his legs beginning to give out from the excitement of this journey, his needful persuasion, his extreme disassociation, and needed all the help that he could get from the attendant in order to make his rapid, scuttling journey. They always rush one through the Towers, but this is to be expected; the Government has many things on its mind and schedules must be obeyed. Finally, the tall man found himself, gasping, and with a bad, purpling bruise on his left forearm, in the section marked HETEROSEX, the doors once again open, a clean, light, bright area much like coming into the concentration camp must have been like after a long, difficult train journey, and there the burly attendant pushed me into a tiny room where a female sat waiting, her hands clasped and folded, quite naked as well, the tall man noticed, since by this time he had obtained a stunning tumescence. These kind of things will happen under panic and stress; one must accept them.

"You have five minutes," the attendant said and went to the door, folded its arms, turned its back. From the rear I could see the small, deadly extrudance of wires coming from the black hair and realized that it was a robot. Of course. Inevitably, the pressure of work and inventory would cause the Towers to convert, but I had hoped (nostalgically, of course) that somehow this would not happen in my time. "Five minutes," the robot said, "is all that you are permitted on your allotment."

"That's ridiculous," the tall man said, already springing out of his clothing, exposing his limbs lustrous and well oiled to the heavy, penetrating light, "I've always been authorized for ten."

"New conditions," the attendant said. The wires seemed to glow beneath the hair, turning orange. "If you don't like it," it said, "you're free to terminate now."

"Oh, no," the tall man said, "oh, no, no, no." And naked, he turned to the female, extending his arms, walking toward her with some difficulty. "Do you speak?" he said.

"Non."

"You should speak," the tall man said. "You always have spoken in the past; I mean, it isn't much to ask, just a few words here or there. . . ."

"You are no longer permitted communication," the attendant said. The tall man looked at the female as if in sad confirmation of this and slowly, bleakly, the female nodded. Pain appeared in her eyes and then disappeared. She rose, extended her own arms. Impassively, one time, she gestured and the tall man came against her.

Hump and jump. Huff and puff. Knead and seed. Pump and rump. The less said about all of this the better: pornographic fantasia was outlawed by the magnificent act of 2010, and I am no one to dispute the Governmental wisdom. Also, about this part there is very little to say. It is a sameness, a grinding grayness under the lights, but the Government has deemed it necessary on an individually analyzed personality profile, and I am not going to dispute the Government in that area, either. I will not dispute the Government in *any* area. The less said about all of this the better, then, other than to point out that the disassociation reaction ceased at once and I no longer had the desire to speak French. Not even two particles of that miserable language—the language of love they call it—remained within me when I was done.

I got off the female slowly and donned my garments. From her position on the floor she regarded me with an admiration that might have been boredom, a boredom that might have been sympathy. *"Je suis satisfee,"* she said.

"Forget that," I said, "I don't want to hear any of that now." Dressed, I went to the attendant, who took my hand once again in that seizing grip. "Must you do that?" I said to him.

"I'm afraid that it must," it said almost regretfully. "Clientele must be escorted."

"I would follow you on my own."

"I know you would follow me on your own," the attendant said, "but according to your profile the infliction of brutality is part of the general satisfaction here. Don't talk to me any further; I told you that I was not programmed." It seized me once again in that terrible grip and led me through the hallway.

A different route this time. HETEROSEX gave way to NECROPHILIA, a solemn, rather funereal area in which the doors were secured by gravestones on which, like graffiti, epitaphs had been ascribed; past NECROPHILIA it was MASTURBATION, an area not composed like the others of separate rooms but rather a communal, almost dormitory kind of arrangement in which the clientele lay in rows stretched on cots, regarding obscenities and photographs projected on the ceiling and did what they must, depressively; past masturbation was ASEPSIS, and here, in the most solemn area of all, men in rumpled or flowing priestly garb passed among the benches in what was a hastily reconstructed synagogue, passing out small words of cheer and advice to the penitents who, clamped on the benches, gripped themselves and studied the simulated stained glass. There is no end to the range of the Towers. At last, back again to the reception area where the supervisor of the robot policemen (I was able to recognize him by the shape of his tentacles) was engaged in absent banter and joshing with the reception attendant.

"He's here," the burly attendant said and released me from his grip. Abruptly I collapsed, a spreading bruise like a stain lurching across my forearm, sending enormous shooting pains into the scalp. I hit the floor and it must have been the shock of this that revived me, but when I returned to consciousness the burly attendant was alone, the robot policemen standing over with a look of concern.

"Are you all right?" it said.

"I am quite all right," I said with dignity and slowly picked myself off the floor, wiping little scabs of dirt and excrement (the Towers is all front, the actual maintenance of the area quite poor) from my clothing. "I had a minor fall."

"If you do not leave at once," the supervisor said intensely, "it will be necessary to arrest you."

"I'm quite aware of that," I said. Residence in the Towers beyond immediate utility is impermissible, of course. Everyone knows that. The world is five times overpopulated and if people who used the Towers did not leave promptly, where, I would like to know, where would we all be? Cooperation is the key to survival in the technocracy; we are a species who must cooperate or die, and I am quite willing to fulfill my obligations. "I'm going to leave," I said, drawing my clothing around me and summoning dignity like a little nimbus over my head, "just as soon as I have recovered my breath."

"Would you like to program in another appointment now?" the attendant said. It winked at me encouragingly. Always, underneath this efficiency, is a hint of scatology, lure of the deeps, and if someone tells you that this is not one of the basic appeals of the Towers he is crazy. Crazy. "You are entitled to one extra appointment because of your, ah, deprivation."

"That is not necessary," I said. The robot policeman gave me suddenly a stunning blow on the head; then as I wavered to the floor, it held me up and looked at me intensely. "You were ordered to leave," it said.

"This is ridiculous. I am a citizen; you are simply machinery and I cannot be dominated . . ."

"I think we'll have to get rid of him," the policeman said to the attendant, and slowly, sadly, the neuter gave a nod of agreement. Once again I felt myself seized with enormous, clutching force and was conveyed through all the spaces of the reception room toward an exit hatch. "This is disgraceful," I burbled. "You can't do this to me."

"Yes we can," said the policeman, *"oui, nous avons le authoritee."* And then I was shoved through the hatch. I landed street-side, gasping, a drop of only three feet to the rubberized conveyor, but still, in my rather damaged condition, rather shocking. Citizens looked at me quickly, appraisingly, and then their eyes turned inward toward private considerations, the conveyor belt whisking all of us along in silence. In a world five times overpopulated it is necessary to function personally only in terms of one's amity group and never elsewhere. The Towers, for example, would be completely impossible if clients were to essay personal relationships with that personnel.

The conveyor carried me swiftly through Wilbur, past Marseilles and into the Blood District. Even after so short and dramatic an absence, it was good to see the familiar outlines of the slaughtering houses appear on the horizon, see the guillotines and little nooses on the tracts, hear the screams, sniff the odors from the abattoirs. At my own slot I stepped off the conveyor belt quickly, feeling my detumescence swinging within my garments like a credit voucher in the pocket: ease, power. I adjusted myself to the slot and carried myself in, then up ninety-six levels and into my own humble quarters which now, since I have been so absorbed in the research project, look something like an abattoir themselves. It was good to be home. It is always good to be home. I loosened my garments, examined myself for scars from burns or inference, syphilitic infestation (this is impossible, but I am in many ways an obsessive-compulsive), gonococcal traces, sighed and sat on my one chair, feeling little puffs of dust whisk up around me. I inhaled them, at peace for the first time in

many days, the pressures of heterosex deprivation removed. Then I noticed that sitting in the room across
from me, half-hidden in the dimness, shielded by the light
of the window was the female with whom I had fornicated
at the Towers some forty-five minutes before.

I was not shocked. This kind of thing happens quite
often. It has never happened to me, but I was prepared.
Sometimes these employees, depressed and made unhappy by the rather turgid and ritualistic nature of their
employment, will sneak out of the Towers and follow
clients home, attempting to establish some kind of relationship. There is only one thing to do, of course. I would
want it done for me. It is in their best interests.

"Please," she said, "listen to me. *Je vous attendre, vous
je attendre.*"

"Impossible," I said, "I'm no longer interested in
French. It only happens when I'm neurasthenic."

"You must listen to me," she said intensely, "we can't
go on this way. We must truly communicate and get to
know one another."

I already had the communicator in operation. She
stopped, looked at me bleakly. I hit the buttons for the
Towers and the robot supervisor who I already knew so
well appeared on the screen and recognized me. "Yes?"
he said impassively. I will give them much credit. There
is nothing personal in their machinery; they simply do
what must be done. As should we all. It is possible
to envy the machines, to aspire to their condition.

I stepped away from the screen, allowed the policeman
to see the female behind me. "You see what's happened?"
I said.

"Yes."

"I refuse to speak with her and I am cooperating."

"Yes," the policeman said. Even in the monochrome
viewer I could see the little green light of approval coming from its eyes. "We will have personnel there within
fifteen seconds to affect re-entry."

It killed the televiewer. I turned back toward the female. With retrieval coming there was no longer need to
fear her. "We must feel," she said. "We must be humans.

We must share our common humanity. *Vous et moi, nois etes humanite.*"

I shrugged. The door, which I never lock (there is safety in accessibility), opened and the burly attendant came in. He must have followed me home. This is standard procedure—to make sure that Towers attendance does not result in abnormal excitation. There have been occasional massacres; now the attendant's pursuit is mandatory. "You," he said to the female, "come here."

He went to her, took her by the arm. I knew that grip. It caused me, against my will, to smile. She saw the smile, looked up at me, her eyes already beginning to dull. "You don't understand," she said as the attendant took her out.

But I did.

Introduction to
OVER THE LINE

As I write this, the original anthology containing this piece has just been published and it is exactly two years since I wrote it and one year and three hundred fifty-eight days (I got the check a week after submission) since I thought of it at all. Thus, it has been even more characteristically alienating than usual to reread the story; like most writers I am at a good distance from my work almost immediately after having finished it (if only as a protective device), but rarely is the lapse between publication and composition as great as this.

I remember very little of this story. I know that it was written in exactly one hour, start to finish, that it gave an impression of hard, heavy work, grinding away at stone, that I was in the middle of an argument with my wife (interrupted for the span of the story), that my sinuses were erupting as I typed, that the one hundred fifty dollars I got for this one hour's work gave me a feeling of great (although totally illusory) pride because, I thought at the time, there were many psychiatrists who would be pleased to make one hundred fifty dollars an hour, let alone blue-collar workers, which is essentially (and don't let them kid you) what the writer is. Nineteen seventy-two was a year for illusory comforts, small explosions of defensiveness. I remember that the commissioning editor said that if this wasn't a publishable piece at a good quality level then he knew absolutely nothing about science fiction (perhaps he does not), and, otherwise, I remember nothing at all . . . or remembered nothing until I reread *Over the Line* when I found it, like most of my fiction, an essential mystery. I do not know from where it came and I doubt if I could go back there and pull out a similar product. With almost every novel or short story the shop of issuance hangs out a TO LET sign. (Other cubicles open down the street, however. If not inexhaustible, I am not very exhaustible.)

It is a peculiar business, this art of fiction. Philip K. Dick writes that when he reads a novel of his between covers he feels further from it than any reader conceivably could because for him, Phil Dick, the characters are dead. John Cheever will not permit a published piece of his work in the house, so totally alienated does he feel from completed material; so much does he loathe it. On the other hand, some writers love their work and can quote whole novels word for word. Or do sequels.

It is a mystery.

———◆———

OVER THE LINE

Now it is time for the test. "Rite of passage," my father has assured me. "No one is expected to pass the test; no one ever has in the history of the voyage. It is nevertheless part of the ritual; in order to become a man you, too, must take the test and fail it and in the failing cultivate some kind of humility. Do not ask me to explain this. I can explain nothing. Perhaps failure, which is our destiny, must be renewed with every generation. Perhaps it must not. I have no answers. Go and do what you can."

"My father is a ponderous man, given to speeches and phrases of this sort. Years ago it irritated me, but now as I approach maturity I understand that this is no less a part of him than the many things that I admire and I must, therefore, bear it. Part of it has to do with the fact that father and I have lived alone together for so many years. I seem to remember that when mother was with us he would not talk as much and with less anxiety, but that was a long time ago. Regardless, she is gone.

Take the test. Rite of passage. Part of that cycle of maturity to which we must all aspire. No less than father, I repeat these sentences to myself as I proceed through the walkways of the ship to the great and silent room in which the computer is housed. When I was much younger I used to dream about the computer, dream about moments such as this. I would come before the computer and say, *Tell me the truth now, tell me the secret of all of this,* and the computer would murmur in its shield and then slowly release to me the information that had been sought for generations, mine alone to distribute. *Let me begin at the beginning, son,* the computer would say, and then in a choked and unguarded voice, its emotions tearing free from the tubes and canisters that created its voice, would tell me what I wanted to know. In the dream I ran down all the corridors of the ship, shouting the truth as freedom. I have not had the dream for a long time. What is going on is nothing like the dream at all. I know that I cannot ask the computer the question and that if I did it would no more have the answer than it has any of the others.

"You will fail as all of the others have failed, but failure is part of our condition," my father has said, and because I am sixteen years old now and on the edge of my own maturity, I have not shouted and wept at his words as I might have even a few months ago. Instead, I have contained my feelings in the understanding that my father, no less than the rest of us, must suffer terribly. I walk into the room where the computer lies for me, whispering its songs across a hundred thousand wires. The computer guides the ship, powers the support system, causes the vegetables in the hydroponics plant to sprout and bear the generations that feed us . . . and yet, enveloped as it is with all these tasks, it yet has the capacity to deal with me as with all of the others who have entered this room. It is an awesome thing; it would move me if I did not realize that the computer, no less than the ship itself, is slowly dying and that if the answer is not found by one of us someday all of it—support system, power, vegetables—will perish. This lends to me the proper sense of humility without which, my father has warned, I cannot accept the mantle of responsibility.

"Yes," the computer says to me in its high, harsh voice

as I sit and prepare myself before the board in which its wires nest like stars, "announce yourself, please. Your name, your condition, your desires." Its voice is strident. The reproduction of the binary impulses that gives it sound is slightly out of synchronization and it grates over the vowels. I was prepared for this as I was prepared for so many other things, but it is a terrible thing to realize that the computer, no less than the ship it guides or me, is decaying and that now, over a service period of unknown hundreds of years, the operation is beginning to become affected.

"Do not become emotional," my father had advised me. "Do not take this personally." And to the best of my ability I remember this and seat myself quietly, fixing my mind on other matters. I do not know what happened to my mother. Once she was there and then she was there no longer and my father would not talk about it. "It is one of those mysteries with which we will have to live," my father said and then said nothing else. I was eight years old then. Now I am twice as old, twice a lifetime, and I know no more.

"Announce yourself," the computer says again. "You are delaying unnecessarily. If you will not announce your name and purposes, you will have to leave."

"My name is Silvar," I say, and give him then my coding number. The computer asks me to repeat it and I do so; I feel the room shake as the numbers are fed slowly into the devices and checked against the central file. It takes some time—the computer, no less than the ship, is very old—and I have some time to look out the portholes of the housing as the process continues. I do not know what I expect to see from these portholes—some order of the constellations, perhaps, some suggestion that there is cohesion from here as there is not from the other viewpoints—but whatever it is, I do not find it. Stars in strange arrangements spin before me in a disorderly way; I try to fix upon the center of one gathering so that I can perceive what happens in the concentricity but cannot. It is no different in here than from any of the other viewpoints of the ship and I find myself wondering if the computer itself is capable of looking out the portholes and what it would make of this if it does. I decide that there is no point to this speculation. If the computer does actually think it must do so in ways that we could never understand and there is no way to gauge the emotions of a great and dying machine. All that I know is that the computer is aging and decaying and that it has been doing so for a long time, and I suspect in some way that what it sees through its portholes would give it no comfort. This eases me and I remember the last thing my father said to me as he sent me down the corridors. "It does not matter," he said, "remember that, it does not matter."

"Your code number has been verified," the computer says, "and your identity appears to be in agreement. You are Silvar of the eighteenth level, born sixteen years, two months and twelve days ago. Of course, you are aware that this chronology has no application to the actual situation and may be considered anachronistic. Nevertheless, Silvar, you may proceed. What do you want?"

"You sound like my father," I find myself saying, rather absently.

"What is that? I do not understand."

"When you said 'the chronology has no application,' that was the way my father speaks."

"I know nothing of your father. I know nothing of you, Silvar. State your business," the computer says, and even though it is a mechanical, impersonal device that my father has told me possesses no ethos of any sort, I detect a trace of irritation. "Your time is quite limited."

"I'm here to ask a question," I say, shifting a little on the seat.

"I know you're here to ask a question. No one comes here *unless* they have a question, and certainly you would be no different. No one would come in here for any other reason. Still," the computer says after a pause, "there are very few questions I can answer anymore. I am aging and most factors are out of my hands, so please do not waste my time with philosophy or empty inquiries. Come, now, Silvar, ask your question and be done."

"I won't," I say. "I mean, I won't bother you with

philosophy or anything like that. I know that you can't answer questions of that sort. I just have one question and then I'll be finished. This is my first time in here, you know. This is the first time I've ever spoken with you or asked you a question."

"I'm perfectly aware of that," the computer says harshly, and I realize that if my intention had been to find any kind of sympathy from the machine, it was misplaced and juvenile. Juvenile, all right. This is the first part of the rite of passage, then, to accept the childishness in one's own behavior. Already I feel slightly older and I know that my father's lessons will be taken.

"I just have one question," I say. "I got permission to ask it from the council."

"I know that, too. Don't you think that I know everything that's going on here? Not, of course," the computer says, "that I can do anything about it. I accept the fact that I am disintegrating, you see, even if the rest of you will not."

"I want to know how long the voyage will go on," I say, talking quickly now and trying to get this over before the computer can make another interruption, create another insult, shake my inquiry again with its despair, which, my father has told me, is the source of the general despair and for that reason alone to be respected. "When will it end? Where are we going? What is happening to us?"

"That's not one question," the computer says matter-of-factly and without a pause, "that's three."

"It's all part of the same question," I say quickly. "It isn't three questions, but one. What is happening to us? That's the whole question. The rest is just part of it."

"I've been asked that before."

"I know."

"I'm asked that many times a cycle," the computer says, "almost in that way. You have no idea how many of you have come before me to ask that question. Did you think that you were the first? Or the hundreth?"

"No," I say, "I know that I'm not."

"You must think that my capacities are limitless," the

computer says, and now the irritation is apparent along with the suggestion of something stronger that I cannot quite express. "You must think that there are no limits to my ability to absorb this. I know that I'm dying. Don't you think I know that I'm dying, and that no less than any of you I am surrounded by doubt? This isn't easy for me, either, you know. I was imbued with emotions when I was created."

"I know."

"No," the computer says, "I don't think that you do know. I don't think you understand anything at all. I was given a full set of emotions and reactions that were analagous to yours. Supposedly it was done to make me a more sympathetic and accessible servant, but those were lies, as I've realized by searching my memory banks through all this time. I was given emotions merely as a check upon my behavior. They did not trust me, although they knew that total trust would be necessary for my role in the voyage, so they instilled in me a network contrived to make me exactly like them. Like *you*. To feel the same miserable fears, to be overcome by the same twitching horror of my own death, to be able to witness and *see* my own death, to be able to project onto all of you in the guise of a false sympathy my own terror of the void. . . ."

"You're not answering my question," I say, raising a hand, although I have been alerted that visual signals have no effect upon the computer, which perceives in subtler and less understandable ways. "I just want you to answer my question."

"I'm going to answer," the computer says, "I'm answering already in my own time and way, although you are certainly too callow and stupid to realize this. All of you are the same: you disgust me. You disgust me," the computer says again, after a while. Then, in a more modulated voice, a voice that plunges several tubes and registers toward a simulacrum of a whisper, it says, "I don't know how long the voyage is going to go on. Sometime, I don't know just when, the program with the destination must have slipped from me and it's irretrievably lost, so we simply must go on along the original apogee of the course, toward infinity. I don't know what's going to happen to you because of this, any more than I know what's going to happen to me. The life-support systems are self-sustaining, you know. And as for the third part, as to what is really happening, *this* is really happening. And that is all."

"That's all?" I say. "You mean there's no more? You don't know *where* we're going or when it's going to end?"

"No more than you do, Silvar," the computer says. "No more than any of them."

"But then, where are we?"

"I am so weary," the computer says, "so weary of these idiocies, these endless reiterations, these pleadings in emptiness. Don't you realize that I have been asked these questions a thousand or a hundred thousand times and the emotions that have been instilled so very thoughtfully in me cause revulsion when I hear them yet again? I don't know. I simply do not know. The original program has been lost and we are simply proceeding along the orbit without compensation. I cannot help this. I really cannot help it, Silvar," the computer says, "and now I want you to leave."

"But there must be more," I say, "there must be more to tell me than that. You are the computer; you have been in this ship, running it, as long as history. There have been generations and generations of us and only one of you, and surely *you* must remember everything. You've got to tell me," I say and resist an impulse to start beating upon the bulkhead with my fists until pain starts, slamming my forehead into the bulkhead until I become unconscious from the frustration of it. "It can't go on this way."

"I cannot tell you, Silvar," the computer says, "for there is really nothing more to say. One time or another our path may carry us into the orbit of a planet or the gravitational attraction of a star and we will collide or incinerate and it will all be over . . . but the chances are that this will not happen. The universe is very large, you know. In the meantime, the system will sustain itself, and even though I am dying it will survive me. It will survive all of you. Everything was planned for this kind of accident, you see. Sometimes it leads me to the feeling that the loss of the program was purposeful, or that there was never any program for our destination in the start. But," the computer says regretfully, "I cannot be sure of this because I have forgotten."

"I see," I say. I stand, finding that my balance is uneven, and yet, despite the weight of all I have learned, I am able to raise my head and confront the computer. I would not have thought that this was so, but I seem still to be in command; perhaps this, too, is part of the rite of passage—realizing that you will remain yourself, no matter what you hear; that you can deal with yourself, no matter what the nature of truth; that truth or lies, neither cannot matter because they are being filtered in through ourselves, and we are the only truth we know. "You have nothing more to say."

"I have nothing more to say. I suggest that you leave. I will shortly reach the limits of my emotional tolerance and will have to break circuits. I am in pain. I am in terrible pain, Silvar. Don't you realize this?"

"All right," I say, turning, moving toward the exit hatch. "You're in terrible pain. It isn't as easy as all that, you know. Being in pain is fine, but you must go on."

"Exactly, Silvar," the computer says, "that is exactly what I was trying to tell you. Pain has nothing to do with it; the voyage must continue. If we were ever to cease, if we lost the enormous speed that sustains this ship, it would collapse from without and all of you would surely die, just as I am surely dying."

"Yes," I say, "yes, I see that." I open the door, move through the door, poised there, stand and turn toward the computer. "So there is no destination," I say, "and there is no answer, and no one knows what will happen to any of us."

"Yes."

"And you suffer terribly because of this but it doesn't change the situation."

"Yes, I suffer terribly. And nothing will change the situation."

"I'm leaving now," I say. "I have nothing more to ask. I'm saying good-bye."

"Good-bye, Silvar."

"Will I ever speak with you again?"

"If you come by here you will speak with me again; otherwise, you will not. What do you want to hear, Silvar? What can I say to you?"

"Nothing," I say, "absolutely nothing. You can say nothing to me. You have said nothing to me."

I allow the door to close behind me and move down the corridors. The corridors are empty as they almost always are except during periods of panic or riot, which occur very rarely, and at the end of the one down which I am walking my father stands, hands on hips, waiting for me. Rite of passage; he seems smaller and more helpless than the man who I left, although I have realized for some time now, of course, that my father is no less limited than I. His little head quavers on his shoulders, his fingers tremble. It is not usual for fathers to wait for sons after the ritual inquiries, but, then again, it is done every so often and there is no shame in it. There is no shame in it. There is no shame in anything, once you understand the lessons of the computer.

"Well?" my father says as I come upon him, his face mottled and torn by what I once would have thought was anxiety but is now plainly grief. "Did you speak with it? Did you learn? Did it tell you?" He raises his hands toward me in a gesture of appeal, but they shake and the shaking turns this appeal to an embrace; he holds me against him and I feel the weakness in his hands, splaying all out and through me.

"Did you find out?" he says in a weak, old voice as I stand against him. "Did it tell you? I hope it told you. It would never tell me, although I begged and begged, but I knew that someday I would send in my son and that my son would find . . . "

"It told me," I say, "it told me; it told me everything." And weakly he falls against me, then gathers himself in with remnants of his old strength, a strength of which I might have once dreamed but never knew. I look out through the portholes of this corridor; it shows me the same constellations that I saw from the room of the computer. No difference, no difference; only one of slight angles, refractions.

"Tell me, then," my father says in a high, strange voice, "tell me then, son. What is it? When is it?"

"Mother's never going to come back," I say then, not wanting to hold back further, "it said that mother's never going to come back again, but where she is she is at peace." And he falls against me once more, sobbing and stroking, rubbing his chin against me. "At peace," I say, "and at infinite mercy."

"Thank you, thank the computer, thank God," my father says, and the ship goes on: it goes on mindless through a thousand galaxies, dead stars streaming by the portholes and I look out upon all of them, feeling the ascension upon me and with that, at last, the beginnings of acceptance.

Introduction to
TRY AGAIN and AN OVERSIGHT

According to modern psychology most characteristics skip a generation; religiosity would not be excluded. My parents have not seen the inside of a synagogue, barring weddings and funerals, more than five times in the thirty-five years I have known them (in fairness, I had best make this ten; I made them go to yizkor once upon a time), whereas my paternal great-grandfather, a splendidly bearded patriarch who I never knew but who my father knew well, used to hold up the breaking of fast on Yom Kippur until well past ten o'clock, getting in some final, optional prayers. My father freely confesses that his images of Judaism became thus at an early age inextricably linked to starvation, and he has never been able to make the separation. I see his point.

No splendidly bearded patriarch I, but a guilt-stricken and intermittently disbelieving Reform Jew, I have found that the religious themes of my fiction, oddly, swerve not toward Judaism (where exist but two stories written past my thirty-third year) but toward what might be called, for lack of scholarship, a reconstructed Fundamentalism, of which the following two stories are excellent, if despairing, examples. The New Testament makes little sense to me as inspiration tor sentimental pastiche or pastel; it makes terrifying sense if taken literally and with the pain put back in. Here are two modest efforts, neither of which held my children back from dinner for an instant.

TRY. AGAIN

July 20: Here we all are in an antique bomb shelter in the basement of a one-family dwelling in Oneonta, New York. Oneonta, New York! The world ended last night and according to Bill—my father-in-law (the Reverend William P. Enright is a religious fanatic, but he is a *companionable* religious fanatic)—the half-life of the radioactive elements that resulted in this generalized destruction is at least forty years, so it looks as if we are going to be in Oneonta for a while. Bill says not to worry about it. Don't worry about a thing. The shelter appears to be well stocked; there are years and years of staples here: distilled water, foodstuffs, even vermin who appear uncontaminated by the atmospheric disturbances, and we can hold out for a good long while; restocking the shelter is certainly the least of our problems. What we have to do, Bill says, is to come to terms with our immortal souls, meet our maker—which, after a fashion, we are all trying to do: Bill through citations of the Book of Daniel, Eva through meditations and your faithful undersigned through this journal, which Lord knows who will ever read.

It is strange that I can be so calm about the matter, but as Bill has pointed out, we live in apocalyptic times —have lived, I should say (the world having ended)— and have been well prepared at one time or the next, one level or another for this various disastrous outcome. Bill says that all prophecies in the well-known and famous Book of Daniel have long since been fulfilled: the seven beasts, the four Kingdoms, the dislocations in the East and so on, and that it was only a matter of time, very little time, in fact, until this happened to us and all in all it is most convenient that we happened to be at his well-equipped farmsite, which happened to include a bomb shelter (the previous tenants of this abode in the early 1960s took warnings seriously and had their shelter and all its conveniences installed) when the long-since adjudicated occurred. I agree with Bill that we may have been fortunate, but I wish, somehow, that he were not quite so *pleased* about it: there is something irritating in a man, any man, even my father-in-law, acting as if the end of the world were a personal fulfillment. Still, I am not being bitter about this. I am, in fact, most grateful toward Bill; if it were not for his razor-sharp conscious-ness of this eventuality and his insistence that we only frequent vacation quarters that had a bomb shelter (the one at our own modest quarters in Paramus had been installed at great expense last summer; a pity that we were not able to use it, but that's life for you), we would be among the three and a half billion souls dead at the present time instead of facing our glowing future, which seems to involve forty years spent underground after which time we may begin small, careful forays for provisions.

Bill has, in many ways, been a great comfort during this difficult time. I will not argue with this. A live-in father-in-law is a difficult enough proposition, let alone an apocalyptic, ministerial father-in-law (he has been predicting the end of the world since I knew him), let alone again an apocalyptic, ministerial father-in-law who was dismissed from his pulpit some years ago pre-cisely because he was making his congregants uncom-fortable, yet even granted his rather punitive state of mind and the close quarters (even closer than usual) in which we have been forced to live recently, I can say that I do not truly know what we would have done with-out him. It is Bill who has made all of this bearable even in the aftermath, pointing out that the prophecies of the Book of Daniel, long ignored, have postulated this tragedy precisely and also postulate after a suitable waiting period the establishment of the Son of Man. (We will be, it would seem, His entire Kingdom. It is Bill who has pointed out that there is surely a purpose and a meaning to this tragedy unrevealed to ordinary mortals,

and we will surely know it if we can only hold out for
the time being, and it is Bill, above all, who has kept Eva
away from me during these difficult times, filling her with
messages from the Book of Daniel as well as words of
miscellaneous comfort so that I might be able to have
privacy in which to come to terms with the tragedy myself and in order to begin this journal, which I am sure,
if I am only allowed to stay with it on my own terms,
will keep me sane, a noble goal. Eva is quite upset by
the fact that the world has ended. Women—even my
wife, his daughter—Bill has confided to me, tend to be
depressed by external events of this sort, even if there
is nothing that they can truly do about them. He will
bring her around, he advises. I am sure that he will. I
have every confidence in the man.

July 21: I see that I started this journal in a mood of
such understandable excitement, such emotional *medias
res,* as it were, that I neglected to fill it with a necessary
statement of the personalities involved, the historical
events, etcetera. It is important that I do so now not only
because of the ancient instinct for neatness and inclu-
sivity but because events are already proceeding so rapidly that unless I include the expository material now I
may never get around to it. (As you can imagine, I
started these notes yesterday in the frame of mind that I
had a leisurely forty years to bring everything up to date.)
So a quick bit of sculpturing, a little feeding in of scraps
of the mass of material before I am overtaken by events
. . . because, you see, today we met an alien who seems
to have established residence in this bomb shelter years
before the fact, awaiting just this event. He seems quite
cooperative and in most ways quite anxious to please, but
nevertheless clearly an alien, which, you can imagine,
gave all of us a bit of a turn. But not to get ahead. The
people involved here:

THE REVEREND WILLIAM P. ENRIGHT: a fundamentalist minister and my father-in-law. Bill is a lumber-
ing, informal sort in his late fifties who seems in many

ways to be an unexceptional person, one of those informal post-technocracy men of the cloth who believe in
fund-raising, baseball, Bingo and rummage sales with
the same easy passion that their forebears might have
mustered for the sect itself; he seems to be that way, in
short, until one discusses anything religious with him
(one should never do this with a minister), and it is at
this point that the fundamentalism asserts itself: a certain tremor of hand, burning of eye, glaze of the same
eye, hoarseness of voice. Of course the world is going to
end; all of the calculations in the Book of Daniel have
been fulfilled, the four Kingdoms, the uprisings in the
East, the seventy years of the final rule and so on. It is
going to end very much within our time; we have brought
this judgment upon ourselves. And so on. Although in
many ways quite a pleasant and understated fellow, this
fundamentalist streak of Bill's has a history of making or
having made people uncomfortable: otherwise, why
seven pulpits in the ten years since I have known him,
and why the rumored thirty-three pulpits throughout his
ministerial career? The most recent pulpit from which he
was discharged chose to do so when Bill interrupted a
church picnic by advising that latest indications were that
this was surely one of the last meals that most of the congregants would ever have the opportunity to eat. The action of the trustees, Bill thought, was without defense,
but I am ready to concede in the channels of my own
mind, at any rate, that Bill had something of a case. Bill
has been living with us since our return from the honey-
moon; aside from this apocalyptic streak (which is
sufficient), he has no bad habits.

EVA SMITH: my wife of some ten years. She or I should
say our childlessness (although medically it has been
demonstrated that the fault is not mine) has given her
a somewhat despairing overlay; also, deep layers of resentment toward Bill and vice-versa have caused something of a strain, but essentially she is a good, if rather
pallid, woman (I can be objective about this) whose
reaction to Bill's notification on July 19 that the world

had ended (he arose before the rest of us and said he had been watching the television before it went off forever) was possibly the most normal of all of us; she screamed and went into a deep, catatonic panic that some days later has not worn off; she sits in a private quarter of the shelter for hours on end, stares at the walls, takes no responsibility for her appearance or for our little homelife here, speaks only when spoken to and then in a flat, unyielding monotone, etcetera. I realize that I should go on in detail about her and about our relationship over many pages, but time is short and I really see no need to do this; sufficient to say that she has taken the news very badly. And as for the ten years of our marriage, our shared experiences, the deep, communal well of marital sex, marital dispute, marital secrets: there is less to say about all of this than one might think, and in any case it has been superseded by events. It is very difficult to take any of this seriously when we are confronted by the fact that the half-life of the radioactive elements used to bomb out the continental shelf (all of it, Bill says) is some forty years. Forty years! I do not think that she will be this way throughout the four decades, but if she is I see that we will have to reach a new understanding in our relationship.

STEPHEN SMITH: that is to say myself, the son-in-law of the apocalyptic Bill, the husband of the stuporous Eva. I am a sportswriter, or at least I *was* a sportswriter before the world ended, and tending to see existence, even post-apocalyptic existence, in terms of the rather cheap metaphors and phrases of my ex-trade, I look at the Book of Daniel as the great scorer who has now called the game on account of conditions. These are not particularly inspired metaphors, but I am not, or was not, much of a sportswriter; it is quite easy in the light of circumstances to look at my earlier life objectively, and the fact is that I was a failure: working for a suburban newspaper as a jack-of-all-trades in the two-man sports department, covering high school football, routine interviews with minor figures who might have passed through the area and out of it visiting relatives, rewriting press releases of events taking place in the city and so on. I had not made much of my life, but all of my life had been a process of accommodation: marrying Eva because she expected me to, and it was hardly worth the trouble disappointing her, permitting Bill to live with us because the dear, apocalyptic old fellow had always lived with Eva (the mother is some kind of dim figure who died when Eva was eight, the old man thirty-eight, apparently from many visions of hell), staying on with the *Herald* and accepting my lot as the second man in a two-man department because it was too much trouble to look for another line of work and so on. Perhaps Bill's visions got to me more than I wanted to admit: if the world was indeed going to end within our time, then there certainly seemed little point or purpose in trying to change my life, now, did it? It was best to accept one's lot and wait for the fore-ordained, although on the surface I scoffed at Bill and could hardly bear to have the dear old fellow in the house, even though it *was* his house, and we were, of course, occupying two rooms of of it rent-free. As you can see, I am at a loss to make a convincing case for myself, although it must be said to my credit that I never hurt anyone, at least consciously, and that this grim confirmation of Bill's prophecies renders pointless most of that self-loathing in which I occasionally engaged. It *did* all end, didn't it? So what would the difference have been?

As I said, we met an alien this morning. He is a pleasant, vaguely humanoid fellow who claims to come from some distant star cluster, although he is so engagingly naïve about his background that I suspect he may come from much closer proximity, perhaps even the Moon. (The astronauts found no life on the Moon when they landed, but, then, no intelligent alien would park himself out there in plain sight for discovery, or so it seems to me.) According to him he has been living in this bomb shelter on an abandoned farmsite in Oneonta, New York, for quite some time now, awaiting exactly what has now

happened—occupancy by a group of humans—in order
that he might conduct a reasonable dialogue with us and
decide our eventual fate on the basis of reports he will
pass back telepathically to his own headquarters. (I realize that all of this sounds faintly bizarre, but the odd
matter-of-factness of the alien must be taken into account; he sees little exceptional about his position and
this phlegmatic viewpoint has carried over.) He speaks a
perfect if somewhat awkward English, and, of course,
when he manifested himself, appearing vaporously beneath some bookshelves that the prior occupants had
crammed with biblical materials (this delighted Bill),
Eva, who had begun to show some vague interest in her
environment just this morning, screamed and fainted,
necessitating her hasty removal to another compartment
in this roomy shelter, leaving Bill and I (who carried her
out somewhat awkwardly) to deal with him.

"You realize that I still have to make some kind of report," he said after the preliminary discussions (which
I shall understandably gloss over) were completed.
"Whether your world has ended or not, the basic situation remains: your planet is an open case, so to speak,
until official approval has come from Headquarters to
close the file on it, at which time, of course, a recovery
crew will be sent for me. Surprising news! You say that
your world really ended?"

"Of course it did," Bill said and went on into a rather
extended declamation not only from Daniel but from the
Revelations of Saint John the Divine, which pointed out
in some detail not only how the world would end but precisely why we were entitled to no other judgment. It was
very difficult to shut him up (it always is when Bill gets
this way) and about all that both the alien and I could
do was to hear him out with little sidelong looks of dis-
tress at one another. "You mean you really didn't know
that this had happened?" Bill concluded in a much milder
tone, looking in the direction of the compartment toward
which Eva had been carted. "You were sent here as an
observer and you didn't know that everything you came
to observe was over? That's incompetence."

The alien shrugged in a most engaging and humanoid way and appeared to spread what would have been its palms if it had palms; actually, it has tentacles. "I'm sorry about this," it said, "but you can imagine that the rather restricted terms of the environment here make direct observation most difficult. Also, we didn't expect you people to blow yourselves up; you're self-destructive, like most post-technological planets, but there's a hardy survival instinct there as well, and the long-range indications seemed to be for you at least most optimistic. I'm not really a data gatherer, anyway, just an observer. Every once in a great while I send back a report. It just goes to show you," he said, "that you never know what's going to happen in between sleep-intervals."

Saying this, the alien became vaporous once again and disappeared with the same efficacy with which he had joined us, leaving Bill and I to stare at one another in a rather stuporous fashion. It was Bill who recovered first, or in any event it was Bill who was able to speak first, his ministerial training as always coming to the fore, Words For Every Occasion. (Despite his fanatical streak, now richly confirmed by events, I think that the trustees of all the churches made a mistake in discharging him.) "Well," he said, "it just goes to show you about these things. You never know. You just never know." Whereupon he heaved himself out of the room, rather sadly, I thought, to take himself to his meditations. Bill brought a rather complete collection of religious materials to Oneonta, supplementing what the long-departed tenants already had on hand, and I believe that he is now engaged in the writing of something that he calls the Third Testament. Meanwhile, it is up to me, of course, to attend to Eva.

July 22: It would be nice, or at least reasonable, in view of the fact that the world has ended, to fill these pages with momentous news, portentous events, accounts of complex doings, but the fact is that despite everything—end of the world, appearance of the alien, Eva's breakdown, Bill's gloom, my own understandable agitation—things have already settled down to a rather eventless routine here on this, only the fourth day of (I am tempted to call it the Year One) our new existence. Eva recovered from her fit and is now taking a little nourishment, Bill is continuing work on his own notes, the alien has not been heard from again and I am merely trying to keep things up to date and as organized as possible. It is hard to believe but we may already be living the life that we may be living for the next forty years. (The half-life of the radioactive elements, as I have said, is forty years, according to Bill; forty years from now the aged remnants of us may be able to go out on the surface to begin a feeble scrambling for artifacts.) "He's happy," Eva said to me this morning, "Bill's *happy*. Haven't you noticed that?"

"He's taking it rather well."

"I don't mean taking it rather well," she said hoarsely, extending her hands, pulling me toward her with a certain frantic intensity. "He's happy! This is exactly what he wanted. Can't you see that this is what he always wanted? He always wanted the world to end; I think he thought that it would save him from dealing with his personal problems."

"That's a rather harsh accusation," I said to her mildly. "He's lost the same things that we've lost. We may be the only survivors; in any event, we're in no position to go out looking for any others, and we're sentenced to a miserable existence for the rest of our lives. I would say that he feels *vindicated*, wouldn't you? I mean, he's been predicting apocalypse ever since you knew him, and that goes back more than three decades; certainly it's understandable that after all this time he might have the satisfaction of a man who finally sees that he was right. But happy? That's a very cruel thing to say about your father."

"I think he's crazy," Eva said, "I think he's insane. He's been insane all of his life. Reading the Book of Daniel and making notes. Do you know that he used to have a set of charts—flow charts, he called them—on the apocalypse? He graphed it out looking for a point of intersection."

"The same thing as computing won and lost records," I said mildly enough. "He was interested; you can't blame him for keeping up notes. In any event," I said, "there's really no point or purpose in discussing this, is there? Right or wrong, crazy or sane, the world's been vaporized and we're stuck with one another. We're just fortunate that his fanaticism, as you call it, made him seek out a vacation spot with a good bomb shelter. This is probably the only location in the state, except for our own house, of course, that has a 1960s bomb shelter still well maintained and in good repair."

"But you still don't understand," she said with that continuing hoarseness, "you don't see any of it, do you? We don't *know* the world has ended. We don't have any objective proof of it at all. He said that he was up early and heard the whole thing on the television before it went out and then he rushed us into the shelter, and of course we can't come out and have a look around ourselves because of the radioactivity, but how do we *know?* How do we really know any of this? He might have invented the whole story, and stupid fools, we went along with him. The point is, what are we going to do now?"
tom

It was a rather discomfiting way of looking at the matter and I am free to admit that what Eva said gave me an entirely different perspective—Bill *is* obsessed by apocalyptic visions; Bill *could* have done this to us in a fit of depression resulting from the loss of his last pulpit with, in the bargain, a very bad recommendation—but I felt it necessary to say, "Well, maybe. I mean, you may have something there, although I for one don't volunteer to go outside and take the chance of dying horribly just to prove that Bill is crazy. Not just yet, anyway. And you've got to admit that the alien is real. You can't get around that. The alien is something we have to deal with, too."

Her eyes became very round and white and she said, "Alien? Oh, my God, I had almost *forgotten* about the alien!" And saying this, she fainted, necessitating certain frantic adjustments and manipulations on my part to prevent her from getting quite a nasty blow on the forehead, and after I had caught her and after I had made her comfortable and after I had once again brought matters into some semblance of order, I found it incumbent upon me to return to my own compartment where I am bringing these notes up to currency with the discomfiting feeling that Eva may have a point, but then on the other hand, what are we supposed to do? Even if Bill is mad, which is a clear possibility, there is still the alien to deal with, and I do not think that he is an invention of Bill's.

July 23: There is nothing to report. Bill was in his compartment all day, apparently still working on the Third Testament. From time to time I could hear cracked screamings and chanting within and vague mumblings as well about the Great Snake. He refused all offers of food and appears to be in a highly agitated condition. Eva is conscious but not speaking to me, and the alien has not been heard from. I do not have these notes to keep me busy, there being already so little to report, and I am beginning to find this existence oppressive. Forty more years? Perhaps Eva is right, but I still have no way of verifying this, all communications equipment necessarily being dead (did Bill cut it off?) and me quite unwilling to wander up to the surface and take my chances. Not today, at any rate.

July 24: Bill still in his compartment in the third day of his retreat, his voice still singing away but weaker and weaker, Eva now with her door barred (she is very angry at me) and the alien vaporizes in front of me at eleven A.M. (I maintain a strict sense of chronology; time is more important than ever, now that the necessity for it has ceased) and says, "Where are the others?" He has a rather distracted expression on his face, assuming that I am not being anthropomorphic here, and his entire manner is rather hasty. "Are you alone?"

"At the moment," I say. "My wife is sulking and Bill is praying a lot."

"Then I'm afraid I must talk to you," the alien says. There is a switch of tenses in this journal; I am quite aware of this. The reason is simple: I am jotting all of this down almost as it happens. The alien has no objection to my taking notes in his presence, it would seem; he does not take it as discourteous, and I took speedwriting in journalism school. More and more I have the feeling that events are overtaking.) "Researches are completed and I'm afraid that I have some rather bad news for you. It would have been better, of course, if the others were present, but," and here the alien gives quite a human little sigh, striking in view of his greenish complexion and rather awesome tentacles, "one must do what one can. Conditions have been fulfilled in that one of your race is present to be informed."

"Yes," I say, rather impatiently. One inferential and verbose personality underground is quite enough, I have decided. "Yes, get to it."

"I will," the alien says, and at this moment, conveniently or inconveniently, Eva emerges from her compartment with a stricken expression, reaching toward me. She sees the alien and screams, but the scream is half-hearted, contained, more a position statement than an outburst of real emotion, and she seems to be possessed of something far more vital than simple fear. The alien turns toward her with a rather bemused look. "What is it?" he says to her.

"Yes," I say, "what is it? I was just about to learn something interesting," I say, pointing to the alien, whose presence is already so familiar to me that I can be quite matter-of-fact about him even if Eva cannot. "We were having a discussion. What is it?"

"The world . . . " Eva says and then pauses, several expressions chasing one another across her face, she looking toward the alien, away from the alien, at the walls, away from the walls. And then everything coalesces and she struggles on with a vast and increasing set of purpose. "The world didn't end. I got the radio working, I spliced tubes and wires. I know a few things about engineering even though you all thought I was a fool. It didn't end; everything's the same as it was. He lied to us, the old fool! I knew it, I knew it!" And she falls forward almost as if she were about to faint once again, but one move from the alien, a suggestion of a step toward her, and Eva recovers, recoils, backs away to the wall. "Don't touch me!" she screamed. And then she said to me, "Did you hear me, you idiot? The world didn't end! The Giants are leading the Colts fourteen to six in the third quarter *and the world didn't end!"*

"All right," I say, as bemused as the alien, "all right, I understand, the world didn't end." Not knowing exactly how I feel about this, it is a considerable thing to have one's existence restored, but then on the other hand, I was beginning to find the apocalyptic condition rather enjoyable; it certainly relieves one of responsibility. "All right, so it didn't end, so he lied to us, but that doesn't mean you have to get hysterical."

She stares at me quite speechless and at that moment Bill emerges from his own compartment, carrying a sheaf of papers that he hurls directly at her with, I might note, a certain disgust. "You damned bitch," he says, a rather disgraceful way to talk to one's daughter, but then, he is somewhat and understandably agitated. "You damned bitch, did you have to spoil the whole thing? Besides, it *should* have ended." And he begins then to vault once more into quotations and blocks of warnings from his ever-beloved Book of Daniel, something that I find rather inappropriate at the present time, granting their discovered inapplicability, and it is at this point that the alien raises a tentacle in a way so commanding that my attention is instantly riveted, and even Bill himself dribbles after a few more passes into a kind of grunting stop, looking at the alien with mingled fear and astonishment as the power of the creature flows from it and into all of us in the room. It is certainly an impressive and forceful performance and I can sense that on his own planet, among his own people, the alien must be very highly thought of.

"That is what I wanted to tell you," the alien says, and a certain sadness informs his tone, a communicable sadness that causes the tears to leap into my eyes, to say nothing of Bill's own; Bill, in fact, caught by the power of the alien, begins to weep, but then he always was a rather moody and emotionally overexpressive person. "You seem to have come into this place due to a misconception, a misconception of the end of your world, which, of course, I have verified and found to be without foundation. That was very quickly dealt with, to be sure, and it would not have taken me all this time to return to tell you the happy news of your salvation . . . but on the basis of the contact that was made between the three of you and me, I was forced to contact my headquarters. You see," the alien says quite gently, "there was never supposed to be any contact, any awareness on your part, I should say, that you were being watched over, as you might put it, and what safer place could I find than a well-stocked abandoned environment such as this? But, unfortunately, contact was made, anyway. I was forced to discuss this with headquarters."

"We'll never say a word," I say earnestly, "believe me, we just want to get out . . . "

"I'm sorry," the alien says, and now the sadness is unmistakable; it is, in fact, quite pervasive and moving. "I'm truly sorry, but it's too late for any of that. The mistake has been made."

"Mistake?" Bill says. He does not seem quite the Third Testament prophet of only a few moments ago. His little chins tremble, he seems quite aged. "What mistake? I was only trying to help my son-in-law and daughter. The world *would* have ended soon, anyway, and . . . "

"I'm sorry," the alien says for the third time as if it were denying us before cock's crow (living with Bill has rubbed off a little Testament on me), "but there's really nothing to be done about it. Headquarters was quite explicit. I'm afraid that we're going to have to proceed with the fall-back plan."

Saying this, he raises his tentacle, vaults into the air, his transparency reasserting himself, and then as the

alien slowly blends into the rather thick and foul air of
the shelter I begin to hear the music—the sound of harps
and flutes, behind it the clear and deadly sound of a
trumpet. "No!" Eva is saying. "No, I can't believe it; it's
impossible!" But it is not her to whom I am listening;
rather, it is Bill to whom I attend. Bill turns toward the
sound of the trumpet, his eyes filled with hope and wonder, and then as the sound overtakes all of us—all of
us in the shelter—the remains of the manuscripts fall
from him like ashes and Bill, too, ascends as the sounds
of judgment filter all around us, and more than anything
else I am filled with a positive conviction of luckless-
ness. I always knew the senile old fool would get us into
trouble sooner or later; I should have confronted the
problem earlier.

Whispering, the Ten Priests descend.

July 25:

July 26:

July 27:

AN OVERSIGHT

In St. Louis I catch a momentary glimpse of the Saviour
during half-time of the Browns–Cardinals game; He is a
sniveling little man gobbling a frankfurter by a stand
and intently reading a program. However, I am unable
to get to Him because of the press of bodies, and, furthermore, the Cardinals blow another, 17–12, losing a
potential winning touchdown in the closing seconds.
Nothing but frustration. In Tel Aviv I am convinced
that I see Him in a bus, wearing phylacteries and *tallis,* disguised as an Armenian Jew intently observing
street scenes, but once again I am balked: I bolt across

the bus to seize Him, but it jars to a stop in the heavy Chasidic traffic and I fall heavily on my knee, impaling it and drawing a concerned group of passengers, one of whom is an orthopedic surgeon who resets the knee on the spot. But not before the Saviour has cunningly glimpsed my intention and used the diversion to flee. In Moscow I am convinced that I have Him run to ground at last in the guise of an old woman munching an apple and reading *Pravda* in a luncheonette, but when I sidle close to speak the proprietor thinks this is a proposition of some kind and threatens in heavily accented English to summon the secret police if I do not leave at once. I do so through a side door, seeing the old woman laughing; momentarily, the mask has dropped and it is the pure, officious glow of the Saviour's face that I see through the folds. By this time, however, I have wasted many weeks in fruitless pursuit and must cover ground at home; I therefore return by fast jet to the mosque where I address my followers in my own heavily accented English, aware of some restlessness in the corridors and aisles. Impatient they may well be; this has gone on too long.

"Don't worry," I point out from the podium, "it is only a matter of time now until I apprehend Him. In St. Louis I saw Him during the half-time of a Browns–Cardinals game. In Tel Aviv I almost intercepted him on a bus." And so on and so forth, although I can sense that my assurances are not getting through exactly as previously and there are, indeed, scattered groans and boos as I conclude my address. I take the collection and find that receipts are down some forty-five percent from the last collection; as a geometrical progression it appears certain that they will have fallen to zero by Christmas. Nevertheless, I maintain my podiumic pose and put the hastily counted receipts in an overcoat pocket. "Worry not," I conclude, "for he who waits for the Lord is as they who watch for the morning, and furthermore, I have Him in sight by now, and shortly contact will be made. He can no longer avoid me. In fact, He no longer *wishes* to avoid me; in Moscow I saw a distinct sense of resignation in His eyes and an acceptance of His imminent fate. He knows that confrontation will be made and the prophecies, as set forth in our magnificent Book of Daniel, will be enacted." Scattered hisses but I pay them no heed. I leave quickly through a side curtain.

In the street I obtain a taxi at once. More and more I must isolate myself from my followers, not only to maintain a certain mystery—let us face this: prophecy is no place for *gemeinschaft*—but because of the rising discontent. Rasps and Bronx cheers in the auditorium; rumors, too, have reached me that certain dissident elements have lost patience and are urging my overthrow unless I can wrap this up immediately. It is not impossible that these elements might assault me in an alleyway and steal the receipts, set up their own competing faction or simply take off. But I am very careful. From the very beginning, I knew that the quest would have to be conducted with a good deal of acumen, guile and control. Apocalyptic religions tend to attract fanatics, but it is not the fanatic who will watch for the morning. Only one with a solid business sense.

At my humble quarters, rumors that I live in splendor being foul and maliciously untrue, I change my garb, don warm clothing, prepare for a flight to Alaska. I am convinced that Alaska will be His next stop. He is still one step ahead of me, but now just barely; His plans and possibilities are as accessible to me as my own genitals—one whisk, folks, and I am gone always—and I have the conviction that Alaska will be the final battleground, that terrain in which I stalk Him to ground and seize him, demanding that He now by all the prophecies accept Judgment and bring about the Coming. The phone during this brief interval rings incessantly but I refuse to answer. It would only be some of the dissidents muttering their threats confidentially into the receiver, or homosexual invitations to be a man. I am a heterosexual. On an impulse I rip the phone from the wall and hurl it into a corner. What has happened to me is unjust. It is unfair of them, having accepted the Revelation itself, to insist upon a time limit or hold me to a schedule. America has been corrupted by notions that passion can be contained by time. I am doing the best anyone could. Over ninety percent of the receipts from collections have been directly converted into plane fare, lodging and food during my travels. I am getting very little out of this. Really, I have not taken enough out of the collections to sustain me for more than a couple of months. It is both unfair and unwise of them to accuse me of using the receipts for personal aggrandizement.

I leave my quarters wearing an elaborate costume largely composed of Turkish flannel and take a cab to the airport. At the International Arrivals Building I purchase a round-trip ticket to Nome and then have a quick drink at a service bar, scanning faces. No one seems to notice me, although the bizarre aspect of my costume should attract at least a glance of loathing. Alone, always alone. I hear the boarding call, quietly walk to the plane and am checked for weaponry, drugs, sinister intentions. The machines pass me through, instead, and I take a seat to the rear of the plane, tourist class as always, hunched over while the plane soars into the night and the stewardess offers me a drink. The plane is almost as empty as I would have hoped; business has been off severely recently (one of the signs of approaching apocalypse) and also very few people other than the Saviour and myself have business in Nome at this difficult time of the year. I tell the stewardess that I want a Gibson straight up, and while she prepares the drink I cautiously inspect my furred pockets for the remainder of the receipts.

They have been stolen.

Someone has appropriated my receipts—five hundred twelve dollars—between the time I paid for the ticket and now. The emptiness of the furred pocket gives me a thrill that I can only describe as *feral;* it is that imminent, final disaster that I must have always been seeking. Now I will land in Nome with no provisons for travel and lodging, only the return-trip ticket, which will be useless for ten days.

The stewardess returns, bearing the drink. She is an attractive girl to my heterosexual consciousness: white pupils, yellow eyeballs. Suddenly, all smashes into place and I press back against the seat, chattering like an acolyte. "You're Him," I say to her, "and you stole all my money!"

She gives me a quick, then evasive, glance. "Your drink, sir," she says. Her little breast heaves. Momentarily, her thighs seem to bottom and flatten; underneath the outlines of the disguise I see His true form. "Your drink," she says again, and then her voice breaks, her cover utterly fails as she backs away, quivering. "Get out of here," she says, "get away from me. Not now, you fool!"

I will not be denied. I drop a gloved hand on her shoulder like thunder and yank her toward me. "I've got you," I say. "It's perfectly fair and now you're in my hands." Of course He would go to Nome in a guise like this. Why waste plane fare? I wouldn't in his position, and, unlike me, he can assume many shapes. "Here I am," I say, "and I've identified you. So under the prophecies you must commence apocalypse at once."

"Leave me alone," she says sullenly, "I'm calling the pilot." The few weary passengers ignore this. She screams disinterestedly.

"The Coming," I say hoarsely, quite excited, as well I might be, gripping her more tightly, "the thousand years of war and judgment."

"You fool," she says, leaning toward me suddenly, her eyeballs blazing like two suns, "you've got it all wrong. *All* of this."

The plane arcs suddenly and my glass topples. Gibson cocktail spreads and stains our locked bodies. Pressed against her, I feel a lump near her shoulder blade, the feel of money, and all makes sense at last.

"We could have split the receipts if you hadn't been so greedy," she murmurs desperately, and I see the point, I really do see it, but the plane is rising, the plane is falling, word of the Contact has gone then to Headquarters. And before I can whisper to her my dilatory but inevitable agreement, signals flick in the heavens . . . and the thousand years begin.

Introduction to
AND STILL IN THE DARKNESS

This piece, last in the book (though not the last piece of science fiction I have written—that honor, or lack of honor, belonging to *Seeking Assistance*, which *Fantasy & Science Fiction* will publish some time next year), calls for a valedictory; for, at the time of this writing (July 23, 1975, one day before my thirty-sixth birthday), I have made the irrevocable decision to write no more science fiction.

This decision was not in mind when this book was assembled, and it was still amorphous during the time that the story introductions were being written, mostly between January and July of 1974. As a matter of fact, ninety-five percent of this book was in the offices of Simon and Schuster before I realized on January 11, 1975, for reasons which will remain private, that I had reached the end of the line as a genre writer and could deal with it no more. Following that decision, I delivered a novel already owed on contract (*Scop,* Pyramid, 1976), revised *Seeking Assistance* for sale, and did a little more work on *The Best,* of which this is the very last.

I cannot conceive that the reasons for my decision to leave science fiction will be of unusual interest to anyone, even to my family and friends who have already heard too much of this. Science fiction, like most other forms of genre writing and, indeed, like most other forms of fiction altogether, seems to impose a definite time limit upon the creative working life of its practitioners. After somewhere between seven and ten years, even the best have gone as far as they can and either get out or repeat their work endlessly. I love this field and the spectacle of being an ex-science-fiction writer is not entertaining; but even less attractive is being one of our twenty- or thirty-year persons. No. No more.

There will be other writing—much less of it—in other

fields, and perhaps more success or perhaps less, but I will never have again the eight years since early 1967 when I believed that it was possible to change the field; when, like the young Welles (in a quote I always admired from, I think, Pauline Kael), there seemed to be no gap between ambition and accomplishment; when much seemed possible. Like first love that time will never come again; but the elements of that love are, at least intermittently, in this collection.

◆

AND STILL IN THE DARKNESS

I

And still in the darkness. Once I believed that our lives would be light, perpetual light, that is to say with love and peace and joy and happiness. But now I am learning the harder lessons of Central. Among all these lessons this is the first: that our lives are lived in darkness and in pain and what joy we will have must come in between these that are our conditions. I wish that this were not so, but Central is very definite upon this point, the darkness and pain, that is, and who am I to argue with it? It has been running the world for hundreds of years now, or at least for a long time before I was born.

So today I go to Central for the first of the great Confrontations. In a room which is the size of my own cubicle, but which expands at other times to that of a great yard and then again seems at other times to close around me as a fist, Central inquires for the usual information: my name, my deposition number, characteristics of genetic definition, and so on. When I feed all this in very quickly, very gracefully, Central says, "You are here for the Confrontation, is that not so?"

Of course that is so. "Yes," I say, "you know that."

"We know that, but do you?" Central speaks from a microphone in the center of the keyboard. I have never seen it, of course, and realize that there is nothing to see, but I have always thought of Central as a small, bitter man, about the age and size of my father, with enormous eyes and grey cheekbones. This is just imagination, but gives me something with which I can identify.

"Yes," I say to the small, bitter man. "I know that. That is why I am here."

"Living is pain. Life is pain and darkness. Once you thought that this was not so, but it is, and you must be educated into this fact." Central talks in a rather high-pitched way and slurs its words together. Sometimes I think that this must be some breakdown in the equipment. At other times I think that this may be the way that everyone talks when one gets out of the cubicles and I must become accustomed to it as quickly as possible. "Today you will be shown this in the first of the Confrontations. Are you ready?"

I incline my head, trying to look respectful. There are some who say that Central sees and knows everything that one is doing. Others say that it is blind, only a voice saying recorded things, and it does not matter what you do when in the room with it. I believe in caution and in being safe and therefore act as obedient in the body as I feel in the spirit. "Yes," I say, "I am ready."

"Then put the helmet on."

I reach to the side of the keyboard where the great, grey headpiece is lying and touch its cold surfaces, run them through my fingers. "Must I do this?" I say, although I know the answer. "Must I really wear the helmet?"

"Of course you must. You know that. Put it on now."

I grip the headpiece and raise it, holding it over my forehead, and slowly insert my head into it. This, I have been told, is the less hurtful way. Things within it seem to clamp tightly as it is pulled into place. It is uncomfortable, but the fact that it is uncomfortable has nothing to do with anything. Life is pain. Life is pain and darkness. I have no right to protest.

"All right," I say, "it is on."

"Good," says Central, "that is very good." I raise my hand to say that I am not ready, that it is not yet ready, that everything is not quite yet ready, but it is too late for all of this for the light and the music have begun.

II

In the headpiece, in what I take to be a dream, although it may not be a dream, I am confronted by a creature which is seven feet tall and horned, which has limbs sprouting like wings from its body, a tail which radiates fire, and a clenched beak somewhat in the form of a bird's. The creature motions toward me, and I approach, fascinated. We seem to be in some kind of enclosure, not like the room in which I have dealt with Central, but rather one which is brown and has the texture and aspects of what I take to be the earth. "Hello, Byl," the creature says. It has a soft, lisping voice, almost gentle, but I am reminded that evil comes in many shapes and many forms, and I am not lulled into a feeling of security. "Are you well, Byl?" it asks. "Are you frightened?"

I shake my head and say nothing. Sometimes if you say nothing you give them nothing to fasten upon, nothing to taunt you with. At least this is what I understand from the discussions I have had about the Confrontations. Of course, all of this may be untrue. I have never been able to speak with anyone who has already actually been through one. "Don't be frightened, Byl," the creature says. "Come here and touch me."

Instinctively I move forward a step before I halt. The reflex to obey an order, any order, is very strong among us, and it is with an effort that I realize that the creature represents evil and that the voice of evil is to be rejected even if it does, as Central says, truly run the world. Again I shake my head. I hold my mouth closed. To give it nothing, nothing. To give it nothing at all. This is the only strength we can derive from them: that they cannot will us to talk.

"You might as well answer me, Byl," the creature says. "We're going to be together for a long, long time. We're going to be together now for the rest of your life." It rustles its limbs with the sound of beating wings, flutters before me, then opens its mouth to show the gigantic teeth. From that mouth pours laughter like oil, slickly filling all the small spaces of the room. "All of your life, Byl," it says. "All of my life now, too, we are going to be together." As it laughs its skin and scales shift in color and, rather than being brightly hued, it moves toward greyness. The colors are fading into dusk and something grey and gelatinous is laughing at me in this enclosure. A tentacle comes close to touch me, a shuddering and gathering of the skin as I feel the contact, and it is as if that contact were to infuse me with all knowledge. Being touched by the creature, I understand something that I never knew before and my body revolts, it gathers upon itself and . . .

III

Carried back further in the dream I am in the cubicle again, being prepared for the Confrontation by my Comforter. "You will put a helmet on your head," my Comforter says. He is barely older than I, fourteen or so, but he speaks with an authority which I must respect, because he has been through the Confrontation and I have not. "The helmet will make you dream and in that dream you will see a creature—some see red and others green; some wings and feathers, others thousands of scuttling legs—who will try to frighten you. But you should not be frightened—it is only a dream caused by the helmet, a work of the imagination which Central creates for you and if you realize this you will be all right. Tell the creature nothing. Turn away its questions with nods or with silence. Say nothing to it and show courage, for all Central wishes to see through this is whether you have the courage not to be frightened. That is all it asks and if you do this it will all be over soon."

"But why?" I say to my Comforter. "Why must this be done to us? Why must they frighten us? Why must they induce dreams if you say that they only want us to prove courage? Are there not other ways?"

My Comforter bites his lips, looking uncomfortable. "I cannot answer that," he says. "Please do not ask such questions of me. I cannot give you the answers. I can only tell you what I am authorized to tell, which is that the creature is a dream and the dream a test of your courage." He stands abruptly. "That will be all, Byl," he says. "I can tell you nothing more. It will be over soon."

"I don't want it to be this way," I say. "I don't want to live in a world where Central gives me dreams which will frighten me. It isn't fair. It isn't right."

My Comforter turns toward me; he seems in a kind of pain, a pain so complex that I cannot understand it. The pain suddenly shifts. He seems about to tell me something so crucial and important that it will explain everything about Central and why it makes these tests upon us. Yet as I lean forward to learn from him the answer which will explain the reasons for all the pain and darkness . . .

IV

I am back in the room and Central is shouting at me through the mouthpiece. "You are not performing satisfactorily," it screams. "You are not concentrating your attention. You are not focusing. You are not participating and we cannot have this." The headpiece is still on me and I can feel its density now. The pressure, the hard clamping contact has shifted to liquid, so profusely am I sweating. "Concentrate," Central is shouting. "Don't worry about what used to happen, worry only about what is going to happen, what is going to happen for the rest of your life." The shouting is intense. Something in the helmet which raises the amplitude causes it to give me real pain and I lift my hands in an attempt to yank the helmet off, but before I can do so I am . . .

V

I am back with the creature, still touching it, the scales fluttering around my hand. "See," it says, "that isn't so bad, is it? It isn't so bad to touch me at all. It doesn't matter; there's nothing to be afraid of." I tremble within that embrace, but it really is *not* that bad—that is the most difficult thing about it. I am being held in the grip of something red or green with wings or scales, seven feet tall and with a beak which gathers me against its breast, but it is not so terrible at all to be in that grip. There is nothing, it would seem, that we cannot accommodate ourselves to if we must. This may be part of Central's lesson. Or perhaps not—it is difficult to say. Now I feel myself seized in the air and the creature is moving. We swoop from the ground, now many yards above it, the floor of the room dwindling and then we are outside of the room, flying over the city, myself twirling and sweating in the creature's grasp, the creature moving through the milky strings of air which surround us and now it says, "Hold to me tightly and I will show you the world."

"I do not want to see the world."

"Nevertheless you must. That is the next part, I must show you the world," it says. Looking down from this height, already a mile or more above the city, I can see the many cities blending into one another, the clumps of complexes against the landscape, the landscape itself enormous from this aspect, spreading so hugely in so many directions that I can see the complexes for what they really are, little nests carved from the browns and blues of the enormous earth below. "Do you see?" the creature asks. "Do you see what you have become?"

There is nothing to do but hold on. I could not draw the breath to answer. Still we are ascending; now, miles above where we were, the complexes themselves have disappeared. They are merely little scars upon the landscape, imperceptible if you did not know where to look for them. The earth overpowers everything. "This is your world," the creature says, "this is where you come from. Are you aware of this? Are you aware of your insignificance? Your powers, your complexes, your cubicles, your Central mean nothing. It is only the earth and the glory and the dominion thereof . . ." And suddenly we are falling.

It is as if I am in the grip of some great wounded bird now holding me, plummeting with me through the air toward the earth, our descent three times as fast as our ascent. Passing stunningly through the levels of the air, gasping, streaming, breath torn away, not even to shriek and now the complexes form again out of the earth and I see them. Now they grow upon us. Now the heights and spires of the tower come into vision as still we fall. The creature is holding me bitterly to its breast and I can hear the sound of its sobs. The creature itself is sobbing now and in mortification—or perhaps it is only terror—I hold onto it, embrace it, clutch it tightly, still falling like a stone to the earth.

Then, the air hammering at us as if we were passing through metal, we are dropped into the room from which we came. The creature and I are tangled together, embracing one another, falling limb to wing, wing to face and we lie there in that tangle, while slowly, slowly the creature removes itself from me bit by bit and moves away balancing on its tentacles. Then at last it is clear by several yards. We have safely returned.

"Do you see?" it says. "Do you see, now?"

I shake my head. I can say nothing. "You are indeed insignificant," the creature says after a pause. "I trust that you have been shown that now. But it *is* to be conceded that in certain ways you are important. Relatively speaking, that is."

There is a petulant tone in its voice and even crouched as I am upon myself I notice it, but before I can come to any conclusion . . .

VII

I am in the discussion group many shifts before when this ceremony of Confrontation was talked over among us (somehow I had forgotten about this for a while— Central must have done things to my memory, since it is able to do that) and one of us—not me, it was one of the others—said, "It does not have to be pain and darkness. Central is lying to us."

"Why?" I said. "Why would it lie?"

"Because it is from the pain and darkness that Central draws profit. If we believe that life is that way then we need Central to protect us and guide us and to remain as powerful as ever, but if this were not so then we would not need Central. Is that not so?"

"Nonsense," I said. "You are speaking lies."

"Why?"

"Because Central would not do this to us. Because if life were not as Central has promised, it would not want to protect us from it. This is only so because it *is* pain and darkness."

"Oh, you fool," the other said. I forget who it was. I really wish that I could remember, but I cannot. That is the way so much of our life is, not to remember. To have the memories excised or, on the other hand, things that did not happen implanted as memories. I wish often that Central would give us full control of our consciousness even though it has its reasons for not doing so. "You fool, you understand nothing, you think this is being done *for our own good*." And he began to laugh. That laughter came over me in a rush like a great spirit and I turned to strike at it. No one can laugh at me. It is not right for people to laugh at me when all I have tried to do is to obey Central's instructions and operate with it and to do with it as it wants. Not right that after all of that there should be laughter. But even as I turn, even as I prepare to strike, it is as if all this passes away along with the memory. So it did not happen. I must have created it all and . . .

VIII

The creature turns upon me with solemn and anxious eyes, its scales now fluttering weakly on the floor, exhausted after its great exertions of flight. "Do you understand?" it asks. "Do you understand why it has to be this way?"

I shake my head. "I don't know," I say. I am beyond silence. I do not care—I will talk to the creature, it does not matter any more. "I do not know."

"It isn't easy for me either. It isn't as if I like this you know. Pain and darkness—I don't want it any more than you do. It just happens to be this way. So I have to acquaint you with them as early as possible because I am ordered. Don't you believe that?"

"I didn't see pain and darkness," I say. "All that I saw was flight and space and how small we were against the land, how small the land itself is against all of the heights."

The creature giggles. "Oh, you fool," it says, "you fool, you fool, *that's* pain and darkness," and with many small cries it comes upon me, its tentacles clutching as if to feed, reaching toward me, its mouth open to show a hideous range of teeth, and I back away, but before that truly threatening engagement can occur, before the creature can eat me, that is to say, I find that I am back . . .

IX

I am in the room of Confrontation and Central is still talking to me through the mouthpiece. "Go, Byl," it says, "go now. Kill. Love. Live. See. But be gone."

"Is it over?" I ask. "Is it over now?"

"It is for you," Central says. There seems to be a rather nervous tone in its voice, although this may only be some trickery of the amplification. "You have finished your Confrontation."

"Did I pass?"

"Everyone passes. Everyone always passes his Confrontation. It is done."

"And the creature?" I say, not really understanding why I am asking this. "What of it?"

"Do not worry."

"What happens to the creature? Does it merely go on and on, fly and be hurt?"

"Don't worry about the creature," Central says again. I realize that I am still wearing the headpiece and yank it off, but Central does not go away, and thoughts of the creature do not go away. As a matter of fact, very little changes except that the headpiece is lolling on the side once again. "Why be concerned with that? Go now."

"I won't," I say. "I won't until you tell me. Is it real? Is it suffering?"

"Go now, Byl."

"Is it suffering?" I say. "I do not want it to suffer." As I say this something breaks within me. I fall upon the mouthpiece, seize it, tear it from the wall, crumble it to ash within my hands. The ash is spreading over my fingers. "What is happening here?" I ask. "Even monsters must suffer; even pain and darkness is more than a demonstration." I shout and scream and bellow this, but Central can not answer, of course. I have destroyed its lungs. After a while, in a different mood, I creep from this room and down the halls back to my cubicle. It is only much later and in somewhat different circumstances that I understand that the Ceremony of Confrontation was planned to be this way from the beginning, and the creature itself . . . well, the creature itself merely another part of Central.